Honey in Her Veins

A Novel

RUTH McKELL

LITTLE, BROWN AND COMPANY
New York Boston London

The characters and events in this book are fictitious. Any similarity to real persons, living or dead, is coincidental and not intended by the author.

Copyright © 2026 by Ruth McKell

Hachette Book Group supports the right to free expression and the value of copyright. The purpose of copyright is to encourage writers and artists to produce the creative works that enrich our culture.

The scanning, uploading, and distribution of this book without permission is a theft of the author's intellectual property. If you would like permission to use material from the book (other than for review purposes), please contact permissions@hbgusa.com. Thank you for your support of the author's rights.

Little, Brown and Company
Hachette Book Group
1290 Avenue of the Americas, New York, NY 10104
littlebrown.com

First Edition: April 2026

Little, Brown and Company is a division of Hachette Book Group, Inc. The Little, Brown name and logo are trademarks of Hachette Book Group, Inc.

The publisher is not responsible for websites (or their content) that are not owned by the publisher.

The Hachette Speakers Bureau provides a wide range of authors for speaking events. To find out more, go to hachettespeakersbureau.com or email hachettespeakers@hbgusa.com.

Little, Brown and Company books may be purchased in bulk for business, educational, or promotional use. For information, please contact your local bookseller or the Hachette Book Group Special Markets Department at special.markets@hbgusa.com.

Print book interior design by Taylor Navis
Interior art: Pear © PinkPurplePlum/Shutterstock.com; Watercolor bee © TD Watercolor/Shutterstock.com; Watercolor bird © WatercolorGardens/Shutterstock.com; Rotting leaf by Taylor Navis

ISBN 9780316595247
LCCN 2025942945

10 9 8 7 6 5 4 3 2

CCR

Printed in the United States of America

For those of you fighting a monster in your head.
May you befriend the beast.

For content warnings, please turn to page 421.

Honey in Her Veins

 *When I am gone, tell the bees I loved them.*

Prologue

There was blood on my shirt.

Sickened, I yanked the damp collar wide, desperate to get it off my skin. Buttons popped free and skittered across the parlor floor. I swallowed the slug of panic in my throat and hit my knees on the hearth's roughened bricks. The tang of iron filled my nose.

"*Hurry.*" The monster in my head uncoiled itself and slipped into my hollows like a hand donning a glove. Nausea rolled up my gullet, but I couldn't fight its invasion. I didn't know how.

The monster had played puppeteer before, but never with so much abandon.

So much violence.

"*We need to burn the clothes.*" The monster steadied my hand, and together we stripped the bark off a log in quick, blunt strokes, then struck a match. A flame glowed at the tip, lighting the fibers orange.

"*Take off your shirt.*"

Numbly, I obeyed, shucking it off and laying it on the log. Soon, the fabric caught. The monster's relief left me lightheaded. "*There,*" it said, shivering in buried delight at the stretch of my limbs. It brought our hand in front of our face and turned it this way and that.

"Stop it," I said with a shudder.

"You feel everything so deeply," it murmured. *"Sometimes I forget."*

I tightened my hand into a fist, wishing I could shove the voice out of my head.

"And go where?" it murmured. *"We are skin and soul. Bone and blood. You could no sooner suck out your own marrow than rip me from your head."*

Something in me caved inward, too exhausted to argue. The monster had always had a cooling, almost numbing effect on me when I got upset. Even this near to the hearth, with the flames crackling up the bricks, I felt only a heavy chill weighing on my chest. If I let it in, the cold would spread until it reached my fingertips, stealing all the bad away.

But the bad always came back, in the end.

With shaking hands, I snatched up the paper I'd left crumpled on the mantel, smoothing back its creases to reveal a phone number scrawled in hasty loops.

Before tonight, I'd all but decided not to use it.

"She is not your home, little death-touch," the monster said with a touch of bitterness in its sweet, caressing tone. Then, more softly: *"I could be, though."*

Every tired muscle in my body yearned to yield to its siren song. It was always the same.

Let go.

Let me help.

Let me try.

But when I closed my eyes, all I saw was the blood sprayed over the chapel wall. The monster really had some nerve to pretend at gentleness after what we'd seen and done tonight.

I stripped off the rest of my clothes to burn. The wedding slacks

Jack had given me reeked of iron, too ruined to save. At the snick of a lock behind me, my heart jumped into my throat. I snatched an oversized coat off the back of the couch and slipped my arms into it as the front door burst open and a large, broad-shouldered man stumbled inside. He slammed the door, hastily spinning the lock behind him, a groan releasing from deep in his chest.

"Jack," I whispered.

The towering giant of a man lurched toward the sink, where he downed a jug of water in one long gulp. His massive shoulders hunched as he bent at the waist and retched into the porcelain basin.

Then he raised his head, wiping his chin with the back of his hand and found me frozen in the doorway to the kitchen. The weight on my chest grew heavier under his stare. "Arthur." His eyes flicked to the hallway. "Where is she?"

"Sleeping," I said softly.

Jack jerked a nod and turned back to the cupboards, fumbling through home-labeled jars of herbs and loose-leaf teas inside. Agony stretched his features taut as he braced one hand on the wall.

"There's something inside him."

The monster's preternatural awareness of any and all signs of life in its proximity sometimes gave me a heightened ability to sense things beyond my natural limitations, such as the whisper of chlorophyll in the window-box plants or the slow chug of a heartbeat upstairs.

And *there*. I squinted, trying to make sense of the squirming mass that twisted between Jack Moreau's ribs, high up where the heart should be.

I sucked in a hard breath. *Is that... rot?*

"*No.*" Wonder crept into the monster's voice. "*Look again.*"

I squinted.

"Damn it." Jack rocked back, a sickly pallor to his face. I'd never seen him like this, bowed from pain as the *something* in his chest wriggled like a worm.

I blanched, instinctively stepping forward, only for the monster to tug me back.

"*Don't.*"

It was right. I couldn't touch him, or any living thing. Tonight had made perfectly clear that there should be no exceptions, not even — no, especially not for Jack's family.

Jack's hand clenched the tea towel draped over the oven's door handle. "Leave me."

"You're hurt," I protested.

"I'm fine," he said through gritted teeth. "Check on Eva." When I didn't move, his eyes snapped to me. "Go."

"But — "

"Now!"

The force of his censure sent me stumbling back into the shadows, shame sickening in my gut. I shoved a fist into my mouth, biting down on my knuckles to hide the sound of a sob. My skin tasted of soap and woodsmoke.

Jack had never spoken to me like that before tonight.

At the sound of heavy feet shuffling, I peered through the open kitchen door, watching silently as Jack pried back the grill of the heater vent over the fridge. The grind of metal fell heavy in the quiet space.

When Jack pulled out a jar of honey, I sensed the *something* in his chest stretching. He buried a groan of pain.

My heart tithed a beat.

The monster was right. I knew decay like I knew my own name, and the pulsing, dark knot inside him may have been distinctly wrong, but it wasn't rot.

With heavy, labored breaths, Jack unscrewed the cap with a loud *pop* and fished out a bit of honeycomb. The moment it slipped between his teeth, the wriggling thing inside him slowed.

I stepped back, heart in my throat as my fingers *tap-tap-tapped* against the side of my leg. The usually soothing rhythm did nothing to stall the catch of my breath.

What had I just witnessed?

My mind flipped through the night's events in a nightmarish zoetrope. Oil-slick feathers exploding from the rafters. Wildflowers bursting through the cracks between the chapel's floorboards. Blood seeping under the body of the man I'd —

"*Stop,*" the voice inside me whispered.

But I couldn't. The monster was right: We were one, and so were our sins.

Jack opened the kitchen door and slipped out into the yard, the lumbering weight of his boots on gravel my only clue to his direction. When I turned, my elbow bumped the landline, nearly knocking the handset off its cradle.

A decision settled inside me. I lifted the handset, unwrinkling the slip of paper still clutched in my fist. I knew the numbers by heart, just as I knew how much I had to lose by making this call.

When I reached for the handset, the monster stiffened. "*What are we doing?*"

I punched the numbers in. My breath caught on the first ring, and I squeezed my eyes shut. If I didn't do this now, I never would.

"We're leaving."

Chapter 1

Eva,
Eight Years Later

Eva plucked a thorax from the water bucket and set it in a bowl of corpses.

They'd finished pulling honey from the northwest apiary yesterday. Most of it went to the extractor, but misfit chunks like these were submerged in water overnight to let the honey slough off, exposing the naked, uncapped comb floating on top. Eva could boil those down and tin them into beeswax candles, salves, and lip balms.

Nothing, however, sold like raw honeycomb. This late in the summer, bottles of the sticky, sugared medicine practically flew off their shelves.

Eva understood. Twenty-five years of keeping the bees with her father and older sister, and still she thrilled each time she sank her teeth into those warm, dripping cells. There was a strangely primal allure to that hint of spice among the sweet, pollen and enzymes sliding down her tongue.

It was hard, when paired with one of the teas in their Honey Shoppe, not to call that magic. Tourists came from miles around for a taste of the honeyman's bottled summertime and a sachet of herbs they fully believed would rid them of their ailments. Dad shrugged off their wilder beliefs, always saying that nature was magic enough.

He didn't disclose his somewhat enchanted green thumb, or his habit of collecting rare and mysterious flowers far up the mountain. Nor did he mention his magical daughter, whose greenhouse was brimming with herbs and florals Eva had cultivated to heal and cure.

"It's not too late, you know."

Eva watched Izzy swirl her finger in the water bucket across from her. "To do what, exactly?"

"Literally anything." Izzy flicked a little water at her. "It's Friday night, and we're *here*." When Eva snorted, her sister leaned closer. "Come on. This'll keep. Let's go dancing."

"At Dawson's?"

If social gatherings with people who'd picked on her in high school were really the lifeblood of small towns, Eva preferred social anemia. She hated crowds. They made her feel like a bug stretched under a microscope.

Besides, the town's nightclub was literally the worst place for Izzy to be.

"We can find a sober bar down the mountain," Izzy urged. "It'll be fun!"

Eva loved her sister, but she'd rather die than willingly subject herself to a night of painful pickup lines and some dry-humping stranger on a dark dance floor.

"I think I'm good here, Iz."

Izzy rolled her eyes, which Eva pretended not to see. *Let the sheriff take her dancing.*

When she'd cleared all the torn wings and insect parts from the dirty honeycomb, Eva turned the bowl out onto a swath of cheesecloth, then swiped her wet fingers over the back of her neck. This summer was a scorcher.

The door to the workshop creaked open, spilling in a shaft of apricot sunset light as Dad stepped in, ducking Goliath shoulders under the door's lintel. Eva's eyes fell to the vee of her father's shirt, where the brunt end of scar tissue and tree root lifted his flesh. The skin split at his sternum, a stubborn sapling pushing through a fistful of viscera and bone. Soft green moss spread over his chest, peeking from beneath the well-worn flannel of his shirt.

Every day, he got a little harder to look at.

"I thought you had an appointment," Eva said.

Dad grunted and shook his head.

The roots of his sapling had burrowed deeper with every passing year, webbing his thoracic cavity into a mesh of wilderness and man. Eva usually tried to hide her worry. Dad and Izzy already treated her like glass ready to break. But her fears lay fallow beneath the surface.

"You rescheduled?" she prodded.

"No." Dad tightened a grimace and sat across from her. "No more appointments."

Eva's heart skipped. She didn't miss the guilty look that flashed across Izzy's face, or the way her sister's eyes dropped to the bucket in front of her.

She knew.

Dad must have seen Eva's face fall, because his expression softened. "There's nothing more Dr. Rosen can do, honeybee."

"But—"

"I'm tired of tests," Dad said. He flicked one of the fluttering leaves. "I'm not going anymore."

Eva's mind spun. There had to be something Dr. Rosen hadn't tried. Some angle they hadn't considered.

"Hey." Izzy took her hand. "It's gonna be okay. Right, Dad?"

Eva squeezed her eyes tight. Glass, again. The pity made her stomach twist.

And made her magic bloom.

At her sudden onslaught of emotion, her gift flung itself wide, finding its mark in a burlap sack leaning against the wall. Eva's palms warmed as bright green stalks carved their way out of the fabric and the pungent smell of onions filled the room.

She swallowed hard. *Focus.* She couldn't lose control when Dad was so close. Her gift could make the roots of his tree push even deeper into his chest. What if they pierced a lung, or slipped into an aortic valve?

Or, or, or.

There were endless possible nightmares, and she'd gone over them all in her head a thousand times.

Breath tight in her lungs, Eva locked away her fear. She couldn't let them see her like this. Brittle. Breakable. Dad had taught her once that she could be more than the storms in her head. Now she had to be. She forced a slow exhale and pictured her anchor: a blue sky full of clouds, slowly clearing.

Izzy squeezed her hand again. That, too, was grounding, even though it hurt to think that her sister had known about her father's decision and had chosen to keep the truth from Eva.

"I want to show you something." Dad plucked a roll of newspaper from his back pocket and held it out. Eva stiffly accepted it.

They weren't done talking about this, but she knew if she pushed now, he'd only bar the door further.

Later, when he wasn't so visibly stressed, she'd bring up Dr. Rosen again.

Dad opened the newspaper to the obituaries. As Eva scanned the line of names, brows furrowed, a honeybee landed on her knuckles.

Connoway.

Heat shot to her spine. Eva sucked in a hard breath, suddenly taut as a bow. No. Not that name. Not his name.

She pulled back, reading again.

Charlotte Connoway.

Relief dulled her panic. The mother, then. Not the son.

It wasn't a local newspaper but something that must have been sent to him. She hadn't realized that Charlotte Connoway had put down roots after so many years of flitting from place to place.

When Eva thrust the newspaper back at her father, the bee flew away. Eva hated the flush up her neck, hated the gentle way both of them looked at her. *I am not fragile.* She wanted to scream it.

Instead, she bit the inside of her cheek, where they couldn't see her bleed. Dad took the crinkled sheet and smoothed it out. "Lottie called me about her illness last month," he said.

Surprise hooked Eva's ribs. He hadn't told her that.

"She wanted to come to visit herself, but" — his voice cracked — "she couldn't travel, in the end."

"Oh."

The resounding silence told Eva she'd said the wrong thing, and awkwardness stirred between the three of them, thick as molasses. Eva should comfort her father. Yes. No matter her own distaste for the woman, Dad had cared for Charlotte.

For whatever reason. Eva turned to her sister, desperate for someone to better guide this conversation. Eva hadn't known Charlotte, not really. If anything, the tidbits she'd gleaned from her former friendship with Charlotte's son, Arthur, had turned her bitter toward the enigmatic woman.

Izzy was sharing a strange look with their father, her eyebrows slightly raised. "Dad," she said. "We don't have to do this now."

Eva looked between her father and sister. "Do what now?" She didn't want to be walked around, talked around, as though she were a bomb that might go off. "Is something wrong?"

"No," Dad reassured. "I'm simply fulfilling a promise."

Eva swallowed. "You're going to her funeral?" she guessed. That would be difficult. It was hard enough to get him down the mountain for his checkups. Eva didn't know how far he could travel.

"Not exactly."

Dread gnawed inside her. Something wasn't right. Eva stood, but her father was an absolute bear of a man, and even on her feet, she didn't meet him eye to eye. "Tell me."

See me. Let me be strong in your eyes.

Dad crooked an unconvincing smile. "She's coming here."

Eva blinked. "What?"

"Well, not *her*, obviously," Izzy cut in.

"Right." Dad stumbled slightly over the correction. "Her ashes are being delivered. I promised Lottie we'd scatter them on the farm. Tell the bees she's gone, like we did with your mom. Remember?"

Eva nodded, a knot in her throat as she clicked together what he wasn't saying. Someone had to bring those ashes back to these mountains. Someone Charlotte had trusted.

There's a strange kind of knowing that comes just before a storm. Pressure crowds between your ears. Old joints ache. The air grows wet and mineral. Eva held her breath so tight her lungs began to burn, that *knowing* drawing back into her mind the very storm clouds she'd tried so hard to shove away.

"Who?" she rasped.

Izzy furrowed her brows. "What?"

And maybe Eva was glass after all, because the question she pushed to the front of her lips made something in her crack.

"Who's bringing the ashes?"

Chapter 2

Arthur

I still think you should have shaved the beard. You look like a muskrat."

I cranked down the van's window and let the breeze sift through my fingers. Appalachia was sweltering, a humid and unbearable heat from which my broken AC offered no relief. Slick with sweat and beyond the point of exhaustion, I had no patience for the monster's vanity.

"This isn't about me," it scoffed. *"Don't you wonder what she'll think of you after all these years?"*

"No." I flexed my grip on the steering wheel, eyes skipping to the royal-blue urn strapped into my passenger seat.

I did not wonder, and I did not care. This was not a social call.

A glowing saffron sunset reached its fingers between the sentinel pine and birch hugging the ditch. Despite my insistence, memories of the last time I'd driven down this very road flooded in. They tasted as bittersweet as the last dregs of an over-steeped cup of tea.

"Do you think she'll like your new tattoos?"

Instinctively, I touched the inside of my forearm where one of the sleeves of ink began. What had started as an act of defiance had metamorphosed into armor with every new design. Little black songbirds flew up my skin, the arc of a wing shading the scar beneath. Woodland details filled in the gaps between the varied species of birds and a curl of honeycomb rounding my left biceps.

The latter had been an impulse, really. A nostalgic dig of the knife that suddenly felt far too exposing. My face went hot.

"I do love it when you pine."

I felt the monster tug our lips into a smirk and quickly rubbed the expression off with the back of my hand. "I'm not pining," I muttered. I simply hadn't expected coming back to feel like some kind of confession. I was a roll of film in a vat of chemicals, exposed too soon to the light. I was —

"Pining," the monster singsonged.

I scowled.

Too soon, we rolled through the town of Audrey's single, blinking stoplight. I kept my eyes forward, unwilling to risk being recognized. Old worn-out buildings in charming pastel lemon and cornflower blue blurred through my periphery. The café. The school. The Honey Shoppe. I told myself the landmarks couldn't bruise if I didn't look too long.

My knuckles whitened as we drove past a pale chapel that was chipping old paint. Weeds climbed up its siding, and a harsh whistle drew my attention to the hole in the roof, where a clutter of dark birds circled overhead. My inhale sharpened to a blade.

Starlings.

While clever, their greedy and invasive nature too often disrupted the local ecosystem with their habit of driving other birds out of their nests. Farmers hated starlings, but my mother had loved them, charmed by their astounding gift for mimicry.

The monster let me stew in my thoughts until we turned off Main Street. We were getting close. I could practically taste the wax in the air, and outside, the road licked a black asphalt tongue around the edge of the Walkers' pear orchards.

Déjà vu wrapped around me, thickening with every passing minute. I hadn't driven this road in years, but my body remembered. Time, it seemed, wasn't enough to patch the wound this place had carved in me.

"*You have such a flair for the dramatic,*" the monster complimented. I rolled my shoulders reflexively — an old habit that never succeeded in shaking its voice out of my head.

My stomach growled. After opening the glove box, I fished through the mess of honey sticks until I found a speckled cinnamon, then popped one end open with my teeth.

I knew I should cry for her. She was my mother, after all. I should have cried weeks ago. Instead, nausea twisted my empty stomach over in knots. My appetite had fled the moment I got the call that she was gone. If that was grief, I sure as hell didn't know how to digest it.

But I could still choke down honey.

"*I could help, if you'd let me.*"

"No." I didn't want the monster's help. It had made such offers before, and they always ended in disaster. Whenever the monster gave in to its own strange appetite, I ended up with the tail of a squirrel between my fingers, or fish scales under my nails. I didn't need another animal husk staring at me dead-eyed and accusing. I knew the monster's work was wretched. Maybe even wicked. But I was worse, for letting it use me, letting it *take*.

"*It doesn't have to be like that. We could —*"

A loud *pop* jolted us both, stalling a surely horrific proposal.

The cab lurched up and down, the van sagging violently to the right. "Shit!" I tapped the brakes and eased onto the road's narrow shoulder. Dust bloomed skyward where the wheel dug into the naked soil until the Volkswagen ground to a standstill.

I sat back, frustration heating my skin. This was the last fucking thing I needed today.

Stepping out into the ocean of heat, I rounded the van, crouched before the ruined tire, and ran my fingertips over the rubber tread until I hit a nail.

"You're kidding," I muttered.

If Fate was laughing at me, it sounded an awful lot like the whir of cicadas.

"Do we have a spare?"

"It's a mess." One more item on a never-ending list of things I'd broken and never repaired.

"So... we walk?"

I didn't answer, nor did I fight when the monster turned my head to the wall of textured evergreens hugging the side of the road. Dandelions speckled the ditch in sunny pops of yellow and wishing fluff. Beneath us, rootscapes stretched to wrap the edge of a warren just out of sight. The monster salivated, tuning our senses to the rolling *tha-dump* of a rabbit's heartbeat, the mammal glow of life pulsing like a toothache behind my gums.

"You skipped breakfast," it noted.

I shuddered. We shared too much, our edges too often blurring together. Sometimes I dreamed of surrender. I could disappear into that cool, relaxing space in my head where I stopped feeling everything so acutely. It would be so easy to give up control. A relief, even, to loosen my grip and let the monster—

"Stop it," I snapped.

It flicked a tongue against my spine. *"Just a taste?"*

I opened my mouth to refuse, then all but choked at the sudden outpouring of life flooding my senses. I looked down to find my hand wrapped around a clump of milkweed.

"Oops."

I snatched it back too late to stop the monster's death-touch. The pink flower heads had wilted to a brown crisp. Relief eased my pounding headache, and I shoved to my feet, the taste of petals still slicking the back of my teeth.

"It's okay," the monster soothed.

I was shaking as I yanked open the passenger door. We'd stolen the life out of those weeds with a single touch. *Flesh to flesh, dust to dust.*

Nothing about that was okay.

It was too hot to leave my equipment in the van, so I tucked the urn under one arm and slung my camera bag over the other shoulder. The bag was Mom's. She'd picked it from a tourist stand at Four Corners the winter we drove west and filled our film rolls with Arizona's red horizons. The pattern of blue and orange fibers on the bag had faded, like everything between us. It was the only thing of hers I'd inherited that didn't hurt. I locked the door and left the van behind, the sweet chemical scent of her perfume washing over me.

We couldn't be more than a quarter mile from the farm. Every step felt heavy under the dark-eyed stares of wild sunflowers growing in the ditch. When I closed my eyes, I pictured the sunflower dress Eva Moreau had worn one bird-watching morning.

The day she'd kissed me.

I exhaled and pushed the memory away.

The word *cottage* did a mighty injustice to the structure ahead of me. Its stone base held solid chestnut walls and a porch that had never sagged a day in its life. At the crest of its gables, a ribbon of smoke seeped from a stone chimney. Beside it stood the workshop where I'd learned how to uncap honeycomb and run frames through an extractor before pouring the honey into jars to sell.

From where I stood at the bend in the road, the greenhouse was behind the cottage, slightly obscured from view, as was the hill leading down to one of the Moreaus' six apiaries. The dying sun soaked the glass in rose-gold light. I stalled in my tracks, struck by the sight.

A hollow of yearning widened in my chest.

I'm not afraid of dead things, Arthur.

I should have gone straight to the front door and knocked. Instead, I took a step off the path, toward the greenhouse, unaware that I was rubbing my honeycomb tattoo until I was nearly at the door.

There was no one inside, as far as I could tell. Greenbrier swathed the walls, a carpet of moss creeping from the outer wall over the doorjamb. When I reached out to touch the handle, the monster stepped in, stalling our hand midway.

"What are you doing, little death-touch?"

The maw of yearning in my chest opened a little wider. "I just want to see."

This wasn't the plan. I'd only meant to pop in, deliver Mom's ashes to her damn honeyman, then get the hell out of here. This little glass house was dangerous.

The monster's disapproval swelled as I shook off its hold and turned the knob, pushing the old door open on creaking hinges. My nose filled: vegetal with summer smells and rich, wild herbs.

My eyes fluttered, and for a moment, I was seventeen again.

Then the door to the workshop burst open.

I jerked back, startled, as a short woman flew like a gale across the yard, her long braid snapping behind her in the wind. Another — taller, with raven-dark hair — followed close behind, her heels sinking into the grass in punching steps. "Eva," she panted. "Would you calm down?"

My heart gave a painful lurch of recognition.

"You want me to be *calm*?"

Even without the flood of wildflowers spilling from her shoes, I would have known the warm rasp of Eva Moreau's voice anywhere. In a blindfold. In the dark.

"This is what not *pining looks like?"*

The monster was right. I'd spent the entire drive here raising a shield in preparation for this very moment. There was no reason to open old wounds. This wasn't a homecoming, and I was the furthest possible thing from a prodigal.

But I hadn't steeled myself for this: the blaze of her, shooting like a fallen star across the garden. Furious. Formidable.

I needed to get a grip. This was fine. I was fine.

"You're sweating."

Neither woman had looked back toward the greenhouse, where I stood, still holding my mother's remains.

"Could you slow down? Hold on. Let me just…" Izzy growled and ripped her high heels off her feet, flinging them to one side.

"I don't want to hear it, Iz." Eva tossed a glower over her shoulder. And froze.

When our eyes connected, the overbearing heat of the day took on a different shape. Instead of clinging to my skin, a flush of awareness, of aching recognition, sank right through to the core of me.

Izzy stumbled into her sister, who caught her before she could fall, then brushed past her, stomping toward me. Bewildered, Izzy spun, seeking the source of her sister's abrupt change in demeanor.

"Ah." Izzy's voice went soft with sudden understanding, but I had eyes only for the woman charging toward me like a bull, cheeks flushed. A nauseating wave of wrongness flooded my senses.

I shouldn't have come back.

Instinctively, I took a step back but stumbled, tripping over a rock. Air rushed from my lungs in surprise, and I hit the ground tailbone first, the urn slipping out of my grasp. It shattered on the stepping stones, spraying ashes across my cheek.

Eva came to an abrupt halt in front of me. "You," she whispered, the pain in her voice like a striking bullet.

A memory flashed before me. In it, Eva was smiling as she coaxed my glove off finger by finger. I could still recall the first brush of her skin against mine, could still see the parting of her lips as she asked me the most dangerous question of all:

You trust me?

Beyond, someone else stepped out of the workshop, casting an enormous shadow across the lawn. I rolled to one side, panting with the effort it took to ignore my aching tailbone, and pushed to my knees, where I began anxiously scooping up ashes before the wind could blow them away.

But the urn, now completely shattered, could no longer hold them.

"Arthur?"

In her mouth, my name sounded almost delicate, the syllables preserved like a flower in a book. My throat went hard with grief.

On my knees, with my hands still cupping the ashes, I felt suddenly like a supplicant come to beg her forgiveness.

I shoved to my feet and tossed my head to one side to get a stray lock out of my eyes, stacking my spine with a confidence I didn't feel.

"Hey, bee girl."

Chapter 3

Arthur

"You." Eva stepped back, her voice thickening with sudden emotion. Accusation filled her eyes as she raised her finger and thrust it in my direction. "What the hell are you doing here?"

Something squeezed inside my chest, and I opened my mouth to speak, only to choke on dead air.

Luckily for me, Izzy swooped in before the awkwardness could grow. "Impeccable timing, Fairy," she chirped. "We were just talking about your arrival."

My eyes zipped from her face back to Eva's, a question budding on my lips, when the size of the figure that had stepped from the workshop registered in my mind. My pulse leapt in recognition. There was only one man on this mountain as impossibly large as he. I hadn't been sure when I'd dialed if the number was still accurate, and part of me had hoped it would ring and ring, that I'd never have to hear his voice again.

But Jack had picked up right away.

Doubt tugged at me. This was a mistake. How could I walk back in after all this time? I couldn't face them. Not now. Maybe not ever.

It wasn't too late to just turn around and go. Mom's ashes had been delivered.

"In the loosest sense of the word," the monster chirped.

I gritted my teeth in annoyance.

At first, I'd thought to ignore Mom's last request and send her ashes through the mail, which had only convinced the monster that I must have been deep in the throes of grief. Driven by a desire to curb my self-destructive tendencies, it had...changed. Grown bolder. The monster had forced me to sleep, dreamless. It had tried to force me to eat to keep up my strength, but despite the gnawing in my belly, everything made my stomach churn.

When the monster had started hunting again, I'd caved to Mom's wishes, and had set a course for Audrey, Pennsylvania, desperate to do whatever it took to soothe the beast into submission.

To prove I was fine.

"Arthur." It wasn't a question that fell from Jack's lips, rather a confirmation. The monster cemented our feet where we stood, preventing me from acting on the impulse to run. Jack stepped from the shadows of the workshop into view.

I froze, my mouth parting in shock. The sight of him stole my breath.

What was I looking at?

A tangle of branches fluttered with leaves. A *tree*. A tree in his — No, that...that wasn't possible.

But denying it did nothing to change what I saw. Where there once had been only a seed, now a whole sapling was lodged in the honeyman's chest.

I gaped, aware of my rudeness but unable to stop.

The monster's wonderment filled our mind. *"Is that an aspen?"*

The question nauseated me. We'd left the farm before we

understood what we'd seen growing inside of Jack. For years, I'd tried to forget and move past that night, but the monster's curiosity had festered deep inside me.

"I know, Fairy. First time's a shocker." Izzy took a step toward me and plucked her shoes from the grass. "You're welcome to come in—"

"No." Eva's stout refusal drew all our attention to where she stood, ramrod straight and twisting the end of her shirt around her finger. Waterweeds spilled from beneath her shoes. "He's not."

"Honeybee," Jack intoned softly, reaching for his younger daughter. Eva stepped back. "Wait!"

But Eva didn't wait. She ripped her gaze away from me and bolted down the path. Jack grimaced.

"That could have gone better," I said weakly.

Izzy shrugged. "Could have gone a lot worse, honestly."

I'd expected a fight. Eva had never shied away from conflict before. Even angry, she had always been warmth. A burn or a balm. She had never frozen me out.

"Is that Lottie?" Jack quietly asked.

I nodded. "Yes, sir." Guilt washed over me as I took in the shattered blue urn.

Jack winced.

I'd imagined this moment many times during my drive, but none of my mental rehearsals had featured me spilling my dead mother's ashes onto the honeyman's sacred soil. Maybe that was a sign. I was stupid to think the monster would give a damn about her last request. Stupid to think coming here would stop it from donning me like a fucking glove.

Stupid to hope for relief.

Silence heavied the air with awkwardness, until Izzy cleared her throat. "Tea?"

I swallowed hard, searching for a protest. They didn't have to do that. Play the host. Pretend. We didn't have to be *fine*.

"Tea," Jack agreed with a nod.

It made the hollow in my belly twist. I couldn't help it. Everything in this family circled back to honey and tea, tea and honey. Jack told me once that healing started with a simmering pot and a spoonful of gold. In this house, tea was a love language all its own, and it spoke when words and other medicines failed.

I crossed on stiff legs to the cottage's front door, stealing glances back to the winding aspen lodged in Jack Moreau's chest. My hands still cupped the ashes I'd scooped off the stepping stones, the breeze teasing away a wisp of the dark cremains.

Our approach startled a trio of gray-and-white kittens out from beneath the bushes. They dashed across the yard and out of sight.

After all this time, coming back should've felt like an intrusion. Instead, the second I stepped into the mudroom, the knot between my shoulders eased. The creaks of the floorboards were a song I didn't expect to recall, the nicks in the wallpaper worn into my memory. I hesitated on the trick step a moment before I realized I still knew it was there.

I didn't expect that, for the house to be so deeply ingrained. But I guess time couldn't steal everything. I'd first found the Moreaus the way a cocklebur found the knit of a sock, too eager to stick where I didn't belong. A weed like that — like me — was hard to pluck out, no matter how long I'd been away from home.

This wasn't home.

I couldn't forget that. No matter how familiar and inviting, the cottage and the family within weren't mine anymore.

Izzy threw a sharp glance over her shoulder and guided me into the kitchen. I tried not to care when she bolted the lock. Of course, they didn't want anyone from town to know I was here after everything that had happened.

"You hungry?" Izzy glanced out the window as she spoke, clearly trying to be gracious in light of Eva's sudden flight.

"No, thank you." But even as I said it, my eyes flicked to the honeypot on the top shelf. Not the one Jack kept hidden in the vent but the everyday pot I'd dipped into time and time again, to slather on toast or stir into tea.

Sometimes I dreamt of it. On bad days, their honey had been one of the only things I could stomach. My summer here had ruined me for other honey. I'd tried other brands and farms, but nothing compared.

I'd spent the last eight years chasing the way it had made me feel. Warm. Alive.

"Why not ask to take some with you? Jack wouldn't begrudge you that."

I gave a minute shake of my head. No, we couldn't beg for favors. We couldn't owe Jack anything more, even if the very thought of raw honeycomb made my mouth water like an animal's.

Izzy plucked a carved wooden box off the side table in the parlor and dumped the contents—pencils and stationery, by the look of it—into the junk drawer beneath. She motioned for me to uncup my hands and let the ashes in my palms pour into the box's velvet-lined interior. I did as instructed, a lump in my throat.

Izzy latched the box shut and rushed from the room. A tap squeaked on in the bathroom, and she returned with a damp rag in hand. She passed it to me, careful not to touch my skin. "You'll stay for dinner?"

I swallowed my guilt and shook my head. This place was a drug. I had to get out before it wormed its way back into my system. I'd spent too many years looking back on that summer with a hole in my gut. "I can't, Iz."

Izzy's mouth pressed into a frown. "You just got here," she said softly.

The sadness in her protest took me aback. I didn't deserve her affection after all I'd put them through. But then, the Moreaus had a thing about taking in strays.

"She's right," Jack said as he filled the kettle and set it on the stove. "Sit down a minute, son."

A flare of heat startled to life in my chest to hear him call me that. Jack's tone brooked no argument, so, like a moth to a flame, I plopped onto the nearest chair, wincing at the discomfort to my injured tailbone.

I cast my gaze over the familiar walls. I'd always loved this warm, close room. It was the kind of rustic, lived-in space that made you set down all your worries. Antique gold frames were littered across cherry-print wallpaper, anything that could be cast iron *was* cast iron, and the burnt-orange tiles featured timeworn cracks like stars that mapped the floor in a tale of teatimes past.

Sometimes I wondered if the Moreaus were too wrapped up in their family bubble to see their own magnetism. They drew people in, even those who didn't want to be drawn, those who fought tooth, nail, and claw to be free of them.

"Like us?"

"You still like it with milk?" Jack asked, ladling a generous spoonful of honey into a mug. My breath quickened. It was pathetic to *want* like this. Too often, I felt like an empty bucket that couldn't get full. Moreau honey had a way of curbing my appetite, just as its keepers had always been able to quiet the monster in my head.

"Should I check on Eva?" Izzy asked softly.

Jack shook his head. "She won't go far."

The words fell like a slap and a soothing hand at once. That was one of the things I liked about Jack's youngest daughter. She was roots. She was soil.

And my return had upset her. Of course it had.

"Where do you think she'll go?" Izzy asked.

"The pond." I didn't realize I'd said it aloud until Jack and Izzy swiveled to face me. My cheeks burned with a new kind of heat. But if Jack remembered my youthful indiscretions with his daughter, he didn't care to rehash them. Small favors.

We sipped our tea, tension brewing in the building silence. Jack swirled his teacup. "So."

My chest panged. "Yes?"

Why had I agreed to this? The room was steeped in discomfort. What could we even talk about? The tree bursting out of his half-buttoned flannel shirt? The pile of ashes spread over the grass?

It would have been so much easier if Mom had simply had her ashes sent to Jack directly. What had she been playing at by playing *us* like this?

Jack took a sip. "I didn't see a car."

I nodded. Right. Yes. That was a safer topic. "I blew a tire."

The weight of my camera bag no longer felt like an anchor. Instead of grounding me, it made the muscles in my shoulder pinch. I switched it to the other side, blinking through a sudden wave of dizziness. When was the last time I had eaten something besides those honey sticks?

"If you have to think, it's been too long."

"Where?" Jack asked.

"Not far. Quarter mile down the road?" I hesitated, discomfort collecting inside me. I didn't want to ask them for help, but Jack guessed anyway.

"You need a ride."

I hated that he was right.

"I can take you in the morning to get it patched. The garage is closed now anyway," Jack said. "Why don't you take your old room tonight?"

The monster perked up. *We're sleeping over?*

I blinked, setting down my teacup to hide its shaking. "Jack," I started, his name a bitter dreg on my tongue. "I can't."

"You can't go anywhere else," Jack said calmly, the leaves of the aspen fluttering in tune with his breath. It made the sapling feel that much more alive. Not only forest but flesh too, human and wilderness twining as one.

I shuddered.

Jack Moreau had always been a little wild. I'd seen him pluck strands of grass from his beard. I'd seen roots pushing from his soles. I'd seen him bleed red-green.

But this was different. This time, I couldn't help the budding fear that this was all my fault. A thundering pressure heavied in my chest. I couldn't stay here when I was the reason their lives were so utterly changed.

"I can drive you to the valley," Izzy offered.

Guilt breathed its spores into me. "No. It's fine." The drive down to Cumberland Valley was nearly an hour long. I could wait until morning. Just a few hours, a quick tire patch, and then I could leave. If I was lucky, I wouldn't see Eva at all. I wouldn't have to figure out if she really did have more freckles or if I'd simply forgotten some of her constellations.

Jack crossed to the window over the sink and hauled it open, reaching through to pluck a scarlet bloom from the rosebush just outside. I cocked my head. Odd that it didn't bloom where he touched it.

Jack snapped off the thorns and held it out to me. "Take it before you pass out."

The monster eagerly stretched up my spine. *"Yes, please. I'm so hungry."*

"I don't want it," I said, tapping the side of my leg.

Maybe, if I'd had more time, more courage, I would have told them about the monster that summer. The Moreaus knew I killed things with a single touch. They knew I hated it. Worst of all, they knew that sometimes killing was the only thing that made me well again. Be it flower, mouse, or snake, they didn't question it, saying I was good inside when the truth was, I was rotting.

Jack held the bloom out, stem toward me. I tried not to look at the tree, or to register the new emerald saturation in his irises, which used to be as blue as Eva's.

The instant the delicate flower touched my skin, its petals shriveled. My vision steadied as the taste of rose spread over my tongue.

Jack stepped back with a crisp nod. "Right. Help yourself to a shower if you like. We'll get a new pair of sheets on the bed. You let us know if you need anything."

"Wait." Beneath the taste of rose, the bite of ashes was still acrid in my mouth. My stomach clenched as I forced out the words. "Can I borrow a broom?"

Pain flashed across Jack's face, there and gone so quick I almost missed it. "I got it," he said gently, bucketing my shoulder with a large hand. The weight of it, the human warmth, shocked my protest away. He was careful not to touch my skin—Jack was always careful—but the pressure alone, the comfort of it, woke in me an old ache.

"I'm so glad you're here, Arthur," Jack said.

Something flickered, deep inside me. Guilt, of course, my eyes flicking to the place where his tree disappeared beneath a mound of torn, scarred flesh.

Grief, too, for the pain I remembered seeing on his face that night. Grief for the years I might have had here, the home I might have built, if everything hadn't gone so wrong.

Still, I wasn't his prodigal, or a stray that had simply wandered off. I'd put myself in exile, and for eight long years I had buried every desire to come back or call or write a damn letter.

I'd been the one to insist on separation. A clean cut was better, I'd thought.

So why does it all still hurt?

Chapter 4

Eva

By the time Eva gave up swimming her anger away, her fingers had shriveled to prunes. She tromped back up to the house. A piercing quiet heavied the air, making every noise feel overly loud as Eva toweled herself dry and wriggled into an old T-shirt and sleep shorts. She had to bite her lip to keep from crying out when she stubbed her toe on the bedpost. Eva crawled under the covers with Izzy, and her older sister turned and curled like a sickle moon around Eva's spine.

The silence was at odds with the buzzing in Eva's ears, her thoughts spilling like honey from uncapped comb. Tucked in the safety of her sister's arms, Eva could pretend.

She wasn't brittle. She was safe. She was soft.

Sleep took her in snatches, never giving any real relief. At the rooster's cry, Eva flipped the blanket off her legs and padded to the kitchen. She rifled through tins of flour and sugar, anxious energy running through her. After a fitful night of sleep, she needed comfort food to stave off her most unpleasant self, and there was nothing more soothing than sweet and sticky food.

Pancakes would do. At least with batter, she got to whip something.

Hyssop meowed loudly at the back door. Eva opened a container of tuna and filled another with water. The latest litter scattered when she opened the door and set the plates out for the kittens and their mother, scratching the furry old queen behind her ears.

Back inside, Eva washed her hands and cut off a square of butter. When it sizzled to a lake in the hot pan, she plopped in three gloopy circles of batter.

Hey, bee girl.

Arthur hadn't looked like himself. He was taller, leaner, rimed in scruff. A frisson shivered down her spine as she pictured his new face, and the soft plea in his eyes.

When bubbles formed in her batter, Eva flipped on autopilot.

She wasn't upset he was back. She was just surprised. Arthur had stayed away so long that after years of no contact — no letters, no calls — she'd assumed he'd never return.

Pressure built at the bridge of Eva's nose. She shook herself, aborting the train of thought entirely. No, she wasn't upset that Arthur had come home.

Come *back.* That was what she meant.

No, this was about the bees. The hives were more than her family's occupation. Every queen, nurse, and drone was part of a deeper legacy that stretched back generations. They were the Moreaus' history and future. They were magic. They were home.

Charlotte Connoway didn't deserve them.

Telling the bees about the passing of a beekeeper or one of their loved ones was a sacred, ancient custom, labeled by some as mere superstition. Not Dad, though. *Heaven's not a place in the sky,* he would always say. It was deeper. Weightier. Real as the soil underfoot. When Mama died, Dad had said the bees would guide her soul back into the earth that had created her, and then he had tied a black ribbon onto the hive box and knelt in the grass, as though it were an altar.

When he had told the bees that Mama was gone, something in Eva unclenched. She could breathe again. It hurt, and she cried, with Izzy holding her far too tight.

But she could breathe.

That's what men pounding their pulpits would never understand. Sacred things didn't hide in churches — they lived in the gentle hum of good, bright creatures, and in anything trying to make life more beautiful for others. At the end of the day, humankind was no more lord of the earth than the tiniest mayfly.

Some cultures centered honeybees in their creation stories. Others, like her family, honored their connection to death, revering the honeybee as a bridge between the natural world and whatever came after a person died. Fields of wildflowers, perhaps, or a bright blue, always-humming sky.

One thing Eva knew for certain, though. There was something special about her bees, something *more*. And maybe it made her petty and mean, but even in death, Eva didn't want to share them with Charlotte Connoway.

"Your pancakes are going to burn."

Eva's gaze snapped to the doorway where Arthur sagged, hazel eyes drunk with exhaustion. His night clearly hadn't been any kinder than hers. Gritting her teeth, she stuck her spatula beneath the bubbling cakes for a peek. *Damn it, he's right.* Her usual perfect gold had darkened while she'd stared on, lost in distraction.

Eva smacked the back of her spatula against a pancake, a wild fizzing in her chest as she pushed the cake deeper into the heat of the pan. She could let them burn. Let him eat them charred.

"Don't look at me like that, Ev."

How dare he call her *Ev* with so much ease, as though the intimate nickname he'd given her years ago was some kind of claim, some proof that he still knew her. How dare he look so tired and indefensible when all Eva wanted was battle. She wanted his armor, so they could fight, but the rough scratch of his morning voice and those sad, bruised eyes hardly made for a fair opponent.

Eva flicked off the stove and began winding her hair back into a braid, twisting her strands into submission. She didn't want to be here anymore. She had enough grief with her own wild magic and her father's ailment. The last thing she needed was Arthur Connoway's ghosts nipping at her heels.

She burned her fingers flinging the overcooked pancakes onto a plate and shoving it down the counter. "Syrup's in the cupboard," she clipped, setting her apron on a hook and all but slamming the kitchen door behind her.

"Thank you." Arthur's voice came muffled through the wall.

Eva scowled at the watercolor sunrise drenching the dewy yard in rich strawberry hues. It was gorgeous, and she hated it. This was so clearly a bitter, gray-sky kind of day.

At the workshop, she slowed, letting herself wilt against the door. It embarrassed her how even that simple interaction had left her raw-edged, the bridge of her nose burning with unshed emotion. She rubbed it with her knuckle and forced the feeling down, dwelling instead on the furious growl of her stomach. In her haste to leave, she'd forgotten to grab a pancake. Clearly that was Arthur's fault too.

It felt good to be mad at him.

At least here she could clear her mind and lose herself to the harvest: comb by comb, wing by delicate wing. Only, when Eva sat on her stool, an empty bucket stared back at her, which meant either Dad or Izzy had finished up last night.

The windows diffused the morning light into a gentle spray across her toes. Dust motes swirled around her still-bare feet, and for several long moments Eva watched the air sparkle and dance. A honeybee found her, as they always did, latching on to the crook of her finger.

She smiled despite her bitter mood. They were so beautiful, it hurt sometimes.

The crunch of boots on gravel drew Eva's gaze to the doorway. The door was open, but Arthur paused on the threshold anyway. His knock was a fragile thing. "Can I come in?"

He'd changed into a dark gray T-shirt, forgoing the hoodie he'd slept in. Eva's mouth went dry, her eyes dropping for the first time to the long swirl of tattoos climbing his arms. She must have been too stunned to really take those in last night. Now they were all she could see, and the sight made an itch crawl over her skin.

When had he gotten those? Whom had he trusted enough to let them touch him?

Taking her silence as permission, Arthur stepped inside, his eyes moving over the equipment she'd washed and laid out to dry after the honey pull. The heavy, cotton bee suits hung on the wall near him. Arthur reached out, trailing a finger down one of the long white sleeves. "Can we talk, Ev?"

Ev.

The short, sharp sound burrowed like an arrow in her skin. He was the only one who called her that.

At seventeen, Eva had loved Arthur Connoway with every cell in her body. She'd trusted him with all of her, and then when she needed him most, he'd fled.

"Sure. Talk."

Maybe part of her did want him to grovel.

Time had sharpened the lines of his face, his jawline slightly softened beneath a dark beard. The new hollows in his cheeks upset her. He upset her, so changed and unfamiliar.

Arthur tugged the sleeve of the bee suit. "I know you're angry."

"How could you tell?" Eva deadpanned, not caring how childish she sounded.

Something unreadable flashed in Arthur's eyes. "Your neck gets pink when you're pissed off."

To her mortification, his words made a lick of heat spread up from her collar. He was right, and at that moment, she hated him a little for noticing that detail. For remembering.

"Why did you come back?"

It wasn't for her — that much was abundantly clear. Eva's chest felt tight. It wasn't fair to still be wounded by him long after she'd stopped caring what he thought of her.

"My mom wanted her ashes brought here," Arthur said, his expression pinched.

He was still so bad at lying.

Eva crossed her arms. "That all?"

His hesitation made her stomach drop. Eva stood and took a step toward him, despite her inner voice warning her away. She was no glutton for rejection, but something in her needed him to keep looking at her like that, as though she were sour to the taste. It was better than Dad and Izzy, who walked on eggshells in every conversation with her. Always so damn careful.

When they were toe to toe, Arthur's throat bunched with a swallow.

"Well?" Eva prodded.

A muscle twitched in Arthur's jaw, and he cut a sharp nod. "That's all."

He smelled like sleep, like bedsheets, like *skin*. Heat spread all the way up to Eva's cheeks. She fought the urge to cool them with the backs of her fingers.

"I should have called you, Ev."

He might as well have cracked an egg on the top of her head. A trickle of feeling rolled down Eva's spine, spreading out into her limbs until her whole body was overwarm.

"I wasn't sure you'd pick up the phone," Arthur said more softly.

Eva barked a laugh, though it didn't feel funny. "I'm surprised you remember our number."

Arthur's posture slumped. "I remember everything."

It was a match. Eva burned on the sulfurous wick of her fury, desperate to be angry instead of sad, to be sharp, if sharp meant she chose where she bled. She resisted the impulse to grab a fistful of his T-shirt and drag him closer. If he felt her nails wound his skin, would he understand? She was a shard now. A jagged piece of what she'd been before.

"I'm sorry."

"I don't want your sorry, Arthur." His name was a barb that dug into her tongue when she spoke it aloud. Arthur's exhale washed over her, maple and sweet. Eva's heart beat fast, reminding her that she was not glass. She was flesh. She wouldn't break for him.

She *couldn't* break for him.

"Tell me the truth," she demanded. Arthur licked his lips, his thumb rubbing the pads of the other four fingers. She'd forgotten that anxious habit. "Why did you come?"

He could have had the ashes shipped.

They stared at each other, Arthur's pupils dilating as he took her in. For a moment, Eva thought he'd give her a real answer. But then his face closed off and he looked away. It felt like a flame snuffing out.

Eva watched him walk away, confusion hurting her chest. At the door to the workshop, he paused.

"It doesn't matter why, Ev."

Her breath rushed out of her lungs. *Bastard.*

Eva watched his shadow disappear, her whole body trembling. It took her several minutes to feel ready to return to the house. When she did, her path was marked by a trail of petite chamomile blossoms blooming in her every step. Irritated, she threw open the kitchen door a little too loudly, and found her father hunched over a jar of vivid blue wildflowers.

"Oh. Sorry, Dad."

Eva's gaze dropped to the tea he'd chosen. Every petal inside had been collected from her father's favorite meadow on the mountain. He used to hike to it every summer when she was a child, mapping caches of rare herbs he'd found en route and bringing home screens of drying blooms to bottle and save. Always blue petals — cobalt, sea, and summer sky. They sold every other herb in the Honey Shoppe, except this one.

Eva couldn't remember the last time he'd made that trip.

"Good morning, honeybee."

Eva's breath hitched at the childhood endearment. She didn't feel like his honeybee right now. That girl thought nothing bad would ever touch her golden little world. She was kind, not cruel and vindictive, as Eva had just been. She was gentle, and Eva didn't feel gentle anymore.

She felt like a knife.

Crossing to where Dad stood, Eva wrapped her arms around his waist, careful not to irritate the skin around the sapling's trunk. It was selfish to touch him when doing so put him more at risk. Eva's gift could hurt her father.

But she needed him today.

"My girl." Dad held her tight against him. "What's wrong?"

So many answers swirled to the tip of her tongue. So much had gone wrong in such a short time.

Dad rubbed a circle over her spine. "Is it Arthur?"

That felt too hard, so Eva shook her head.

"Lottie, then?"

Yes. That was an easier, simpler anger to face. Eva nodded into his chest.

"Oh, love." Dad pulled back and cupped her cheek, his hand so large it swallowed half her face. "Does it bother you to share your bees?"

Her heart gave a needful tug forward. Yes, it bothered her. But even more, she didn't like the way he asked, like she was a child learning to share.

"I don't know."

Eva had spent many afternoons talking out her worries as she leaned against one of the many painted hive boxes, her head tilted back against the wood. Sometimes she fell asleep to the sound of their hum and woke with a dozen or more bees perched on her body. They didn't sting her. They simply let her melt into their world.

Dad clearly wanted more, but thankfully the teakettle saved her from having to answer. At the soft whistle, he stepped back and plucked her favorite teacup out of the cupboard. Her mother, always the artist, had painted a cluster of forget-me-nots on the pale white porcelain, to match the hive boxes outside.

"I don't need tea, Dad. You should sit down and rest."

He ignored her protest and reached for the honeypot on the top shelf. "You'll feel better if you drink."

Frustration flared in her. Dad always did this. He thought medicine was something found in roots and petals, and maybe it was, maybe it should be, but the feelings inside her wouldn't be chased away by anything he could bottle up. She wasn't like Arthur, who had always been so eager to accept her father's remedies, putting his faith in their tinctures and balms. Peppermint for stomachaches. Feverfew for migraines. Calendula for bee stings. Arthur had been a sponge to all of it.

But more than anything, he'd loved tea.

"I wonder if he missed this," Dad said softly as he slowly turned the wooden honey dipper over her teacup. When the heat made his glasses fog up, Dad lifted them off his nose and hooked them on his collar. Eva's eyes tracked the movement.

Root. Skin. Flesh. Forest.

She ripped her gaze away. "I doubt it."

Her father flicked her a look, securing the lid of the hinge-top jar back on. He'd cut himself shaving, leaving behind a tiny smear of red-green blood on his jaw.

Eva still remembered the day the sprout in his chest had broken skin. She'd been hanging herbs in the greenhouse when Dad had bellowed in pain. She'd found him, passed out, with blood smeared over his hand, as though he'd tried to dig it out himself.

Eva blinked, her vision blurring. Sometimes it was painful to remember what he'd been like before. Arthur's reappearance had unearthed old and tender wounds. A dark pool of blood staining hardwood. A body on the floor. Starlings in the rafters.

Her father, forever changed.

"Lottie loved this tea," Dad said, his voice catching. "I named it after her, you know."

"What?"

Dad seemed to catch himself. "Oh, never mind," he said as he held out her teacup.

"But you just said —"

"I know," he cut in. "But those are just memories, honeybee."

She wanted to protest, to demand he go back and explain what he'd meant by that. He had named his blue tea after Charlotte? Eva thought it didn't have a name.

Her father laid a hand on her arm. "Let it go," he said. "I'm just sad today."

Guilt shut her up quick. Of course he was.

Eva raised the teacup to her lips, her chest warming at the first sip.

"You and Arthur talk yet?" Dad asked.

She nearly spat out her tea. It burned up her throat to her nose. "What?"

"I'll take that as a yes," Dad said too calmly. "The two of you make things right?"

Eva's throat closed with a sudden, hard lump of emotion. No, they hadn't made things right. She didn't think they ever would, and if she was being honest, she wasn't sure she even wanted them to.

"I'm taking him to get that tire patched this morning, before we scatter Lottie's ashes. I don't know how long the boy will stick around after that."

The way he eyed her made her feel as transparent as the glass in the windows. Eva broke their eye contact and took a sip of tea, hating the way her body reacted to those words. She wanted Arthur to go. So why did the thought of him leaving again still sting?

The silence in their little kitchen seemed to grow heavier with every passing second. Dad's expression shifted, worry lines creasing the planes of his face. "He isn't doing well, is he?"

The man at their door last night had been near unrecognizable from the boy Eva remembered. Even this morning, she'd been forced to acknowledge the signs of self-neglect staring her in the face. The deep exhaustion bruising Arthur's eyes. The too-thin frame. He was underweight again, and tapping, like he always did when he was anxious.

"No," Eva admitted, setting her teacup back onto its plate. *Not well at all.*

Chapter 5

Arthur, Before

Mom and I wintered in the southern states, tuned to the sun like a migrating flock. I turned seventeen only days before the warming spring weather woke her need to uproot us again.

The sun chased us north into the Blue Ridge Mountains. I looked up from my book in time to catch a glimpse of a fading sign naming our destination: AUDREY, PENNSYLVANIA. It wasn't the worst pit-stop town I'd seen, though it was quite out of the way. Pastels washed Main Street in soft, childlike hues, Victorian-style storefronts fringed in frost-white trim, like something from a storybook.

Cute.

"Why are we here, exactly?" When I'd asked before, Mom had been very cagey about this little detour, but I was used to her impulsiveness and hadn't given it much thought until now.

Mom parked beneath a wooden sign featuring a painted yellow bee. "You're staying with a friend of mine for a while."

The monster slithered up my spine, its cold touch raising the hairs on my nape. I could practically taste its suspicion. The monster had been with me most of my life, twined between bone, sinew, and something else...something soul-deep and far too delicate to protect on my own. That's what the monster was for.

"A friend?" I repeated, sounding far calmer than I felt.

Mom killed the engine and turned to face me. She wore her slightly too-bright smile. "You'll like Jack," she strained. "I promise."

My heart beat a staccato *no*. No, no, not again. She'd left me before, of course. My mother was a bird, and sometimes birds flew away, leaving their younglings behind in a nest.

"Is this one my father?" It took guts to ask, heat crawling up my neck.

Mom shook her head. "No. Jack and I, we never —"

"I don't need the details." I sank into the embroidered seat cover, chest deflating, whether in relief or disappointment, I wasn't sure. My mind raced. I couldn't remember her ever mentioning a Jack, and I didn't know if that was good or bad.

"He's smart," Mom offered. "He can help you with calculus."

"I finished calculus."

She opened and closed her mouth. "Well, he's...got a daughter your age."

"Is she pimping us out?" the monster asked.

"Maybe the two of you could be friends," Mom pushed.

"He already has a friend."

I shooed the monster's grumble away. It had never liked sharing, but I wasn't in the mood for its jealousy right now.

For the vast majority of my seventeen years, I'd spent my life on the road, camping and hiking. Mom liked the freedom of van life. She collected boyfriends in every state and rocks from every national park. I collected books and Polaroids but never a friend who lasted. It wasn't worth it when we never stayed in any one place for long.

"Eva is different," Mom said, encouraged by my silence. "She's like you."

Like hell she is.

I looked away. No one was like me. Sometimes I wished I could find someone who was. Someone who craved death as much as they feared it, who knew what it was like to hold rot in your hands. But that was selfish, to wish my curse on someone else.

Still, sometimes it was hard not to fear that I was the only person in the world this broken.

"*Wholeness is much like a puzzle, little death-touch. Do not confuse its many pieces for brokenness.*"

My fingers ticked a familiar, anxious rhythm against the side of my leg in a desperate attempt to calm the voice in my head before it got louder.

"I just…" Mom trailed off. Her frown made her delicate, drawn-on brows curve like the jut of a wing in flight. "I can't keep doing this, Artie."

I closed my book and held it to my chest. The Edgar Allan Poe anthology weighed heavy against my sternum. I liked the pressure of it, how that beating, maddening heart under the floorboards hid the crack in my own chest.

I'd tried to be small for years. I'd tried to be light as air, but I was still too much for her.

"You're coming back." It wasn't a question, and I hated that my voice trembled like it was.

Mom's fingers wrapped a little too tightly around the door handle on the driver's side. "Let's go inside. You'll like it here. I promise."

I determined I would not.

A little bell announced our arrival. The Honey Shoppe was all warm wood and glinting glass. Amber-colored jars lined the shelves, each tied with a neat burlap bow and a rustic label: MOREAU HONEY. Behind the counter, soldier-straight rows of jars full of brightly colored loose-leaf teas broke up the overwhelming glow of gold. My gaze snagged on a gingham cloth by the window, where a loaf of focaccia had been cut into cubes, toothpicks spearing the crust. A folded white card invited shoppers to slather on the house-whipped honey butter.

My mouth watered at the smell.

"Don't touch anything," Mom murmured. When she turned her back, I swiped one of the samples and popped it into my mouth. Surprise and pleasure at the taste spread through me. The herbal undertones were rich and earthy. Rosemary, perhaps?

You haven't eaten today.

I speared another sample, my stomach growling as my eyes skated over the labels detailing the various flavors of tea lining the shelves. Some I recognized, like rosehip and dandelion, while others — like meadowsweet or usnea — were unfamiliar to me.

"Is your honeyman in today?" Mom asked the girl behind the counter. She had raven-dark hair that stretched all the way to her waist.

"Not today, no. He's…" The girl paused and cocked her head. "Mrs. Connoway?"

"Charlotte, please." Mom's smile could have melted a candle. "I'm surprised you recognize me. Missy, isn't it?"

"Izzy." The girl looked faintly stunned.

"Izzy." Mom nodded pleasantly. "I was so sorry to hear about your mama."

"Oh. Thank you, ma'am."

The bell rang behind us, signaling another customer. When Izzy caught their eyes, her bewildered expression fled, replaced by a sudden tightness around her own eyes.

"Whatcha doin' here, Lenny?"

I turned, not realizing how close the newcomer stood until the bone of his shoulder knocked hard into mine. "Watch it." He shot me a glare before turning to face the girl behind the counter. "Your sister 'round, Moreau?"

I didn't hear her reply, anxiety sparking in my chest as I crossed my arms and pushed past him, almost tripping over my feet in my desperation to get outside, away from those too-gold walls.

I'd touched him.

Panic strobed through me, and my heartbeat quickened as the door swung closed behind me.

"Hey. Take a breath, little death-touch."

But I couldn't. The anxious trill of my thumb down my fingertips wasn't enough to soothe the rising flood. It was so hot today that I'd left my jacket in the car, and I was certain that when the stranger had knocked into me, his bare arm had brushed against mine.

My next inhale came too shallow, too quick. I should have been more careful.

"He was fine. You would have felt if he wasn't." The monster paused, its presence soothing the center of my chest like ice to a swollen wound. *"It takes more than that, and you know it."*

It was right, of course. Simpler life-forms, like flowers and fruit, withered with a single touch, the glow of their fading light sparking new life in me. Animals like voles or robins took longer to kill, due to their size and complexity. I didn't know how long it took to kill a human being, but surely it would take more than a mere brush of skin.

And the monster was right. I would have sensed it.

Still, I couldn't help feeling shaken. I wasn't used to being touched like that.

The monster sighed and opened our awareness to the threads of life in the weeds growing through the cracks of the sidewalk. "There," it said.

I looked and saw a sunflower stalk swaying near the passenger side of the van. Making sure no one was looking, I took the stalk between my fingers. The petals shriveled, and a vegetal pulse bled to autumn on my tongue.

I sighed in relief, panic ebbing away. "Thanks."

We rode in silence past a flowering orchard, potholes bouncing us out of our seats. I tasted sunflower the whole way. Soon, a house emerged. It looked like a cottage drawn by a child who'd never seen one before.

"How do you know him?" I asked when Mom put on the brakes.

Dust plumed around the Volkswagen's windshield. "We're old friends."

"Bullshit."

"Language," Mom shot back. The old van door creaked on its hinges as she got out and slammed it shut behind her. "I trust him. Isn't that enough?"

I didn't know how to answer that, but I followed her to the porch, not knowing what else to do. Wildflowers of all sorts grew in place of grass: ironweed, yarrow, and heavy-scented lavender that made my nose itch. Each delicate plant whispered to the beast in me and tempted me closer. It would be so easy to slip off my shoes, to crush them underfoot and let the monster feast.

Instead, I pulled my gloves out of my pocket and slipped them onto my hands.

The air vibrated with the steady thrum of honeybees as Mom raised her hand to the door. Before she could knock, however, the door sprang open and a giant man holding a toolbox filled the entryway, gray suspenders stretched over a broad, muscular chest.

All three of us jumped in surprise.

The man rocked back, his toolbox clanking as he stared at Mom. "Lottie?"

I blinked. Displeasure knotted my neck in promise of a future headache.

"Jack!"

I didn't like the delighted way she had said his name. Not at all.

The giant's bewilderment slowly melted into a broad smile. "It's really you. Do you want to — ?"

"Can we?" Mom let out a laugh as the two spoke over each other. She cleared her throat and tried again. "Can we come in?"

"Of course!" Jack sprang back — oddly spry for a man his size — and emphatically motioned us in. I caught him studying me in the hallway mirror and shivered, feeling suddenly as overexposed as a canister of film held to the light.

The pale green cushions on the kitchen chairs were old and pilling. I kept my gaze on Jack as I sat. I didn't like the way he looked at my mother. It was too soft, too...eager.

I tapped the side of my leg, but the anxious habit brought no relief.

"Can I make you some tea, Lottie?"

Her smile spread across her cheeks. "You always do."

When I coughed, they startled, as though both had forgotten I was there. Awkwardness thickened the air as Mom jerked her chin my way. "This is Arthur. My son."

Jack's eyes widened. "You have a son?"

"*Wow.*" The monster's irritation bled into me. I was tempted to give in to its temper and tell this stranger to fuck right off.

Mom cut in. "Jack, is there a place we can speak alone?"

The monster and I turned our head to stare at her, indignant.

"I suppose." Jack cleared his throat again, shooting me a look. "Storm brought a branch down on the greenhouse roof." He extended the toolbox. "We were just about to start on repairs, if you could bring this out to my daughter?"

I didn't move.

"Artie. Please." Mom turned her gaze to mine. "Do this for me."

Sometimes I hated how I loved her. Even knowing that she wanted to leave me, I couldn't help the gut-clench desire to please her anyway. Maybe if I did, she'd stay.

"We'll be right behind you," Jack added quickly.

When I snatched up the toolbox, Jack's shoulders relaxed. He nodded to the kitchen door. "There's a path leading straight to it, if you follow the stepping sto — "

I took pleasure in slamming the door on his instructions. The moment their voices started up again, however, I quietly pressed my ear to the wood. Only muffled words came through.

You safe?

Could have called me.

Sorry.

Emotion hard in my throat, I stepped back and crept down the clearly indicated path. This place was a fucking Eden. It put me on edge. I didn't belong in a place so full of life. With every step, the monster pressed against the confines of my skin, willing me to trail my fingers through the swaying flora. A fluffy gray-and-white kitten froze in place when it saw me. It didn't outwardly look afraid, but the monster's awareness revealed the animal's heartbeat racing.

It was almost a relief to see a little glass house come into view. Almost, until I remembered what greenhouses were for. I would find no relief from the living there.

With a scowl, I flung open the door.

A girl crouched below a hole in the ceiling, sweeping broken glass. Her long golden braid kissed the floor, wispy curls frizzing a soft, round face. She looked up, clearly startled to have been disturbed. "Who are you?"

A cotton clothesline strung with drying herbs bisected the room. Two beautifully stained wooden counters faced each other, each lined with pots in every color, shape, and size. A rich, earthy smell assaulted my nose, and my eyebrows shot to my hairline at the sight of bright green moss carpeting the floor in a layer so thick I couldn't see what lay beneath.

I thrust out the toolbox. "No one."

This place was too vibrant. It pulsed with life, sang to me, yearned for my touch. The monster was practically thrumming with excitement at our proximity to so much greenery.

I had to leave.

The girl took the toolbox, eyes dropping to my hands. It was too hot for gloves. Her lips parted as though to speak. I didn't give her the chance, turning to go. But in my blind rush, I miscalculated my proximity to the garden tools slumped near the door, and when my foot came down on the tines of an ancient rake, it snapped up and smacked me in the nose.

I barked a cry of pained surprise.

"Oh my gosh!" the girl gasped. "Are you okay?"

No. My face was broken.

"I'm fine," I grunted, even as a groan of pain bubbled up from deep in my chest.

"You're bleeding!"

I shook off the girl's concern, stepping away. "Don't come any closer."

"Let me get you a rag." She either hadn't heard the mumbled words or had chosen to ignore them. "Here —"

"I said don't *touch* me!"

The girl startled to a stop. The look on her face reached through my cloud of pain. Shame hooked in my chest. *Shit.* I'd scared her.

I should apologize.

"I don't like to be touched," I said instead.

"Oh."

When her eyes widened, the monster pawed at my ribs, almost feline. *"Can you get a little closer?"*

I groaned internally.

"She's got freckles."

The girl turned her palms up in surrender. "It's okay. I'll stay right here."

A honeybee flew past my ear and landed on her braid. I blinked, surprise flicking through me as I took her in more fully, now that the shock was wearing off.

She was covered in bees.

I counted seven on her overalls alone, more on her braid. One even crawled out from behind the shell of her ear.

The corner of her mouth tugged upward in a smirk. "They won't hurt you. If you're nice." She coaxed one onto her fingertip and held it out for me to see.

The monster leaned in, holding our breath.

"I'm Eva," the bee girl said.

Chapter 6

Isobel

The way Arthur wrapped the black funerary ribbon around his knuckles put Isobel in mind of a boxer preparing to fight.

A fence marked the boundary between her family's property and the Walkers' pear orchard. Heavy golden bulbs swayed in the breeze, the smell of harvest thick in the air. During the transition into fall, it was common to see one of the orchard hands out between the rows, twisting pears into tightly woven buckets.

Isobel cast her eyes over the property, searching for the familiar shape of Dane Walker between his pear trees. She hadn't seen him all week, which wasn't usual for them, and though she missed him, just now a part of her hoped he'd stay busy a little longer.

Eight years had passed since the Walkers had laid eyes on Arthur. Eight years of her lying.

Closing her eyes, Isobel let her concerns about that reunion slide away, donning the mask that would help her through today. It wasn't hard. Izzy was a persona she wore often. Izzy the older sister, the daughter, the family glue. It was the role they expected and needed her to play, and since it was a close fit to who she wanted to be anyway, it wasn't hard to slide into.

Stepping forward, Isobel carefully unwrapped a blue scarf from around the wooden box Dad had swept Charlotte's ashes into. The design on the ornately carved lid resembled a beautiful dark bird.

Arthur would like that.

"Here." She held it out. Arthur took the box, appearing resigned. Isobel bit her lip. "I'm so sorry about your mom."

She'd spent a lot of time thinking about mothers. Her own was long gone, taken by a tumor they hadn't caught in time. Isobel had been young, Eva younger still. Their mother hadn't been there for most of their milestones, but she still held a place of reverence in their home. Their love was a harvest of memories and warmth.

Arthur's relationship with his own mother hadn't been like that. The love between him and Charlotte — if you could call it love — had more closely resembled a variant of orchard blight.

Isobel wanted to tell Arthur that Lottie had been proud of him, but she was a little afraid that the words would stick on her tongue. Sometimes polite words were more empty than kind. And maybe the threat of their neighbors appearing at any moment had put into her mind all the lies she'd upheld with a smile, or maybe she was just sick of false platitudes, because in that moment, all she wanted was to give Arthur something real.

So instead, she said, "I missed you, you know."

Arthur's eyes widened. "Oh." His jaw worked. "I...um..."

"You don't have to say it back, Fairy."

The door to the cottage shut, and two figures appeared at the top of the hill. One giant. One small.

Isobel waved.

Though her stepfather and sister were complete physical opposites, they still somehow managed to move through the world in the exact same way. Firm steps, searching eyes, fingers trailing through the field of swaying purple coneflowers. Eva wore her favorite cornflower-blue overalls, wildflowers embroidered into the pockets with colorful thread. They had belonged to their mother once. When Eva grew into them, the overalls had become her armor.

Where Dad's expression was open, however, her sister's face was screwed into a glower. By the way Eva fixed her gaze on Arthur, one would have thought she truly believed she could burn a hole in the back of his head.

Isobel sighed. That was a mess she couldn't clean up.

"Stick around for a bit, after, won't you?" she said to Arthur. Maybe it was selfish to ask, with him still obviously grieving, but Isobel had a hunch that if she didn't say something, he might just bolt again, now that the tire was fixed. She knew how sticky it was to graft in family members like cuts of scion wood. She'd done it with Dad, when he had married her mother. She'd done it again with Arthur.

She could be a little selfish. Despite the tension sitting heavy in the air, despite his years of distance, Arthur was still theirs.

After a moment's hesitation, Arthur nodded.

Isobel's shoulders dropped in relief. "Talk later, then," she said. At the very least, he wouldn't leave without saying goodbye this time.

A breeze moved through the orchard, making the leaves on the pear trees dance. In another month or so, the golden turn of the seasons would spice the air with the sweet-sick tang of mulch. As a girl, that had meant bottling jam and quilt nights with the old ladies from her mother's book club. Later, the smell would remind

Isobel of the night Dane Walker had married her best friend under a sea of sparkling stars.

When Dad and Eva reached the hive boxes where Isobel and Arthur stood, Dad held out a rose. Eva bristled, twirling the end of her shirt around her finger so tight it had to be cutting off circulation. Her younger sister had never been good at hiding her feelings. When Arthur hesitated, however, his gaze sliding from the honeyman to his youngest daughter, Eva's patience snapped. "Just take it," she muttered.

As though pulled by a string, Arthur lurched to obey. Isobel clocked the movement, tucking that morsel away in the back of her head.

Still magnets, then.

Eva's grim expression grew ever more sour as the rose desiccated in Arthur's hand. Dad, however, ignored his youngest's mood, taking his glasses off to wipe the lenses clean on his shirt before replacing them on the bridge of his nose. He cut a striking figure against the azure sky, chalk-pale branches twisting out of him like some eldritch sacrifice. It sent a chill down Isobel's spine. "Ready?" he asked.

Arthur unwound the ribbon from around his palm. "What do I do?"

"Tie it around the hive box," Dad said.

Arthur knelt in the grass and did as instructed. Even from here, Isobel could see his hands were shaking as he cinched the knot. The bow sagged limply against the wood.

Arthur looked up. "Now what?"

For just a moment, the clear expression on Dad's face clouded. There was so much buried in that look. If the town gossips were to be believed, her father's history with Lottie Connoway had been...complex, at best. Dad hadn't told her much, but Isobel remembered the whispers.

Dad cleared his throat. "Do you have anything to say to her?"

A war of emotions flickered across Arthur's face, but he only shook his head. Dad took a knee beside him. "I know how hard it is to miss her," Dad said. "I've been doing it a long time."

Arthur's back was ramrod straight. He nodded tightly and unhooked the latch on the box's lid. "Let's just get this over with."

Telling the bees was an old tradition rife with superstition. If you didn't tell the hives when one of their keepers died, you tempted Fate to curse you with a bad crop, a hive box full of wax moths, or worse —

Another death.

Isobel didn't put much stock in all that, but she did know the power of grief.

Isobel's lips curled into a smile as she studied the fading designs on the hive box. Dad had built them from scratch, and together, they'd painted the boxes white, with little blue flowers detailing the sides. Forget-me-nots. Her mother's contribution, painted with a shaky hand.

Her smile faded. That was one of the last memories Isobel had before they told her that her mother was sick.

"For the bees to guide her soul, first you tell them she is gone," Dad said to Arthur. "It lets them grieve with us."

Arthur's mouth tightened at the corners, but otherwise he did not move a muscle.

Dad went on. "After that, you can sprinkle her ashes. Set her free."

Arthur shut his eyes tight, nails digging into the wood of the ash box. "Why don't you just do it?" he muttered.

"What?" Dad asked, surprised.

"She would have wanted it to be you, anyway."

A beat of heavy silence weighed down the space between them. Isobel watched her father, holding her breath. Dad shook his head. "No," he said. "It has to be you, Arthur."

"I don't think I can."

"She needs *you*," Dad repeated. He held Arthur's gaze. "Whenever you're ready."

Chapter 7

Arthur

It was happening again. The sea of grief. The lapse in control. I didn't want the Moreaus to see me coming apart like this, as naked as the day I'd burned the bloody clothes. The woman in that urn hadn't given a shit about her black hole of a son, collapsing inward and swallowing anything light and good.

So why did I still care about her?

I shouldn't have even been the one to do this. All morning, I'd fought the slow rise of dread in my chest as we prepared to spread her ashes. Jack's words made the anxious feeling calcify. I couldn't move. I couldn't breathe.

Whenever you're ready.

I wasn't ready.

"Arthur?" Izzy's concern bled into her voice.

I shoved to my feet and thrust the box full of Mom's ashes into her hands. "I need a minute," I rasped.

The monster weighed as heavy as fresh, ripe fruit between my ribs as I stomped toward the house. I had to consume something, fast. The last time I got this hungry, I woke one morning with a crow stiff with rigor mortis stretched between my hands, my bare feet dark with forest soil.

I felt smaller and smaller with every step forward. I used to want that. The smaller I made myself, the easier I was to handle, and for so long that was all I'd wanted to be.

"Don't cry for her."

"I'm not!" I snapped back, forgetting to lower my voice. Maybe it didn't matter. I was far enough from the Moreaus now that they likely wouldn't hear me talking, presumably to myself.

At the top of the hill, I gripped the iron gate, surveying the cottage and the state of the yard, grown even more wild since that morning. The weathervane rooster atop the cottage wore the daytime moon like a crown jewel on its head. Errant skeins of prickly greenbrier stretched down the trellis and onto the porch, where scarlet bee balm spilled from a hole in the siding like the innards of a butchered pig.

All Eva's rage.

The wildness shouted her name. In a sea of bad feelings, it was strangely grounding to latch on to something so concrete, even if that something was her bitterness toward me.

Her golden, gentle magic had always felt like something out of a folktale. She did impossible things, like pulling seeds from deep in the earth with nothing but desire and will. She woke the world up with every footstep, every laugh.

But she wasn't laughing now, and the wildflowers her magic had yanked to the surface had a wretched kind of violence to them, their stems slightly twisted, the roses and greenbrier overpacked with thorns.

I wondered what she'd do with me, if given the chance. I doubted she'd be gentle, after all I'd done, and all I'd left her to bear alone.

The monster stopped me in my tracks and made me bend and pick a flower, wrapping my fingers around the bright red cluster of petals. *"You need to consume."*

I swallowed hard. It was better than killing an animal, but still, I hated that I needed it. Hated even more that I was scared of what I might become if I refused.

So I crushed the flower in my fist and let it wither. The fragile bloom hardly sated the gnawing and desperate hunger inside me.

But it was something.

I went inside.

Once, this cottage had been my sanctuary. I tried to ground myself by focusing on the details I remembered: the faded cherry wallpaper, the familiar snick of the door, the sag and groan of the floorboards, every scuffed one holy simply because it was something I wanted that would never really be mine.

Coming to a halt in front of the hall mirror, I stared, desperate to find something of myself in the reflection, instead of the beast. My hair had grown over my ears, my beard was in desperate need of a trim, and dark circles rimmed my eyes... but they were still *my* eyes.

This body was still mine.

"Of course it is." My reflection smiled.

I clenched my hands into fists at my sides. "Get out," I whispered.

"You called me here." The monster's lazy, reptilian stretch made me shudder.

Is that all I am? A skin, to be molted?

"You're lying."

The silence that followed bore the weight of a thousand moments just like this, when I'd reached instinctively for the monster, needing it to bear a weight I couldn't bear myself. I hated myself for being so weak, but my body was heavy, and some days, it took effort just to keep going.

The monster helped with that.

"*That's right.*" Like a heartbeat, it gently pulsed in the center of my chest. "*I am the one who has walked beside you. I have been there to sit with you in the dark—*"

A dark it created.

"*I am the home you are looking for. Not this place.*" It paused. "*Not her.*"

I struck the face in the glass.

Pain erupted in my knuckles, the shock of the impact running a current up my arm. A large crack spidered my features in the mirror, fragmenting me from nose to jaw.

"Who's there?" someone called out. The sound made me jump, and heat washed over me as I realized I wasn't alone. Tightening my fist, I paced to the kitchen's open doorway, blood slicking my knuckles beneath my glove.

The intruder stood by the edge of the sink, facing me. In one hand, he held a jar filled to the brim with little blue flowers. In the other, a scoop.

"Connoway?" Shock rippled across his face at the sight of me. Then he shoved the tea to one side and ripped a chef's knife out of the block on the counter. "What the hell are you doing here?"

The monster's fury rose in an instant, sinking shards of ice into my bones. "*What are we doing here?*" it inwardly seethed.

"Lenny," I said, the word as cold and dead as a corpse. I didn't miss the way his grip tightened over the hilt of the knife, or the way his gaze skipped over my shoulder nervously. My eyes narrowed. "Whatcha got there?"

"None of your business."

I huffed in disbelief, the hairs on the back of my neck lifting in unease.

The monster threw itself at the wall between our wills, clawing for escape until my eyes watered from the strain of holding it back. *"He's in her house!"*

I know.

Just seeing him here felt like sacrilege.

"You gonna let me by?" Lenny took a step forward. "Or are you here to finish what you started before you skipped town? It won't be so easy this time."

"I don't know what you're talking about."

Lenny's gaze darkened. "The hell you don't."

The monster flicked my gaze to the breadboard, where a long serrated knife lay beside a half-eaten loaf of focaccia. *"Pick up the knife,"* the monster urged.

I didn't.

Lenny stepped forward, our mutual hatred charging the air. A sudden warning rang between my ears when he shifted his weight. "You really thought you could just show up here?" Lenny snatched my camera off the counter with his free hand and drew his arm back. "I know what you did, Connoway!"

He's going to hit me.

I ducked a split second before Lenny slammed my camera into the cabinet. The hard crack it made at contact was so loud it bored into my ears, and as splinters of wood and shattered glass sprayed over the counter, the woodsy aroma of oregano burst in my nose.

My camera. Shock was a delicate blade to my heart. *He broke my camera.*

Lenny pinned me against the wainscoting and slid the blade of the knife against my throat. "I saw it all," he growled.

The monster flared. *"Don't touch him!"*

But Lenny couldn't hear the voice in my head. Adrenaline pounded in my veins, and I pushed Lenny off me and tried to scramble away, afraid of what we might do to stop him. What I might do.

Lenny had to be lying. He'd been black-out drunk that night.

Glass crunched beneath my shoe, and I tripped over the pieces of my camera and lost my balance. For a split second, I went airborne.

Then my face slammed into the counter's edge.

My brow split, a shock of pain stealing my breath. My ears whined with a harsh tinnitus, and hot blood ran down my face, blurring my vision in one eye and pooling on my upper lip.

The monster licked the blood away. *"Enough,"* it gritted out.

I struggled onto my knees. "Please," I whispered as more blood dripped onto the woven rug beneath me. "Don't do this."

I didn't want to hurt him.

The monster poured into my hollows, furious and cold. *"Yes, we do,"* it snapped.

As it stole my will, I felt myself become a passenger in my own body. It was always strange how loud the silence felt.

Numbness crawled up my fingertips into my palms. Into my forearms. My chest. Soon, my tether to my senses fell away entirely. Gone was the ache in my knuckles from punching the mirror. Gone was the floral-scented air. Gone was the taste of copper from where I'd bitten my tongue. Weightless, I shifted from a man of flesh to a creature preserved in ice.

I couldn't move. I couldn't breathe.

I could only witness.

Lenny's chest rose and fell in angry bursts as he leered over us. "I know your girlfriend's secret too. No one believed me before, but now — Ah!"

The monster yanked on the cuff of Lenny's pants, forcing him to throw out his hands to catch his fall. Trapped inside myself, I could only watch as the monster leapt onto Lenny, throwing a clumsy punch to his jaw. Lenny's head snapped back, smacking the tiles.

The monster growled — not in my head but in my very throat, a hoarse, unpracticed sound that shocked me to my core. *"Why are you here?"* The monster's demand slipped past my own lips, feeling strange and foreign on my tongue. *"Why are you in her house?!"*

Horror collected inside me. It had never stolen my voice before. "Arthur?"

Lenny's eyes darted toward the sound of Eva's voice, and he tried to call out for help, visibly alarmed. The windows exploded inward, thorny vines pouring in and knocking the basil plants off the windowsills.

For a moment, I was seventeen again. I was a killer, and I didn't care.

Eva appeared in the doorway, hair unbound and wild eyes bright with alarm. At her feet, the floorboards cracked and moss spilled out quick as flowing water across the kitchen floor. The sight of her filled me with shame. I didn't want the bee girl to see me like this, but I wasn't in control of my body anymore.

The monster licked more blood off my lip, but I tasted nothing. I *was* nothing, just a husk to be molted.

Eva rushed toward us. "What are you doing?"

"He deserves to feel pain," the monster snarled. When Lenny tried to wriggle away, the monster dug its grip into his forearms. We were brutal, furious and violent and
 empty

enraged.

"Arthur, stop!" Eva shrieked.

I would have cried out in frustration if I could. I wanted to scream and tell her this wasn't me, tell her I was in here, I was broken, I was *sorry*.

The monster shucked off my gloves, its dark intent flooding the body we shared. *Wait.* A full-body panic tore through me. *Wait! Stop!*

The monster didn't stop, reaching for Lenny.

A pair of impossibly large hands locked over my arms in an iron grip.

Jack.

The monster struggled. *"Let me go!"* it barked aloud.

"No," Jack huffed. The monster thrashed, but Jack Moreau was stronger than the beast. "Take a deep breath," he commanded. "There's a place in you where the darkness doesn't reach, Arthur. Find it!"

I trembled within my prison of ice. He didn't understand. I *was* the darkness. You can't run from the parts of yourself you hate.

"What's going on?" a voice I didn't recognize called out.

Jack squeezed even tighter. "Don't let go, Arthur."

The monster didn't like the way Jack's branches dug into our back. Hurting us. With a snap of our teeth, it ripped an arm free and grasped the closest branch.

And snapped.

Chapter 8

Arthur

Jack Moreau bellowed in pain.

The agony in his voice was a shock to my whole system, cracking the monster's ice in a moment. Sensation flowed back into my fingertips, pain replacing numbness.

"Jack?" I mouthed his name, blinking fast. Red-green sap oozed from the branch I'd broken. It smelled almost autumnal, as sweet and rotten as mulch gathered under a carpet of leaves.

At first, the big man simply stared at me, his face draining of color. Then he fell to his knees.

"Dad!" Eva shoved me out of the way as she rushed to his side. I caught my balance on the countertop, shattered glass digging into my now-exposed palm.

Before my eyes, the leaves on Jack's aspen began to change. Their edges curled inward, green bleeding into a vibrant yellow. Some chipped off and floated to the floor.

Eva took his face in her hands. "Say something," she begged.

But when he tried, no sound came out, his mouth gaping open only to close again. Pain sketched over his features.

"I'm sorry," I whispered, feeling smaller than I ever had.

At the sound of my voice, Eva stiffened. She whipped toward me, eyes red. "What have you done?" she snarled.

I was going to be sick, my mouth opening and closing with no words to fill it as my gaze flicked back to the man I'd hurt. Jack stared at his youngest daughter, rapidly blinking, a shudder moving through his enormous frame.

A pair of heavy boots drew my eyes up.

I rocked back, a wholly different kind of confusion falling through me. I shook my head, certain I was imagining the tall man with copper hair standing in the doorway to the kitchen, gun in a holster and sheriff's badge at his hip. Dane Walker's eyes cut first to his brother, still gasping in pain against the wall, before the lawman's gaze landed on me.

A flash of surprise took over his face, before he quickly smothered it into a neutral expression. "Stand back," he ordered, motioning me with his chin.

"Dane." I wasn't sure when Izzy had entered the room. She turned her palms up in surrender as she came to stand between us. "What are you doing?"

"I'm arresting him."

"You can't!" she fired back.

"Isobel," Dane Walker said in a low voice.

"It was an accident," Izzy said, turning pleading eyes on me. The tiny kitchen was taut with tension, made all the worse when Jack let out a groan.

"Need...the honey."

"Daddy?" Eva's hands fluttered uselessly over Jack's chest, as though she wasn't sure whether she should touch him. "What did you say?"

Instead of meeting her worried gaze, Jack kept his eyes steady on me, his expression pleading, glasses slightly askew. "The honey," he rasped. "Lottie's..." He coughed hard, coughed again, until red-green spittle smeared over his hand. Soon he was wheezing.

Izzy rushed to the phone. "I'm calling an ambulance." She looked directly at Dane Walker. "Don't touch Arthur!"

"I have to take him in," Dane said.

"You don't understand," Izzy snapped. "You *can't* touch him. No one can."

The air pulsed around me. No one had ever said that out loud. The summer I had lived here, the Moreaus had kept my secret. No one had told a soul what I could do, that I killed things, even when I didn't want to.

Dane looked between me and Lenny in quick assessment. His younger brother had taken a step back, still seething and looking for all the world like the human equivalent of a coiled snake. Maybe Dane could sense that. Maybe he finally understood what I'd known for years about the bastard he'd given so many fucking chances, and for once, he'd see through Lenny's bullshit.

But I couldn't depend on that. I still felt the monster in my tingling palms, the remnants of its cold invasion stretching up my arms. My knuckles ached, and blood dribbled from the cut in my eyebrow. I licked my lips instinctively, and a wave of self-loathing rolled over me.

It tasted good.

Izzy turned to Lenny. "Why are *you* here?"

"Isobel—"

"No, I want to know."

Their voices faded into the background as I stepped forward

and slipped my gloves back on, careful to make sure all my skin was covered. I knew what I had to do.

"Take me in," I said as I stretched out my hands.

"What are you doing?" The monster spoke inside our shared mind for the first time since losing control. I ground my teeth.

Coming here had been a mistake. Clearly, my hope that fulfilling Mom's last request would help me shuck off the monster's control had been woefully misplaced. Or maybe I was just too far gone to be saved. Either way, today had proven that I couldn't trust myself to hold the monster off.

I couldn't let it out again.

The monster carved a nail down my ribs in desperation. I imagined it splitting me open, peeling back the skin and viscera to reveal the heart beneath. Would it find anything still beating? At the end of the day, under all my fruitless struggle to be someone good, I was nothing but meat. Nothing but bone.

"Don't do this," the monster begged. *"Please, I... I'll be good!"*

Pity was a chasm I would gladly fall into to swallow that voice. "I don't believe you," I whispered, not caring who heard.

With a click, Dane placed the handcuffs on my wrists. "You have the right to remain silent," he said. "Anything you say can be used against you in a court of law."

Instead of taking root, the sheriff's words slipped through me like grains of sand in an hourglass, my full attention fixed on the giant man slumped against the oven. Jack's teakettle had fallen, water spilling out its spout.

"You have the right to an attorney and to have them present during any questioning. If you cannot afford an attorney, one will be provided for you."

I felt Eva's glare bore into my skin. Shame swelled hot inside me, and I dug the toe of my shoe into the layer of moss growing over the kitchen tiles at my feet.

"Do you understand the rights I have just read to you?"

The question snapped me out of my daze, and I looked up at the man I'd murdered eight summers before.

"I understand."

Chapter 9

Arthur, Before

Mom lifted the strap of her camera bag over her head and slung it across my shoulder, careful as always to not let her fingers touch my skin. "There's a fresh roll inside," she said.

My chest tightened, and I thought of the summer she'd rented out a darkroom and taught me the painstaking process of photo development. The sharp bite of chemicals had filled my nose as we'd loaded the film reel into a developing tank. Mom had explained each step, so patient with me then. Developer first, to expose the image. A stop bath to neutralize it. Fixer to remove all unexposed silver halides and make a picture permanent.

It was chemistry to her. Magic to me.

"Be good for Jack," Mom said softly.

Emotion clogged the space between my ribs, making words impossible.

As she stepped off the porch, Mom wiggled her fingers, a sad little smile playing at the corners of her mouth. Jack walked her to the Volkswagen, quietly saying something as he opened her door that I didn't quite catch. Mom huffed a laugh and shook her head.

"I'm sorry about your nose."

I all but jumped out of my skin as Eva appeared, holding a bright yellow plate and a trio of blueberry muffins, her smile rueful.

Jack was speaking again. I strained to hear, my attention slipping off his daughter. Mom scrawled something on a scrap of paper spread on the dashboard, then held it out to Jack, who pocketed it.

"Do you like blueberries?"

"I... What?"

The bee girl set the plate down and hopped onto the porch rail, her legs swinging underneath her. It seemed a strangely childlike gesture for someone who appeared to be my age. Sixteen, maybe seventeen at the most?

"I should have asked, before. I'm not bad at streusel, if you'd prefer that."

She was making it so hard to focus. I shook my head, though I didn't have anything against muffins, really. I'd simply lost my appetite.

Jack stepped back, and Mom slammed the door shut, her plastic smile slipping. As the Volkswagen rolled, spitting dust in its wake, the last string of hope in me snapped.

"Do you — "

I turned and bolted into the mudroom, fleeing the incessant line of questions.

Jack had put me in a spare room off the kitchen. Its main features included towers of fabric stacked against the wall and an old metal sewing machine thick with dust.

I locked the door and plopped down onto the bed. The pillowcase smelled like lemons.

I slept fitfully, hating how Mom filled the empty space even when she wasn't there. I hated that I cared, when she clearly didn't give a shit about me. Who the hell dumped their kid off with a stranger, anyway?

The sewing room was a saccharine prison in Pepto-Bismol pink. For days, I avoided the Moreaus, stewing in my irritation as I read my books behind a locked door. But it seemed the more pages I turned, the more my anger calcified into something duller, something hard and cold. The monster was numbing me up again. It was the only real defense we had. When you can't change something, you have to find a way not to care about it so much.

Jack kept a plate of leftovers for me on constant rotation in the fridge. I didn't have the heart to tell him how the ribs and chicken thighs turned my stomach.

Every morning, a yellow plate of pastries was left outside my door, which I ignored.

On the fifth day, however, the smell of pancakes reached into my dreams. I woke to the waft of maple syrup. When I rolled, squinting, my eyes fixed first on a plate of fluffy golden pancakes on my side table, then on the bee girl perched on top of my dresser.

"Good morning, sleepyhead," she chirped.

I bolted upright with a gasp. "You're...you're in my room!"

She used her toe to point to the steaming offering. "You didn't eat my muffins."

My mouth gaped open.

"You didn't eat my scones." Eva scowled and hopped off the dresser. "I'm not making you croissants. They're too hard."

"What are you—?"

She cut me off. "I'm sorry I broke your nose."

When she pulled her braid over her shoulder like that, she exposed a whole new bouquet of freckles. I caught sight of a honeybee nesting in her hair. More stirred on the windowsill. A twinge of discomfort flicked through me. Intellectually, I knew bees were a vital part of our ecosystem, but they bore a remarkable resemblance to wasps, and wasps were, objectively, assholes. I still hadn't forgiven the mean little bastards for an incident last spring when a nest in our campsite fell from its branch and the hive blamed me for its shoddy construction. I was sore and swollen for days.

"Can you not do that?" I asked, pointing to where Eva was swirling a finger through the air. A honeybee chased it, seemingly entranced by the movement, until finally it landed on her nail.

The bee girl cocked a brow at me. "What, this?" She blew on the honeybee, coaxing it into flight again.

I stiffened. "Yes."

"She won't hurt you."

"If you're nice," the monster finished, remembering what she'd said before. It shared none of my apprehension. On the contrary, the beast seemed delighted, even charmed, by our visitor. *"You really should have eaten her muffins."*

"Don't say it like that." I realized too late that I'd spoken the words aloud.

"You talk to yourself. A lot." Eva snatched up the plate, thrusting the fork in my face. "Now. Eat this and forgive me."

A honeybee perched on her knuckle. I swallowed a biting retort and snatched the fork and plate from her, annoyed at her dogged persistence and somewhat perplexed that she seemed somewhat insulted. I hadn't meant to hurt her feelings, but I also wasn't interested in being her friend.

The monster flicked me. *"Be nicer."*

I sighed. Maybe it was right. At the very least, fighting off her aggressive hospitality was getting a little exhausting. I didn't know if her stubbornness was a farm-kid thing, but it was becoming clear that she wouldn't relent until I accepted an olive branch.

The first bite of pancake melted in my mouth. The sweet and salty contrast of butter and syrup made my eyes roll back a moment. I barely hid a groan.

Eva smirked, but she didn't say anything, just held out a glass of milk to wash it down.

"You are very persistent," I muttered, stabbing another bite.

"Sure am."

I nodded to the bees in her braid. "What's the deal with that, anyway?" They followed her everywhere. It was deeply unsettling.

Eva pursed her lips, seeming to consider. "I'll tell you, if you answer a question."

I paused with a bite in my mouth, surprised. "What question?" I garbled.

The monster heated my cheeks. *"Would you chew your food?"* it gritted out. *"You're embarrassing us."*

"Your touch. It...hurts things?"

I swallowed a too-large bite. How the hell had she figured that out?

Before I could answer, Jack peered around the corner. "Eva," he chided. "I told you not to bother him."

Eva looked at me sweetly. "Am I bothering you, Arthur?"

I fumbled a reply, finding the word *bothering* wholly inadequate and hating the trickle of feeling that my name in her mouth sent up my spine. She said it like a secret.

"See, Dad?" Eva smiled, all innocence. "We're just eating."

Jack plucked a green sprig from his hairline. I did a double take. *Is that a sprout?* "Eat up, then. Got a lot of work to do today."

When he left, I turned to Eva. "What work?"

She smiled. "We're uncapping honeycomb. You'll love it."

When she turned to go, I snatched my jeans and a dirty T-shirt off the floor, dressing quickly, then followed the bee girl down the hall, irritation sparking.

She plucked two aprons off a hook in the mudroom, tossing me one of them. "We'll start with uncapping the wax from the hives in our own backyard." A strand of hair fell into her eyes as she tied the strings at the small of her back. "Then we'll move on to the apiary just north of the Walkers' orchard."

I clutched the linen apron, worn soft from years of use. "I don't work for you. Or your father."

Eva shrugged. "Your loss. There's nothing like fresh honeycomb, believe me. And spring's harvest is the sweetest. Though" — she slipped into a pair of sandals — "autumn has the deepest flavor. If you stay here long enough to see the asters and goldenrod bloom, you can try that too."

"I'm not staying," I snapped.

I didn't realize I was trailing after her until the door to the cottage clapped shut behind me. Eva opened the chicken coop, and for some reason, I followed her inside. Immediately, the swell and beat of too many hearts pressed against me. The monster was wide-awake, its alertness to signs of life making the close space insufferable.

"Do you like birds, Arthur?"

My face snapped to hers. The question was innocent enough, but something about the too-easy way it had rolled off her tongue caught my attention.

"Yeah. I do," I said carefully.

The hens were calm as Eva reached into the nesting boxes and gathered egg after egg, setting each into the wide, square pockets of her apron. An Orpington with deep rusty hackle feathers poked her head through the coop door. I loosed a breath. This bird wasn't free, but she was soft and feathered, like all my favorite things. "If you touched one of them," Eva said casually, "would it hurt?"

My stomach corkscrewed. *Why would she ask me that?*

Eva waited, but I couldn't — wouldn't — answer. My mind filled with a hundred different times when the beating heart of something alive had painfully slowed to a halt because of me, killed to sate the hungry thing that lived beneath my skin. I couldn't tell her that even though I hated myself for it, it felt good, necessary on a cellular level.

I couldn't tell her that like a shriveled sprout in the dirt, I needed nutrients, nourishment, *life,* and that when I was desperate, I would take it every time.

I couldn't tell her I craved it.

"What about me?" Eva didn't move closer, but she may as well have. I felt her attention like a weight and stepped back. "Would you hurt me?"

"No," the monster rasped inside my head.

I swallowed. "I don't want to hurt anyone, bee girl."

Eva's lips puckered, like she wanted to ask more, then changed her mind. She led me out of the coop, the back of her heels striped in dark green excrement.

I squinted into the too-bright light. Asters bloomed a path down from the cottage, their petals uncurling like soft little stars. I could have sworn they weren't there before. When Eva bent and picked one, she scratched the head of the same fluffy gray-and-white kitten I'd seen my first day here. It nuzzled her leg, purring loudly.

"I can feel it when they die, you know." Eva's eyes met mine.

I sucked in a breath when she held the flower out. "Will you show me?"

"I...I can't—"

"I know you do it. I want to see." Eva wiggled the flower's stem. I watched the aster lengthen, the cut vine curling back to wind around her wrist.

"*The flowers respond to her,*" the monster said in amazement.

Eva's expression grew more serious. "I'm not afraid of dead things, Arthur."

That irritated me more than anything else. I snatched the aster from her and tore off my glove. I didn't know how she could feel what I could do, but she was wrong to think I was anything less than a plague.

And I would prove it.

The instant the aster touched my skin, it wilted in my palm and its energy moved into me, unseen.

Within me, the monster straightened. *"It tastes like honey,"* it whispered in wonderment.

Eva watched, transfixed. I waited for the fear to come. I waited for disgust. Gingerly, she took the weed back, holding it up to the light, and I watched, mouth agape, as the dead thing came back to life again and bloomed for her.

"So." Eva's triumphant smile was a confirmation. "You're like me."

Chapter 10

Eva

Her father was a ghost of himself.

The sheriff had taken Arthur away hours ago. Since then, Dad's condition had worsened, his graying skin and the deep bruises under his eyes slowly turning a sickening shade of green.

He slept now, his breathing even. Unable to settle, Eva paced the room, winding the end of her shirt around her finger. A seed of panic had taken root in her heart.

Arthur had hurt him. No, Arthur had nearly *killed* him!

Eva shut her eyes, not wanting to feel it anymore. The shock. The grief. She'd always been able to fix the things that Arthur broke, but she couldn't fix this. She'd tried reviving the sapling, but the aspen didn't seem to hear her, the pale and brittle heartwood hollowed of life.

Dad's heart still beat, lost somewhere within the mesh of roots inside his chest cavity. His sluggish pulse gave her little comfort. Eva couldn't rest, afraid if she closed her eyes for even a moment, he would slip away.

She curled her fingers again into the hem of her shirt, pressure building behind her eyes. For so long, Eva had feared Arthur's return as much as she'd yearned for it. He was always ruining things. Ruining her. When he had shown up yesterday, Eva had feared he'd find a crack in her armor and slither beneath. She'd thought the most precious thing he could break was her heart.

She'd been wrong.

A soft knock drew her attention to the doorway, where Izzy stood holding a teacup.

"Dad always says a hard day should end with tea."

Eva accepted the cup without speaking and swallowed the whole thing down so fast it burned her throat.

"Oh, sweetie." Izzy laid a hand on her shoulder. "Take a break. I got him."

"I can't," Eva croaked out. It didn't matter how tired she was, or how terrified she felt sitting here, obsessively checking his pulse, watching his breathing, waiting for him to wake.

She couldn't leave.

Izzy sighed. "I promise to call for you the instant anything changes."

Eva hesitated, the back of her tongue feeling scalded and raw.

"Go on, then," Izzy softly urged.

As though released from a spell, Eva finally did, squeezing her sister's hand on the way out the door. She didn't go to her room, drawn instead to the kitchen, where she surveyed the mess with raw, stinging eyes. Glass and aromatic herbs littered the counters. Her socks squished soundlessly on the moss-laden tiles as she stepped through the wreckage and out onto the porch in a search for fresh air and an open sky.

After Dad had refused an ambulance, they'd called Dr. Rosen, who agreed and advised them not to move their father, promising to send someone from the hospital to the house instead. She'd said Dad's size and strange condition left too many variables, and besides, he'd made it clear he wanted to die on his own land.

That's when Eva had hung up the phone.

Wind chimes sang—in warning or blessing, Eva couldn't tell. Her eyes landed on the greenhouse, and a sudden crush of emotion drew out the long, slender leaves of the hyacinths planted on either side of the porch, purple flowers popping into bloom. She walked toward the greenhouse, blades of grass wisping against her ankles with every step. A lump grew in her throat when she pushed inside and her nose filled with a familiar concoction of herbs and spices.

Eva couldn't create life out of nothing. Her gift merely coaxed existing seeds and bulbs in the soil out of dormancy. She'd limited her garden to local flora so as not to introduce any invasive species to the area, but in here?

She could grow anything she wanted.

Past the bags of fertilizer and a clothesline strung with drying sage lay a pile of books Eva had long neglected. She rifled through the stack. A homesteader's field guide. A historical romance novel she'd read a dozen times. A book on local songbirds. When she opened that one, the pages made a loud, unsticking sound. Something old and tarry had been thumbed across an image of an oriole. Eva touched the bird. *Probably sap.* They used to take this book into the woods on birdwatching days.

But when she took a whiff, she realized she was wrong.

Honey.

With a hard swallow, Eva recalled her father's painful gasp as he begged her for honey. *Lottie's honey.* Eva had never seen him so desperate, and it scared her not to understand.

She was missing something.

Honey in Her Veins

At the bottom of the stack, Eva found a folder full of pressed flower heads, and her heart skipped. Dad had built her a flower press for her eleventh birthday. He had made a big show of it, and the two of them had spent the afternoon collecting and preserving blooms while Dad told her stories.

Eva frowned, rubbing her thumb over a pink petal. The smooth and delicate silk wrinkled under the pressure.

Dad had a whole trove of heartbreaking folktales. Eva still remembered her favorite, about a honeyman who found magic in the wildflower fields on their mountains. He tried to take the magic home in sachets full of seeds, but by then the forest had already wriggled into his veins, and the seeds bloomed instead, spilling flowers out his pockets.

Eva sniffed, then immediately wrinkled her nose, forgetting the tale as the smell of rot hit her. She tracked it to a pot of heirloom tomatoes. Just this morning, they'd been heavy with bulbous fruit, but the weight of her emotions had over-ripened them. Now a sour flavor stained the air, and a rime of mold coated the tomato skin in fuzzy white-blue patches.

Eva pushed out a breath. "You are in control."

When she sat back on her haunches, a steel box shoved far into the shadows under the counter caught her eye. Cobwebs silked the backs of her fingers as she dragged it forward. Eva shook them off, goose bumps stippling up her arms. A bit of dust sprayed out when she popped the lid, making her cough. Eva waved it away and lifted one of the thin green notebooks from the stack inside.

Dad's journals.

Eva ran her thumb over the smooth laminated cover. In his giant hands, they had always seemed so small and trivial. Now this one weighed heavily in her grasp.

Something gnawed at the back of her mind.

Her father kept a detailed record of his life and business. He'd shown Eva some of the charts he made, tracking the patterns and preferences of their bees so they could better serve their needs as keepers. He kept logs of their apiaries, too, and made sketches of the trails he took up the mountain, noting the herbs he found along the way.

Eva lifted the cover page, then stopped herself. She'd never intruded on his privacy before, and even the thought of doing so now made her itch. But something nagged at her.

Her father's stories weren't always children's tales. They could be wicked, thorny things. In some, the honeyman was punished for trying to steal away the magic he'd found. Dad's imagination made every new retelling more fantastical and jarring. Perhaps the honeyman's lungs filled with waterweeds or he sprouted honeysuckle from his ears!

A shudder moved through her.

They were just stories.

And yet while Eva had studied cures to common ailments, nothing she'd tried had ever worked on the aspen tree rooted inside her father's body. Her father's condition wasn't exactly one you would expect to find in an anatomy book or a tome on ancient herbal wisdom. It was strange, and wrong, and horrifying.

What are you hiding, Dad?

Eva skated her thumb across the cover again. She knew there were things he'd never told her.

Or maybe he had.

Eva let out a breath. "This is crazy," she said aloud, needing to physicalize the turn of her thoughts, to ground herself in reality. Those were just stories!

But what if she was wrong? What if there was something more, hidden in his half-truths?

She didn't want to break his trust, but...Eva flashed to the strain of his lungs as he had succumbed to sleep. She pictured the withered tree in his chest, its heartwood barely pulsing.

Chest tight, she flipped the journal open.

At first, Eva found nothing of significance between the pages. There were detailed annotations and instructions for new hikers and seasoned veterans of the woods alike. Dad had a way of spotting treasures others would pass by. Troves of hidden ginseng untouched by sang hunters. Fields of bloodroot, which blossomed only a few weeks a year. Goldenseal, which had become so popular now that people often forgot you could overharvest a good thing.

But Dad never did. He had taught her that the most important thing a person could do was protect and shield vulnerable things. Precious things.

Things too sacred to be cultivated.

Eva skimmed through the more personal entries. Part of her ached to linger and soak in the details Dad had written about her mother. These pages were a window into the woman who'd given Eva life, but they weren't hers to read, and she couldn't help but feel the press of time.

When her eye caught on a bulging envelope wedged between the other journals, Eva paused. She reached for it and peeled off the address sticker holding it closed, then slid the contents onto her lap.

Photographs.

Her breath caught, and she flicked through them quickly, her hands unsteady. Some of the photographs had light leaks, or the occasional blur. She'd never seen this roll developed, but she recognized each one of these moments, and the memories made the center of her chest ache.

Arthur had taken these.

There were shots of the cottage, both inside and out. Shots of her father tending the bees. Shots of Eva pulling weeds from the garden. Eva snipping herbs in the greenhouse. Eva lifting the binoculars to her eyes as she searched the canopy for birds. Eva grinning as she lay on the dock of their pond, her cheek turned toward the camera.

She remembered that afternoon. They'd spent it sunbathing on the dock, playing truth or dare. Her cheeks warmed when she remembered how, precisely, that game had ended.

The last photograph made her breath catch. Arthur had taken it during the golden hour. The sun had made everything in the garden glow. Eva held a bouquet of dandelions in her hand, ready to be dried and jarred for tea. She was laughing at him, not sure how or when to smile, one hand out to block the camera's view.

This had been the day Eva realized she wanted Arthur to stay.

Grief scalded its way up her throat. Burning, burning, *burning*. Eva wanted to scream, but the sound that escaped was more of a sob. Dad had no business developing these. She'd thought the roll of film Arthur had left her had been lost in the months of grief after he left. Eva had tried finding it, then tried forgetting. She didn't want them. She didn't want *him*.

Frustration rose inside her, and Eva hurled the photographs away. They flew apart, fluttering — briefly — like wings. No, what she'd wanted was to matter enough for him to stay, to write to, to give a damn about the state of her heart after that night in the chapel when everything changed.

The flight of the photographs knocked down a few sprigs of tied-up sage. When her breathing returned to a normal rhythm, Eva got on her knees and collected the herbs and photographs from the floor.

She didn't want to hold the greenhouse in such high regard, because if she did, it meant she was still holding on to Arthur. He was all over this room. When Eva closed her eyes, she could still see him hanging herbs on the clothesline. Snipping tomatoes. Coaxing a ladybug onto the tip of his glove.

And there, in the corner. There was a hidden place where the greenbrier climbed the wall outside, blocking their view of the house. It was the perfect place to hide, and they'd used it well. Eva flushed at the flood of memories. Arthur always had the coldest hands. It had been such a sweet relief, in the summer heat.

Why did he come back?

If he'd just stayed away, her father wouldn't be hurt. Arthur wouldn't be stuck behind the very bars he'd run from in the first place. And she wouldn't be here, hating him for it.

As Eva dumped the photographs back into the open bin, her eyes caught on a purple envelope she'd never noticed before. Curious, she opened the flap and slid out a card. The handwriting was unfamiliar. Eva's eyes dropped to the bottom of the page, where the name of the sender was scrawled in curling loops.

The air rushed out of her lungs.

Lottie.

Chapter 11

Arthur

A silver sleeve of Pop-Tarts sat on a bench near the door to the holding cell where I'd been left, waiting, for hours. I bounced a knee, holding a cloth against the cut in my eyebrow.

"You need stitches."

I didn't answer. I didn't want to talk to the monster right now.

The motion sensor had long since flickered off, casting the spartan room in pitch blackness. The darkness was cold, so like the icy state the monster had forced upon me when it tried to take its vengeance on Lenny Walker.

The monster bristled. *"You wanted to hurt him too,"* it said.

But I wouldn't have. That was the difference.

With the chemical burn of cleaner stinging my nose, I replayed the events at the cottage. The memorial service I couldn't finish. The fight with Lenny. The slip in control that allowed the monster to puppet me like a violent doll under its command. And Jack. Large, wonderful, powerful Jack hitting his knees, face distorted in pain because of me.

The shock of hurting him had ripped me free of the monster's hold too late to stop the flow of death into his tree, and into him. My poison hadn't killed him—yet—but the agony of what could have been left a buzz of anxiety crawling over every inch of my body.

I hated small, tight spaces and how trapped they made me feel. It reminded me of how it felt when the monster took me over, as though even my skin was too tight to comfortably hold my pounding heart. I'd wanted to rip myself open and yank my skeleton out of my skin, carve off the viscera and breathe, breathe, breathe.

I was too small a container for all the bad inside me. Even tapping the side of my leg brought no relief from the pressure weighing heavy on my chest. This wasn't new. I'd always known something wasn't right about me, but I'd never known how to fix it. I didn't even know how to start. I'd tried carving the monster out, tried starving it out... but it was in my bones.

Eva's face flashed before me. I'd seen her furious, I'd seen her soft, and wild, but fear was an emotion I'd sworn never to inflict on her again, and I'd broken that promise less than a day after my return.

The door to the hall snicked open, and a man wearing a navy tie cinched to his throat stepped inside, triggering the motion-sensitive lights back on. Dane Walker had been a newly appointed deputy the summer I'd come to stay with the Moreaus. Somewhere along the line, he'd acquired the position of sheriff. It should have been impressive.

But dead men weren't meant to get promotions.

When Dane dragged over the Pop-Tart bench, sitting spread-legged on the other side of the bars, my already chilled body went full subarctic. I couldn't help the hollow ache, or the confusion spilling into goose bumps across my skin, at the sight of Dane Walker, hale and whole.

Not a dead man after all, but still my ghost.

"You did the right thing, Arthur."

I didn't answer. The only reason I'd given myself up was because I was terrified of the monster inside me getting out again. For so long, I'd tried to minimize the damage I caused just by existing, but it wasn't enough. I wasn't a strong enough cage.

But I couldn't tell him any of that.

Dane surveyed me carefully. "I want to help you," he said.

Suspicion collected inside me. "Why?"

"I don't know." Dane scrubbed the back of his neck. "Jack always thought you were innocent. Isobel insists on it. And I'd like to avoid any more trouble."

That was just like the man I remembered. Never one to actually face the problem if there was a way to avoid it. No wonder Lenny had walked all over him for so many years.

My stomach soured. "Where's your brother?"

Dane's eyes widened in surprise. "What?"

"Is he here?"

In the permeating silence, I could almost hear the tick of my heart, speeding faster. It wouldn't surprise me in the least to hear that Lenny had gotten off scot-free. Maybe I deserved to be locked up, but so did he. Lenny had trespassed into the Moreau family home. Lenny had been the one to start the fight.

"He should be in here too," I snapped.

"Arthur—"

"No." Lenny couldn't get away with doing whatever he wanted just because his brother was the sheriff. It wasn't right. "He attacked *me*."

Dane studied me, then sat back, unhooking a pad of paper from his pocket. He flipped it open and clicked a pen. "Do you have any witnesses?"

"Your brother does a lot of things without witnesses." The words seemed to unlock something inside me, and before I could stop myself, more raced out. "How are you even alive?"

It came out like an accusation. Maybe it was.

My first summer in Audrey had ended in a nightmare so horrifying that I couldn't even think of it without bile rising in my throat. By the time I'd grabbed Eva's hand to run that fateful night, I'd been certain Dane Walker was dead.

When a trail of blood from the cut on my brow leaked down my cheek, the monster darted our tongue out to lick the hot, iron bead off the bow of my lip. Questions pushed to the forefront of my mind. Eloquent questions, like *How the hell?* and *What the actual fuck?*

Most pressingly: *Why have I spent my life running from your ghost?*

"Frankly," Dane said, his expression inscrutable, "I was hoping you could enlighten me."

"Excuse me?"

The monster pushed its presence into my hands to stall the anxious tap of my fingers as Dane sat forward, rubbing the center of his chest. I tried not to think about the kind of scar that would form over a wound like that. "I remember pieces from the reception," he said. "It's all scattered, broken up." Our eyes locked together. "But I remember you."

The monster swirled in my belly. To quell the sickening churn, I braced my head between my knees. Cold whispered through me. *"I could make the pain go away. You just say the word."*

I squeezed my eyes shut. Summoned the strength to refuse. To linger. To stay *Arthur*. I didn't realize Dane had asked me another question until he cleared his throat and I looked up to see him watching me expectantly.

"You're just like them, you know," Dane said, frustration leaking into his voice. "All four of you bend over backwards to keep each other's secrets. What am I supposed to do with that?"

I didn't answer. I couldn't. He'd made it sound like I still belonged to the Moreaus, when nothing could be further from the truth.

"You bruised my brother up real good. He could press charges," Dane said, visibly exhausted. "It would be in Jack's right to press them as well, if he wakes."

The mention of Jack cut like a thorn.

"How is he?" I pressed.

"Stable, for now."

The monster stirred nausea in my belly again. I needed to soothe it before I was sick. Fill the emptiness. "Can I have a Pop-Tart?" I asked, my voice cracking.

Dane hesitated only a moment before tossing me the foil through the bars. I tore open one end, my hands shaking, and was hit by the artificial smell of strawberry sugar. Nostalgia rose inside me. Mom had always kept a box of these on hand. They were her favorite flavor.

"It's strange," Dane said. "Secrets don't usually survive in a town this small. Tongues slip, you know? Everybody knows everybody's business."

I tensed, swallowing a large bite of the too-dry pastry.

"Things were messy enough when you left," Dane went on. "The doctors didn't know what to make of my scar, or Jack's condition, and my ex-wife didn't want the press looking deeper into our lives." He took a breath. "There was an investigation."

I'd known there likely would be, and that I'd been a coward to leave town the way I did. Audrey was a snow globe that was constantly shaking, obscuring the truth with false snow. But I'd hoped to draw the town's ire when I disappeared, giving them a scapegoat to take the pressure off the Moreaus.

Apparently, it had worked.

Dane watched me intently. "My brother remembers things from that night much more colorfully."

What a diplomatic way of saying Lenny had been drunk off his ass. I struggled not to squirm beneath Dane's stare.

"Why did you run?" he asked, his calm expression belying the urgency of his words.

Before I could dredge up a lie, the sound of rising voices came from just outside the holding cell. A knock sounded, and a guard peeked in. "We have a visitor," he said.

"Not now, Grayson."

A pale sheen of sweat glistened on the man's forehead. He looked visibly uncomfortable as he cleared his throat. "I told her to come back tomorrow, Sheriff, but she insisted."

That's when I noticed the lichen slinking over the door's threshold, and the smell of spring filled my nose.

Eva.

Dane must have clocked the edge to his deputy's voice. He looked up, then sucked in a hard breath, his eyes darting back to me a moment. He stood. "Five minutes." At the door, he looked back at me. "I meant what I said, Arthur. We can help each other."

Then he was gone.

In the doorframe he vacated, the bee girl stood with her arms crossed, her expression a whetted blade. Eyes bloodshot, mouth hard, she stepped toward me, the door to the holding cell clicking heavily into place behind her.

When Eva reached the bars, she slipped what looked like a letter out of her pocket and shook it at me. "What the hell is this?" she seethed.

Chapter 12

Eva

Arthur looked even worse than before. In the jaundiced light of the holding cell, his already worrisome pallor looked even more sickly as his eyes latched on to the envelope containing Lottie's note to Dad.

Eva had braced herself for lies. She knew there was something hidden just under the surface, something her father and sister weren't telling her. But no matter how broken things were between her and Arthur, she expected that he at least would be honest with her.

Eva took the note from its envelope and pressed it flat against the bars. "You know what this is?"

"No."

A crack split in the wall above his cot, spitting dust onto Arthur's pillow. He popped to his feet to avoid the debris, surprise flashing over his face.

"Why did your mother bring you here that summer?" Eva had to fight to contain the swell of anger rising like a tide inside her chest. "How did she know my father?"

Arthur's eyes dropped to where she'd wrapped a fist around

one of the bars between them. Bright yellow lichen grew where her palm touched the cool metal, spreading like a sunlit disease. "Ev, I swear, I don't know."

Eva's anger exploded into blooms. Weeds grew in the cracks in the floor, filling the empty spaces with furious green. Wildflowers ripped into life almost violently. She couldn't stop the tide of growing things.

Nor did she want to.

With a snarl, Eva thrust the paper into Arthur's hands. "Read it."

Tension scored the planes of Arthur's face, and he cut a glance to the wilderness spilling at their feet and up the walls before giving Charlotte's letter to her father his full attention.

Eva flicked a look at the clock. They had four minutes before Dane came back.

Arthur frowned. "They wrote to each other?"

"Every week, for years," Eva snapped. She didn't believe his innocent little act. There was clearly more to their parents' history than Arthur had ever divulged. How dare he keep it from her. Eva's chin trembled. *How dare he lie.*

Something green and covered in thorns pushed through a crack in the wall as a tear slipped down Eva's cheek.

"Ev, I didn't know."

She didn't believe him.

Long past feeling guilt over snooping, Eva had torn the greenhouse apart searching for more letters before raiding her father's office. The volume of letters she found stuffed into boxes and filing cabinets had overwhelmed her. How long had they been in correspondence?

Dad had slept on, his breathing steady but his heartbeat weak.

"You heard what he asked for at the cottage, didn't you?" Eva reached through the bars and snarled her fingers into the front of Arthur's shirt, dragging him down to her. Her lips curled back. "He didn't just ask me for honey, Arthur, he asked for *Lottie's* honey. You must know something about that!"

The clock on the wall ticked in the beats of silence.

"Please," Eva whispered, not caring how pathetic she sounded, or if she was making a fool of herself coming here, expecting him to have the answers. There was a bitter weed digging into her most tender places, as sharp as the vines now snaking through the brick wall into the jail cell. The pain inside her pushed its own thorns deeper with every minute that passed.

The silence stretched so long that for a moment, Eva felt herself falter. She clocked the time. One minute, at most, before she had to leave. One minute wasn't enough.

But then, Arthur swallowed hard.

And she knew she was right.

"What?" she demanded as the jangle of keys sounded just outside the door. They were out of time. She shook him by the shoulders. "What do you know?"

"I-I'm not sure." Arthur's eyes darted back and forth, seeing something that wasn't before them now. "But I saw something, the night we..." His jaw worked. "The night I left."

"Something?"

"You were asleep when Jack got home that night. He wasn't well," Arthur said. "When he asked me to check on you, I stayed and watched instead. And, Ev, he did something...strange."

The door behind them unlatched as someone just outside — the guard, or maybe the sheriff — pushed it open.

Arthur's eyes flicked over her shoulder. "I didn't understand it then," he said quickly.

"Just say it!" Eva's impatience lit like a wick to a flame. The crack above Arthur's cot widened, allowing more vines to snake inside, their snarled tips splayed against the painted bricks.

"There was a hidden jar of honey," Arthur said.

Hidden honey?

"Where?"

"Time's up," Dane Walker said.

Eva's panic spiked. Arthur knew something — she didn't know what, or why Dad had kept it from her, but if there was any chance that he could help her father, she couldn't let that pass her by. "*Where*, Arthur?"

"In the vent." He licked his lips. Blood, dried and new, caked a path of switchbacks down his cheek. Her eyes fixed on the split of his brow. It should have been cleaned up by now. It should have been stitched.

But no one would touch him, she realized. No one but her. Maybe Izzy's warning had scared them away, or maybe news of his return had reignited old rumors and sparked old fears. Audrey had never been very good at welcoming outsiders, especially those who were... different.

She straightened. "I'm getting you out of here."

"Eva," Dane said, crisp and stern.

She ignored him. "Stand back," she said to Arthur as she squeezed her eyes shut, trying to focus her gift, to take the chaos and guide it into something sharp and intentional. Lichen and mushrooms spread over the walls at her call, filling the room with the scent of rotting summer.

She breathed it in. *The cracks.* That was it! Her eyes snapped open again, all her focus trained on the split in the bricks over Arthur's bed. There was a network of roots beneath the building, twining deep into the ground. At her nudge, they trembled and reached upward.

The ground beneath them shook.

"Whoa," Dane Walker said, and Eva turned to see the sheriff steady himself against the doorframe. Dust rained from the ceiling, chalking the air.

Crack.

Another split formed in the brick wall, this one leading all the way down to the floor.

CRACK.

Eva lost her balance at the next shake, falling against the bars. Someone shouted out in the hall. Spider-legging roots crawled out of the cracks, brown and feathery, seeking, *seeking...*

Eva's breaths were ragged, her feet slipping over the now-slanted floor. She cut a gaze to the outer wall, beckoning her power forth. The rootlings already splayed against the bricks squeezed tight.

And the wall buckled.

Chaos broke loose. Eva covered her head with her arms to protect herself from the rush of falling debris. An alarm blared, strobing the cloud of swirling dust in the holding room with blinking red flashes. The world around her seemed to slow as she squinted, searching for Arthur. He lay on the other side of the bars, head between his knees.

Behind her, Dane let out a grunt.

It brought Eva back to another night, one far too sharp to remember right now. She shook her head to clear it away and dropped to a crouch beside the sheriff, her hands shaking as she unhooked the key ring from his belt. The jangle seemed to rouse Dane, and he tried to push onto his elbows. She scrambled away, the smell of green, blooming vegetation filling her nose as she tried one, two, three keys in the lock on the holding cell, searching for the right one.

"Eva?" Dane asked, blinking. He looked disoriented but not wounded, and relief collected inside her to see that she'd controlled her magic. He'd be okay.

"I'm sorry," she lied. In truth, she felt triumphant.

The next key clicked in the lock. Relief flooded through Eva as she stepped into the holding cell, shoving the door closed behind her.

"Wait!" Dane coughed, pulling himself to his feet, only to sway against the wall. "Stop!"

Eva chucked the keys into a corner he couldn't reach. Then she circled Arthur's wrist with her hand and yanked him to his feet. "Come on!" she yelled. He stumbled awkwardly behind her, both of them stepping through fallen debris. The roots around her seemed to pulse, responsive to her will. Eva all but pushed Arthur through the hole in the wall, then followed quickly after. Dane shouted at them through the bars. In seconds, another voice joined him. *The guard.*

They had to go, now. Eva pulled Arthur after her.

"What are we doing?" he panted.

"Running!"

It seemed good enough for him. Arthur stumbled down the street beside her. Adrenaline pumped through Eva. There was nowhere to hide. The only reason they'd gotten this far was the lateness of the hour, but even this late on a Saturday night there were usually a few stragglers in the streets, leaving Dawson's Bar on wobbly feet.

Fear slithered up her body. They had to hide!

Arthur tugged her hand, pulling them into a narrow alley wedged between two worn-out buildings. Eva wanted to protest. They didn't have time to stop, time to think!

"Breathe," Arthur demanded. He walked her deeper into the shadows, looking every bit the fugitive she'd just made them both into. Dirt-smudged. Guilty. Panicked.

Well, maybe not as panicked as her. Eva pulled the end of her braid, every breath coming faster, harder, *faster, harder.*

"Arthur," she whispered in disbelief. "I think I just broke you out of jail."

To her surprise, he laughed — a short, humorless sound. "You sure did, bee girl."

What had she been thinking? Eva's chest fluttered, and dark spots constellated her vision. She wanted to be angry with him, not whatever this was. Her insides buzzed with furious and protective feelings as her gaze landed on the cut on his eyebrow again.

They hadn't even cleaned it.

Eva felt a little faint, the rush of the jailbreak crowding into her thoughts. She didn't know what to do next, hadn't thought this through. She didn't break rules.

"Ev?"

Shouts came from somewhere down the street. People were flocking to the jail, people who soon would be looking for them. For her.

She couldn't breathe.

"Ev." Arthur's voice came as though from underwater. Eva blinked fast but failed to bring him into focus. "Ev, I think you're having a panic attack."

She couldn't get enough air. It hurt to try.

"Shh." Arthur gingerly cupped the back of her head and held her to his chest. His voice was an anchor she didn't expect. An old tether. It pulled at something deep inside her that Eva wanted to keep buried. She squeezed her eyes shut.

Be here. Be now.

Arthur's thumb skated over the back of her skull. "Take a breath with me?"

Together, they inhaled. They exhaled.

"Remember the storm clouds," Arthur whispered, turning his face into her hair. "The rain comes and goes, but you, *you* are the whole sky, Ev."

Eva couldn't believe he remembered her telling him that.

They had to go. Eva felt the pressure of impending consequences, but Arthur didn't hurry. With every exhale, his breath warmed the skin behind her ear. As Eva's panic eased away, she became more and more aware of how wrong his delicate touch was. They weren't like this anymore. They weren't anything close to okay, much less...tender.

She sucked in a hard breath and stepped out of his embrace. If Arthur was affected by the distance she put between them, he didn't show it on his face. "Tell me again what you saw that night."

She had to help Dad, before it was too late.

Arthur's eyes flicked down the alley. "Now?"

Eva jerked a nod. They didn't have time to waste. Arthur had to get away from these mountains, and as far from Audrey as he could. But she couldn't let him go until she knew what he'd witnessed. "Tell me."

Arthur pursed his lips. "I think his tree started growing that night."

Eva sucked in a breath.

"He was in so much pain, after what...what happened," Arthur said quietly, a pang in his voice. "When he didn't think I was looking, he pried open the vent above your fridge and took out a jar of honey. He ate it, and…"

"Yes?" Eva asked, breathless.

Arthur swallowed. "It was miraculous. Like he'd taken medicine."

Her mind swam with this new information. Sometimes they had return customers who came raving into the Shoppe, claiming their honey had cured them of some ailment or another that no medicine had ever touched. It was lovely, really. Eva thought it was all that bottled summertime stuff Dad was always going on about. The power of sun and soil and belief.

But what if it was real?

A tightness corded itself around her chest and squeezed. *What does it mean, if it is?*

"We need to get into that vent," Eva said, forgetting herself for a moment. There was no *we* between them, and besides, the cottage was the first place the sheriff and his deputies would look.

Arthur's van was there, though, parked in the cottage's driveway after he and Dad had returned from getting the tire patched that morning. He needed that van to get away from here.

"Okay." To her surprise, Arthur nodded, his attention shifting to the other cobwebbed end of the alley, where the forest had crept in, vines curling up and over the corners of the building in a shallow layer of emerald ivy.

Eva blinked. *Did I do that?*

"We'll have to be fast," Arthur said, meeting her gaze. "Can you run?"

Chapter 13

Arthur, Before

The hive boxes at the bottom of the hill behind the Moreau cottage looked like a mouth of crooked teeth ready to swallow the surrounding coneflowers swaying in the breeze.

After returning the eggs to the kitchen to be washed, the bee girl had led me across the yard to what looked like a workshop, chatting easily as we walked, unbothered by the trail of clover she left in her footsteps. I couldn't get her words out of my head.

You're like me.

"Just in here," Eva chirped, rolling the door to the workshop open. The instant I stepped through, the smell of melting sugar drew me up short. *No, not sugar.* My mouth watered, the warmth of the little room folding around my body. *Honey.*

"We have six apiaries," Eva said as she tied her hair at the back of her neck. "The one you saw coming in."

The mouth of teeth.

"And five more scattered across different farms we collaborate with nearby."

I nodded, curious despite myself. My eyes moved over the room, taking in the setup of equipment. It was rustic but very clean, with a surprising amount of light flooding down from a set of what looked like handcrafted skylights.

My inspection halted when I met the gaze of the dark-haired girl standing at the sink.

It turned out the cashier Mom had spoken to at the Honey Shoppe had been none other than Eva's sister, Izzy. She seemed older than Eva and me by four, maybe five years.

Izzy studied me, spinning a rag inside an empty honey jar before setting the jar on a cloth. "So," she said, "Sleeping Beauty *can* leave his room."

"Yes."

Izzy crossed her arms over her chest. "You live in a van?"

The question caught me off-guard. I nodded.

"Why?"

Eva made a little sound. "Iz."

But her older sister clearly had no qualms about putting her suspicion on full display. She tipped her chin up, waiting for my answer.

"We travel," I said. When the silence stretched, I cleared my throat. "A lot."

"Travel where?"

"Around."

This was, by far, the longest conversation we'd had in the last two weeks. Izzy's eyebrows knit in clear irritation at my evasion. I didn't particularly like her verbal dissection either.

"I remember your mom. It's been a long time since she up and left this place."

"Hey." Eva speared her sister a warning look. "Would you back off?"

"I think we deserve to know a little more about our guest."

I huffed. "What, you afraid I've got an ax on me or something?"

To my surprise, Izzy didn't laugh. She tilted her head to one side, considering.

"Seriously, Iz?" Eva's cheeks were aflame. She turned to me. "I'm so sorry. Izzy's girlfriend watches too much true crime."

"Granted," Izzy hummed. "But my point stands. We don't know anything about him."

Something about Izzy Moreau's protectiveness put me in mind of a badger all too keen to tear out throats if a predator got too close. It was strangely grounding to feel that for once I might not be the most vicious person in a room.

"Left my ax behind," I said.

Eva coughed a laugh, and Izzy's surprise melted into a quicksilver grin.

Jack ducked under the workshop's too-short doorframe. "In pairs," he said, passing each daughter a corded knife, which they plugged into opposing outlets. All three beekeepers sat on a pair of benches facing a wide, shallow basin, Izzy across from Eva, Jack across from an empty seat he motioned for me to take. I sat, feeling a little self-conscious.

Jack set one of the frames into a pair of clamps between us and nodded to the blade in his hand. "We use a hot knife to cut the comb away." He did as he described. The layer of waxy cells protecting the honey made a delicious crackling sound against the hot serrated edge before tumbling into the bin.

The smell of warm honey and melting wax intensified.

"Leave the comb in the bin for now. When you've cleared a frame, set it in the extractor." Jack leaned back to indicate the steel cylinder in the corner of the room. Then Paul Bunyan held the hot blade out to me.

I blinked. "You trust me with a knife?"

The monster winced internally.

Jack lifted a brow. "Should I not?"

"He'd prefer an ax," Izzy deadpanned.

"What?"

I laughed nervously. "Nothing."

"Whatever you say, Fairy Eyes." Izzy turned to her sister. "They are, aren't they? Vivid hazel. Damn."

The bee girl flicked me a too-quick look. "He's too tall for a fairy."

I flushed, not sure whether to take that as a compliment or an insult. Then Eva smiled at me, and a seed of warmth sprouted between my ribs.

Jack passed me the knife.

Once I got the angle right, it wasn't a difficult task, and it was strangely satisfying to watch the comb release all that hot dripping gold. Jack was patient, explaining the process to me as we went. The extractor would spin the bulk of the honey off the frames, he said, making it easier to bottle and seal.

A truck honked in the yard behind me. I craned my neck around just as a lanky, copper-haired boy my age leapt from the vehicle's bed. Recognition flickered through me first, followed by displeasure. It was the asshole I'd bumped into at the Honey Shoppe. He was clearly of some relation to the driver; they had the same red hair, the same steel eyes. A tiny woman with sleek black hair cropped to her chin slipped out from the passenger side.

Jack raised a hand in greeting. Izzy popped to her feet and went to greet them, hugging the much shorter woman. They each took a bin full of greenery from the back. When Izzy led them past the workshop door, she paused. "Arthur, meet Dane and Lenny Walker, our neighbors. And this is June."

The prim, petite woman held a comically large box of greenery. She wiggled her fingers in greeting. "Good morning," she strained.

Jack stood. "Let me help you, Junie."

Izzy elbowed the taller Walker brother. "This lucky bastard managed to convince my best friend to marry him. Can you believe that?"

"It took some work." Dane chuckled good-naturedly. "Still not sure I deserve her."

"I'm sure. You don't."

"Hey—"

"You are *both* my favorite people," June cut in, rolling her eyes as she passed the box to Jack. "Now quit yapping and help me bring these boxes up to the house, hmm?"

Izzy met her father's gaze. "June wanted a look at the back fields for her bouquets."

"I'll go with you." Jack looked at Eva. "You finish up here with Arthur?"

I jumped at the sound of my name.

When Eva nodded, the group filtered out of the workshop. All except the younger brother I'd recognized. Lenny's gaze shifted between Eva and me, his pupils expanding and his nostrils slightly flaring. "This looks cozy," he said.

I bristled, his voice instantly grating, and noted that he stood a bit too close to be polite. From where he leaned against the wall, he had a full view down Eva's shirt, and by the flush crawling up her neck, she knew.

And she shrank.

This was none of my business. This wasn't my town, or my family, or my home. So why did it bug the hell out of me that when the bee girl spoke, she'd lost a bit of the fire I'd seen that morning?

"Lenny," Eva said, "what are you doing here?"

"You haven't returned my calls."

"We've been busy," she said, quieter than I'd heard her all week.

"With what?"

Eva glanced at me, but what could I say?

"Anything," the monster urged.

"Pancakes," I blurted out.

"Anything but that."

Eva snorted a laugh. It was short and breathless, and she looked as caught off-guard by it as I was, but still, a warm feeling collected in my chest.

Lenny, meanwhile, was regarding me the way one looked at a bit of shit on their shoe. "I see," he said.

When he returned his focus to Eva, her smile fell, all her mirth doused like a candle flame squeezed into a ribbon of smoke between finger and thumb. The monster's preternatural senses attuned to a nervous uptick in her heartbeat.

Was she afraid of him?

The very thought had me glued to my spot on the bench, despite the growing awkwardness and the distinct impression that I should not be here. There was something weird about this guy. I didn't like the way he charged the room with static, setting all my nerves on edge.

I didn't like the way Eva paled the longer he stared at her.

The monster nudged me. *"Do something."*

Talking wouldn't help. I wasn't good at using my words like weapons. But I knew how it felt to be dismissed. An idea formed, and my grip tightened on the hot knife we'd been using to slice off the comb. As nonchalantly as I could, I plucked a new frame from the top of the pile, setting it in the clamps. The monster helped me keep my gaze calm and even, the message clear. *We have work to do,* my body language said. *So, kindly remove your sorry ass.*

Lenny's expression flickered with annoyance, but he tried to ignore my subtle dismissal. "So long as you're not avoiding me."

Beside me, Eva's comb knife slipped into the bin below. "Course not," she said, a little too fast. Overhead, the half dozen honeybees that had trailed after her all morning seemed to buzz a little louder. Their agitation made the hairs on the back of my neck rise.

Lenny, however, didn't seem to notice. If anything, he looked relieved. "Of course not." He smiled, and I immediately hated it. I wanted to shove a palmful of honeycomb right into his teeth. "Why would you?" he said with a laugh.

Eva made a sound like she meant to laugh it off too, but the little cheep that came out of her more closely resembled that of a wounded bird. For a painful moment, the monster's awareness of her discomfort made my heart pound harder in my chest, too. Her bees frenzied faster as I shared in her silent anxiety, looking between her and Lenny.

He continued to lean against the wall of the workshop, mouth crooking in a confident smile. "Let's go out tomorrow," he said, as though I weren't there at all.

"Oh. I-I can't," Eva said, stumbling over the words.

But Lenny bulldozed on. "Eight o'clock. There's a drive-in movie down in the valley. I'll pick you up at — Ow!" Lenny reared back, holding his wrist against his chest. His cavalier swagger bled into shock, then anger. "The hell?"

Even from here, I could see the pink already-swelling center of a bee sting.

"Oh, sorry," Eva said in a near monotone. "One of our queens mated with a hot-blooded drone. They've been pretty aggressive. The next brood cycle should calm down."

"This fucking hurts!"

I flinched back at his sudden outburst, at the sheer volume of anger. The bee girl, however, stacked her spine. "Do you have any vinegar back at the farmhouse? You'll need to put some on that right away."

The asshole looked between us again, eyes furious. "Vinegar?"

"Mm-hmm. Quicker the better," Eva said.

I looked at her, struck by the sudden change in her pitch, the way her eyes wouldn't quite meet mine.

She was lying.

"Lenny! We need you!" his older brother called from the house, just out of sight.

With a scowl, Lenny stepped back. His eyes landed on me again, and I had the impression that he was seeing me differently than he had when he'd first arrived.

"Eight o'clock," he repeated, keeping his eyes on mine even though he'd spoken to Eva. I bristled inside but held his gaze. The monster helped steady the squall of my emotions, allowing me to simply lift a brow.

His answering scowl felt good. It stroked something wretched inside me that wanted to see him displeased. When his brother called again, Lenny strode away, hugging his wounded arm to his chest.

The instant he left, Eva's shoulders dropped. A strand of blond had escaped her braid, obscuring her expression from view.

The monster spun around my spine. *"I didn't like that,"* it said quietly.

Neither did I.

"Vinegar, huh?" I asked nonchalantly. Eva's gaze snapped to mine. I pretended her eyes weren't suddenly red, as though she were holding in tears. She plucked the knife from the bin, nicking a bit of gooey honeycomb off the blade before she thrust it toward me.

"Eat this," she commanded.

And because I was glad the fire had returned to her eyes, I didn't fight her. I accepted the sticky mess, careful not to let our fingers brush, and cautiously brought it between my lips. The sweet, pungent honey glazed down my throat. I chewed until the wax shrank to a gum that made my teeth squeak.

"Really good," I said.

The knot between Eva's brows unknit. "Nothing like it," she said.

I couldn't help but think that there was nothing like her, or anyone in her family. The Moreaus weren't supposed to be like this. Kind. Funny. They weren't supposed to distract me from the ache in my chest.

"So, what do you think?" Eva asked, a notch too brightly, sweeping her arm out to gesture toward the workshop at large. "Better than the old sewing room?"

I huffed a laugh, surprised. "Yes."

"Fewer mothballs, at least."

She was quick, and funny. I couldn't stop the hitch of my smile. "Less pink."

The bee girl had a bright laugh. The peal of golden sound seemed to wrap around me, warm as the summer heat. Maybe that explained the sudden flush to my cheeks.

The monster rolled in my belly. *"Little death-touch. You made a friend."*

Chapter 14

Arthur

We dashed into the trees, the blare of the jail's alarm slowly fading behind us. A heavy blanket of clouds had obscured the moon and any stars, making the air feel heavy and thick, charged with the promise of an oncoming storm.

"*Hurry!*" The monster's urgency pushed me faster into the belly of the Walkers' orchard. It was a hell of a gamble to use their land as a shortcut, but we didn't have much of a choice. Soon, the cottage came into view. We hopped the low-lying fence and all but slammed into the porch rail, doubling over to catch our breath.

"Just show me the vent and you can go," Eva panted. "Follow the farm roads down to the valley. Dane won't expect you to know that route."

I watched her swipe a curl off her forehead, a strange feeling in my chest. Eva had asked me to stay many times; she'd never asked me to run.

There were no vehicles in the driveway, save my Volkswagen, sporting a newly patched tire. We hurried to the kitchen door and slipped inside. The sight stopped me in my tracks. Moss carpeted the floor and walls. A textured stripe of oyster mushrooms crawled up the cabinets. Rose vines and greenbrier littered the floor, and everything smelled fecund and floral.

"What happened here?" I asked.

"I happened," Eva said.

The monster could sense only one other heartbeat in the house. I didn't know where Izzy had gone off to, but she wasn't at home.

Eva still wore the overalls she'd had on earlier today, the intricate floral designs embroidered on the pockets now marred by strange dark flecks. I flashed to the last time I had stood in this room, my mind filling with the cracking sound Jack's branch had made when the monster snapped it in two. The way a red-green, almost resinous substance had dribbled from the broken end, smelling of sap and iron.

Did she know she wore her father's blood?

My camera sat on the counter, a starburst of cracks obscuring my favorite lens. Anger sliced through my gut as I remembered Lenny slamming my camera into the cabinets, remembered the crunch of it under my foot.

Purple envelopes littered the table, the same shade as the one Eva had shoved in my face at the jail cell. My heart gave a lurch.

Mom's letters.

"So?" Eva asked expectantly.

I picked a path through the mess, carefully dragging a chair to the fridge. At first tug, the vent didn't budge. "We need something to pry it open," I grunted.

Eva disappeared down the hall. My eyes followed her, stalling on the open doorway to Jack's bedroom. I could see the uneven rise and fall of the sleeping man's chest. Without his leaves, the branches twisting out of him appeared more like the fingers of some eldritch monster.

I shuddered. When Eva returned, I accepted the offered flathead screwdriver, wedging it behind the vent. The metal screeched as I pried it away, and I reached in, hand fumbling.

"Anything?"

I frowned, lifting onto my toes. Jack was taller than me by a lot, but not even he could have reached much farther. Dust caked a slick grime onto my fingertips as I searched the hollow.

But the vent was empty.

I drew back. "It's gone."

"What?" Eva tugged my sleeve and scrambled to replace me on the chair.

"Ev, there's nothing there," I insisted.

"There has to be!" There was heat behind the sheen in her eyes. I couldn't even blame her. I'd given her hope and then snatched it away.

"Maybe... he moved it?" I suggested.

"Well, we can't exactly ask him, can we?" The bite of her words was undercut by the break in her voice, grief clouding her expression.

It hurt to see her so defeated.

But then a new resolve seemed to fall over her, and Eva straightened, tugging on the straps of her overalls as she bit her lip. "The fields," she whispered.

"What?"

A car door slammed outside, and we whipped in tandem to see a deputy step out of his vehicle. Eva gasped and ducked out of view of the window. She snatched her tennis shoes from where they'd been discarded on the moss-covered floor, slipping her feet out of her sandals and stuffing them into socks, then the shoes, urgency in every movement.

When she started rifling through the envelopes on the table, I flicked an anxious glance to the door. Footsteps crunched the gravel outside.

"Aha!" She held up a thick wad of folded paper in triumph before stuffing it into a pocket of her overalls.

"What is that?" I asked.

Eva wore determination in every line of her face. "His atlas."

"Wha—"

She cut me off. "Come with me," she said, circling her fingers around my wrist as she dragged me to the cellar door and pried it open with a squeak. Her thumb was warm and rough against the tendon there, just a nudge from my pulse. It sent a shiver down my spine.

No one else could touch me like this.

The cellar was old, used mainly for storing camping supplies and bottled fruit. The instant Eva opened the door, a solid wall of cold rushed up the stairs. Eva descended first, steps creaking. I instinctively curled my toes in my shoes as I followed her down, gripping the rail for balance, braced for a rogue spiderweb to find my face at any moment.

The tug of a chain bathed the sparse gray room in yellow light. I closed the door behind me seconds before a loud knock came at the front door. Panic ran through me. "Is there another way out?"

"Yes." Eva rushed to the camping shelves and heaved a tent bag off and into her arms, stirring dust.

"What are you doing?" I hissed.

Eva unzipped a hiking pack and began stuffing things inside. She tossed a look to the sleeping bag on the top shelf overhead. "Get me that, will you?"

"Eva—"

"I promise I'll explain!" Her hands shook as she yanked the zipper closed and hoisted the backpack over her shoulders, the tent curled under her arm. When I plucked the sleeping bag off the shelf, Eva nodded to the back wall of the cellar. Unlike the other walls, made from heavy stones, this one contained a slanted hatch made entirely of wood and iron braces, with steps leading up to it.

I remembered this door now, an old, steep-angled entrance we'd never used, and rarely saw, because it had always been covered in greenery. I moved up the steps and tried the handle, but it was locked.

Overhead, we heard the squeak of a floorboard. I sucked in a breath. That wasn't the heavy groan of Jack's feet, or the click of Izzy's heels. A chill swept over me.

The deputy was in the house.

"You got a key?" I pressed.

"Dad kept it in a turtle, I think." Setting the tent bag down for a moment, Eva crouched and rifled through the keepsakes on the adjoining shelf. Ceramic clinked too loudly. I winced, glancing back in the direction of the stairs.

"Hurry, Ev!"

"I'm trying!" She rattled something loose and thrust it into my hand, turning her attention to the lock.

My fingers smoothed over the glossy ceramic figurine. "This is a frog."

"That is not helpful." Eva shoved the key into the lock, gritting her teeth. When it clicked, she let out a laugh. "Here, help me lift the door."

Together, we shouldered open the escape hatch. It took effort at first. The door hadn't been opened in years, and weeds had grown over the edges. As we forced it open, the popping sound of roots filled my ears, and loose sediment spilled into the cellar. I held my breath as I peered outside, anxious that I could see neither the road nor whatever backup the deputy had brought to the cottage.

Eva rolled the heavy tent bag out onto the grass and looked at me. "Get your keys ready. We'll run to the van."

"They'll catch us."

Eva's mouth pinned down in a fine line of determination. "No. They won't."

And maybe it was just an echo of all that stood between us, unhealed, but it felt, in some way, as it had years before when she'd asked me if I trusted her. I took a breath, fishing my keys from my pocket. "On my mark. One, two—"

"Fly."

"Run!"

We bolted toward the front of the house.

"FLY!" the monster sang again. It breezed through me, giddy at the wind rushing through our fingers.

Someone called out to us, but I didn't look back as I yanked the driver's door wide and tossed first the sleeping bag, then the heavier tent bag inside.

Eva leapt into her seat and slammed her door. "Go! GO!"

I jammed my keys into the ignition and turned. As the van coughed to life, the man Dane had called Grayson burst out the front door, flanked by two other deputies. Eva swiveled in her seat, and in my rearview mirror, I watched the earth buckle under one of the patrol car's tires. Weeds slithered up and around the wheels as Grayson yanked the car's door handle, surprising him so much that he cried out and jumped back.

I laughed in disbelief. "Was that you?"

"I'm sorry!"

"Don't be sorry! That was...wow." I'd never seen her use her magic with such precision. The sight of her power, of the forest bending to her will, stole my breath.

Eva flushed a violent pink. "I guess it comes in handy sometimes."

I turned my attention back to the road, feeling suddenly lighter. "I guess it does."

Chapter 15

Eva

Eva spread the atlas she'd taken onto the dashboard and squinted at her father's minuscule scrawl in the margins. The tentative hunch she'd had when she found this map stashed away with his letters from Charlotte solidified a little more as she traced a heavily circled mile marker, and the note beside it. *Aspens.*

"Take the north road," Eva said.

It was the quickest way to the trailhead, and rarely used by visitors. After Arthur dropped her off, he could follow the back roads all the way down to the valley.

She expected Arthur to push back and demand more information. Instead, he only nodded, gripping the wheel. They'd gained an advantage by disabling the patrol car back at the house, but Eva knew the sheriff's men would call for backup soon. The oncoming storm might delay them, but she couldn't rely on the incompetence of the county's paltry sheriff's department, not with so much on the line. They needed to hurry.

After another mile, Eva turned to him. "Do you remember my father's stories?"

Maybe it was a mistake to crack open the door like this, but she needed someone to reassure her she wasn't crazy for thinking there was something more to those old tales than simply a child's entertainment.

"Remember?" Arthur snorted. "They gave me nightmares."

"Do you remember the honeyman who found a field of magic flowers?"

"Sure," Arthur said. "He stole their magic or something?"

"Right." Eva took a breath, tapping the mile marker on the atlas. "Well, I think *this* might be that meadow."

Arthur's eyebrows shot up.

"Dad used to hike here every summer to collect a rare blue flower he dried into tea," Eva went on, desperate to lay her theory out so he could see all the pieces. "He hasn't been since the…accident."

"A blue flower?" Arthur murmured. "Like the tea blend Lenny had back at the cottage?"

Eva's thoughts slammed to a halt. "What?"

Arthur's gaze jumped to hers. "I found him in the kitchen with one of your jars."

The words brought an instant wash of unease. Eva hadn't known anything about that.

"Sorry," Arthur said when the silence between them went on a beat too long.

"It's fine."

But it wasn't fine. Eva hated that Lenny Walker still had the power to catch her off-guard in the worst of ways. She hated that he'd come into her home and rifled through her family's things. She hated that she was finding out only now, with Arthur glancing worriedly over at her as he drove.

Eva plucked the envelope she'd brought to the holding cell

from her pocket and unfolded it, trying to pull his attention off her face. "I never knew what those flowers were called, before this letter."

To her relief, Arthur let her guide them back to the topic at hand. "Oh?"

Eva nodded, transported for a moment to her kitchen as her father's words unraveled inside her again. *I named it after her, you know.* She bit her lip. It felt like giving away a piece of her father she'd only just found, and wanted to keep for herself.

But the secret wasn't hers alone to inherit.

"He called them Little Lotties," Eva said.

Arthur sucked in a breath, surprised. "For my mom?"

"Yeah."

Her father had kept the details of his friendship with Charlotte Connoway largely to himself, and before now, Eva hadn't cared. She bore no love for the woman who'd made Arthur feel so disposable.

"He wrote that the flowers there have healing properties. That's why he hoards the tea," Eva went on. She twisted a loose thread at the waist of her overalls around her little finger, pulling it taut. "What you said, before, about the honey? About it helping him…" Eva trailed off, feeling suddenly foolish.

This was just superstitious folklore.

But it was also the only shot she had.

"You think the honey I saw him eat that night came from those fields?" Arthur guessed.

Eva nodded. "He's never planted those flowers at the cottage. He must have established a hive up there." The pain the sapling caused could have prevented him from making the trip again, cutting off his access to the healing honey.

The possibility made something in Eva's chest go tight. How much of Dad's pain had he buried over the years? How much better might it have been if he'd had this honey all along, if he'd trusted her to help him? She wasn't fragile! She could handle knowing he was in pain, even if she was the reason—

Stop.

Eva corked the thought before it could play out. She'd show him just how strong she could be.

"I'm going to the meadow he wrote about," she said in determination. "And I'm going to bring more honey back."

She expected Arthur to scoff or to laugh at her. Instead, he fell silent. A storm had gathered overhead, heavy dark clouds lower in the night sky now. At the first drop of rain, Arthur leaned over, popping open the glove box between her knees. He fished out a honey stick and stuck it in his teeth, then handed her another. "Want one?"

"You just have these on hand?"

A flush peeked from beneath the collar at his neck. "Just take it. I know you get snacky."

In minutes, the sky unzipped, raindrops pelting the windshield. They drove slowly through the pounding storm. Soon the road changed to a rough and unpaved surface, making Eva's already too-full bladder more unbearable. When she couldn't stand it any longer, Arthur pulled off to the side of the road. Eva dashed into the trees to relieve herself, and by the time she returned, her clothes were utterly soaked.

"Here." Arthur tossed her a warm, heavy flannel shirt.

She wrapped it around her shoulders, teeth chattering. "Can we turn on the heat?"

He shot her a look of apology. "Heat's broken."

"Oh."

The air in the van pressurized as the storm grew more intense, lighting up the night sky overhead with brilliant cracks of lightning. Eva yawned to pop her ears as they slowed to a crawl. When the road turned slick and muddy, Arthur eased onto its shoulder. "We've got to stop," he said as he brought the van to a halt.

"What? We can't!"

"If we can't drive in this, neither can they. And we *can't* drive in this." Arthur patted the wheel. "My girl's got a delicate suspension."

Eva's helpless laugh did nothing to stall the anxiety building in her chest.

Arthur's hand lifted off the wheel and stretched toward her for a moment before he seemed to change his mind and set it awkwardly on the dash instead. "Hey. We'll leave as soon as the rain lets up, okay?"

"Promise?" Eva felt like a child demanding his word, but she didn't care.

"I promise." He smiled wearily, his eyes a treasure box of hazel. Stone. Soil. Grass. Gold. All the colors of the earth, ensconced in his irises.

"I like the beard," Eva blurted out. Impulsively. Stupidly.

Arthur's eyes widened in surprise, and he touched his jaw self-consciously. "It's new."

"It's nice." Her neck flamed with hot discomfort. Eva hurried on, eager to change the subject. "Do you have a medical kit?"

"In the back," Arthur hedged.

"Good." She pointed to the gash in his eyebrow. "You need stitches."

He stiffened. "The hell I do."

"You want to risk infection?"

"If you stitch me up, I'll surely risk infection."

Sometimes he made her want to scream. "Medical kit. Where is it?" Eva demanded.

After a tense staring contest, Arthur grumbled and climbed into the back portion of the van. Eva craned her head to see, but his living space was obscured in shadows.

"Ev!" Arthur cried out in sudden alarm. "There's a cat in my bed!"

She twisted in her seat. "What?"

"Why is there a cat in my bed?!"

She scrambled over the divider, awkwardly trying to find a way to fit her body into the cramped space. A neatly made bed had been elevated off the van's floor, with storage space cleverly positioned beneath it. Outside, rain plonked hard against the van's vintage roof. Arthur had pressed himself against the back door of the Volkswagen, chest heaving as he stared at the blanket on his pillow.

The blanket twitched, then rolled over. A little gray kitten batted at the coverlet's rust-colored tassels.

Eva gasped and scooped up the kitten, tucking it into the wide chest pocket of her overalls, kangaroo-style. "Oh, you little rascal!"

"What? Why is it...?" Arthur fumbled his words. He looked, ironically, like the very creature currently making him freeze up, his body pressed far from the object of his fear into the side of the Volkswagen.

"We left the windows rolled down. She must have climbed inside."

"This is *your* cat?"

"One of Hyssop's newest litter, I'd guess."

"Ev, I can't have a cat. You know I can't have a living thing."

It shouldn't soften her toward him when the years still sat like an open wound between them. But Eva couldn't help but recall the tattoos of songbirds she'd glimpsed on Arthur's biceps back at the farm. Had he continued to practice controlling his gift, as they'd done together as teenagers? Or had those swirls of ink become the closest he got to touching anything living?

She swallowed the traitorous need to know and scratched the kitten's soft little head. There were too many things she and Arthur had left unsaid, too many hurts still festering, for her to ask such a question.

"We can't turn her out in this." Eva nodded to the torrent as the kitten bumped her chin with its forehead, already purring. "Can we, little one?"

Arthur remained frozen, watching as Eva rewrapped the kitten in her blanket and set it on the passenger seat.

Eva pointed to the mattress. "Sit."

Even that felt too intimate. How many times had they arranged themselves in this exact position, trading care for bee stings, cuts, and burns? There were other wounds now that first aid couldn't fix. Hurts that scraped down to the bone.

Arthur plopped down obediently. "Wash your hands," he muttered.

To her relief, the poorly stocked first aid box did have a suture kit. Eva clicked on a flashlight she'd grabbed from the cellar. It had a wide base that let it stand upright, its beam bouncing off the van's ceiling and lighting the space around them. After locating a pack of alcohol wipes from the first aid kit, Eva cleaned her shaking hands. Then she gently rubbed a disinfecting wipe over the pink, raw skin of Arthur's wound. He winced.

"Try not to move," Eva muttered. "You'll make it worse."

"You don't have to do this, Ev."

"You'll scar if I don't."

Arthur gave a harsh laugh. "It wouldn't be the first time."

The words made her chest squeeze so tightly she had to turn away, shakily threading the needle.

"That's huge," Arthur protested, his voice pitched up in alarm.

She couldn't disagree. The sharp silver tip looked deadly against the broken flesh of his brow. Eva swallowed hard. "Ready?"

"Definitely not."

She hesitated. "Do you want to go back?"

"No." The word was hard as stone, and Eva saw him as he'd been in the holding cell, blood leaking down his brow from a wound no one had dared to touch. It made her angry that fear of him had made his needs so easy to ignore. No one deserved that. Not even him.

Eva shored up her courage. She could do this. How hard could it be, really? She'd cross-stitched before, had quilted with her Gran —

"Ev." Arthur cut into her thoughts. "The anticipation is worse."

"Right. Okay." She inched a little closer and tilted his chin up with a finger, a shiver running up her back. Any nearer and she'd practically be positioned between his knees. It would be easier to reach him. Easier to stitch. But she couldn't seem to get herself to come any closer.

Arthur was wrong. The anticipation was *not* worse. The second the needle pierced his skin, his eyes flew open and he barked a cry of shock and pain. "Fuck!"

"I'm sorry!" Eva bit the inside of her cheek so hard the copper tang of blood spread over her tongue.

Arthur's chest rose and fell in harsh, staccato breaths. His eyes locked on hers. "Again."

Her hands trembled. When the steel tip broke through skin on the opposite side, Arthur groaned. Eva pulled the split edges together as softly as she could, still too rough.

Arthur grabbed her by the pockets of her overalls, his expression seared in pain. "Stop," he whispered. "Please."

"Okay." Tears leaked down Eva's cheeks. "I stopped."

Up till now, every touch they'd shared had been functional. Practical. Not this. Arthur dragged her so close that her legs brushed the insides of his thighs, denim kissing denim as he shuddered in pain. "I'm sorry," he rasped. "I just...Can I...?"

Eva took his hands off her pockets and set them on her hips. "You can hold on to me."

This was a liminal space. They couldn't dwell here, no matter how soft it felt. There was too much pain in it. But just for a moment, they could drift. He could touch her. She could let him. And after, they wouldn't speak of it.

Arthur's grip tightened, his thumbs rubbing her hip bones. Eva tried to ignore the shiver that rippled over her skin as she steadied her forearm against his shoulder. "Three more stitches and I will close it. That's it."

"Fuck," Arthur cracked out again, the curse almost delicate. "Do it."

It was so much worse than she'd imagined. Worse than the first stitch, by far. When they'd fought at the cottage, Eva had wanted him without armor. Now she had it. The universe laid

Arthur Connoway bare to the bone, every inch of his face etched in anguish. He tried and failed to bury the guttural sounds of his pain as he held her body like it was his only anchor, clutching her hips so tightly Eva had to bite her lip to keep from crying out.

He would never forgive himself if he thought he'd hurt her.

Bile rose at the back of Eva's throat when the thread slicked pink. She hated that the only word she had was *sorry*. She hated the raw, animal edge to his groans, and the stripes of tears salting his skin.

The suture kit had no scissors, so when she'd finished, Eva leaned in and carefully bit off the end of the thread with her teeth. Arthur flinched as she blotted the edges around the wound with another sterile wipe, his eyelids shuttering.

"Done," she whispered.

Arthur didn't release her right away. Raindrops streamed down the window behind him, and though Eva still wore the flannel shirt he'd given her, the sight of the deluge sent a chill across her skin.

It was easier to look at him when he wasn't staring back. Eva let her eyes map the contours of his face. They were sharper than she remembered, his body hardened with time. Arthur would never be a large man, but in the years that had separated them from that fateful summer, his once gangly body had turned lean with muscle.

When he didn't move after several long seconds, Eva laid her hands over his and gently pried his fingers off her hips. Arthur startled back to himself with a little gasp. His eyes were open windows, and she saw the pain behind them, a wound she couldn't stitch up.

Arthur snatched his hands back. "Thank you," he strained.

Eva didn't mean to sleep, but the rain lulled her down anyway, Arthur's flannel shirt wrapping her in warmth. She dreamed of the two of them as they'd been eight years before. Arthur used to take her out in the mornings with a pair of binoculars and his old Minolta camera. They'd listen to birdsong and wait for just the right shot.

Her nose wrinkled. If she didn't know better, she'd swear she could still hear those calls. Orioles. Robins. Starlings. Arthur didn't like that last one. He said starlings had a penchant for stealing the nests of other birds. For someone who cared about *home* so much, his disdain for such behavior made sense, though Eva couldn't help but find the birds beautiful anyway, with their dark rainbow of slick, oil-hued feathers. Besides, they could mimic the calls of other species, meadowlarks and killdeer and —

Eva gasped awake, realizing with a start the birds weren't in her dream at all but all around her. Where was she? Instantly disoriented, Eva shot up in the makeshift bed and whacked her head on the roof of Arthur's van.

Oh. That's right.

"Hey! You okay?"

Eva moaned and rubbed the spot, holding her palm up with a nod. "Yeah. I'm good." She felt more embarrassed than anything. An orange Afghan had been draped over her body. She must have twisted while she dozed, given how it now compressed her legs in a cocoon. At the end of the mattress, the little gray kitten made enthusiastic biscuits with the blanket. When Eva flexed her toes, the kitten pounced. Eva yelped a laugh.

The side door of the van had been left open. Outside, Arthur crouched over a propane stove, stirring a pan of golden eggs. When their gazes latched, the corners of his mouth lifted. Eva felt the smile like a hook in her chest.

"Hey." She yawned wide and looked around. She'd never seen the van's interior before, and it surprised her just how colorful it was. How neat. "The rain stopped?"

Arthur nodded, somewhat rueful. "I tried to wake you."

Even in a tight space, there was room to breathe, clutter corralled behind home-crafted pine cabinets. Curious, Eva opened the one nearest her. Instantly, her eyes fell on a pair of binoculars she recognized, folded and tucked into a ball cap.

She bit her lip, then quietly shut the cabinet.

The air had that fresh, washed-out clarity that comes only after a storm. So did Eva's mind, now washed free of all but one single, urgent thought: They had to run, now. She'd slept through the sunrise. The return of daylight and clear roads meant their reprieve was over, and at any minute the sheriff's men could come around the bend. Eva scooped up the kitten.

"What time is it?" she asked.

"Almost six." Arthur's mouth twisted wryly. "Don't look so worried. You slept through the drive, but if Jack's notes are right, we're close to the trailhead." He pointed to a post just beyond the Volkswagen. "The mile marker is there. Figured you'd want to eat first."

Stunned, Eva turned, taking in the overflowing sea of chalky aspens tinkling in the wind.

He was right. This place was a perfect match to her father's notes.

Aspens were a special tree, one of a small handful of species that reproduce by sending out sucker sprouts from their roots to clone themselves into existence again and again. The unique system affords them greater longevity and resilience, as they function, in essence, as one cooperative organism.

Her magic had a way of sensing where it might reach out and encourage things to grow. Now that Eva was paying attention, she could feel the energy of the aspen roots vibrating underground, not unlike a busy crowd of people, or a hive of bees working together for survival.

"Here."

Eva eyed the plate he gave her, her stomach growling. "You don't eat eggs."

He lifted a shoulder. "I'm trying to."

Arthur wasn't strictly vegan, but his aversion to animal flesh made him very selective. She, on the other hand, was absolutely weak for all forms of breakfast food.

"You sure?"

"Of course." He said it like a joke, but Eva noted he'd given her the lion's share, and while she wolfed her eggs down, he stirred his with a grimace.

She didn't press him. The summer Arthur had stayed with them, Dad had told her anxiety could be hard on a person's stomach. So could grief. Arthur lost his appetite in all sorts of ways.

Her eyes dropped to the fingers he tapped on the outside seam of his jeans. That was the same too. It had always been her biggest clue to his emotional state. When Arthur was upset, he tapped that same rhythm over and over.

Her eyes followed the dip in his throat as he chugged a drink of water from a bottle he must have kept in the van, then wiped the moisture off his lips. Between her shoes, the kitten pounced on a bright green beetle.

Silence spread like a balm while they ate, sweet petrichor rising off the rocks and soil. When a honeybee landed on Eva's knuckle, she twiddled her fingers to make it take flight again.

The kitten rubbed against Arthur's leg. His expression puckered, tart with unease as he held perfectly still.

"She likes you," Eva noted.

"She doesn't know I'm poison."

He had spoken so quietly Eva wasn't sure he'd meant her to hear, so she pretended she hadn't. "Wanna name her?"

"Not a chance, bee girl."

After breakfast, Arthur offered Eva a spare toothbrush and his toothpaste. *I can do this,* she thought as she scrubbed her teeth and spat in the dirt. *I've gone camping before.*

"Ev?"

Every time he said her name, it got a little easier to hear. That didn't mean she liked it. "Yeah?"

Arthur stood at the open door of the Volkswagen, hands stuffed in his pockets. "I don't think you should do this alone."

Great. One more person who didn't believe she was capable.

"Thanks, but I'll be fine," Eva said, ignoring the voice niggling at the back of her mind. For all the time she'd spent in the woods growing up, she'd never camped alone.

Arthur's eyes burned with an intensity she'd never seen as he stepped forward. "I want to go with you."

The words hit like a bullet to her ribs. Stunned, Eva's lips parted. "What?"

"I want to help."

Eva shook her head. "You have to leave." The words were gravel in her throat, words she never thought she'd say. But they'd lost too much time as it was with the storm. There were only so many roads through these mountains. "If you don't go now, the sheriff—"

"I know."

The words were resigned, and Eva realized with a start that Arthur wasn't running to freedom at all. And how could he be? How long did she really expect to keep him out of the hands of the law with the charges laid against him? Against them both? Sooner or later, Dane Walker's deputies would catch up, and then what?

She swallowed hard. Arthur had apparently already grasped what she'd refused to accept: This moment, this reprieve, was nothing more than a delay.

"What happened to Jack is my fault," Arthur said as he stepped toward her and lifted a second hiking pack she hadn't clocked before. He'd clearly gathered his supplies together while she slept. "If you really think something up there can help your dad, then... please. I owe it to him."

She stared at him a moment, then her eyes flicked to the pack. He'd already secured the tent onto it. Eva didn't know how far the meadow was, to be honest, or if she had sufficient supplies for an overnight stay. The realization made her flush.

"I have food packed," Arthur said, as though reading her thoughts. "You can change clothes too, if you want. Take anything of mine."

Eva looked down at her overalls. The denim was worn soft with years of use, the colorful threads on the embroidered flowers—fuzzed with touch and time—now stained with flecks of her father's blood. She hadn't thought to change earlier, too shocked after what had happened, but now the sight of the blood made her sick.

She should have been grateful for his offer of help. Instead, defensiveness rose inside her. "You don't have to do that."

"I do."

A knot bloomed in her throat, making it hard to snap back at him. Eva didn't want him to atone. Nothing he did could give back the years she'd had to live with the consequences of his actions. Arthur looked strangely fragile under the weight of the pack, all skin and bones and sweat. They hadn't even started yet.

Eva fought to quell her mounting exasperation. This would be a disaster.

And it wouldn't fix things.

Eva bent down, scooping up the kitten. "Fine," she conceded.

Arthur's earnest expression wobbled. "You're taking the cat?"

As if on cue, the kitten chose that moment to let out a hungry mewl. Eva stroked the back of her head. "Of course we're taking the cat."

Chapter 16

Isobel

The storm had everyone on edge. Dane pulled together a search party willing to work in the inclement weather. While his crew searched the surrounding area, Isobel kept watch over her father at the cottage. Dr. Rosen had urged her over the phone to let him continue to rest. It was vital, the doctor had said, to eliminate unneeded stressors so his body could heal.

So when Dad woke that night in a fit of panic, asking after Arthur, Isobel did something she never thought she would.

She lied to her father.

"We posted his bail."

Dad's immediate look of relief made Isobel's stomach churn with guilt. "I need to see him," he said, his voice faint.

"Um...you can't, just yet." Isobel scrambled for something believable. "Arthur was...Well, he was so upset about what happened." True. Isobel swallowed her nerves down a dry throat. "He and Eva went for a drive."

A bad lie, by her standards. No one would willingly choose to drive in this storm.

"They drove down to the diner," she amended. "To work things out."

When the worry knitting her father's brow eased, it almost made the deception worth it.

"Good," Dad said, sinking back against the pillows propped beneath him. His eyes were drooping again. "They'll be okay, you know."

But Isobel didn't know, and she felt suddenly sick. What kind of person lied to their wounded father?

Shortly after midnight, Dane called off the search until the storm let up, for the safety of the search crew. Isobel dozed in a chair by her father's bed through the night, too anxious to leave his side.

She needed a drink.

When she phoned the next morning, Dane tried to reassure her that he would find her sister soon.

Isobel wasn't so certain.

Though Eva would be loath to admit it, Arthur Connoway had always been able to reach a part of Eva that Isobel couldn't. Her sister's first experience with love hadn't grown solely from attraction but from a desperate need to be seen. Arthur had fed Eva's curious mind, stirring her to compassion and a deeper understanding of the world and her place within it. He had taught her to be more careful with living things, his deadly touch making him keenly aware of how fragile a life truly is.

Eva might not have forgiven Arthur for running away, but if she thought he was in trouble, Isobel had no doubt her sister would jump to his aid. And while that was courageous, it didn't mean it was *smart*.

The violence of last night's rain had destroyed some of the

flowers in their yard, the tallest and flimsiest stems pressed flat into the mud with their once-silken petals now crumpled and strewn around them. Izzy stood on her front porch, taking in the mess outside. The inside of their cottage wasn't much better, still covered in the flora that Eva had grown during the disastrous events of yesterday.

With the craving for whiskey sitting on her tongue, Isobel turned her attention first to putting the kitchen to rights. She started with peeling the newly grown layer of moss off the tiles and walls. The spongy texture of the moss pressing into her palms gave her something soft to focus on, rather than the worry cutting up her insides. Broken glass clinked against the tiles as she swept the floor clear of debris. She was almost glad for the shards, glad to have something shattered that she was capable of fixing.

Isobel was plucking a rogue cluster of turkey tail mushrooms that had started growing on the hallway wallpaper when she saw the mirror. The glass looked as though it had been struck by an angry fist. Her chest tightened, and she flashed to yesterday, when Dane had led Arthur away, his bloodied knuckles drawn behind his back in handcuffs.

Determined to hide her worry and keep up the facade that all was well, Isobel prepared a lunch platter to share with her father. They ate it while he still rested in bed, a little more color leaking into his pale cheeks. Dad asked her about Eva and Arthur again. Biting her lip, Isobel forced a smile she didn't feel and cheerfully said that the two of them had gone down to the valley and had asked that she pass along a hello to Dad when he woke.

Eager to escape her guilt over the lie, Isobel spent the afternoon outside, tearing out weeds and clearing up debris the wind had blown into the yard during last night's storm. There was nothing she could do about the patrol car Eva had taken out of commission, its tires sunk deep into the ground, with a layer of flora snaking up its doors and around its hood, as though the whole thing was being swallowed. They would need assistance and heavier equipment to break it free and tow it off their property.

The sun seemed to be trying to make up for yesterday's cloudy weather. By the time Isobel hung her tools in the greenhouse and called it a day, she was sweating, exhausted, and more than a little achy in her lower back.

Dad went to bed early, still looking too pale. When she tried to check on him, he shooed her away, so Isobel retreated to take a shower, eager to cleanse the layer of grime off her skin.

While she was showering, Dane left a message on her voicemail. He'd had no luck on the search today.

Dusk had fallen over the sky like a bruise by the time Isobel slipped out onto the porch and sank into her mother's old rocking chair, the knot of worry in her chest cinching a little tighter. The woods sang around her, the air smelling sweet and clean. Isobel rocked in the chair and tried to tamp down the feeling of helplessness she'd been hiding from all day.

It found her anyway.

Through the orchard, she watched the main lights in the Walker farmhouse click off one by one, until only Dane's office light remained.

Isobel pushed to her feet, carried by a sharp and sudden need.

For distraction.

For escape.

She grabbed the closest shoes she could find and marched to the fence line dividing their properties. The usually pristine rows of trees were looking a little beat up, a smattering of golden pears thrown to the ground in the storm.

Halfway to the farmhouse, she knew she'd chosen the wrong pair of shoes. The kitten heels sank into the softened ground. It was pride, maybe—or perhaps adrenaline—that carried her to the back door, where she bent and fished out the secret key from under the mat.

The brass lock stuck on the first try, drawing her frustration to the surface.

She needed a drink.

No. Isobel shook her head. No, that was why she'd come here instead.

When the key finally turned, Isobel all but fell into the back hallway of the farmhouse. It was dark, save for the gap beneath Dane's office door hemorrhaging golden lamplight.

She crept down the hall, trying to avoid the creakiest floorboards. She didn't want to wake Dane's daughter, Esther. Evidence of the little girl was everywhere, from the dirty handprints Isobel knew were on the walls to the pile of tea party bric-a-brac abandoned along the baseboards.

Isobel needed to fall apart, and she feared if she didn't come here, she might go somewhere else. Dane Walker was the least of her vices, and unlike alcohol, he could kiss her back.

Bad days like today made her miss the secret drinks Priya used to slip her from behind the bar at Dawson's. Days like those were long gone. Isobel had never told her ex-girlfriend about her sobriety, but in a town this small, Priya knew.

Isobel smacked her tongue against the roof of her mouth. She could still taste the whiskey she wanted so badly—whiskey she hadn't had in over eleven months.

When she opened the office door, she found Dane glued to a spread of papers on his desk. He wore a pair of navy slacks and a pressed button-up with the sleeves rolled up to his elbows, each turn made with careful, measured precision. Isobel shivered. She'd read far too many romance novels in her thirty-two years not to appreciate a well-chiseled cliché.

"Knock, knock," she said softly when he didn't notice her entry.

Dane jumped, his attention snapping to where she stood. For just a moment, he looked as frazzled as she'd felt since the jailbreak yesterday. "Isobel."

The knots in her shoulders loosened a little. To everyone else she was *Izzy*, but not to Dane. She loved the slow, unhurried way he said her name. Always three syllables: *Is-o-bel*. It was her favorite mask. Isobel was confident, sexy, sober, *brave*. Most importantly, Isobel didn't keep secrets from the people she loved the way she'd done with her father that day.

She didn't lie.

"Is everything okay?" Dane asked. Anxiety flashed across his face, and he sat up a little straighter. "Is your dad...?"

"He's fine," she assured him. "Well, not fine, I guess, but he woke up enough to eat and move around a bit today."

"Good." Dane sank against the back of his chair, visibly relieved. "That's good."

It was obscene, really, how well the cinnamon scruff highlighted his jaw. Isobel could see from here the dark circles rimming his eyes. He seemed as exhausted as she was, though clearly too anxious to sleep.

"What are you working on?" she asked, stepping toward the desk. She should have known he wouldn't actually take a rest, even after a long day. If anything, Dane worked harder when he was frustrated.

"Don't…" Dane leaned forward and tried to cover the pages he'd been perusing, too late. Isobel had seen the title of Dane's witness statement, taken the morning after his wedding. Her mouth went chalky. That wasn't at all what she'd been expecting. Why was he digging back into all that, tonight of all nights?

"This is a cold case." Isobel tried to hide the shake in her voice.

"Not to me," Dane muttered. "There's got to be something here that I missed before." He tapped the pages. "It all comes back to her."

A tingling dread stole up Isobel's spine. Her sister was wild in a way few understood. That night eight years ago had changed her too. Eva refused to speak of it, but she revealed the loss in the violence of her flowers. Her magic used to be gentle. Now it trembled, ripping buds into bloom instead of coaxing them.

"Eva's emotions run high." Isobel tried to keep her voice light, though it felt like a betrayal to speak this way. "It's a wonder she hasn't brought more buildings down by accident."

"It wasn't an accident."

Isobel bit her cheek, refusing to let her stress show on her face. "Oh?"

"She meant to get him out." Dane shook his head. "What I don't understand is why. I told Arthur I wanted to help. I just wanted answers, and he was supposed to—" Dane cut himself off and lowered his volume, glancing toward the door to the hallway. He took a deep breath. "He wasn't supposed to run. Not again."

Isobel felt frustrated too. If Eva had simply waited, or asked for help, they might not be in this situation at all, and the stories

Isobel had fabricated for Dad could have actually been true. Isobel had planned to post Arthur's bail the next morning. When she'd heard the alarms, she'd rushed to the scene, but had missed Eva and Arthur. By the time she'd returned to the house, they were already gone.

"I'd given up, you know," Dane said, letting out a mirthless laugh that sent a little chill across her skin. "On finding the truth of what happened that night. But then he came back."

Isobel swallowed hard as her eyes dropped to the center of his chest. She knew the scar that lay beneath, a mirror position to her father's tree.

"I have to know," Dane whispered.

She was nearer the desk now, and Dane reached out and took the hem of her skirt between his first and middle finger. A seeking touch. A bid for comfort. Dane sighed. "I know you must want answers too."

Of all Isobel's secrets, this was the only one that made her feel like she might actually be a bad person. She knew how this had haunted Dane, she knew it hurt, and still she buttoned her lips, family obligation clogging her throat. "I do." Her gaze dropped to the Band-Aids on his arms and neck. Souvenirs from falling debris and thorny vines that had grown over the hole Eva made in the jail wall.

"He's the last thing I remember," Dane quietly said. "I don't know what to do about that, Isobel." When Dane met her gaze, the guard he usually kept up fell away. His expression was almost tentative. Questioning. "I know you care about him."

It was more than that. Arthur belonged here. Her family had chosen him as much as he'd chosen them, and she couldn't sever a bond like that.

Her breath came a little faster as she thought of what Arthur had done to her father, and for a moment, it was hard to breathe for the lump in her throat. But Arthur hadn't meant to do that. He'd just made a mistake, and Dad?

Isobel swallowed her fear. He would pull through, like he always did.

Dad would want her to forgive Arthur for what had happened today. He always said that just as scion cuts were grafted onto a damaged tree to preserve it, people sometimes came into your life who changed you forever, and healed you in ways you couldn't anticipate. Arthur had never been a charity case to them. From the moment he'd shown up, he'd filled a hole in their family they hadn't even known was there.

Still, when Isobel closed her eyes now, she saw Arthur snapping her father's branch, the horrible sound so much like a breaking bone.

"I care about you," she said to Dane, stepping closer so she could knit her fingers into his hair. "And I want you to get your answers."

Wanting, she'd learned, wasn't always enough. But sometimes it was all you had.

Dane dropped his forehead against her stomach, his shoulder blades squeezing together as he tried to hold back a wave of emotion. Dane Walker felt things in silence. In stillness. In strength.

If only she could siphon off this grief.

Isobel took a long, deep breath, scratching her nails lightly over the nape of his neck. "This is eating you up."

"I have to figure it out."

"I know," Isobel said quietly. She closed her eyes. "But not tonight."

Dane didn't answer, but he leaned into her a little more.

"Why was Lenny at the cottage yesterday?"

He hadn't answered her when she'd asked him before. Arthur had distracted them when he'd offered himself up for arrest. Isobel wasn't used to seeing Lenny around. For years, he'd gone off with friends of his own, living somewhere down in the valley. It was only a year or so ago that he'd started showing up here again on a regular basis, picking up odd jobs now and then.

Lenny had told his brother he wanted a fresh start.

Dane pulled back, an expression she couldn't quite parse flashing across his face. "I asked him to pick something up for me."

"Oh?"

For a moment, she didn't think he would elaborate. Then Dane sighed. "Jack's tea helps with my chest pains."

Of course. Her father had a remedy for everything. But why hadn't he told her? An uneasy feeling sat at the back of Isobel's mind. "Were you in pain yesterday?"

He grunted. "I'm fine."

Isobel bit her lip, choosing not to call him on the obvious lie as she weighed what he'd said. Even if Lenny was sincere in wanting to turn over a new leaf, Eva wouldn't like it if he started showing up on their doorstep regularly. Next time, Isobel would deliver the tea herself.

"You can tell me, you know." She brushed a bit of lint off Dane's shoulder. "When you don't feel well."

In response, Dane's hand found its way under the flowing hem of her skirt, and he traced a line from her outer thigh all the way down to her calves. The springs in his chair creaked as he pushed back and, one by one, eased off her pinching shoes. He swiped a tissue from its box on his desk and wiped the mud off the heels.

"You've got a bit of a Prince Charming complex," Isobel hummed.

"I know my job." With a gentle tug, Dane pulled her into his lap. "And it starts with undressing you." When she laughed, he nuzzled her neck with a little growl. "I fucking love that sound, Isobel."

She craved him like this, needful and devoted. It healed up something inside her to feel so wanted. There was honesty in the push and pull of craving another person. She had to lie about so many things, but she'd never lied about *this*. There was truth in the way they lost themselves in a heavy-lunged kiss, truth in the way Isobel gasped at the scrape of his teeth down her earlobe, the soft bite sending a strobe of bone-melting desire between her legs.

This was better than Dawson's. Better than whiskey, by far.

She loosened the knot of Dane's tie and let her fingers linger there, gently brushing the curve of his throat, the skate of her nails raising goose bumps across his skin. A gravelly sound vibrated against her fingertips. "You will be the end of me," he muttered.

"I think you mean 'Get on the desk.'"

He grunted assent and reached behind her, gathering the witness accounts on his desk into a slender pile and slipping them into his top drawer. Then he lifted her by the hips and set her firmly on the smooth, hard wood of the desktop.

Anticipation hummed through her body as Dane planted the soles of her feet on his thighs. He kissed the inside of her knee, massaging a hand down a calf Isobel hadn't even known was aching. It pulled a groan from her.

And a wicked grin from him. "You like that?"

"Shut up, Charming."

When Dane stood, he brought her legs with him, wrapping them around his waist as his tie slithered to the floor. Isobel shivered as Dane brushed his nose down the line of her jaw and roughed a kiss to her chin, then dragged his thumb down her lip to coax her mouth open for deeper plunder.

Isobel loved when he touched her like this. When he made her feel like *his*. Opaque. Real. Keepable.

"Want to go upstairs?" he asked, breathless. Isobel thrilled with the power of it. Dane Walker was a stone, uncrackable, yet he cracked for her.

"No." She urgently worked the rest of his buttons free and ran a finger down the raised pink scar on his sternum, right over his heart. Dane's skin stippled with goose bumps as she craned her neck and loved her mouth against the ruined skin. An apology, to soothe the lie. "Here."

A rumble of assent sounded from his chest. "I can—"

Someone pounded on the front door, cutting him off.

Dane swore under his breath and pulled back. His lips were slightly swollen, and colored by her lipstick. Isobel rubbed a red spot staining the corner of his mouth.

"Do you need to get that?"

"No," he muttered, going back in for another deep and hungry kiss just as the visitor knocked again, more urgently this time. He growled in frustration. "Yes."

His clear irritation warmed some baser part of her, but she nodded to the hall. "Go."

He hesitated just a moment, then pressed a kiss to her lips. "Stay here."

The order shivered up her spine. As he retreated into the hall, she tucked her blouse back into the waistband of her skirt. The drawer he'd set the witness accounts in was slightly ajar, and for a moment she went still, her eyes finding the edge of the stack of papers.

The intruder's third knock was so loud it made Isobel jump, and her gaze shifted to the clock. It was late. What could possibly be so urgent? Unless... Isobel's heart sped up a beat. Unless one of Dane's deputies had news to report on the search?

But it wasn't a deputy at the door.

"Len? What the hell—"

"We found Connoway."

Isobel snapped to attention. She paced to the door, careful not to let her shadow spill into the hall.

Dane closed the door behind his brother. "What are you talking about?"

Lenny's elation was palpable in every word. "His van was spotted on the north road," he said, slightly breathless.

A wash of unease filled Isobel, who didn't like the thought of Lenny Walker wandering in the dark in search of her baby sister. Not at all.

"Len." Dane sounded pained. "We talked about this."

What was that supposed to mean?

"I'm not looking for *her*," Lenny said.

"For what, then?" When Lenny scoffed, Dane pressed harder. "For justice? Revenge?"

Isobel's nails dug crescent moons into her palms as she held her breath.

"I'll bring them in, Len. That's my job. Not yours."

"Then why aren't you doing it?" Lenny shot back. "They could be anywhere by now! You should still be out looking—"

"I've been out all day!" Dane snapped.

Lenny went on as though he hadn't heard him. "But instead you're here, looking like..." Lenny paused. "What are you doing, exactly?" he asked, suspicion leaking into his voice.

Isobel's cheeks bloomed with heat.

"I have Esther tonight," Dane said evenly.

"June could take her."

The mention of Esther's mother was a bruise. June had been her best friend, grafted to her heart from early childhood. Later, Dane had been looped into their group, but from the beginning, it was June who'd held Isobel's hand when she was scared, June who'd made her laugh so hard it hurt, June whom she'd promised to love forever.

And when the divorce put Isobel in an impossible place between two of the people she cared about most, it was June who'd walked away from all their history.

They didn't talk now.

"Len," Dane said gently, a different kind of exhaustion leaking into his voice. "You have to stop. This...this *obsession* isn't good for you."

Isobel looked up at the sudden, quiet shuffling of footsteps down the hall on the floor above them.

"You have a chance to be different," Dane went on. "Don't go down this path again."

The stairs creaked at the press of a small foot. "Daddy?" a musical voice called from the top of the stairs.

Isobel peeked around the corner, catching sight of Esther rubbing her eyes, her unicorn stuffy tucked under her arm.

The little girl yawned. "What's happening?"

"Nothing, baby. Come here." Dane held out a hand, and Esther hurried down the stairs to his embrace.

It made Isobel ache. This was the kind of family she wanted to build. The kind she'd had growing up. Steady. Warm. Sure. But Isobel couldn't belong to these two like that. She wasn't ready. She wasn't sure she ever would be. And besides, they deserved someone more reliable than her.

Someone without secrets.

She thought of June again, and her chest went tight. That's who should have been here.

"We're going to find him," Lenny said. "With or without you."

Dane stiffened, but he didn't let his smile budge with his daughter there. His voice stayed calm. "We?"

"Avi will come with me. I know he will." Lenny pulled the front door wide, letting in a gust of wind that made Esther gasp. He ruffled his niece's hair, eyes going soft for a moment.

Isobel held her breath and waited for Dane to stop him. Instead, he simply watched Lenny flip up the hood of his jacket. *Don't let him go*, she silently begged. This was obviously going to come back to bite Dane in the ass. Why, after so many years of being burned by his brother, could Dane not just say no?

"Please, Len." Dane's voice was rough. "Don't be stupid."

When Lenny's eyes moved past his brother toward the shadows in the hall, Isobel yanked herself out of his line of view, heart pounding.

The front door clicked shut.

Isobel let out a breath and pressed her palms to her eyes.

"Daddy," Esther said after a moment, "I'm thirsty."

Isobel peeked around the corner again as Dane stood, his daughter wrapping her limbs koala-style around him. "Let's get you some water."

"Popsicle," she said into his shirt, the sound muffled.

"Popsicles are for daytime, kiddo."

Isobel waited until they passed the office where she hid before slinking back down the hallway, her shoes clutched in her hand.

She knew that after Dane tucked his daughter back into bed, he would come looking for her, but Isobel couldn't wait when her sister was out there unaware of Lenny's pursuit.

She retraced her steps to the door where she'd snuck in earlier, slipping one of Dane's jackets off its hook. It was chilly after dark. As she quietly exited the house, she slid her arms into the sleeves.

Rows of Walker pear trees striped the field behind the farmhouse. Isobel squinted, her focus zipping to where someone moved, almost catlike, beneath the light beaming over the barn doors. The silhouette of a man cut a path swiftly down the street.

Isobel's eyes narrowed.

Not this time, you bastard.

She set off in quiet pursuit, turning only once, when the flicker of a porch light behind her revealed Dane Walker framed in his doorway, peering out into the night.

Chapter 17

Arthur, Before

The green sepals cupping the rosebud unwound in a slow pirouette, leaving behind a splash of petals in Eva's palm. I watched the display of slow and gentle magic from nearby, a smoker dangling from my fingertips.

The perceived smell of fire had driven the bees to gorge on their stores, and a swarm of them, now drunk on their own honey, buzzed overhead. Despite what their hardwired panic would have them believe, the smoke was no disaster. Honeybees had a tireless work ethic, collecting nectar from dawn to dusk to be converted into honey and sealed in wax back at the hive. But sometimes they brought too much. An overabundance of nectar-producing flowers in the forest — *the honey flow*, Jack called it — had overwhelmed this apiary. It was our job as beekeepers to give them more real estate.

Eva tipped her head up, as though daring the sun to gift her more freckles. Across the yard, Jack set down a stack of supers. The shallow boxes contained the frames on which the bees stored their excess honey. Adding more supers reduced the chances of the hives swarming and splitting in two.

"It's too hot today," Eva complained, wiping a bead of sweat off her temple. "Let's swim."

"Sure." I swatted absentmindedly at what I thought was a fly until it stung my jaw, making me yelp.

Both Moreaus looked up. After a quick assessment, Jack nodded to his youngest daughter. "First sting is a rite of passage. Take him inside and show him what to do."

Eva perked up and flounced my way, tugging my sleeve. "Come on."

My jaw throbbed as we walked back up the hill to the cottage. "Another angry brood cycle?" I asked.

"What?"

"That's what you told Lenny after he was stung, right?" Despite my early hesitation, the beekeepers' sun-soaked world had woken my curiosity over the last few weeks. I was hungry to learn.

Eva's face turned pink. "I did tell him that," she said slowly. "I also told him to put vinegar on the sting."

"Are we not doing that?"

She laughed. "Not unless you want it to burn worse than it does now." She scooped up Hyssop — a recent rescue from a cat shelter, I'd learned — and brought her inside, filling the kitten's water bowl before the two of us unzipped our bee suits down to the waist, letting the arms dangle so we could cool down.

I pinched my T-shirt at the sternum and fanned in a bit of air. Heat aside, I liked the bee suit. It felt like armor. For the first time in a long time, I felt content.

Eva nodded to a chair. "Sit."

More than content.

I sank obediently onto the curved, stained wood, worn soft from decades of use.

Glass rattled as she dug through her cupboard, searching among her jars of herbs. The bee suit swung low over her hips, sleeves flopping against rainbow socks and grass-stained shoes.

This was our game. I watched her, and she watched me. We'd been playing it for weeks, trading glances like playing cards, the *unspoken* breathing down our necks like a creature ready to swallow us whole if we didn't give it voice. I knew it wasn't just me. Eva's freckles connected when she blushed, and she played with her braid when she was nervous. Best of all, her magic betrayed her, her emotions pulling flora to the soil's reef. Once, I had caught her staring at my hands, wildflowers sprouting in the grass at her feet.

"How's the swelling?"

I felt like someone had taken a match to my skin. "Fine."

"Liar." I could hear the smile in her voice as she plucked a jar between her fingertips. "Aha!" When she turned, my eyes snapped to her face. "Calendula!" Then she closed the distance between us and stepped between my knees, eyes bright as an afternoon sky. Eva unscrewed the cap to the little tin and swirled her finger in the yellow mixture. When she reached for me, I leaned away.

"What are you doing?"

Eva paused. "I have to apply this."

"I can do that."

"I know." Eva's voice colored with sudden embarrassment. "But I...want to."

The air between us thinned. For weeks, we'd danced around the no-touching rule. The bee suit's heavy cotton let me pretend I could be close to her, but it was all a facade. Eva Moreau couldn't really touch me, though she walked the line. Tugging my elbow. Bumping my hip. "Ev," I strained. "You can't do that."

"Maybe I can." When she stepped closer, the smell of coconut shampoo and fresh-cut grass filtered through my nose. Her eyes sparked as she gingerly traced her fingertips down the back of my glove. Even through the waffle knit, goose bumps rose on my arms. "I bring dead things back to life all the time."

"I'm not dead, bee girl." But she could be if I let her touch me. I was no flower; I was flesh and bone and, currently, a lot of rushing blood.

I could hurt her.

The chair creaked as I leaned into its ancient back, creating distance. Eva closed it with a single step, so close her knees kissed my inner thighs. One of her hands was tucked safely in its glove, the other unbearably naked. "Do you not want me to?"

"That's not it, and you know it."

A flicker of vulnerability passed over her face. "You're afraid of me."

"She is monstrous too, in her own way."

I bristled at the admiration in the monster's tone. *No, she isn't*, I silently snapped back.

The Moreaus straddled an interesting line between friend and foe in the town's ecosystem, drawing whispers wherever they went. Eva got the brunt of it. Her sister didn't have the gift she and her father shared, and for whatever reason, Jack had proven capable of hiding his ability to make things grow when the situation demanded it.

Not like Eva. Wilderness burst from the earth everywhere the bee girl stepped.

"I'm not afraid of *you*, Ev."

Eva flipped my hand. "What, then?" A honeybee sat in the hollow of her throat, the sections of its wings putting me in mind of a gothic window's delicate tracery.

"I'm afraid... you want something you can't have."

"Can't?" Eva's throat pulsed a slow, hard swallow. "Or shouldn't?"

"Does it matter?"

Her gaze pinned me like a bug to Styrofoam. "It does to me."

The sketch of her fingernail made my glove feel like it wasn't even there. I gripped the arms of the chair. "Ev, I — "

"Just let me try. Please."

A better person would have pulled away, instead of just sitting there, eyes fixed on the determined set of her mouth as she peeled the cotton free and set it on my knee.

I wasn't a better person.

I was me.

The monster curled deeper inside me, both of us as terrified as we were desperate to let her touch us. Just once.

Please, I begged. *Don't hurt her.*

The monster shook inside me, its ever-awareness tuned to the thrum of her pulse, so near our skin. *"I won't, little death-touch,"* it said as Eva rolled down the edge of my glove. *"I promise."*

The bee girl's eyes softened. "You trust me?"

I could still say no. Deny it. But she was full of light, and like a sunflower, I couldn't help yielding to her. My body spoke for me anyway; I sat with my legs spread, palms open, face upturned. There was no use lying when *trust* was written all over me.

Still, my heart beat in my skull, and my skin pulled tight everywhere, anticipation like a drug. I wanted to let her want me. To see me. I wanted the crush of another person's skin reassuring me that I wasn't alone.

"Yes," I whispered. I wasn't usually one for faith, but she made me want to believe in something bigger than my own broken pieces.

Eva took my hand in hers.

Like sparklers, the nerves in my fingers lit up. A current of feeling rushed up my arm to the center of my chest. I shivered with something deeper than cold. Something raw. Something new.

I stared at Eva. She twitched a smile, seemingly content to exist under my magnifying glass. I'd been doing it for weeks, cataloging finite details:

The splash of freckles dusting her nose.

The circular fingernails she never left unbitten.

The rosy shade of her neck when she blushed.

The easy curve of her mouth when she smiled.

I'd pictured this moment, of course I had, playing pretend when I had nothing else. My imagination, however, had failed me dramatically. I tried to memorize the slide of her warm, smooth fingers through mine, feeling clumsy beside her confidence. I didn't know how to do this.

Eva bit her lip, softly teasing a strand of hair at my nape between her fingers. The skim of her nails sent a frisson down my spine. Was it supposed to feel like this — so good that it almost hurt?

Then her smile dimmed. She dropped a gentle touch to the scar on my inner forearm. "How did you get this?"

I drew back, shame chasing the sunshine away. "What?"

"I'm sorry. You don't have to talk about it." Her thumb drew a bridge over the long-healed wound, her voice turning rough. "I just want to know you."

Her touch felt like fire, but the heat was good. Painfully good. I didn't deserve that.

"It doesn't matter," I whispered.

The world had every reason to hurt me. I was the poison under its skin, killing and killing with every touch. But it wasn't the world that had taken a knife to my skin and tried to carve the badness out.

That had been me.

The monster soothed a touch to the center of my chest, easing the ache in my heart. *"No more."*

I swallowed hard, hoping it was right. I never wanted to be that Arthur again.

Eva's gentle touch pleased the monster. She was soft as feathers. *"And so alive,"* it breathed. It didn't reach to touch her, but I searched her eyes anyway, looking for some sign of death, some form of desiccation or decay.

I saw only blue.

And slowly, my disbelief sprouted into wonder.

I wasn't supposed to be able to do this. I couldn't touch anyone, but here I was, touching Eva Moreau, with no consequences whatsoever.

Eva set her palm on my chest.

"What are you doing?" I might have pulled back, run away, if she hadn't all but pinned me against the table: a butterfly, dead and spread for examination.

"Dad taught me this trick," Eva said. "Sometimes, when I start to feel very panicky, I close my eyes and picture a sky full of storm clouds, slowly clearing."

It was hard to think about storms when I looked at her.

"I think... sometimes it helps to remember that *you* are not the storm, you know?" Eva said, absentmindedly moving her thumb across my shirt. Our gazes clicked and held. "You're the whole sky," she said, softer now.

I swallowed hard. "Why are you telling me this?"

Something I couldn't name passed over her expression. "You're like me," Eva said as she leaned closer, until I was certain she had to feel my heart racing beneath her palm.

I was staring at her mouth. I couldn't stop. It was round and full and slightly swollen, as though she'd been chewing her lip.

"I want you to feel safe here, Arthur."

The words were so earnest, and it hurt to realize how much I wanted that too. To be safe at the cottage. To be safe with her.

"I know, bee girl," I whispered.

Eva's mouth creased into a reluctant smile. "Good." She reached past my shoulder for the calendula cream and set it in my palm. "Help me with this, won't you?"

It took a moment for her words to process. Oh. *Oh.* I sat up straighter and held up the balm, my cheeks flaming nearly as much as my swollen jaw. Eva swirled her finger in the paste and smoothed it over the sting. I took in her vital signs. Flushed skin. Clear eyes. Even breathing. All clear indicators of life. Still, the clamp in my chest wouldn't loosen. It didn't make sense. Why could I touch her when I couldn't touch anyone else?

"Am I hurting you?" I whispered.

"No." Eva smiled. Her bees stopped humming. When I looked up, I found a half dozen clustered on the dusty blades of a long-broken ceiling fan. One particularly fat honeybee scooted closer to the carcass of a moth that had died upside down, tiny feet still gripping the wood grain.

"Do they ever sting you?"

"Rarely," Eva murmured. "And I'm a quick healer."

I'd noticed that. She never really seemed to get sick either.

I winced when Eva smeared the healing cream a little too roughly over the wound.

"Sorry," she said.

"It's fine," I murmured, quietly reveling in the touch. I felt dizzy from the soft pleasure of contact, *real* contact. Skin on skin, reverent and nervous. I didn't want her to pull away, even if staying close cost a little pain.

"I found a robin's nest in the woods yesterday," Eva said, drawing the words out as her thumb lingered at the hinge of my jaw. Our eyes met. "Maybe tomorrow... we could go see it?" Her words were tentative. "I know you love them, and I — "

Her words faltered at the gentle press of my thumb to the side of her leg. I didn't even realize I'd done it until she looked down. "I do love them," I whispered, heart pounding.

In the almost painful beat of silence, I cupped my hand more fully around the back of her knee. A trickle of pink stole up her neck. *This is too much.* I tried to pull away.

"No. Don't stop," Eva rasped.

And just as it had when our hands touched for the first time, a current of warmth melted from the top of my crown all the way down to my toes. I couldn't refuse her. I didn't want to, didn't even know how. Eva leaned into my touch, and my eyes shuttered, my hand gently squeezing the muscle of her thigh. A sweet sound of surprise burst out of her.

I didn't expect the flicker of pride in my chest. I'd made her feel something good. And I wanted to do it again.

Eva drew in a shaky breath.

If Jack Moreau was my lighthouse, his daughter Izzy was the relentless tide pushing me back to shore. And maybe I needed them both, but the bee girl was different. Not a beacon. Not a wave. She was the seafloor, home to broken, sunken ships. I wanted to drown in her graveyard of blue, to cut gills in my flesh and rebuild my lungs on her.

I squeezed the muscle of her leg again, hungry for her approval. The sliver of space between us pulsed. *Wanting* was its own heartbeat, and it thrummed everywhere we could have been touching but weren't.

Jack's tenor rumbled through the back door. "You two still in here?"

We sprang apart.

"Almost done!" Eva squeaked, cheeks florid with color. I doubted I was any better.

As Jack stepped inside, he plucked a green tenderling from his scalp with a wince. His eyes flicked our way and stopped. Heat rushed up my neck. Did we look how I felt? Scraped bare? Exultant? *Debauched?*

The monster snorted. *"You held hands."*

I shook my head the barest amount. I'd done far more than that. I'd let down my guard. I hadn't been careful, and worse —

Eva plucked the lid to the calendula cream off the table and screwed it back on, then went on her tiptoes to replace it in the cupboard. She touched her cheek with the backs of her fingers.

Worse, I wanted to not be careful again.

Chapter 18

Arthur

I'd spent a lot of time over the years thinking about homes. When we were seventeen, Eva had told me that home was simply wherever we put down roots and grew, but that was easy to say when you grew things just by existing. It was harder for me. I couldn't stormproof my thoughts like people did their houses when the weather turned inclement. I'd tried. I'd taken Eva's advice countless times and tried to let rainy thoughts pass through without judgment.

But it was hard. I'd never had a brick-and-mortar house, and my body was my only true constant. If I was my own home, I wanted to board up my windows and keep the monsters out, not let them in.

But you couldn't keep out a monster that lived inside you.

The aspens seemed to undulate around us as we hiked, the dark knots in pale bark giving the uncanny impression of eyes watching in my periphery. They never moved when I looked at them straight, but I felt them watching, and the hairs on the back of my neck rose.

Maybe I was being paranoid.

I tightened the straps of my pack and tried to ignore the ache in my plum-bruised knuckles. Before leaving the van on the side of the road, we'd wrapped my hands in clean white strips of linen from the first aid box. More bruises dotted my body in places I hadn't really had the opportunity to examine, most of them scuffs and scrapes acquired in the jailbreak.

But the stitches were by far the worst of it. They ached with every step. The monster tried to help, but even it couldn't numb all pain, and honestly, I didn't want it to. Being numb too often meant I was slipping into the monster's hold again. At least when I was hurting I knew I was *me*.

The touch of wind curled through the trees, brushing my skin in a way that made me feel at once too cold and far, far too hot. I couldn't tell Eva that after the stink I'd made about coming along. She might make me turn back, and I couldn't do that.

There were so many things I couldn't fix; I just wanted to do this one good thing for Jack. And then I would leave, since that was clearly what Eva wanted. If her sour response at the trailhead hadn't made that perfectly clear, then her silence since had certainly done the trick.

The ghost of a song moved in the breeze. If I didn't know better, I might have sworn it was a voice. I shucked off the feeling. Maybe I was truly, finally losing my mind.

"*No*," the monster said. "*I hear it too.*"

That didn't exactly comfort me.

The monster's unease pressed against me like a second skin. "*Maybe this was a bad idea.*" It didn't like how many places on our body were hurting. It didn't like that we were headed away from civilization. Most of all, it didn't like this forest.

But unsettling trees or not, I had to do this. We owed it to Jack to at least try.

"*You could let me help you.*"

"No," I muttered.

A strange flicker of vulnerability entered the monster's voice. "*Why do you fight me?*"

I didn't answer. It knew why. My deepest regrets had been sown by the monster's impulsive judgment. Its sense of justice lay on a monochrome scale of black and white, measured only by what hurt me, which was, objectively, a terrible metric.

"Stop." Eva held up a hand, nose pressed to the atlas. I slapped a mosquito. The uptick of humidity was a beacon to the little vampires.

"What—" A tremor rolled beneath my feet, stalling my question and forcing me to step back. A root snaked out from the soil, flailing like a cut worm split by the blade of a shovel. I sucked in a breath and stepped back.

Eva turned. "What's wrong?"

I pointed, mouth agape, to the wriggling root just as it slunk back into the dirt. "There. It moved!"

Eva squinted, following my finger. "What do you mean?"

"I mean it *moved*, Ev!"

"Okay, okay," she said, eyes widening in surprise at my vigor. Worry clouded her features, but I couldn't tell if she believed me. I was sure of what I'd seen.

There was something wrong with this forest.

Or maybe... it was just her gift? Eva could be making the roots move without even realizing it. The moment I thought it, I relaxed.

We'd been able to do little to hide the trail of flowers that grew behind her as we walked, leaving an irregular pattern of goldenrod, asters, and bright orange butterfly milkweed weaving through the aspen trees. Most likely, no one would even come up that road. And if they did, who would be smart enough to connect a trail of wildflowers to her anyway?

It would be fine.

I licked my lips, the skin so dry it had split. The subtle taste of blood mixed with the salt of sweat on my tongue.

"Let's take a break. Get a drink," Eva suggested.

I didn't fight her, sinking onto a fallen tree nearby. My hands shook as I unclicked the hiking pack and dropped it in the grass. The kitten leapt onto it.

The animal had taken to Eva at once, which didn't surprise me. Unfortunately, she'd also taken to *me*. I arched in stress when she trotted toward me, purring contentedly.

"Go on," I murmured, tossing down a shriveled leaf. The kitten pounced on that too.

We shouldn't have brought her. There were too many creatures in these woods that would gladly make her their next snack. If she survived those, she still had to face me: a killer who made her purr.

"She's probably getting tired." Eva unzipped her pack and rifled through the contents inside before pulling out a loaf of sandwich bread. She tore a slice into little pieces. "What should we call her?"

"I don't want to call her anything." Naming was claiming, and she would never be mine.

"Maybe... Puff? Snowball?"

"Snowballs are white."

Eva snorted. This was the longest conversation we'd had since leaving the Volkswagen. She'd taken me up on my offer of a change of clothes, eschewing her bloodstained overalls for a clean T-shirt and shorts. "You care a little," Eva said. "Admit it."

It was strange how quickly those words drew my monster up. I shrugged, unwilling to argue, but the simple tease made the beast in me bristle. It held my spine a little straighter, hissing in my ear. *"You care too much."*

I shivered.

"You care what people think of you."

"Socks is a good cat name," Eva mused, oblivious to the sharp-tongued voice in my head. She laughed when the kitten jumped on a piece of bread she'd tossed.

"You let people eat you up." The monster's self-righteous anger crowded my thoughts, squeezing me out like a lemon.

"Stop it," I whispered.

Eva shot me a look. "What? Do you have a better suggestion?"

"You let them consume you."

The permanent fixture of honeybees over Eva's head seemed to pulse, growing louder. When our eyes clicked together, Eva blinked. "Are you...okay?"

"You let them spit you out and —"

"SHUT UP!" I pressed my hands to my ears, a hard lump in my throat. "Stop talking!"

Eva jumped, eyes blowing wide, and a loud buzz sounded just beside my ear. I batted it away on instinct—and felt a stinger sink in. The monster faltered, and with its retreat came a rush of feeling. Shock. Breathlessness.

Pain.

Eva stepped forward. "You're stung."

"I'm fine," I growled, shaking as I braced my hands on my thighs.

"Liar."

She crossed to the trunk of an aspen tree and ripped a bit of cheatgrass from the soil.

"Unsophisticated palate," the monster muttered, displeased with her choice of plant.

When Eva got back to me, she held it out without a word. I took it and let the green stalk wither against my skin, hating the short-lived relief it brought to kill the plant. "I'm sorry," I muttered. I hadn't meant to yell at her.

Eva nodded, not meeting my gaze. "Let's just keep going."

Jack had left fastidious notes. Eva pointed out the highlights as we passed. Ginseng, she said, was a big deal in Appalachia. Sang hunters who cared only for the herb's market price took everything they found, overharvesting be damned. When we passed a cache Jack had marked, Eva bent and pushed her fingers into the soil. Green shoots sprouted, tripling the trove. She left it all in the ground, always one to give instead of take.

Not like me.

At some point, my breathing grew too labored to hide.

"You need to stop?" Eva asked. "Take another drink?"

Water wouldn't stop my body from feeling like I'd squeezed it through a paper shredder. My vision went slightly out of focus as I shook my head. It was these damn aspen trees. The endless sea of white bark and rippling green leaves swayed around me like an optical illusion.

"You have grown too accustomed to self-neglect." The monster's annoyance cut down my ribs. Before I could stop it, it slipped into the muscles of my arms and sloppily jerked my bottle from its pouch in the pack. Screwed off the lid.

I flushed with distress and tried to rip away from its hold. *Fine, I'll drink!*

The monster didn't release me.

Let me go.

"Push me out."

My eyes widened. The monster had never demanded that before.

"Maybe I deserve a chance to pilot this ship, if you won't captain it properly."

"Here, have an apple." Eva tossed one my way. I had no athletic skill, but the monster snatched it from the air. A bruise marred the fruit's dark, carmine flesh.

"Eat."

But even looking at the apple made me feel a little nauseous. It seemed the more space the monster took up inside me, the less appetite I had, though its presence didn't fill me. If anything, it did the opposite, carving hunger into a hollow I couldn't fill with food.

"Don't make me into some kind of villain. You have to push through, little death-touch," it snapped. *"You're too hot, and probably dehydrated too. You need to drink."*

The very thought of water made me smack the roof of my mouth with my tongue.

Eva planted herself on a rock, angled so when she leaned back, the pack squished under her. The pink glow of a sunburn striped her forehead. It wouldn't last long, the way she healed. She eyed me. "You don't look so good."

"I'm fine," I mumbled.

"Drink." The monster roughly jerked the open water bottle to my mouth. It sloshed down my chin, but some made it in. I swallowed hard enough to hurt.

"Now eat."

The crunch of apple skin sent a shudder down my body. Too

much like the tear of sinew off bone. But it took only seconds for the sugar in the juice to offer relief.

Eva unclicked her pack and crossed to me, pressing a hand to my forehead. "Are you dizzy?"

"No," I lied.

Eva clearly didn't believe me. "Let's take a break and set up camp. We're not going to make it to the meadow today anyway."

"I can do it," I gritted out to both of them.

Her gaze turned steely. "A good hiker resolves a problem before it gets worse."

"He's bad at that."

My flush intensified. "I'm a good hiker," I muttered, pride wounded.

"Good." Eva lifted the straps of my pack. "Here, you unclick."

I buried a groan of relief as the weight slipped off my shoulders and landed with a clunk in the dirt. "Sorry," I mumbled, though I wasn't sure what exactly I was apologizing for this time. It was an easy state to slip into. Sorry for being difficult. Sorry for being me.

I wiped a bit of sweat off my forehead and took another swig of water, watching as yet another honeybee landed on Eva's shoulder. Even out here, they flocked to her. The wings on the little insect fluttered. Above us, the canopy shifted, the sun finding the honeybee's wings. It was so ordinary. So painfully beautiful.

My eyelids drooped. For just a moment, I let myself drift, seeking a foothold where my body wasn't an open flare of pain and discomfort.

"Arthur!"

Startled, my eyes snapped open. Eva arched an expectant brow. "You keep zoning out."

"Oh."

Eva studied me a bit too closely. "What's going on with you?"

"Nothing."

"You've been fidgety and unsettled all day."

"Maybe you're unsettling, bee girl."

I hadn't meant to say it aloud, and certainly not with a touch of irritation. Eva's eyes blew wide in surprise. Chagrined, I took a quick, brutal bite of the apple. The flavor soured on my tongue, just like the rot spoiling inside me.

"What aren't you telling me?" she demanded.

She shouldn't ask questions like that. She wouldn't like the answers.

"I'm just hot. And tired."

"You're developing a fever."

"Really?" Eva challenged. "Is that all?"

For a moment, I thought what a relief it would be if she knew and understood. Not only about the monster but also about the fear that lived inside me, fear of what the creature's existence said about the state of my soul.

"Just say it," Eva said. "It's clearly eating you up."

Her word choice delighted the monster. *"At least one of us gets to eat."*

I braced my forearms on my knees and shook my head. "Forget it."

It was one thing to daydream, but I couldn't tell her about the monster. I'd take that with me to the grave.

"You're ashamed of me?"

I huffed. Why did it sound so surprised?

Eva switched tactics. "How're your stitches feeling?"

They hurt like hell, but I wasn't keen to bring that up again. She'd feel awful, and both of us would have to sit with the memory of sitting too close, sharing air, my hands splayed over her hips. It was instinctive, excusable, once. But we couldn't do that again.

"Already feeling better," I lied.

Eva didn't look like she believed me, but she crossed to me, bent beside my pack and lifted it onto her shoulders.

"What are you doing?"

"I'll come back for the other one when we find a place to set up camp," she said, ignoring my question. When I tried to argue, she put up a hand. "Just...let this be easy. Okay?"

My jaw tightened. "Fine."

We followed the nearby burbling to a river. I wanted to sprawl on the bank, feet in the water, and let the mosquitoes have me. It was worth it, or it would be, if the bank hadn't been covered in tall, feathery reeds I didn't dare touch.

"Take off your shirt," Eva said.

"What?"

"We need to cool you down."

I bristled at the monster's smug satisfaction but obeyed without further protest. When Eva returned from the river, she wrung the shirt out over my head. The trickle down my neck was blissfully cold.

"Back on." As Eva dangled the damp shirt in front of me, her eyes strayed to the honeycomb tattoo on my bare biceps. Somehow her unwillingness to comment made it feel even more incriminating.

The kitten pounced on a silverfish in the dirt.

"Take off your shoes."

"You know, you've gotten a little bossy." But I couldn't deny how much better I felt when the shoes came off. I carefully rested my arches on the laces. Sometimes I dreamt of grass between my toes. It was a luxury I'd experienced only in snatches, and always just for a meager second, before the monster stole all the life out from whatever touched our skin.

Eva sank down beside me and we drank from our water bottles, the wind kissing our cheeks. The breeze blew a golden strand over Eva's sun-rosed skin. She tucked it back. "You put the first aid kit in my pack, right? You got any aspirin in there?"

"Yeah." I hadn't told her my head was pounding, but of course she'd picked up on that. When Eva was certain I was cooling down, she left to fetch the other pack. The kitten apprehensively watched her leave, but one look at me and she settled, pawing at a line of ants.

"You're a funny bug," I murmured.

Mom's memorial service felt far away, a distant memory from years past, instead of yesterday. So far, our hike had not gone well at all. In fact, I wasn't sure how it could have gone worse.

At the rustle of wind, a strange feeling licked up the back of my neck. It was not unlike the feeling of the monster's awareness expanding inside me to reveal the thump of a rabbit's heart, or the ocean song of mycelium.

But this wasn't the monster.

Arthur.

I stiffened at the musical lilt to my name and turned, unease collecting inside me. That voice had worn a groove in my brain I'd never be rid of. A broken-promise voice. A bedtime-story voice. A should-have-been-dead voice.

At first, I saw nothing but the green expanse of forest around me. When something moved to my left, I whirled, catching sight only of a fluttering branch. I blinked, thinking that I'd simply caught a bird in flight. But there were no wings or shaking leaves, and the monster sensed no heartbeat.

The outstretched arm of a branch bent inward, like the joint of an elbow.

"Arthur!" This time my name came on the verge of panic. I shook off the feeling of wrongness, blinking hard, and the tree became just a tree again, solid and still.

The voice melted back into the wind.

"Arthur!" Eva crashed through the trees and burst into view. "It's gone!"

"What?"

"The pack," she panted. "It's gone!"

Chapter 19

Arthur,
Before

Audrey's weekly farmers' market drew a hungry crowd from Cumberland Valley. They came in droves to fill their woven baskets with pears from the orchard and goods from the Honey Shoppe. Harvest season provided the town with a much-needed financial boost. With Jack up the mountain collecting samples of flowers to dry into tea, the task of selling the Shoppe's stock fell to his daughters, and to me.

I managed the cash register, more than eager to lessen the risk of skin-to-skin contact. Citrine sunlight spilled in through the bay window, and an acoustic guitar thrummed outside. Through the crowd, I caught sight of Eva's bouncing, messy bun.

"Excuse me."

My attention snapped to June, Izzy's friend and Dane Walker's soon-to-be bride. She lifted her sunglasses onto her forehead, a crinkle of tension knotting her otherwise perfectly smooth brow.

"Sorry, yes." I cleared my throat. "How can I help?"

"I'm here for the wedding candles. Izzy said she left a note?"

I snapped my fingers. "Yes. Hang on. I think she put them in the back."

The storage room was a welcoming mess of jarred pollen, honey sticks, and a bee-balm lip salve that sold like…well, like honey cakes. *When autumn comes,* Eva had said, *we'll sell those too. You'll love them, Arthur.*

The idea of still being here when autumn hit was hard to wrap my mind around. I couldn't picture the bee girl in the cold.

Sometimes my mind drifted to my mother. Hope was a scab I picked and picked. Would she come back for the holidays?

I bent, thumbing the handwritten labels along the shelf edge as I searched for the box, the slide of my thumb over tape the only sound in the quiet space. Not here. I stood, turning, eyes surfing upper shelves stuffed with glass jars of honey, steel and brass infusers, and biodegradable tea bags you could fill yourself.

When the bell dinged in the Shoppe, I glanced up. I was taking too long. *Where are those damn candles?*

Through a gap in the curtain, I watched as Lenny Walker stepped toward the counter, carrying a large crate full of golden pears. Eva trailed behind him, picking at the hem of her shirt. "On the counter," she said stiffly.

Lenny lowered the crate with a grunt, then turned to June. "Dane's looking for you."

"Oh?" She sounded surprised.

My toe stubbed into a box sticking out from underneath the lowest shelf. I crouched and peeled off Izzy's note, scrawled with instructions: *Three dozen votive candles for Walker reception.*

Lenny took one of the pears in hand and tossed it once. When he caught it again, he buried his incisors into its flesh, his eyes trained on Eva all the while. "Something about the band calling to cancel?"

"What?!" June shrieked. Lenny shrugged and took another bite, pear juice bursting through his lips.

June launched out of the Honey Shoppe, visibly alarmed. The instant she was gone, Lenny crossed to the door.

But he didn't leave. He bolted the lock.

A whisper of alarm went through me.

"What are you doing?" Eva asked uneasily.

"I'm not a bad guy, you know." Lenny tugged the blinds, tension pulling his back muscles taut, then turned toward her, eyes hard. "You didn't have to stand me up like that."

When he stepped forward, Eva stepped back.

"I just want to talk," Lenny huffed, exasperated. "I've been trying to talk to you all fucking summer."

"I-I don't want to talk to you."

"Dammit, Eva, it was just a kiss!"

I knifed to my feet.

When Eva tried to shoot past him, Lenny grabbed her around the waist. He took her jaw in his grip and pressed his lips hard to her mouth.

"Hey!" I barked out as I pushed through the gap in the curtain.

Lenny jerked back.

I snatched a jar of honey off a shelf and chucked it at him. Glass shattered at his feet where it landed, shards skittering under the display tables.

"Get out!"

Lenny released Eva. She gasped as she fell against the counter's edge.

"OUT!" I roared again.

I felt the monster in every pulse of adrenaline, and it took all I had to fight back the lapping desire to rush forward and seize Lenny by the throat. Already, I could see it in my mind's eye. He'd turn purple, the monster squeezing our hand around his neck. He would —

Stop it, I inwardly snapped.

Flushed, Lenny swiped his mouth, his eyes still dark with cruel intent. When I stepped forward, he turned on his heel. The bolt resisted him, sticking in brass, before he jerked the door open and fled.

My vision hazed, and tinnitus pealed bright in my ears. I crossed to the door and re-bolted it, adrenaline rushing through me. The monster thrashed inside me, demanding I go after the coward. It wanted me to hurt him. *I* wanted to hurt him.

But then Eva let out a sob and rushed past me to the storage room, hiding her face in her hands.

My anger crumpled. I flicked the sign to CLOSED and steadied a palm on the door. Tried to bury the fury stretching its wings inside me. I could do that, for her.

I gave us both a minute to collect ourselves before going after her. When I pulled back the burlap curtain, Eva turned away from me. She white-knuckled the shelf, a raw sound breaking past her lips.

I felt like an intruder. I hadn't earned the right to her bare emotion like this, but I was here, seeing it anyway.

"I'll pay for the jar," I said softly.

Eva turned. Tears striped her cheeks, and her bottom lip was swollen. She tried to speak once and had to start over to get the words out. "I don't" — *hic* — "care about the jar!"

I nodded, scared that anything I said would only make her feel more cornered. Eva's eyes shone under the ancient, swinging bulb. Her breaths quickened into short puffs. Too quick. In seconds, alarm washed her features.

She was hyperventilating.

I moved to her on instinct, hoping I wouldn't scare her too. To my relief, Eva fell against me. She clutched my T-shirt, hitching sobs.

"Help her, little death-touch."

Cupping the back of her head, I thought back to the day she'd tended my bee sting. If I couldn't find the right words, I could steal hers. "Think of the sky," I whispered. "The storm clouds. They move through you, right?"

"I can't...can't breathe!" Eva gasped.

When I pulled back, I realized her bottom lip wasn't only swollen — it was bitten. The skin had darkened where Lenny had buried his teeth. A rush of anger made me dizzy, but I swallowed it down, for now, and placed Eva's hand over my heart, as she'd done before.

"Do you feel that?" I said softly.

Eva nodded fast.

"Good." I inhaled, deeply. "Can you try to breathe with me?"

Together, we inhaled. We exhaled. Time seemed to flatten, keeping us suspended as Eva's frantic breathing slowly evened out.

"Okay." Tears spilled down my cheeks. "You're okay, Ev."

It was a lie. Nothing was okay right now. Lenny's words turned over in my mind. *It was just a kiss.* I thought of the blank expression she'd worn the day Lenny had walked into the workshop, the day her bees had stung him. I thought about what she'd told me the very day we met.

They won't hurt you. If you're nice.

The monster's anger steamed down to aggressive worry as Eva leaned her weight into my chest. I rubbed circles over her back, counting in circuits of eight. Stretching time. Slowing her down.

The monster's ability to sense the life around us turned Eva's heartbeat into a drum. Slowly, the rhythm lost its frantic edge. Our breaths moved in tandem. Eva slipped her arms around my waist. Somehow, that touch, so trusting, reached deeper than anything else had.

"You're okay," I whispered again.

I turned my face into her hair, not daring to plant a real kiss there but needing the reassurance of her touch. Eva melted into me. Could she feel my heart pounding too, with our chests pressed this close?

"I'm sorry," Eva husked.

"No. You did nothing wrong." I drew back. "He was way out of line. You know that, right?"

She hiccupped.

"Eva," I said carefully, "has Lenny ever done that before?"

Her eyes shimmered as they stared into mine, and for a long, trembling moment, I thought she wouldn't answer. At last, she nodded slightly. "Once."

My heart dropped into my stomach.

"Last day of school. He...he cornered me by the lockers." Eva choked out the words.

The door to the Honey Shoppe rattled. Eva jerked in my arms, but it was only Izzy, who called through the door. "Let me in, lovebirds! We have a wedding emergency."

A panicked look overtook Eva's features. "You can't tell her!"

"What?" I shook my head. "Ev, we have to."

"No!"

I stared, stunned. Eva Moreau was the most fearless person I'd ever met, and the anxiety painting her face now was wrong, all wrong. Hatred burst under my skin for the boy who'd made her cry like this, who'd *touched* her without permission.

My eyes fixed on her swollen lip. "We need to tell someone."

If I'd thought she looked panicked before, it was nothing on the terror that seized her now. "Not Izzy."

"Helloooooo," her sister called, wiggling the doorknob. "Is someone in here? Market's still going."

Eva turned desperate eyes on me. "Please, Arthur." Her voice was fainter than before. "I just want to forget it, okay?"

I hesitated. This... this didn't feel right.

Eva took my hand and pressed her lips to my knuckles. It wasn't a kiss, not really, but it was warm and pleading. "I don't want to be another thing my neighbors talk about," she croaked. "Please."

She was looking at me with so much fear. So much hope. No one looked at me like that.

I didn't want to disappoint her.

"Okay."

Relief melted over her face. "Promise me."

I nodded. "I promise."

The moment the words slipped past my lips, I knew they were a mistake.

Chapter 20

Isobel

Dawson's Bar was the last place Isobel should be right now. Of course that's where Lenny went.

Outside the door, Isobel hesitated. The flickering rainbow lights shining through the glass cast her pale skin in every color of ruin and play. It beckoned her to shuck off her worries, to enter.

To stay.

She steadied herself with a long breath. She'd gone almost a year without drinking, and it felt good. She didn't want to go inside, but Lenny was in there, and Lenny was looking for the people she loved most.

Isobel still held her shoes in her hand, her bare feet muddied from her pursuit. She walked to the nearest patch of grass and wiped her soles clean, slipping the heels back on before she wrapped her hand around the doorknob and pushed in.

She wouldn't drink. She was just getting information.

The crush of people made it difficult to spot her target, so Isobel angled to the bar, where a familiar face was mixing drinks.

"Izzy?" When Priya recognized her, her whole face lit up with a golden smile. The bartender was even more dazzling now than she'd been when she and Izzy had dated, and she was by far the most attractive person in the room. Married life suited her.

"Hey, Pree."

Isobel hadn't started drinking in earnest until after they'd ended things. Life had taken a dark turn for her family after Dane and June's disastrous wedding reception. After Arthur had left and her father's tree had sprouted from his ribs, Eva had fallen apart entirely. Her family had needed Isobel to hold them up, so she had. She'd dropped out of college and come home to bear more of the workload on the farm. She'd taken on full responsibility for the household's upkeep, broken up with Priya, and held her sister while she grieved. When the noise got too loud, Isobel had discovered that a round of shots made things quiet again.

But none of that mattered, because she wasn't here to drink.

Priya had tied her cropped black hair into a tiny bun on her nape. "What can I get you?" she asked. Isobel didn't miss the nervous edge to her smile.

"Lemonade and fries?"

Visible relief melted the tension on Priya's face. "You got it." She worked quickly, her eyes straying back to Isobel as she scooped the crinkle cuts into a basket. "Are you doing all right, Iz? I heard about your sister."

"I'm fine." Isobel thumbed a water stain on the counter, desperate for a distraction. "How's Molly?"

To her relief, Priya took the bait and her face split into a broad grin. "She's good. We got a dog."

Isobel's plastic smile softened to something real. "Oh yeah?"

"Yeah. Peggy's collie had her litter last month. I think I've been replaced."

As they laughed, Isobel searched the crowd.

"You lookin' for the sheriff?"

"No, I..." A familiar flash of red hair caught her attention, and Isobel turned. *There.* Lenny was seated across from Avi Dawson, Priya's brother and one of Lenny's oldest friends. They spoke too quietly for Isobel to hear, but the lines of their bodies were carved in tension. When Avi downed his last bit of beer, the two men stood.

Dammit.

Isobel left her place at the bar and rushed to stand between them and the door.

"Out of my way, Moreau," Lenny said.

But Isobel didn't move, didn't so much as break eye contact, even though a whisper of danger made the skin on her arms pebble with goose bumps. "No."

Avi scoffed. "The hell she means, *no?*"

The words made Lenny's cheeks turn pink. "Move. Now," he clipped.

Isobel shook her head. "I don't think so."

It was about time Lenny learned that he didn't get to have something just because he wanted it. Dane believed Lenny had changed, but he'd also been acting as his brother's keeper for as long as Isobel had known the Walkers. Love could blind you to the truth. Isobel had watched this play out so many times before. Lenny screwed up, people got hurt, and Dane always took the fall.

It was time to break the cycle.

"Is there a problem here?" Priya asked, coming up behind Isobel and brushing her palms on her apron.

"The problem," Avi said, his body language twitching with irritation as he lifted his chin toward Isobel, "is *her.*" He looked down his nose at Isobel. "You're not even supposed to be here."

"Izzy is always welcome here," Priya snapped.

He was right, though. This room was overwhelming. The low, pulsing lights. The smell of cheap beer. The memories thickening the air around her. Isobel's mouth watered, the taste of a whiskey dancing on her tongue, a delicate temptation she shouldn't — couldn't — give in to.

Isobel searched inward for the right mask to fortify her, but it was difficult. All these people knew her as the party girl she'd been before. She was Izzy here, not Isobel. Between these walls, she became all the versions of herself she'd tried so hard to let go of. Not wanting to let her discomfort show, she lifted her chin. "I know what you're doing."

Lenny cocked his head, his gaze dropping to his brother's jacket around her shoulders. "It was you," he said. "In the office."

Isobel stiffened.

Lenny's mouth pulled up in a sneer. "So. *You* were what he was so busy doing tonight. Figures."

Isobel glared to hide the creep of a flush up her neck.

"You Moreaus are all the same, you know," he said flatly. "You think you're all so *good*."

To Isobel's surprise, the words, like a knife, found a chink in her armor and slid beneath. When she tried to answer, the words stopped in her throat, her mind crowding with doubts.

Maybe he was right. She'd done a lot of things she wasn't proud of over the last eight years.

Lenny came a little closer. "But you know what?" His breath ghosted against the shell of her ear. "You're just like me."

"That's enough," Priya said uneasily.

Lenny ignored her. "You and I both know what really happened that night," he went on in a low voice. "And fucking my brother won't stop him from hating you when he finds out you've been lying to him."

Isobel slapped him.

The next few moments happened very fast.

Lenny seized Isobel by the hair and ripped her away from the door. She tripped over an empty chair, knocking a tumbler off the nearest table as she fell. Her knees hit the linoleum, pain strobing through her.

"Hey!" Priya barked.

Isobel's heart beat hard. She stared at the shattered glass on the floor before her. Only when a carmine drip oozed beneath her knees did she realize she'd cut herself.

"Bitch," Lenny muttered. He grabbed Avi and the two of them tore into the night, Priya shouting obscenities after her brother. Isobel stared numbly after them. She touched the aching place on her scalp where Lenny had tugged hard enough to pull some hairs out by the roots.

Priya crouched beside her. "Fuck, Iz, I'm so sorry."

"Not your fault," Isobel said, her voice cracking.

Priya signaled someone over Isobel's shoulder. "Call the sheriff."

"No!" Isobel snapped, a lump balling in her throat. She didn't want to see Dane right now. "I'm fine. Just...give me a minute." She stood and sank down onto her stool, the room throbbing around her. People were looking at her. Normally she didn't care, but Lenny had cracked the shell of her mask, making it impossible to pretend she was unaffected. Usually when Isobel felt this out of control, she turned to Dane. But Dane was too busy seeking answers to questions he shouldn't be asking.

Isobel closed her eyes, letting the world fall away. She was sweating, her skin as slick as her mouth was dry. A shiver of thirst narrowed her world to the taste of whiskey on her tongue.

But she couldn't taste it. She only remembered.

An out-of-towner sat on the stool nearest her, an amber shot of something good in front of him.

Don't. It was Dane's voice in her head, but Dane wasn't here.

"Pree!" Isobel flushed with conviction. Just one drink. Maybe two. That's all she needed to take the edge off and get control again. "Double bourbon. Neat."

Priya hesitated. "Iz, I don't think that's a good —"

"Now." Isobel snatched up the stranger's glass. "I'll pay for this," she promised him, before throwing it back. The liquid burned its way down her throat. Oaky. Warming. Wonderful.

She let out a sigh, already feeling more herself.

Izzy couldn't help but giggle at the words the strange man spoke into her ear. Not a local. Not a very good flirt either, but his breath tickled the hairs on her neck as they danced to the beat of a song Izzy hadn't heard in ages.

"You want to go somewhere more private?" he asked a bit too loudly.

Izzy patted his cheek and shook her head. "I just want to dance."

At some point after Lenny had left the bar, she'd lost her grip on her Isobel mask and slipped into *Izzy* again. This was who she was, after all, under all her good intentions. This was her true face.

The thought made her ache. She didn't want to be Izzy. And she didn't want to be sad. But it felt good to forget, just for a minute, to lose herself in dance and in the feeling of being desirable, even if it was only in a stranger's eyes.

She saw a flash of red hair in the crowd, there and gone. The lightness in her chest dissipated when the stranger closed a hand on her waist and tugged her back. "Come on, Lily. Stop teasing me."

She blinked. Took him in. Only moments ago, he'd looked so harmless. Young and carefree, nervous even. Now he looked irritated. When his hand went south to grab her ass, she pushed away.

"My name is Izzy," she slurred.

The answer wasn't quite right, even to her ears. Her words, in the voice of a stranger. She turned to walk away, but the man grabbed her wrist. She drove her heel onto his foot, causing him to howl with pain. Thrown off-balance, Izzy fell back a step and slammed smack into a broad stone chest.

A very *warm* broad stone chest.

"Isobel." The voice was hard, and Izzy's stomach swooped low. "Are you okay?" Dane demanded.

He smelled expensive. It was something in his soap she hadn't been able to identify, a clean and masculine scent that had a way of clinging to all his clothes. It wafted into her nose as she leaned back against him, a grin stealing over her face. "I'm great, Sheriff."

"What the hell are you doing here?"

Before she could answer, the stranger whose foot she'd stomped on aimed an accusatory finger at her, the bass swallowing his insult as Dane took her by the elbow and led her off the dance floor. A muscle tensed in his jaw. "Why did you leave the house? I've been worried sick!"

That was far too many questions, and the answers felt... hard. So Izzy shucked him off and strode toward the bar, cheeks and neck and heart aflame. Everything was soft-lit and spinning. She made to pick up another drink, but Dane was right there, and he slammed the glass back down on the sticky counter, next to a fleet of lipstick-kissed glasses. His favorite shade—Rose Coquette—wasted on a room of people Izzy didn't want.

She spun to face him, fire-eyed. "Go away."

"No." He sounded angry. He sounded hurt. "We have a deal."

Damn their deal.

They'd made it years ago, after his divorce was final. A pact, for old friends. He'd just been promoted to sheriff, and he'd gotten a call about a woman dancing on the bar and singing a very loud, music-free rendition of "Jessie's Girl" on repeat. When Dane had found her, she had passed out on the linoleum with a sticker on her cheek.

A blizzard had made the road up to the cottage dangerously slick, so he'd taken her back to his shoebox apartment. Esther had slept in a crib in the kitchen. Izzy had taken the scratchy couch, nursing her pride and a burgeoning hangover in a pair of borrowed gray sweatpants she'd never given back.

The next morning, he'd held her hand while she'd called to find an AA meeting. After that, she'd promised to tell him whenever she wanted to drink. Day or night. In return, Dane had opened up to her for the first time since his split with June had soured their once-easy trio. He'd confided how afraid he was of failing both Lenny and his daughter. "I'm not good at being the glue," he'd told her miserably. "Not like you."

She'd reassured him that night, and many nights since, "You're a good dad." And, begrudgingly, "a good brother too." That was still true, even if Lenny was a human fungus parasitizing Dane's forgiving nature.

Izzy didn't want to admit that she needed his help tonight.

"Why did you leave?" Dane asked again.

"I... I don't know. I had to follow Lenny—"

"To a *bar*?"

She flushed. "At least I did something."

Izzy was primed for his anger. She wasn't prepared, however, for him to soften. Dane stepped closer and folded his arms around her. "That you did," he whispered, ghosting a soft touch to the bruise on her arm that Lenny had left behind. "You brave, terrifying woman."

Izzy was frozen, afraid to let herself sink into his touch.

Dane pulled back and held her by the shoulders. "But what if he'd hurt you, Isobel? Hurt you *more*?"

"Why did *you* just let him go?"

"I didn't," Dane said, clearly appalled.

"But you're not out looking for him."

"I was looking for you!" The strobing, colorful lights overhead cast his pale skin in strange and sickening hues. Dane's expression was earnest. "I had to make sure you were okay. I have deputies out searching for Lenny."

"He'll go after them," Izzy said.

Dane paused, then nodded. "I think so too."

It was all so hard to think about with her head still spinning. Izzy backed up, reaching behind her for a stool to settle on.

"I know you're worried about Arthur and your sister," Dane said. "But we'll find them, Isobel."

"I know." She believed him. So why didn't his words comfort her?

Dane hesitated. "I brought Esther to June's on my way over so I can stay at your place tonight if you or your dad need anything."

Thoughts of her father pierced through the haze. She hadn't meant to be gone this long. How much time had passed?

"I'll rejoin the search tomorrow morning."

Izzy huffed. "I don't need a babysitter." She spun to face the bar and snatched up an abandoned glass of beer, which Dane immediately plucked out of her hand.

"Hey!"

"You don't want that, Isobel."

The syllables of her name slid over his tongue in the most intoxicating way.

In her boozy haze, his eye contact felt deliciously bold.

Dane rolled up his sleeves. Careful. Precise. Ridiculous, given the venue. She let out a wet, derisive snort. If Prince Charming was trying to keep his shirt clean, he'd come to the wrong place. The surfaces in Dawson's were always sticky, the air always thick with booze. Drinkers spat their sunflower seeds onto the floor and threw darts at a hay bale with a spray-painted boob in place of a target. If you hit the nipple, you got a free beer.

He didn't belong in a place like this.

He didn't belong with *her*.

Dane lifted her chin. His touch made the rest of the room around them blur. It was a little unfair he could pull her in like this when her focus was in tatters. She wanted to undo him, not the other way around.

Tears came to her eyes. *Dammit.* Izzy never cried unless she was drunk. "Why do you still defend him?" Izzy was proud of the words because they didn't slur. Drunk Izzy didn't slur. Drunk Izzy didn't wobble. Drunk Izzy didn't get sad.

Dane sighed. "I think drunk Izzy should have some water."

She frowned. Had she said that out loud?

Dane signaled to Priya, who appeared holding a bottle, the traitor. "Drink," he said.

A hiccup closed her throat. "I was" — *hic* — "drinking." She made to push his offering away but knocked the bottle over instead.

Dane caught it, then unscrewed the cap with a sharp twist. "Drink water, love."

Izzy consented to a grumpy sip, still waiting for his answer.

"I do not defend my brother. I'm… trying, failing maybe, to make amends."

"With him?" she scoffed.

Dane's eyes never strayed. "Is that so hard for you to understand?"

Lenny's words rang between her ears like the world's most repulsive tinnitus. *Fucking my brother won't stop him from hating you when he finds out you've been lying to him.*

"Yes," she admitted.

"You have Arthur, though."

She rocked back. "What?"

"I'm just saying, you know what it is to love a… complicated person," he said. "It's one thing I really admire in you."

"Arthur isn't complicated!" Izzy snapped. He was, in fact, all too easy for her to understand. So was Lenny. Both of them had taken their grief over the loss of a parent, the loss of love, and sharpened it into a weapon.

The difference was who they pointed the blade at.

She shoved away from the bar. "I don't want to be here anymore."

Dane followed her out into the empty street. "Isobel, wait."

"I don't want to fight," she said, head aching.

"Are we fighting?" Dane challenged.

She didn't turn to face him, but the sound of his footsteps over the pavement warned her of his approach. Delicately, Dane put his hands on her upper arms. When Izzy leaned back into his chest, he wrapped his arms more firmly around her.

"They're not the same," she whispered.

The Arthur she knew had only ever tried to make life a little better. She'd missed him so much, and now he was back and her father was hurt because of him, and Dane was bent on chasing him down.

Everything about it felt wrong.

Dane kissed her hair. "Let me take you home, love."

She turned, but Dane was a blur. Damn these tears. Damn his stupid shirt and his stupid perfect smell. Izzy wanted to see him come undone. She wanted to pull the wild out of this careful, measured man. "Is that an order?"

"Do you want it to be, Isobel?"

And though he'd said her name already that night, something about the shape of it on his lips now loosened the tension in her chest. She took a deep breath, savoring the syllables.

Dane smiled, unaware of how such a little word could so deeply rearrange her. "Come on. We'll negotiate a truce on the way, hmm?"

And maybe it was the alcohol plying her, or maybe she was tired of carrying it all alone, but when he pulled his keys from his pocket, she stepped forward and slipped back into the person she wanted to be.

Battered, but still fighting.

Isobel, again.

As they drove through Audrey's single stoplight, Dane reached across the console and took her hand. Isobel let him rub his thumb over the ridges of her knuckles. For diplomacy and all.

Dane gave her fingers a squeeze. "Everything will be okay."

Isobel said nothing, wanting to believe him.

Chapter 21

Eva

It could have been an animal.
The words beat a frantic rhythm in Eva's head as she cleared a fire pit. The slink of vinyl and the clatter of tent poles rang out behind her. When Arthur swore, she peeked and caught him nursing a smashed thumb. Gloves on, of course. With a rock, he hammered the stakes of their tent into the ground.

At least they still had that. With the disappearance of her pack, they'd lost one of their sleeping bags, their first aid kit, and half their food. Too stressed and frustrated to speak without sniping at each other, they'd stopped talking altogether.

A strip of bark flared, then caught flame. Eva blew on the ember to make it grow. They still had an hour of daylight left, but the mountains got cold at night this time of year, and Eva needed to busy herself with a useful task to distract from her spiraling thoughts.

It could have been an animal.

But wanting something to be true didn't make it so. If an animal had smelled the food still in the backpack and dragged it off, wouldn't there have been some kind of mark in the soil? Eva hadn't seen any tracks. It was as though the pack had disappeared into thin air. She thought of the sheriff, who certainly would have pulled together a search party. But if Dane and his deputies had tracked them down, they wouldn't hide in the trees or steal supplies. They wouldn't keep their presence a secret.

She could make neither head nor tail of it, but the sensation of being watched made the hairs on the back of her neck stand up. She cut a glance over her shoulder to the trail of wildflowers she'd left in her footprints. Anxiety buzzed inside her.

This forest was unlike any other she'd been in. Eva couldn't put her finger on what about it unnerved her, exactly, only that it seemed somehow more…conscious. Not like an animal but *more* than any stand of trees she'd ever come across. The communal hum of roots beneath the surface had started to grate against her skull.

She needed to shut down her brain. To stop catastrophizing.

It was hard not to let her father's stories creep back in. As she worked on their fire, Eva's memory drifted back to other hearthside moments in their cottage, when Dad would gather both his girls on his lap with a giant bag of chocolate-covered popcorn and tell them stories about his fictional honeyman.

"He used to be an average-sized sort of fellow, until magic stretched him into a giant."

That one had made Eva giggle, and Dad had tickled her ribs.

"He spoke the languages of trees. He knew the sounds they made when they were happy" — Dad had pointed to the crackling log in their fireplace — "and when they were in pain."

A flame caught and licked across the lichen-covered log Eva was hovering over, pulling her from the memory she'd all but forgotten. She moved back, giving the fire space to grow as she stuck a finger in her shoe and lifted her heel out to give the growing blister some relief. Usually, such wounds healed faster than this, but even her quick healing couldn't quite keep up with the torment of too-small shoes over miles and miles.

A zipper whined behind her. She turned to see Arthur kneel inside the tent and unroll their single sleeping bag. When his back muscles flexed taut, her mouth went dry.

At least they'd switched packs, or else they wouldn't have the tent at all.

The kitten had curled up like a pill bug in the grass. The cans of chicken they'd planned on giving her had been in the pack too. Eva had peaches, but she was pretty sure she'd read somewhere that cats shouldn't have peaches. So, for now, her sandwich bread would have to tide the kitten over.

Guilt wormed inside her as she wondered again if they'd made a mistake. Between Arthur's stitches, the rough terrain, and the kitten's hungry mewls, it certainly hadn't been the strongest start to their quest.

Worse was her father. Eva hadn't told him goodbye. What if his body gave out before they could return? Had she surrendered her last days with him for nothing?

No. No, they could still do this. They just had to get to the wildflower fields.

The fire hit a water pocket in the wood and sparked a bright scarlet. Eva dug a few cheese sticks out of her pack. Tonight, they would eat and rest. Tomorrow, Arthur would be well, and together they would finish the trek to the meadows.

They had to.

The tent door fluttered in the breeze as she approached.

"I can sleep outside," Arthur offered cautiously.

Snapshots flicked through her mind: the withering branches of her father's tree, the depression in the grass where her pack should have been. "It's not safe," she said carefully.

"It's not safe for me to be inside either."

"You won't hurt me."

It felt like a confession to admit she still believed that, despite the ache of the last eight years. It also felt a little bit like a lie. They both knew he *had* hurt her, his absence a bruise that time couldn't fade.

"You won't," Eva said more firmly, unsure which of them she was trying to convince.

Arthur's eyes dropped to the kitten. "I could hurt Bug."

She blinked. "Bug? What are you...?" She glanced at their furry companion. "You named the cat!"

Arthur flushed. "No."

"You did!"

"She's been pawing at bugs all day!" Arthur said with a defensive sweep of his arm.

Eva snorted a laugh. She couldn't help it. "You named our cat *Bug*."

"*Our* cat?" Arthur countered indignantly.

It was just enough to send her over the edge. Eva bent over giggling, tears salting her cheeks.

Arthur's ears reddened. "Forget it," he muttered. "She can be Snowball."

"No, no, I think it's cute." Eva pushed herself up, swiping away the moisture in her eyes. Honestly, it felt good to cry for something funny for a change. "Sorry. I do, I... Sorry." Another laugh slipped out of her. She pointed to her face. "This isn't about you."

The emotional release made newborn blades of grass push out of the soil at her feet. She scooped Bug up and followed a sulking Arthur into the tent, her lips still trembling with laughter.

"What do we do about this?" He nodded to the remaining sleeping bag they had to share.

It was a good question. The cooling temperature would leave them both shivering without a few extra layers. Luckily, they still had the clothes in Arthur's pack, including the flannel shirt she'd worn in the van.

"Unzip it," she decided. "We'll dress warm and sleep underneath."

"And the cat?"

Bug arched her back and pawed the floor of the tent, widening a sudden yawn.

"Oh, she'll sleep with me. We cuddle now." Eva nuzzled the animal close and dropped her voice to a whisper. "Isn't that right, Bug?"

Eva used to love camping, priding herself as a child on her hardiness to the outdoors. It was something she and Dad had shared. So it irritated her no end that no matter what she did, no matter how the last few days had depleted her stores of energy down to the dregs, she couldn't fall asleep.

She blamed the pine cones digging into her back. She blamed the cold. Most frustratingly, she blamed her proximity to the man beside her.

Arthur's presence was distracting, from the telltale *snluuf* of his snores to the chocolate curl hanging over his nose. It took everything in her not to fix that lock of hair. Not that Arthur would have noticed, since he apparently slept like the dead despite the rough terrain and shivering cold.

Eva rolled over and stared at him in the dark.

He'd given her a sweatshirt from their remaining pack, taking for himself the flannel shirt she'd worn last night. The shorts he'd given her had started to chafe her thighs, and after he'd fallen asleep, Eva had dug through the pack and pulled out the softest alternative she could find: a pair of boxers.

In desperate times.

At last, she gave in to the urge and reached to delicately lift the lock of hair out of Arthur's eyes. He didn't even stir. She studied his profile. Dry lips. Harsh cheekbones. A pained grimace, softened by sleep.

Eva couldn't believe he'd wanted to come with her. It was so unlike him to stick around.

Rolling onto her back again, Eva closed her eyes. On her other side, Bug slept in a T-shirt nest between Eva's back and the tent wall. Eva ran a finger softly down the kitten's spine and tried counting sheep. She tried flexing and releasing first the muscles of her toes, then her feet, then her legs. She tried clearing her mind to a blank slate, but the harder she tried to sleep, the more awake she became.

With a huff, she finally surrendered and rolled onto the balls of her feet, ankles cracking. *This is ridiculous.* She eased the zipper open, glancing back. Arthur and Bug were both fast asleep, turned away from each other with an Eva-sized gap between them.

She quietly slid the zipper closed again, willing to chance a brief separation to relieve her screaming bladder.

The air outside tasted infinitely fresher. Eva craned her neck up at the stars. You never saw them this vivid down in the valley, where light pollution made them fade. Here, the constellations told a story older than honey itself.

When her skin goosed with cold, she rubbed her arms and dug out the roll of toilet paper from the backpack, slipping her feet into her shoes. She quietly tiptoed past the tent to do her business, grateful that the forest was never truly quiet. Night music filled her ears and settled her. The burbling river. The orchestra of crickets. The snore of pickerel frogs. If Arthur were awake, he could tell her what species of owl hooted in the trees.

For a moment, Eva let go of her fear of the unknown, forgetting the missing pack and the gnawing sensation of something *other* watching them where they slept. Forests had a way of making her feel small in a good way. Here, she was just another part of the ecosystem, and all she had to do to be worthy was exist.

A tear surprised her, slipping down her cheek. Why was that feeling so hard to hold on to?

"Ev!" Arthur called out.

She stiffened and turned in the direction of their campsite. "I'm here!" she called back, a knot tying in her belly. He sounded alarmed. Was it Bug? *Oh no.* "I'm here!" she called again, stomping back through the underbrush.

He gave another shout. Eva's heart tripped, and then she was running through the trees. In seconds, her entire body became aware of something distinctly *wrong* moving beneath her feet. The ground was shaking, the compact dirt giving way beneath the press of her soles.

She broke into the clearing and gasped.

The tent was sinking.

The soil, once solid, had buckled beneath it, pulling the tent into a crater of its own weight. Already it stood more than a foot lower than it had been.

A groan sounded from the trees themselves, and Eva's mouth fell open at the sight of thick, meaty roots ripping themselves out of the soil, spraying sediment that made her blink and cough. They undulated, as fluid and powerful as tentacles stretching from the heart of a kraken in the deep. One of the roots speared itself through the tent wall, the ripping sound of torn vinyl shooting a bullet of fear and adrenaline straight through Eva's heart.

The kitten yowled from inside the tent.

Eva rushed to the quickly forming pit, slipping over loose dirt as she slid down the dirt wall, disturbing a colony of ants into a panic. She felt the frantic skitter of their legs down the back of her sweatshirt.

"Ev, what's happening?"

"I don't know!" This was unlike any sinkhole she'd ever seen. Unlike a sinkhole at all, really. And the *roots*. She had no words for their conscient, wild behavior. As she watched, the long, fibrous arms of once-buried roots wrapped around the crisscross where the tent poles met.

They tugged upward.

The tent's suction with the ground released with a pop. Eva called out in panic, trying to force the tent door open, only to find the zipper teeth stuck. Soil sloughed off the vinyl walls, and gravity dragged Arthur down to the bottom. Bug yowled.

The trees groaned as they lifted the tent even higher.

Eva dug her fingers into one of the holes the tree roots had punched in the vinyl and yanked, tearing the fabric. "Help me!" she called out, and then Arthur's hand brushed hers through the gap, and together they ripped the hole wider.

Arthur fell through with a grunt, knocking Eva into a snarl of roots. He held a wadded-up T-shirt in his arms, from which Bug burst free, panicked. The kitten clawed up the side of the pit and disappeared.

The aspens lifted the tent higher into their canopy, shredding it into an unrecognizable flap that stuck in the branches like a flag blowing in the wind.

Eva's heart pounded, but she hardly had time to take in what had just happened. The pit was still sinking, and those octopean roots were folding over and over one another, settling back into place by weaving a thatch above her and Arthur.

Something with too many legs wriggled inside her bra. She shrieked, tearing a centipede out and, in her panic, crunching its middle beneath her fingers. The severed halves fell to the earth.

Arthur made a sound Eva had never heard before. It was small and pained. "Ev?" he whispered, his voice pitching upward.

That's when she remembered. He didn't like tight spaces.

"It's okay," she repeated, her mind racing for a way to get them out of this. Her magic would only make the snarling roots grow thicker and more wild. That had happened once, with Dad. He'd tried to push her to talk, and when she snapped that she didn't want to, her flood of emotions had made his tree roots plunge even deeper into his chest cavity. He'd spent a weekend in the hospital.

After that, Eva had learned to hold things in. It was better for everyone, especially him. Maybe Dad and Isobel were right to treat her like glass. Glass was fragile, but when it was broken, it was sharp, and dangerous. Like her.

Through the dim light, Eva made out the shape of Arthur, one hand anxiously clutching the fabric of his shirt.

"You should crawl up there," she said. "Your touch will kill the roots."

"No." They were closer than she'd realized, the heat of his refusal ghosting over her cheek. "Ev, I-I-I can't."

"You have to." More insects, dislodged by the wriggling roots overhead, fell down. Eva couldn't see them, but she felt the scurry of tiny legs, startled pincers nipping her flesh. She scratched at her arms. "Arthur, please."

He didn't budge, seemingly frozen in place.

Eva felt like a monster for pushing him. Arthur had only ever wanted to be good. He didn't want to hurt anyone or anything, and he was clearly panicked, his breaths coming hotter and faster against her skin. They were nearly cheek to cheek.

An idea struck her. It was mad, reckless even, and so, so unwise. But he was frozen and she needed to shock him out of it. "I won't let us die like this," Eva said.

Then she pressed a hard kiss to Arthur's mouth.

It was clumsy in the dark where they collided. His warm, chapped lips parted in surprise against hers. He whispered her name, a soft, fractured *"Ev"* so light it almost wasn't there at all. His obvious confusion stirred something buried inside her. There had been a time when Arthur Connoway knew exactly what she felt for him. She'd made it her mission to prove how vital he was to her by touch and taste and so much trust. She'd given him the parts of her that no one else had access to. The rough, the raw, the needy.

This kiss was not that.

This kiss was a ghost.

It lasted only a few seconds, but the haunting pressure of his lips sent a chill over Eva's skin. A thousand other kisses echoed through her, kisses she'd fooled herself into thinking she'd buried. But no. She remembered and remembered and remembered.

When Arthur's hand found the bend of her waist, Eva broke away, shaking. "You can do this," she whispered. Her palm was still pressed to Arthur's chest, and she felt where his breath caught, the trip of a heart beating faster.

Even with her eyes adjusted to the dark, she could make out only the shape of him. His neck ticked, his silhouette shifting in clear agitation.

"No," he moaned. "Not now."

"It has to be now," Eva said, a tremor running through her.

Arthur shook his head. "Not that. Not you. Ev, I—" He cut himself off, the words strangled as his breath came harsher. In the dark, he felt like another person entirely. Someone sharper than the boy she remembered. "There's something inside me. It won't let me...I can't..."

When he didn't continue, Eva prodded him. "Can't what?"

But Arthur only shook his head again, his hands twisting into the hem of her sweatshirt. Eva gently took his wrists in her grip. When her thumbs ran over his pulse points, Arthur twisted, pinning her back against the wall of dirt and shackling her hands above her head.

"Your heartbeat," he muttered, "is so loud."

Eva trembled. The tone of his voice had downshifted from its usual warmth into something hard and full of gravel.

The ground continued to groan as the cavity that had opened up in the earth began to close again, the spill of loose dirt flecking her arms and putting Eva in mind of the sands of an hourglass rushing to fill any empty space gravity provided them.

Above them, a shelf of hard-packed earth jutted from the side of the pit. Using strength she wouldn't have guessed he had, Arthur gripped it and hauled first her, then himself, up onto it. "You're not dying today, Freckles," he said with a grunt. When they were on the ledge, he thumbed the dip in her waist. "If he won't save you, I will."

Chapter 22

Arthur

Cold shot through my veins, a hard freeze working a path up my body from toes to crown. In seconds, the fear I felt, pressed between the walls of sinking soil, gave way to a much worse kind of claustrophobia as the monster fit itself into my hollows.

I tried to suck in a breath, tried to push back, but the monster held fast, its relentless determination disconnecting me from my body in the space of a moment.

The trickle of raining sediment lifted away. The pain I'd felt released, leaving me untethered, weightless to the point of nausea. I shivered as even that physical anchor sloughed off, leaving me wholly detached from my body. I became nothing. Just a scrap of detritus in my own head.

Terror gripped me.

The monster reached to grasp a root squiggling out of the dirt to the side of Eva's head. Upon contact, the roots curled back from the deadly power coursing through me. That was all I *could* still feel: cold, bitter death.

"Can we get on your shoulders?" the monster asked Eva.

I couldn't smell the dirt coating the both of us in a dark rime of earth. I couldn't feel the warm pressure of her body against mine, as I had when she'd taken my face in her hands and kissed me.

Kissed me.

For a moment, our connection point had felt like the first drop of summer. She was a warm flash of heat.

But then she was gone and I was ice again.

Eva nodded, bending into a crouch. I felt the monster's intention move through me as it stepped both our feet onto her shoulders. It was careful to position our weight so as not to knock her off-balance. I couldn't feel my legs shake. Maybe I had stopped trembling, or maybe the numbness had stolen that too.

"*Okay?*" the monster asked her. It was strange, and awful, to hear my voice speak without my consent. To watch my body move and act as an observer, the claustrophobic weight of my own mind pressing in around me like walls closing in, while I was trapped inside myself like a prehistoric insect caught in amber.

Eva nodded. "I'm okay."

The monster dug our fingers into the soil, clawing every possible hold as it lengthened our body to our full height and reached overhead. I couldn't hear its thoughts anymore, alone in my head again. I tried to push against the membrane where our wills met. I tried to find one pulse of warmth. To grit my teeth and stay, stay, stay.

But I was already gone.

"*Almost there.*"

A scream built inside me, but with no release, its pressure became panic.

With a cry of triumph, the monster grasped one of the lower-hanging roots. "*Got it!*"

I couldn't feel where our fingers stubbed into the fibrous

rootscape, but the moment the monster ripped the life from the interweaving vines, a face flashed before my eyes.

It was my mother.

Her face twisted in shock, then pain, her eyes blowing wide. When the roots shrank back, she disappeared, swallowed by the dark.

Grunting, the monster split a window through the roots, sending debris of unearthed flora, moss, and insects raining down below. It wrestled our forearms onto the surface and scrambled up, rolling onto our back.

For a moment, we stared at the dark sky, and though I couldn't hear the monster's thoughts anymore, its triumph coursed through me.

Let me out, I begged.

No answer. Instead, the monster rolled onto our knees, plucking a long stick from the underbrush and extending it down to Eva. With the monster in control, I couldn't feel the strain it took on my muscles to haul her out of the pit. I couldn't even feel the burn in my stitches anymore.

Let me go.

I couldn't get out of my own head. I couldn't get free. Fear built in whatever shred of *me* was left, trapped behind the will of something stronger.

"You did it!" Eva's smile was painfully bright as the monster helped her out of the pit. The pride it felt was reflected in her eyes too.

The icy grip holding me still seemed to get even colder. Couldn't she tell there was something wrong with me? Was there so little of me that wasn't monstrous that she couldn't even see that *that* wasn't me?

The grove of aspens around us had withered, their chalky husks hollowed of life. Soon, the dead wood would likely become the home and feast of a dozen other species, fungus and insect alike making a home of what had once been only destruction. But just now, the trunks were empty of life.

The monster's gaze fell to something lying in the grass. It stepped closer. When the dark, feathered form took shape, a spike of nausea reached deep into my frozen state to make me gag.

It was a nest. Dislodged, perhaps, when the trees had uprooted themselves to bury us in soil. Or perhaps it was the monster's doing. Perhaps its deadly touch had traveled up the roots and trunk and branches until it found bone and blood and flesh.

Something rustled to my right. The leaves had turned yellow and fallen to the earth, like drops of gold in autumn. The monster reached for the flapping, wounded mother bird thrashing in the brush there.

STOP!

Seemingly oblivious to my protest, the monster lifted the injured robin into the cradle of our palms. I couldn't flex a single muscle, no matter how panicked I was.

But I still felt the bird die.

And it felt good.

Eva approached cautiously. She gently took the bird and set it in the grass. "Hey," she said, watching me too knowingly. Of course she did. Eva knew how precious birds were to me. "You okay?"

"Sometimes death is a mercy."

Her eyes widened at the callous words.

"Are you sur —"

"*We should probably get going.*" The monster cut her off and nodded our head at the dead aspens. "*Ground might not be stable.*"

For a moment, I thought Eva might protest. Her mouth puckered. Where she touched me, I could almost feel again, the numbness pushed back by a glow of warmth. I couldn't breathe, hope pushing through like sprouts from a dormant bulb. If I was ice, then surely she was sun.

I worked my lips without sound, unable to form the words at first. There had been a moment, down in the pit, when I'd tried to tell her the truth: There was something awful and deadly inside me, and I was afraid that I no longer had control of it.

The monster hadn't let me get the words out.

Sensation trickled in slowly, painfully, like blood returning to a numbed limb. "Please, Ev," I rasped.

The monster ripped away from her touch, but it was too late. The ice had melted, and for the first time in minutes, I took a deep breath. My lungs felt burned, my throat raw.

My stitches were agony.

"Please," I repeated, my knees giving out.

Eva caught me on the way down. "Oh, hey, hey. Take a minute, okay?"

I nodded, the world spinning in dark shades of night around me. Eva rubbed a circle over my spine as she waited for me to speak.

I searched for a way to explain, afraid of the monster cutting me off again. "Do you ever feel...hollow?" I finally asked.

Eva's hand slowed over my lower back. "What do you mean?"

I didn't know how else to say it. "Like something inside you is...missing," I roughed out, letting my eyes close. "Something important."

When she didn't answer, I looked up. Eva's cheeks were pale against the moonlit sky. "Yeah," she said softly.

It was ridiculous, to cast my shadow over her light. The bee girl didn't know what it was like to wonder if she even had a soul, or if the emptiness inside was merely a sign that her soul was rotten. She had honey in her veins, not death. Not rot.

Not like me.

The kiss we'd shared sat like a phantom between us now. I couldn't help the drop of my eyes to her mouth. She had a bit of dirt smudged on her chin. I wanted to reach out and clear it away with the pad of my thumb. I wanted to touch her again. I wanted to tell her I was sorry.

More than anything, I wanted another chance to show her I could be *good*.

But then I thought of the nest of hatchlings, their delicate bodies broken and still. I thought of how easily the monster had taken the life of their mother with a single, pitiless touch, and my mouth closed, the words dying just as easily on my lips.

I didn't deserve absolution.

The monster squirmed inside me, the membranous layer between our wills stretching thin. I knew if it pressed, it could take me over again, no matter how deeply Eva's warmth touched the ice inside my heart.

"Let's follow the river," Eva said, rising to her feet. She whistled for Bug, and to my surprise, the little fluff monster darted out from between the trees. Relief unfurled inside me. She was okay. "The atlas showed it curving around the meadow."

The atlas. We'd lost that too, lost everything we weren't wearing when we went to bed. I looked down at my socked feet, poking out beneath a pair of fuzzy checkered pajama pants. Eva wore my old sweatshirt and a pair of boxers repurposed into sleep shorts.

Heat bloomed up my neck. "Right. Yeah, let's go."

Chapter 23

Isobel

The instant they pulled up the drive to the cottage, Isobel knew something was wrong. Dane sucked in a breath and leaned forward. "Holy shit," he breathed.

All her work in the yard that afternoon had been undone, leaving a mess of flowers, vines, and tree roots upended from the earth. The abandoned patrol car, now entirely smothered in grasping flora, had sunk so deep the front bumper and tires were entrenched in the soil.

Isobel blinked several times, trying to make sense of the scene with only the moonlight to illuminate it. The ocean of greenery almost looked to be swallowing her home in the same way it was devouring the car, wrapping the cottage in a summered maw of greenbrier, moss, and rose vines.

"The porch," Dane said. "It's too low."

Isobel followed his finger, a stone dropping in her belly as she realized he was right. The wooden steps had splintered, and the sloping deck now stood nearly level with the ground.

Her house was sinking.

The ground beneath them seemed to groan, forcing Isobel to grab the dashboard. Outside, the trees shook, their branches swaying. A loud ripping sounded from their left, where the old aspen stood. Only when the dirt cracked and large, fibrous arms rolled out from its base did Isobel realize the ripping sound was roots.

She kicked the car door open.

"Wait!" Dane shouted. But Isobel didn't wait, stumbling out. Her vision swam, but adrenaline cleared her thoughts to a pinpoint, and she dodged one of the swaying roots, dirt spraying her square in the face. She spat, and the wind blew it back onto her cheek.

Disgusting. She wiped her face and stumbled forward.

"Isobel, stop — " Dane caught up to her and grabbed her by the arm. He looked panicked. "You can't go in there!"

The dark made everything far more disorienting. The aspen groaned behind Isobel, and she pushed against Dane's chest, panic collecting inside her. "My dad is inside!"

Dane's face paled. He looked from her to the cottage. Isobel pushed past him. The door didn't open at first, as though the shifting ground had thrown the frame out of alignment. Isobel threw her weight against it, her feet slipping over the ruined porch, until at last the door popped free.

She spilled inside and fell against a wall ribbed once more in turkey tail mushrooms. The spongy give of the fruiting bodies under her palm made her shudder, and she righted herself. The darkness felt thicker here without the moon, the ruptures in the ground seeming to have cut off the house's electricity.

Where are you, Dad?

Fighting a dizzy spell, Isobel lumbered to the kitchen, which appeared to be empty. Beneath her, the rust-orange tiles had cracked, and dark, loamy earth spilled from the fissures.

This wasn't like Eva's magic. Instead of sprouting flowers, there was only soil and the muscle of roots pulling down the bones of their home.

"Dad?" Isobel called out, her voice rough. The alcohol still swimming in her veins made everything about this strange and frightening scene a little harder to sort through. At the sound of a cough, her gaze snapped to the stairs leading up to the little attic.

He was in Eva's room.

Isobel hurried up the narrow staircase, her foot slipping once on the trick step. Dane caught her before her knee could slam down onto the wood and hoisted her back up just as her father's silhouette filled the doorframe.

"Dad!" A shock of relief went through her. "What are you doing up here?"

"Eva should've come home by now." Worry was evident in his voice. "Where is she?"

Isobel's mouth went chalky.

"She's gone, Jack," Dane cut in, urging her father back into the cramped little room at the top of the stairs.

"Gone? What — "

The whine of strained glass rang from downstairs, and Isobel looked back just in time to see a kitchen window burst in, spilling soil into the sink.

They were trapped up here.

"No time to explain," Dane grunted as the house shuddered, the whole stone entity sinking another foot into the ground. "We have to get out, now!" He made straight for the casement window, their only exit still available.

In the dark, Isobel could barely see the swirls of greenery Eva had painted on the wall, to match her view of the gardens outside.

"The lower level is too sunk to get out safely. We'll have to jump," Dane said.

"Jack, you first." He guided her father to the window. Dad looked more than a little disheveled with his hair mussed and his glasses askew.

When the house shook again, Isobel's vision swam, and the rime of fungi coating the walls seemed to swirl around them. This was the absolute worst time to be a little bit drunk.

Dane gritted his teeth, bracing his weight to help balance her father as the floor began to tilt. Isobel slid against the wall with a grunt. Her stomach didn't like this. A sharp pang of nausea rolled up her gullet, and she grasped the nearby windowsill, retching out onto the lawn. Her whole body shuddered, and a wave of fresh shame rolled over her.

She hated feeling so out of control.

When she pulled back, Dane touched her elbow in support. His eyes were as firm as his comforting grip. Isobel squinted at his shirtsleeve, where a bit of blood had seeped through from the nick in his arm. She must be seeing things, because in the light of the moon, it looked almost... green.

"Dad. You go first."

The ground was still a good way down, but Izzy didn't dare risk waiting any longer. What if the roof collapsed next?

But when they positioned him in front of the glass, a new problem presented itself.

"I don't fit," her father gruffed.

The buzz of alarm inside Isobel spun into panic. "You have to!"

The grass split open, torn by the roots as the front of the house lifted.

He gripped a primary branch from his sapling and snapped. His howl of pain chilled her to the bone.

"Dad!"

Her father caught his breath, and then, through gritted teeth, he chose another and snapped that one too.

"Jack, that's enough." Dane caught her father's hands. He looked pale. "Let's get you down."

Even with the tree pruned down nearly to its base, it would be a tight fit to get her father through the window. "I'll go down first and help catch you both," Dane said. They didn't have time to argue the point. The house groaned as the once-stable foundation sank a little lower into the too-soft dirt beneath it. Isobel's stomach swooped as she caught her father by the elbow. He braced against the wall with a nod and a grimace.

Dane hopped down, the mound of ruptured loam and topsoil catching his fall. "Jack, you next."

They puzzle-pieced him through the window in the world's worst game of Tetris. Dad's breaths came in short, hard bursts of barely concealed agony.

Isobel's throat tightened as she steadied him, then let him drop below. Dad landed with a solid thud.

"All right, love. Your turn."

She had one shaky leg up on the windowsill when her eyes, having adjusted somewhat to the darkness of the room, snagged on a small wooden box on Eva's bedside table.

The ashes.

How had they gotten there? She hesitated, then swung her leg back over just as the house gave its mightiest groan yet.

"Isobel!"

The cottage's whole frame shook, knocking Eva's bookshelf

onto the bed. Izzy gasped when a heavy stack of books struck her shoulder, knocking her down. The floorboards splintered with the impact of her body.

She pushed herself to her knees, moving as carefully as she would on thinning ice as she dug through the toppled pile of books, looking for the box. Moments later, Dane reappeared in the window. He took in the scene, then, without a word, scooped her up and bolted back to the window.

"No, wait!" Isobel protested.

"No time," Dane grunted.

A horrible popping sound came from somewhere deep in the bowels of the house as the two of them clambered over the sill. The ground was only a few feet below now, but Isobel landed wrong on her bruised shoulder and let out a groan.

Dane was over her in an instant, his eyes panicked. "Are you hurt?!"

"Just a bruise," she gasped.

The sight of his fear melting away was a physical thing. Dane gathered her against him and placed a desperate kiss to her cheek, then her temple. "Don't do that again." His voice was ragged.

Isobel's bottom lip trembled. "I'm sorry." She hadn't even gotten the ashes. They were still in there somewhere, trapped beneath the rubble. A sob bubbled up her throat. Dane cupped her cheek and kissed her again, his relief palpable.

Her father had moved closer to the fence that shouldered the Walkers' land. He was on his hands and knees, his spine curved in a question mark. As Isobel approached, she caught the acrid scent of stomach bile. Dad, breathing heavily, wiped a bit of sick off his chin. His branches wept a bloody sap into the soil below.

She fell to her knees beside him and took his trembling hand in both of her own.

Behind him, the earth gave an almost animal groan as it swallowed down another foot of her home. Then it stopped. The settling silence echoed like a bell in the space between Isobel's ears. Not even the birds sang, the yard rendered in total silence, as though the land itself was shocked by what it had done. Isobel's eyes drifted up to the lonesome chimney and the weathervane rooster sitting crooked on its arrow.

"Isobel." Her name came out rough as sandpaper, the look in her father's eyes pleading — no, *terrified* — as he seized her arm and held her close. "Where is your sister?"

Chapter 24

Eva

Eva couldn't stop thinking about the kiss.

It wasn't that she cared for Arthur still. She'd simply never really gotten closure the last time he left, and now that the old wound had been bared to the sun again, the heat of it stung.

Eva kept her eyes on the riverbank, mindful of the microgreens pushing through the soil with her every step. They couldn't be far from the meadow now. Soon this nightmare would be over. Once they found Dad's legendary honey, they could heal Arthur, heal her father, and put this horrible week and all it had dredged to the surface behind them.

Arthur would run, no doubt. And Eva?

She would forget him. She would try.

Her body was a living ache of little wounds. She'd thought she was tired before, but after another night of almost no sleep, her steps fell a little too heavily. The waning adrenaline left her with little resilience, and her eyes burned, a stinging tear of exhaustion sliding down her cheek.

But she kept going. That's what she was good at, wasn't it? Pressing on. Moving forward.

Soon, the smell of overturned earth and rich, dead wood gave way to the fresher scent of morning. The river rushed to her left, and Arthur followed behind her. Having lost his shoes, he hiked in socks that were surely getting damp in the dewy grass.

When the sunrise turned the sky violet, Eva caught sight of a honeybee and followed its flight path across the river with her eyes, where it landed on a cluster of wildflowers snugging the other bank.

She stopped, her breath catching in her chest. "Arthur. Look."

He came up behind her, not quite close enough to touch, and followed her pointing finger. There, just beyond the thicket of green pine and lurking aspen, Eva caught a glimpse of color.

Little Lotties. They littered the ground, but Eva had almost missed them entirely, the deep indigo and violet shades of the rare flower mimicking the sky above. That was her meadow. She was certain of it. Eva rushed to a log that had fallen across the river, stepping eagerly onto its slippery surface to get a better view. Her stomach clenched as she took a step on the slick rime of bright green algae covering the makeshift bridge.

"What are you doing?" Arthur asked.

"We have to cross!" Eva held her breath as she took one more step, then another, a flood of white water rushing below her. It was deeper here, the water rougher. A fall would be dangerous.

"Ev, wait."

She was done waiting. She kept going, and after a moment, when she heard the sounds of Arthur relenting, she looked back to see him teeter slightly as he stepped onto the log, throwing his arms out to either side. He was pale, and clearly didn't share her confidence, wobbling forward and warily glancing at the river.

Eva looked forward. They would be fine.

But as soon as she thought it, the log bridge shifted beneath her, rolling slightly to the left. It wasn't wedged as firmly on the other side of the river as she'd thought. Eva caught a hard breath and tried to regain her balance.

Arthur cried out in alarm. Eva turned toward him instinctively, and when the log beneath them rolled again, her foot slipped on the algae.

The two of them plunged into the water below.

Her ankle smacked the stones. Eva cried out, swallowing a mouthful of water at the shock of pain. The strength of the rapids flung her downriver. The river was deceptively deep here, even more than she'd thought when she stood on the log bridge.

Through the rheumy film of water, Eva caught sight of Arthur floating nearby. She kicked toward him, but her good foot slicked uselessly along the riverbed's loose slurry. When she finally broke the surface, she gasped in a wet and painful breath and flung her arm out. Arthur's hair slipped through her fingers, and he surged downriver.

"No, wait!" Eva garbled. Her ankle screamed in pain as she pushed off the stones toward him, finally managing to get ahold of his T-shirt. As she tugged his limp form against her, something caught around her wrist.

A root.

Eva gasped at the way it slinked up her arm, squeezing tight and pulling her downward, under the water again. Sediment rushed through her fingers.

"Help!" The plea hardly made it past the shape of her lips when a second root wound around her knees, pulling her down to the river bottom. Alarm spiked within her, and too soon, her body protested its lack of much-needed oxygen.

She ripped her arm free of the root, instinctively thrusting her gift deep in the earth, deeper than she'd ever gone. The banks erupted in color: vivid mosses, thick reeds, and watercolor blooms filling the space.

For a moment, she felt triumphant. Then a thickly muscled vine encircled Arthur's waist.

"No!" Eva shouted. "Let him go!" She snarled a long tress of grass growing on the bank in her fingers and used it to keep them from flowing any farther downriver.

A figure standing on the opposite bank caught Eva's attention. She blinked, confused. It was a woman, but something about her was wrong. Her body was made not of flesh but of tree branches woven and bent as though to imitate the shape of a person.

My son.

The voice rang through the clearing, finding Eva in peril. The roots binding her tightened, and Arthur woke with a hard exhale, expelling water from his mouth. When he clawed at the vine around his stomach, the woman on the bank screamed. The shape of her was unmade in an instant as the branches snapped back into their places, rigid and... and *dead,* Eva realized. The roots burning Eva's skin slackened and fell away as the figure disappeared, the trees that had made her now as stiff and dead as the grove of aspens Arthur had killed.

Had she been the one to attack them? First at the pit, now here?

Eva hauled Arthur onto the bank, her ankle screaming as they both crawled up the muddy slope and fell onto the grass. Every inhale was a knife.

The wildflowers her gift had yanked into bloom lay beneath Arthur in a colorful carpet. Where his skin touched, they faded, only to bloom again under the heavy rush of relief Eva felt. He made things die, but she brought them back. Life and death. Always a tug-of-war between them.

"Breathe," Eva commanded, flattening her palm to Arthur's chest. It rose and fell in a stutter, but he was breathing still, his face pale but with color slowly returning. Something slinked up and over his wrist, filling her nose with the scent of fresh, damp peat. The root was small and tentative, barely brushing over his pulse point, as though it, too, was searching for signs of vitality.

But that was absurd.

"GET AWAY FROM HIM!" Eva snatched the root up and twisted it hard, snapping it from the soil. It was already dying, doomed by his skin. Eva felt the echo of its last thread of life wisp away as Arthur drew its light into himself. He had corrupted it. Poisoned it. For a moment, with his hot breath fanning against her cheek as she leaned over him, Eva was certain he was poisoning her too. What else could make her feel such a burn?

She laid frantic touches to Arthur's torso and arms, afraid that he was hurt because of another choice she'd made. "I'm sorry," she whispered.

Arthur gathered her weakly against his chest. Her ankle was throbbing, but when he brought her hand to his lips and pressed a kiss to her palm, Eva forgot the pain, and shivered at the scrape of his teeth.

She liked his teeth.

"S'okay," he croaked.

But it wasn't.

They were both still dripping, shivering from the cold of the river. Or maybe it was the pressure of so many feelings kept inside that made Eva shake.

"I never should've left you," Arthur whispered. "I know you said you don't want my apology, but... fuck, Ev, I wish I'd stayed."

The words should have been a balm. Instead, they were gravestones. If Eva really were made of glass, this confession would shatter her.

She drew back. Water dripped off Arthur's brow, running pink from his reopened wound. The stitches weren't holding, and the dribble marked a path down his cheek. He opened his eyes and met her gaze. "I wish I could go back and make a different choice," Arthur said softly. "For you. For us."

And something did shatter then, but it wasn't the splinter of heartbreak she feared. Instead, Eva's anger fractured. There were two griefs bisecting her heart now: The fury she'd held on to all these years, bitter and spent. And the newer, sharper ache of grieving what might have been, if only they'd been a little braver.

"At the very least," he said, "I wish we'd had a better goodbye."

She thumbed a bead of scarlet blood off his cheek. Arthur found the small of her back with a gentle hand, and for the first time since his arrival back in Audrey, Eva realized he was in pain too, a kind that reached far beyond the physical aches they'd incurred on this mountain.

"Let's find that honey," she whispered.

Arthur nodded and sat up, twisting as he searched the bank full of vivid blue Lotties. Despite the peril of the river, they'd somehow both ended up on the opposite bank. Their meadow had to be close by.

Bug yowled in displeasure from the other side of the river.

"We'll come back!" Eva called out.

The reassurance did nothing for the panicked little kitten, who tentatively pawed the ground beside the very log the two of them had fallen off. Eva's heart jumped into her throat when Bug leapt onto the log. Arthur stiffened too.

But the kitten's journey across the river was not nearly so eventful as theirs had been. She bounded across, then shot toward the two of them. Eva scooped her up with a laugh of relief. Bug's paws were wet, her usual gray fluff slightly damp. "That was brave," she murmured. In response, Bug nuzzled her neck, digging her claws in deep enough to make Eva yelp.

The bright flare of emotion clogging her throat drew even more of the delicate blue-violet flowers to the soil's surface. Eva plucked one, bringing it to her nose to smell. It was home, it was Dad, it was tea and comfort and summer.

Arthur helped her shakily to her feet, only to stiffen when Eva cried out. "What is it?"

"My ankle. I hurt it when we fell." And from the look of it, she'd gotten a nasty sprain. The joint was already swelling, hurting more and more with every second now that she was upright, the blood rushing down into her foot.

Arthur pursed his lips for a moment, then disappeared into the trees. He'd lost one of his socks in the river, and his bare foot left a trail of wilted flora in his footsteps.

When Arthur returned, he held out a long walking stick, and they slowly hobbled forward, their still-dripping pajamas hanging loose off their bodies as they made their way uphill in the light of the rising sun, Bug trotting between them.

They were so close to the meadow now. Eva could feel it, and her heart seemed to crawl up into her throat. Beside her, Arthur's breathing got more ragged. "Do you need to stop?" Eva pressed.

Arthur shook his head. "We keep going."

Eva was torn between wanting to reach out and make amends with the forest around her and wanting to hide from whatever strange thing was chasing them through these woods. First the tent. Then the river. The branches that had folded themselves unnaturally into the mock of a woman on the bank.

A drop of water traced down Eva's spine, drawing out a shiver. Something in these woods was festering like a rotten wound. Something, or someone, wanted to hurt them. Eva knew she was likely dehydrated, her mind fuzzy and full of fear, but she couldn't help the way her thoughts spun over themselves, landing time and time again in the same impossible place:

The figure on the bank had called Arthur *son*.

"There." Arthur pointed ahead.

As she leaned on her makeshift cane, Eva followed his gaze up a slight rise dotted with blue-violet flowers. There were more at the top, seemingly nestled in a bed of green. Eva's heart quickened.

That has to be it.

More Little Lotties grew at her feet with every step, propelled into growth by the swell of her emotions. They hurried up the hill, her ankle throbbing. She didn't care. They were almost there!

Her cheeks hurt from smiling, a bud of relief unfurling in her chest. But when Eva threw Arthur a grin, her excitement withered. Arthur marched with eyes half lidded, his dark hair sticking up in every direction. He didn't look like himself. He didn't walk like himself. Eva didn't know how to explain it, but sometimes he seemed to slip away from her completely. It made her uneasy, and she couldn't say exactly why.

Feeling her eyes, Arthur looked over. "Almost there," he panted.

A lump formed in Eva's throat as she reached out and grasped his hand. "Almost there."

When they crested the hill, Eva's jaw dropped. Arthur swore in quiet awe.

It was an artist's palette. Wildflowers painted the ground in a vision of violet, gold, and blue. There was snakeroot and southern harebell, even the sunny pop of yellow spreading avens. But the crown jewel was the Lotties: They swayed in the wind, royal and delicate, their whisper of life reaching out to where Eva stood.

The honeyman found a garden of everlasting life.

Eva shook her father's stories out of her head and limped toward the hive boxes peeping through the mass of blooms. Disbelief hooked behind her ribs as she twisted the hem of her shirt around her finger.

They'd actually found it.

"Those your dad's?" Arthur asked, using his chin to indicate the hive boxes.

"Yes." Eva's vision softened with the sudden blur of tears. "It's my mother's design." The floral pattern on these hive boxes, as well as on those of their other six apiaries, had been created as a nod to the delicate forget-me-nots on the side of her mother's — and Eva's — favorite teacup.

Arthur swayed a little, his arm brushing against hers. His skin was hot. Too hot. Eva turned to face him and sucked in a hard breath. He looked worse now than he had at the river. "You're burning up," she said.

"*You're* burning up," Arthur muttered.

They had to get him that honey, now.

Eva hobbled to the nearest hive box, wincing as she pulled

off the cover and set it and the walking stick down in the grass. Her skin tingled with anticipation. She knew they were both in a rough state, between the bites, the blisters, and the bruises, not to mention what appeared to be a quickly advancing infection from the injury on Arthur's brow.

But this would make all of it worth it.

Her eyes locked with Arthur's. "Ready?"

At his nod, Eva lifted the first frame out of the super, giddiness building in her chest.

But the frame was empty.

Chapter 25

Arthur, Before

"You're still not ready?"

I shot Eva a look of exasperation as I tugged on my shoes. "How are you so awake this morning?" We'd been up past midnight, watching movies and stuffing our bellies with popcorn. It wouldn't have mattered, except today was Sunday — or "bird-watching day," as the bee girl had dubbed it weeks ago.

She wiggled the last bite of a pancake in my face, then popped it into her mouth. "Easily."

Eva was a bear until she got her morning pastry. Last week she'd nearly bitten my head off when I stole the last slice of brioche. The girl did not like to be toast-teased.

"Insufferable," I muttered.

Eva hooked my chin with a finger and tilted my face up. Instantly, I began clicking through her features. Round cheeks. Damp hair. A masterpiece of freckles.

She deserved analog. Soft focus, hazy light, rolls and rolls of film.

When her lips puckered, I realized I was staring at her mouth.

"Suffer me, then," she whispered, leaning in to plant the faintest kiss on the corner of my mouth.

My breath caught, and the mudroom hazed around me.

Before I was ready, she pulled back and flashed a dimple, brushing her palms over the pockets of her sunflower-patterned dress. "Five minutes, sleepyhead, or I leave without you." Then she slipped out the door, leaving me speechless.

She'd kissed me. Actually *kissed* me.

After a long moment, the monster nudged me. *"Let's go, little death-touch."*

It was kidding, right? I touched my lips. "I can't?" I was frozen in this spot, probably forever. Stuck in the feeling of Eva's mouth on mine.

Wait, no.

Not on my mouth, exactly. On my…cheek? My neck heated. Was that on purpose? Had she missed? Maybe she only meant to kiss me as a friend, and I turned my head wrong—

"Calm down."

A new fear uncoiled inside me. She'd run away so fast. Did that mean she regretted it?

"She woke up early. For birds," the monster said, exasperated. *"I don't think she regrets it. Now finish your laces."*

Right. Okay.

I yanked the knots to my boots tight and scrambled to follow after her. The strap of my Minolta hung comfortably over my shoulder as I rounded the corner, where Eva stood facing the woods, her new book on local songbirds tucked under her arm. When she heard me coming, she turned, smiling.

A warm glow stirred in my chest. "Ready?"

In answer, she shook a packet of wildflower seeds.

It was Eva's idea to practice controlling my death-touch. I'd never tried before, afraid I would slip up and make things worse somehow. But Eva eased that fear, bringing the plants I killed back to life with a simple touch of her own.

As we angled for the path, Eva opened the packet and poured a handful of seeds into her palm. In seconds, the seeds cracked. Thin sproutlets pushed out, spinning themselves into long green threads. By the time we reached the clearing I'd chosen, Eva held a palmful of white candy-stripe creeping phlox, their pale roots dangling from her wrist.

She extended the bundle to me. Anxiety buzzed in my chest as I accepted the fragile blossoms. "Slow," Eva reminded me.

It took only a second of contact with my skin for the first creeping phlox to wilt. I bit my lip and closed my eyes, trying to halt the starving thing inside me that *wanted* so badly. It felt unnatural, at first. It always did. The monster's appetite was all-consuming. It wanted me to suck the life from the little flowers and crush their skeletal remains in my fist.

It wanted me to take.

I thought of the sky, as Eva had taught me. Storms moving through me, instead of sucking me down. I thought of the earth. It was easy with the monster's awareness so tuned in to the woods around me. Water rushed from the damp soil into nutrient-seeking roots. Sunlight bathed the hungry leaves. Inches away, Eva's heartbeat thumped. Anxious. Eager. It was an anchor, and I tethered myself to it until my breathing slowed.

When I looked again, I found three little blooms still blushed with pink.

"You're getting better," Eva said.

I passed the bundle back to her. In seconds, it was green again. I wanted to argue. Three blooms out of nine didn't feel like enough, and neither did I.

A peachy sunrise cast the glade in hazy soft-focus, dew-glossed spiderwebs sparkling in the grass. Birdsong constellated the woods around us. I grinned and swung my leg over a fallen tree, motioning her to sit in front of me.

This was the reason we woke at such an ungodly hour.

When Eva was properly situated, I lifted the Minolta strap and draped it over her neck.

"Ready?"

Eva nodded, rubbing her thumb over the advance lever, as I'd taught her.

Somewhere above us, a bird released a syrupy trill. I leaned closer, wrapping my arms around Eva and notching the settings into place with my thumbs. "What's that?" I asked her.

"Robin?"

I nodded, my nose brushing her hair. When I whistled in perfect imitation to the songbird, goose bumps pebbled down Eva's arms. The monster watched them in fascination.

"Now, that is a sight to behold."

"Show-off," Eva muttered.

I grinned.

As a kid, Mom's job-hopping had left me plenty of time to wander the woods alone, practicing the calls of any and every bird I came across. I'd thought she would like that I'd spent so much effort learning their songs. Mom always did love birds.

My throat lodged with emotion. I'd been with the Moreaus for three months now, and I was fine, happy even. Still, not a day went by that I didn't think of my mother and worry.

She hadn't called once.

A new *chirrup* painted the air, and Eva sat up. "What was that one?"

"Tufted titmouse."

"That's a funny name," she said, lifting the camera and squinting through the viewfinder.

"You see your bird up there, Ev?"

"I see...a blur."

I buried a chuckle. "Here. Switch with me."

While I scanned the canopy for movement, Eva flipped through the pages of the bird identification book she'd picked up, still so new that the slick pages stuck together. The breeze tossed a dark gold strand of hair onto her cheek. There were endless variations to the colors in her hair. Yellow, wheat, molasses, gold. It refused to stay straight but didn't quite curl, caught somewhere in between. Usually in the heat she wound it into a braid, but this morning it tumbled freely down her back.

When she found the page with the tufted titmouse, her face lit up. "It's so cute!"

I watched the way her fingers ran over the edge of the illustration. They weren't even real feathers, but she touched it so delicately they might as well have been.

Eva leaned back against my chest and took the camera from me again. I cupped her elbow instinctively to steady her.

"There," she whispered.

Something rustled the leaves. To my surprise, a little gray-and-white songbird alighted on a branch nearby. We held our breath in tandem—I felt the seize of muscle, so closely was her back pressed to my chest.

Had *she* done that? I knew the bees were attuned to her, but never in our weeks of bird-watching had a bird come so close as this. The monster tuned our awareness to the rapid pulse of the tufted titmouse's heartbeat. I didn't even mind. There was no temptation, no hunger.

Not for that, anyway.

"No," the monster murmured softly into our shared mind, almost teasing. *"You hunger for something else now, don't you?"*

As Eva peered through the camera's viewfinder, my eyes dropped to her mouth. The bow of her lip, the soft parting of breath.

Suffer me, then.

Eva snapped a shot of the bird, then lowered the camera to her lap. She looked back at me, our faces drawn closer than I'd planned on. Just a breath and my lips would graze her nose.

The monster preened at the sudden speeding of her pulse.

"I've always envied them."

Eva stilled. "Songbirds?"

I nodded.

"Because they're free?" Eva asked.

No. That's why Mom loved them. She wanted, *needed*, wings.

"Some species migrate at night," I said. "Daytime thermals affect the atmosphere, but after dark, the air cools. It makes it easier for them to find their way back home."

Eva's gaze dipped. "That's really cool."

Was she looking at my mouth?

The monster gave me a little nudge. *"If you can touch her, you can taste her, little death-touch."*

Cheeks flushed, I plunged on, unwilling to take romantic advice from the creature in my head. "They have a biological compass?" I hadn't meant to make it into a question. I just felt nervous. "It brings them back home."

Eva twisted toward me more fully, letting the Minolta hang from her neck. "You're thinking about your mom, aren't you?"

I shouldn't have been surprised she'd picked up on that.

"Where was your home before you came to us?" she asked.

Home had never been a where at all. I shrugged, scuffing rough bark with the toe of my shoe. "I didn't really have one, bee girl."

What I did have was a lifetime of days spent on the road with Mom. Some of those memories were good, others dull. Far too many were sharp with the disappointment that no matter how I tried, I couldn't get the one person I loved most to see me. I couldn't get her to look past her need for escape and find a home in what we already had.

Eva bit her lip. "That isn't fair."

No. I supposed it wasn't.

Suddenly antsy, I moved to dismount the log, but before I could, Eva caught me by the shirt. "I don't think any home worth its salt would run from you, Arthur."

I huffed. That was easy for her to say.

"What?" she pressed.

"That just isn't my experience."

Her eyes were blue fire. "Trust mine, then," she said. "Real love doesn't run so easily. And home is a thing that grows, wherever you are."

"I don't grow things, Ev."

Maybe for her, love was something you watered and dug up for harvest, but I wasn't like that. It was easy to paint the world in pretty colors when nothing was permanent and you could bring things back to life just by willing it.

But my love killed.

"You're so determined to see your gift as a curse," Eva said, as though she could hear the very thoughts in my head. "But every tree that dies and becomes a snag in the woods provides life to hundreds of creatures below it. You are like..." She seemed to search for the word, and when she found it, she lit up. "Like mulch!"

The monster snorted. *She's terrible at flirting. Worse than you are, which I didn't think was possible.*

Softening, Eva reached out and lifted my chin with a finger. "Are you really so afraid of yourself?"

"Of course I am." I swallowed hard. "I ruin things."

She was close enough for me to inhale the maple syrup on her breath. Close enough for me to kiss. I didn't realize I was tapping on her arm until her fingers curled over mine.

"I mend things," Eva whispered, leaning in.

Our mouths brushed, soft as a butterfly's wing to a flower, light and so delicate I could easily pull back and pretend it hadn't happened at all.

"Don't you dare." The monster was breathless, at my mercy for once. A thrill surged through me.

Eva angled her head and brushed her lips over mine again with more purpose, her skin warm and soft and seeking. An exhale rushed from me, and when I moved too fast in my sudden excitement, our teeth clicked together.

"Oh! Sorry," Eva said with a little laugh.

"That's okay." I pulled her back to me, resting a hand on the bend of her hip to steady the both of us. Eva melted into the embrace, leaning fully against my chest as she tilted her chin and caught my mouth with hers again. She laughed, and it was sunshine.

This was actually happening. So many weeks of wanting to kiss her, to touch her, and still I couldn't believe that I was here with the bee girl in my arms.

"What are we doing?" she whispered, a smile still spreading her cheeks.

"What I should have done a month ago." I deepened the kiss, instinctively sucking in her bottom lip. The pleasure of that simple indulgence sent a flush over my skin, my body hardening in response. I moved closer as Eva grasped the hair at my nape, her excitement tasteable. When she parted her lips against mine, I groaned.

Her tongue was a delicate agony.

Eva broke away. "You wanted to kiss me a month ago?"

"Yes."

She play-smacked me. "You jerk!"

Then she kissed me again.

I hadn't thought it possible that she could hunger for me like this. I fought my baser instinct to lick the salt off her skin, instead carding my hand back into her loose, soft waves.

Eva drew back again, panting slightly. "I thought it was just me. I didn't know that you... that you wanted..."

Her words were honey, summer-scraped. The sweetness was almost too much.

"I do, Ev."

I'd tried to ignore the wanting, knowing soft and stolen moments like these would only make it all hurt more in the end when I had to leave.

Eva chewed her lip. "I want... more of this," she said slowly.

I frowned, sensing a *but*. "What is it?"

I'd never seen her look so nervous. "I don't want to go fast."

Immediately, I flashed back to the altercation she'd had in the

Shoppe with Lenny. Something in me still felt bruised when I recalled first her fear, then her panic that someone would find out.

Not for the first time, I worried I'd made a mistake by promising to keep that secret.

"Of course we can go slow, bee girl."

"You mean it?"

I nodded and pulled her against me again, pressing my face into her hair. "I only want what you want too." That was already more than I'd ever hoped for.

The tension in her shoulders dissipated. Her relief made me ache, and a new layer of disdain for Lenny Walker grew inside my heart. She didn't deserve to feel the way Lenny had made her feel. She shouldn't have to worry that wanting — or not wanting — was something to fear.

I breathed into her loose golden waves. "Slow is perfect," I whispered, rubbing a circle over her back as the words she'd spoken only minutes before came back to me.

Home is a thing that grows.

Maybe trust was too.

Eva trusted me to keep my mouth shut about what Lenny had done. So, I would. But I would hate him for what he'd done to the girl I was starting to love. It hurt to recognize the look I'd seen on her face that day and to know exactly how he'd made her feel.

Scared. Immobile. Frozen.

That was something I could understand. The claustrophobic feeling of not having a choice had stuck its roots in me long ago.

Resolve settled in me like old seeds packed under a heavy weight of soil. I wouldn't let that happen again. I wouldn't let him near enough to hurt her.

Chapter 26

Arthur

The honey was gone.

I stared as Eva tore frame after frame out of their hive boxes, growing more frantic by the second. *It's all gone.* Blood pounded in my ears, and the world seemed to thin, stealing my breath until the center of my chest ached with that single, nauseating truth.

There was no honey.

No cure.

No escape. Not for Jack, and certainly not for me.

The words ran viscous through my mind, slipping through the cracks between my will and the monster's, and I imagined the membranous barrier between us growing sticky.

Eva limped to the hive box farthest from where I stood, an audible sob slipping out as she tore off the top. I flinched at the cracking sound of the wood as storm-damaged splinters flecked off into the grass.

"It's all gone," she rasped.

A chill swept down my spine, the monster's touch as gentle as a rime of frost on a window deep in autumn. Hands shaking, I bent to lift a discarded wooden frame from the grass and tried to fight off the monster's trickling cold. Mildew speckled the rough-cut grain, the wood slightly warped from exposure to the elements. Wax moths had eaten a tunnel through the cells, leaving silky, weblike strands behind. The sparse remaining comb fragments had turned brittle and dark with age and neglect, the hives turned to ruin without proper care.

Bug jogged on soft paws through the carpet of swaying grasses and deep blue flowers, looking around curiously. She seemed oblivious to the source of Eva's tears, and to the emptiness swelling inside me, content to play in this new, colorful place.

The monster didn't say the obvious, that we were too late — many years too late, by the state of the frames. Instead, I felt its hope sink into a cool resolve inside my chest.

In my current state of overwhelm, it would be such a relief to just...let go. Let the monster have me. I already felt myself slipping — I always did when everything felt like too much. The monster had always been there for me, hadn't it? It never let me fall or break. It was an escape.

The frame slipped from my fingers, thunking into the grass at my feet as the meadow kaleidoscoped in a swirl of blues and greens around me. With a start, I realized I was *tap-tap-tapping* the side of my leg again. It took effort to flatten my palm, and I closed my eyes and slowed my breath. Told myself to stay.

Stay here.

Stay present.

Stay *me*.

My resistance only drew its pity to the surface. "Little death-touch," the monster began, its concern a familiar weight in my chest. Cold. Horrible. Caring. I hated everything about this...this *thing* inside me that was so wrong and unnatural. I hated that it cared so much when no one else ever had. I didn't want to always need fixing, a broken and pitiful thing so lost in my own head that the simplest gust of wind sent me spinning.

I didn't want to need something to catch me. Especially not something —

"Like me?" the monster softly asked.

I clamped my bottom lip between my teeth.

"You've tried so hard to be rid of me." The monster coiled inside my chest. *"But you don't need fixing."*

No. I needed a fucking exorcism.

The monster's presence had once been a relief. I was young when it had first come into being, just a boy with no other company but the voice in my head and the deadly power in my hands. Together, we'd staved off the loneliness that reared its ugly head whenever Mom had worked too late, or when she hadn't come home at all.

This wasn't friendship anymore, though.

The monster saw itself as medicine, but medicine could poison too. A cup of tea soothed so many ailments, but how many herbs acted as poison if administered in too high a dose? For years, the monster's protective nature had over-steeped inside me, turning whatever kinship we once had bitter and toxic with self-loathing.

"Arthur —"

"Stop," I whispered, too quiet for Eva to hear. I was so tired of its voice. Its soft encouragement. Its brutal demands. It was too much to hold so much contradiction inside me.

"I just want to help."

I kept tapping against the side of my leg. "I know." A quiet seed of despair split open in my chest. "But whenever you try, someone gets hurt."

Cold washed over me, touching every place the monster and I pressed together, hand to glove, soul to body. I wasn't sure which one of those I was anymore, but I knew I had to resist. For all its talk of care, the monster could be ruthless, even cruel, when it felt wounded.

"I don't hurt you."

It had taken control at the cottage, then again in the pit. It would do so again. I knew it.

I needed to stay in control.

Stay me.

I gritted my teeth. "You hurt me every time," I said under my breath.

Eva turned toward me then, wholly unaware of my inner struggle. Her eyes were bright with tears, and the empty frames lay in a scattered puzzle at her feet. Wild grasses pushed taller where she stood, green blades splitting from their roots in testament to her breaking heart.

"Arthur, please," the monster whispered. I shivered. It was so rare to hear it say my name. A hot tear rolled down my cheek, in stark contrast to the ice in my bones. *"Let me help you,"* it urged again, its sadness swelling inside me. *"You need to consume."*

"No," I snapped, and this time Eva heard, though what she made of it, I didn't know. When she looked at me, I turned away.

Sometimes it felt as though the weight of the whole Earth was pressing on my chest. It felt like being buried alive. I didn't know how to escape that feeling without the monster's help, but I knew that I wanted to find a way.

I didn't want to go numb anymore. Maybe once doing so had been my only means of survival, but that wasn't living. Eva had shown me that back when she'd taken a boy no one wanted and accepted him as hers.

Even though our mistakes had changed the shape of who we were to each other, I would never forget how her kind of love had rearranged my view of the world. It had made everything brighter, and had made me want to live brighter too.

Squeezing my eyes shut, I pushed the monster back. It was difficult. My body was worn out, sore in too many ways to count.

The monster snarled in frustration. *"You don't know what you're doing!"*

That had always been the case.

"You need me!" it called out, fainter now as I smothered it in pure resolve. This wasn't a long-term solution — I knew that. I wasn't even sure it would last the day, especially with the fever and infection worsening. Maybe the monster would keep clawing away, hungry to devour my pain, as the wax moths had done to the honeycomb, until only a brittle shell of me remained.

But for now, for as long as I could, I wanted to be my own.

My knees gave out, the weight of my body sinking down into the soft earth below. I sagged against the abandoned hive box, eyes closing. "I don't need you."

Another storm was brewing across the dark and frothy sky. The instant the first drop fell, I felt the monster's desire to wipe it off our cheek, but I fought that too.

This body was still mine.

The clouds opened just as the plonk of Eva's walking stick and the shush of her feet sounded in the grass behind me. In seconds, the slow dribble quickened to a roar.

"Arthur?"

A stream of raindrops was already cooling my too-warm skin, making a shiver roll over me.

"Arthur!" Strong hands gripped my shoulders and shook. "You've got to get up!"

"Bee girl," I whispered, eyes fluttering.

Eva hauled me to my feet and nodded to the other side of the meadow. "I think that's a shed."

To my bewilderment, she was right. Beyond the sea of rippling violet flowers, there was a simple wooden door, smothered in a mound of green ivy. Eva dragged me toward it, leaning heavily on her walking stick. All the while, the monster's hunger for the life around us swelled and built inside me. These flowers were different. They seemed to glow with life. My mouth watered, the monster's thirst stretching through me. It wanted to take the tender petals between our fingertips. It wanted me to get on my knees and rip the plants up, to sink my teeth into the roots and suck the meadow dry.

Mortified, I clutched my shirt with my free hand to keep it still, and together, Eva and I hobbled up to the door of the strange abandoned shed. Bug followed close behind us. As we came nearer, my gaze fell on a circle of stones arranged in what had clearly once been a fire pit, though now the protective ring was covered in a rime of moss and lichen, and wildflowers bloomed where the flames had once burned.

The shed had been built on the flat ground at the bottom of a slope. Wedged between its back wall and the rising hill sat a pile of chopped wood, covered in a tarp that had frayed and been eaten away to nothing more than a scrap now.

Eva tried the door. "It's locked."

Of course it was.

She nudged me. "Check the top of the doorframe."

Wind whipped the rain sideways, throwing skeins of ivy into our faces. Water dripped down my chin as I ran my hand over the top of the doorframe. "No luck." I pulled away, watching the ivy shrivel back at my touch, green leaves crisping to brown remains. I should have felt shame. I did feel shame, somewhere under all my exhaustion.

Eva crouched, picking up stones near the base of the door and turning them over.

"What are you doing?" I asked her.

"Looking for — aha!" Eva pulled a smooth-looking stone from the dirt and brushed it off. Mud streaked her fingers. Eva's face lit up in fierce triumph as she held up a ceramic figurine. "The turtle!"

She flipped a panel on its belly, slid out a hidden key, and unlocked the door.

We spilled into the tiny room. It was thick with must, the scent of ozone filling my nose and the press of humidity clinging at once to my skin. The shed was windowless, only the barest of slivers of light coming through the cracks between the planks of wood siding. I could make out only a few details in the dim. The decor was stark, leaving little but a camping cot stripped of its bedding at the far end of the room. Bug darted past our ankles, straight for the hollow beneath the cot, with a yowl that spoke to her displeasure at getting rained on.

The second I stepped in, a trapped, panicky feeling twisted inside me. I froze in place. Eva paused too, and her eyes flicked to the open door.

"Tight spaces?" she whispered.

I swallowed hard and nodded once, embarrassed that she'd clocked my reaction. The room was small, but it was also dry, and that was a vast improvement.

The onslaught of rain picked up a notch as Eva's gaze moved past me to the field we'd abandoned, her expression wilting into the same despair I'd seen as she'd torn frame after frame from the empty hive boxes. "I can't believe it's gone."

"I know."

Crying made her blue eyes brighter. When she looked at me, a frisson ran a current of awareness over my skin. "What do we do now?"

It was a far more vulnerable question than any other she'd posed since my return to Audrey. Somewhere up this mountain, we'd inadvertently slipped back into former versions of ourselves, clinging to something familiar, as though that would help us survive.

I flashed to the kiss we'd shared in the pit, when she'd tried to snap me out of the same claustrophobic pressure that was eking back into my thoughts even now, inside this small, dark space. That moment sat between us now, making it difficult to pretend that everything we'd once been to each other was truly dead and buried. Love, like infection, had a way of festering until the soft remains turned septic with neglect.

Love could be gangrenous. After my mother died, the monster's love had spread like an infection. In its eagerness to keep me from hurting, the monster had smothered my grief again and again, until I was left feeling nothing at all.

I'd come back to Audrey, desperate to feel again. I'd dreaded seeing Eva, knowing how our love had rotted away, too. But now she was looking at me with flushed cheeks and eyes full of tears, asking for reassurance.

"We'll figure it out." I took a step forward, an ache opening up in my chest. My throat closed around the words.

So many things to say to her, and none of them came easily.

My eyes fell to the round bow of Eva's lips. She'd lost her scrunchie in the river, and her loose, damp hair was plastered against her neck. "I don't know how to make things right between us," I exhaled through my nose, suddenly flustered. "Maybe I shouldn't try. It's just... I miss you so much, bee girl."

Eva's eyes grew wider, her mouth puckering. My own mouth felt as dry as cotton. But she deserved to hear that, at least once. She deserved to know that she had been loved. That I would choose infection now if it meant I had once been hers.

The air between us sat heavy and thick with the smell of rain. Of fresh things.

"Is it too late for us?" I asked. The wind rushed in at my back, chilling my still-damp skin.

Surprise rippled across her face at the question.

"Sorry." I stepped back, suddenly flushed. "That was out of line. I shouldn't — "

"Stop," Eva commanded, and I did. She closed the scant distance between us, her fingers splaying over my abdomen. The door snapped shut behind me, plunging us into darkness as Eva pinned me against the damp aged wood.

When her mouth pressed to mine, the world narrowed to a thread.

My hands found her waist before my mind properly processed what we were doing, my lips parting for the dip of her tongue. She kissed too urgently to be soft, her warmth like the sun, magnetizing me closer.

"Arthur," Eva whispered. In her mouth, my name was a sentencing, and a trickle of fear ran down my body. But I wanted her judgment. I wanted atonement. I wanted her, sharp or soft.

The rain beat against the door behind me as we held each other a little tighter, our bodies damp and our breaths ragged.

"You left me alone, after all that happened." Eva thumbed the side of my mouth, her breath a hot caress on my chin.

"I know."

My response seemed to irritate her, and she kissed me harder. The metallic slide of iron spread over my tongue, and I flinched, licking the split in my lower lip. The salt of her was a luxury. So human, to sweat and bleed, to want and wound.

"Is that all you have to say?" she asked.

I pushed off the door. Eva grabbed my hips, limping us back toward the cot. "No," I whispered.

When the backs of her calves hit the cot, Eva turned us and pushed me down onto the makeshift bed. A spark of pain erupted in the swollen skin around my stitches, making me wince.

"I have a lot I want to say to you, bee girl."

A zing of awareness shot up my limbs as Eva stepped between my knees and knit her fingers into the hair at my nape.

"Sometimes being angry at you was the only thing I had to hold on to," she whispered.

I swallowed. "Be angry, then, bee girl. Be furious with me, but don't let go." I wrapped my arms tightly around her middle, yearning to draw her in completely and bury my face in the soft ravines of her body.

Eva gently touched my forehead, but the skin was too sensitive, and I flinched back without meaning to.

"Your fever is worse," she said.

"It's fine. I just need to rest."

"*You* need *antibiotics,*" the monster snapped inside our head.

The weight of her hand against the side of my neck anchored me enough to push the voice away again. It wasn't forever, but every second of silence was precious with her.

I could tell she didn't believe me. Eva carefully knelt on the cot, her knees straddling my lap. I held on to her legs to keep her steady. "Tell me," I roughed out. "How do I earn your trust again?"

"I don't know." Her hands moved up my chest to the narrow rise of my shoulders. It felt wonderfully wrong to be so close, her ministrations almost reverent. Almost right.

"I missed this too."

I didn't mean to say it.

Eva's knees cinched tighter against my hips. "That's the fever talking."

I shook my head. "You know it isn't."

"Do I?"

How could she not? There was no moment in which I was with her when I did not find myself bending in heart and body like a sunflower to the light. But saying that would ring hollow when my actions years ago had told her otherwise.

"You know me," I said softly, unsure if that was really true, or if I merely wanted it to be.

Eva brushed her fingertips down the beard growing along my jaw, her voice turning rough with emotion. "I knew a boy."

I caught her fingers in mine and pressed her palm to my heart. It still beat for her. Maybe it always would.

She'd known me as the boy who'd taken her out to hear the birds, who'd lost himself in the sanctuary of her world, who'd teased her and laughed with her, and touched her with tentative hands.

But I'd buried that Arthur. I'd sloughed him off like an insect voiding its chrysalis. How I wished I could get back to the boy she had loved. If I could be him again, maybe I could survive being a monster too.

"Do something for me?" Eva asked, her voice hushed.

My heart skipped a beat. "Anything."

Her hesitation felt like the strike of a gavel, weighty and full of my fate.

Eva's exhale washed over me. "I want what you took away eight years ago." She curled the hand pressed to my heart into a fist, her voice husky and rough with feeling. "I want a better goodbye."

Chapter 27

Eva

Eva's body hummed with the things she hadn't said. *I want. I want.* Like a heart, it beat inside her, steady and stubborn and strong.

She wanted to know why he'd tattooed a bird he hated into his skin.

She wanted to know who he spoke to when he thought she wasn't listening.

She wanted to know where he'd gone when he left these mountains.

She wanted to know who he'd become when he stopped being hers.

The boy Eva remembered had been more conscientious about preserving life than any other person she knew: Everything was finite, so everything was precious. Eva wanted to know if he still believed that, after all this time.

"A better goodbye?" he echoed.

A lump grew in Eva's throat as she nodded, turning her hand and moving her thumb over the pulse point in Arthur's wrist.

It would hurt. She knew that. There was nothing good about goodbyes.

"What did you have in mind?" Arthur asked. He sounded the way she felt. Nervous. Needful. Full of want and fear.

Eva scooted a little closer and guided Arthur's hands to her waist. "Touch me."

He splayed his hands over her ribs.

"More than that," she chastened.

And so he slipped his hands beneath her sweatshirt, still heavy and damp from the river. One hand wrapped around the small of her back and tugged her close to keep her from falling off the cot. The other sculpted upward, and Eva sighed as he relearned the soft plane of her stomach and the valley between her breasts, aching from the pleasure she found in his touch.

The air between them pressurized with desire.

"Kiss me," Eva husked.

Arthur moved at a glacial pace in the dark, so careful even now, making Eva's body tense with anticipation. It was better that she couldn't fully see him. Instead of becoming self-conscious, Eva felt grounded and present. She touched the soft give of Arthur's beard under her fingertips, the edge of a sharp jaw underneath. She heard the catch and pull of his breath, so honest and rough it made her breath catch too.

Wanting was contagious.

Arthur's kiss left the taste of rain on her lips. It settled her nerves. Glaciers were slow, but they carved whole valleys with their movements. So did he. Arthur took Eva's face in his hands, pressing his lips worshipfully to the corners of her eyes. When a tear slipped free, Arthur caught it on his tongue, a low hum radiating from his chest.

He felt so good.

Eva's shoulders dropped, and she wound her arms around his neck.

As a girl, she'd lived on folktales. They were the water to her family's roots, and she'd grown up on stories of bargains and broken hearts. Even Dad's stories often ended in tragedy. When she was young, Eva thought it terribly romantic to love what you were destined to lose.

Now she called bullshit. It was easy to say that you'd die for someone, but what Eva really wanted was the kind of love that stood its ground when things got difficult, the kind of love that chose to live.

For years, she'd fed her anger to survive, picturing her heart like a garden made to wither in the cold, and she'd blamed Arthur for killing the part of her that had believed in their story.

But his touch awakened something in her again.

As Arthur moaned into the skin of her neck, pressing his lips to her body and making goose bumps erupt down her arms, Eva wondered if maybe she'd been wrong all this time. Gardens never really die, after all. Seeds lie dormant, and soil goes fallow, all in the faith that one day, when the conditions are right, it will bloom again.

Eva crossed her arms and pulled the damp and dirt-stained sweatshirt over her head, leaving her in nothing but a sports bra and his boxers.

Arthur let out a breathless laugh. "I'm so glad you decided to sleep in those."

"I needed shorts," she said defensively. "It was only meant to be for one night."

"I'm not complaining." He ran a finger over the top of the

waistband, sending a shiver across her skin. "You are so beautiful, Ev."

Warmth rushed over her skin. "Fever again?"

"Fever wouldn't make me a liar."

True. If anything, Arthur seemed to be letting more things slip. At least he had an excuse. Eva didn't know what had come over her to explain the words tripping from her lips. "I missed you too, you know."

Arthur groaned, slanting his mouth over hers again.

The energy in the room seemed to shift, a sudden uptick of urgency underlying every new touch. Eva's restraint was unspooling by the second, every press and catch of his lips undoing her, shaping her, rebuilding her into something new. She clumsily helped Arthur out of his shirt. He was shivering, his clothes too damp on his chilled skin. She needed to get him warm.

Arthur lifted the sports bra over her head. The physical relief turned to pleasure as he warmed a path across her collarbone with his lips. The reverent brush of his fingertips up the curve of her breast was enough to drive Eva mad. An ache gathered between her legs. When his thumb brushed her nipple, she gasped, and he licked the hollow of her throat.

"So fucking beautiful," he murmured.

Eva loved his dirty mouth. She tipped her head up, letting her eyes briefly close as she rolled her hips, seeking the relief of friction.

It was strange how this moment straddled the line between known and new, the past and the present colliding with simple shocks of touch. Eva had plenty of stolen memories she'd created with Arthur in every corner of her family cottage, the greenhouse, even the Honey Shoppe. He'd made his mark on every place that mattered to her.

Maybe that was why his absence had been such a ghost, haunting her through the years.

The cot was too narrow for Eva to stretch out the way her body craved, so she planted her hands on the wall instead. Moss softened under her palms, growing in the dark. Arthur gripped her waist.

"Am I hurting you?" Eva asked, all too aware of her still-throbbing ankle hanging off the cot behind her and how it underscored every moment of pleasure. Arthur was in even worse shape.

"No."

"Because we could slow down," Eva said, worried now.

"If you want," Arthur panted.

When Eva lifted her body and dragged it against his, Arthur let out a long groan. When she did it again, he seized her by the hips. "Ev," he begged. "Please, tell me. Do *you* want to slow down?"

"No," she whimpered.

Arthur slipped a hand between her legs, his fingers gliding over the front of the boxers. A shock of pleasure stole her breath. Eva covered his hand with one of her own, guiding him to the place she wanted. Arthur nodded in understanding. It was an agonizingly slow reacquainting, and Eva thought she might die from the relief of it, and from the way his focus narrowed on the sparest details as he learned, anew, what she wanted.

"Fuck," Arthur whispered, dropping his face into the crook of her neck.

Eva clung to him, rendered speechless by the promise of relief building inside her, only to retreat again.

Arthur tugged at her waistband. "Please. Let me take these off."

And Eva realized *this* was the groveling she wanted. Arthur's impatient desire made her feel strong, wholly in charge of her own body and the pleasure she took from his touch. She lifted her hips and let him pull the boxers down her legs, savoring the pressure of his hands on her skin.

Her body hummed at the return of his fingers to where she needed him most. She was silk to a flame, her fibers undone. She was honeycomb under a heated knife, her spine arching as she melted against him.

When Arthur sucked the delicate spot beneath her ear, his exhale hot on her skin, Eva gasped.

Her climax crashed through her like a tide against the shore. She moaned in gratitude as Arthur kept kissing her neck, her jaw, all the while working his fingers inside her until the bliss faded to a distant ache, and she slackened against him.

A better goodbye.

Arthur gathered her close. He still burned, a steady fever hiking ever higher. When Eva licked her lips, tasting salt, she realized her cheeks were wet. A little more tension fell away, and she thought for a moment that it would be so cleansing to cry all the grief out.

But the pressure of Arthur's embrace chased away her desire to weep. Eva slumped against him, wholly wrung out. She took great pleasure in feeling the spread of goose bumps rising at her touch. "Well. We definitely didn't slow down," she murmured.

Arthur barked a laugh that made Eva's chest feel warm and bright.

He should always laugh like that.

When the pain in her ankle outweighed the temptation to stay wrapped in his arms, Eva extracted the pretzel her limbs had made around him and slid off the cot, her muscles warm and tired.

Her eyes had adjusted a bit to the dark. The storm grew more boisterous outside. A clap of thunder boomed directly over their heads. Bug let out a yowl.

"Hang on," Eva said softly to the kitten, kneeling on the floor beside the cot again and blindly sweeping her hand under the bed frame. A mistake. Bug swiped in alarm.

"Ow!" Eva drew her hand back and sucked the wounded skin. "Sorry, girl."

"She scratched you?" Arthur asked.

Eva nodded, then remembered he couldn't see. "Yeah. She seems scared of the storm." She bent, more cautiously this time, squinting into the deep shadows under the cot. When lightning flashed, Eva caught a glimpse of movement: Bug pressed into the corner.

She saw something else under the bed as well. Eva frowned and reached to glide her fingertips along the straight, smooth edge of the object she'd missed before. It was some kind of…box? No. Her thumb caught the cool edge of a metal latch on the side. A trunk?

"I think I found something."

Eva hauled the trunk out, the bottom scraping loudly against the floor. Bug jumped, yowling in protest. Eva undid the heavy latch, and the lid came unstuck with an audible crackle, the wood groaning as she lifted the top free. The smell of must and old, worn canvas filled her nose. Eva recognized it, flashing in an instant to the camping trips she'd taken with Dad and Izzy growing up.

"What is it?" Arthur asked.

Eva reached inside, fumbling as she tried to make out the items. Her fingers closed around a cool metal cylinder. She huffed a laugh and held up a flashlight in triumph. "Supplies!"

Chapter 28

Isobel

It had been eight years since Isobel last saw her father like this, his pallor bleached to a stark bone white, smeared in red-green blood that smelled strangely more like sap.

It was just past dawn. After the cottage had stopped sinking into the ground, Dane had taken Isobel and her father back to his farmhouse, where the three of them now sat at his kitchen table. Isobel still felt shaken, and her father's hands trembled as he raised a glass of chocolate milk to his lips, a bit of liquid sloshing up the side.

"Please, Dad," Isobel said when he put down the milk. "Let us take you to the hospital." It scared her to see him like this, half rotted, more forest than man with every breath he took.

Her father shook his head and took off his glasses, eyes on the box of ashes in the center of the table as he rubbed the lenses clean, then replaced the glasses on his nose. "How long has Eva been gone?"

"About thirty-six hours," Dane clipped.

Isobel felt the heat of her father's gaze and looked away, knowing he'd puzzled out that she'd lied to him when she told him Eva and Arthur were safe.

"Do you know where?"

Isobel fought to remember what Lenny had said when he'd shown up at the farmhouse only hours before, but the headache brimming behind her eyes made it hard to focus. She took a sip of water.

"They were last spotted on the north road," Dane said evenly. "We have reason to believe both Eva and Arthur abandoned their vehicle and pursued a trail up the mountain on foot."

"How far up the north road?" Dad pressed.

Dane clicked his tongue. "A few miles?"

"I need to see it." He made as though to rise.

"Dad, stop." Isobel tugged his arm back down. "What you need to see is Dr. Rosen!"

"And just what is she going to do with all this?" He gestured to the aspen stump in his chest. "A dead man, rotting in his own skin?" His laugh was humorless. "Dr. Rosen has already tried everything."

"But maybe — "

"She can't fix this," he snapped.

Izzy paled. It didn't feel like they were talking just about his injury. "You don't know that," she whispered softly.

The fight seemed to leave her father then, and he slumped back into his chair. "Now you sound like your sister."

The sting in those words was worse than an outright accusation. She'd messed up.

"You recognize that location?" Dane asked.

Her father grimaced. "Maybe." He tried to take another sip of his milk, only to realize the glass was empty. Isobel popped to her feet and dashed to the fridge. Colorful magnets held Esther's crayon drawings to the steel surface.

She returned with a new, full glass, which Dad drained all in one go. Little scales of bark flaked off his cheek, and his eyes were shot with green veins when he met her gaze. "What did your sister say, exactly, before she left?"

Isobel chewed her lip as she thought back. "You were badly hurt. She was upset that you kept asking her for honey."

"Honey?" Dad let out a low curse.

Dane looked between them. "What does that mean?"

A feeling of unease stirred in Isobel's stomach as she watched her father's face lose a bit more color. "It means we need to hurry." His chair legs squeaked against the tiles as he pushed back and rose. "Sheriff, you drive."

"But—"

"Izzy, please." Dad's expression softened into need. "I can do this. I *have* to do this. And after...I'll go wherever you want me to go."

She straightened. "To the hospital?"

He sighed. "Yes. Fine."

It was the best she was going to get. Isobel stood and plucked Dane's keys off the hook on the wall. "Then let's go."

Even with the branches of his saplings snapped off, Dad was almost too big to fit inside the back of Dane's patrol car. He didn't complain, though. When they turned onto the north road, he started speaking, so softly that it could have just been for himself. "The Appalachian mountain range is one of the oldest on Earth, you know."

Dane shot him a quick, inquiring look but didn't interrupt.

"Ancient places are something of a breeding ground for the

unusual, but I didn't believe the impossible stories I'd grown up on until I stumbled into one myself." As he spoke, Dad's voice fell into a cadence she remembered from the many nights he'd spent weaving bedtime stories for her and Eva when they were little. "It was my first summer out of college, and a buddy and I were meant to go camping. When he bailed, I went up this road alone, until I hit a stand of aspens."

The car rattled and bounced over a muddy pothole.

"There was something strange about those trees. They felt more alive than the forest surrounding my family's farm. I couldn't help the feeling that they were...watching me. And there was this voice," Dad said, his words slowing. "It knew my name. I could hear it, not in the wind but from the roots beneath me. I followed it for miles, until I found her."

"Her?" Isobel said, twisting to face her father in the back seat.

Dad nodded. "The spirit of the wood. She was a woman, once, given the gift of everlasting life so long as she remained in the meadow where I found her."

"I don't understand," Dane said.

Outside, the wall of trees began to change from pine and poplar to the pale, chalky white hues of aspens. Isobel sifted through her father's words with a frown. "What did you do next?"

Dad's voice turned wistful. "I freed her."

Isobel wanted to ask more questions, but around the next bend, Arthur's Volkswagen came into view. Dane sucked in an audible breath and pulled onto the shoulder of the road. His keys clicked together, the only sound to break up the silence in the car as the three of them got out and walked to the sagging vehicle.

Dane knelt and ran a hand over the tread of a flattened tire. "Slashed," he muttered.

Lenny's face flashed through Isobel's mind. He'd come up this road. That had to have been done by him and Avi Dawson.

Dane straightened and tipped his chin toward her father. "So, Jack. Where did they go?"

Her father stepped past both of them. His movements were slow, his breaths still too shallow, but he wore a grim determination as he lifted a finger to the trees. "There."

At first, Isobel didn't understand. Then her eyes fixed on a trail of wildflowers starting at the edge of the road and stretching deep into the trees. Where the rest of the undergrowth was sprinkled only with occasional goldenrod, the wending line of flowers was lush with the sunny blooms.

A trail not of breadcrumbs but of seeds coaxed to life. Isobel's heart gave a jolt.

Eva.

"There is a flower that only grows in a meadow up this way," Jack said, falling back into his story. "For years after I freed the spirit of the wood, I ignored her warnings and utilized its healing properties by drying it into a tea, as I had for so many other herbs I collected. I even cultivated a few hives up the mountain that pollinated a field of the blooms, concentrating its life-giving power into—"

"Honey," Isobel said in a hush, the pieces clicking into place.

Her father nodded, his eyes still fixed on the trail his youngest daughter had left behind her in the grass.

Isobel's mind whirred. So that's what he must have been doing every time he took a solo trip up the mountain. He'd never permitted her and Eva to tag along on those particular hikes like he did on others.

"Why didn't you tell us?" Isobel said softly.

The question made her feel like a hypocrite.

Dad's brows drew into a slow frown. "Because this story doesn't have a happy ending."

Most of his stories didn't. Isobel opened her mouth to respond when a voice called out roughly.

"Is someone there?"

Instantly, Isobel's body went on high alert.

"Please," the voice choked out, anguished. "Help me."

Dane swore and jogged forward into the trees. "Avi, is that you?"

Isobel followed behind, her eyes sweeping the brush.

"Lenny!" Dane bellowed, but his brother didn't reply.

Avi let another sob slip free, an anguished moan drawing their attention. When she saw him, Isobel gasped.

Avi was face down, one hand clutching a clump of grass as he tried to haul himself forward. A depression the width of his body carved a clear path behind him. How far had he dragged himself? What had happened?

Why was there blood caking his face?

A burgundy stain smeared down his cheek, mixing with the soil beneath. But that's not where Isobel's focus landed. Her breath stalled in her throat at the sight of his left eye, gouged of its ball and the fluids inside it. Flowers spilled out of the empty, bloody socket.

"The hell?" Dane muttered as he rushed to the injured man's side. There had to be other wounds too, Isobel realized, that prevented Avi from rising. His pants were ripped, and though one of his legs was scrambling to thrust himself forward, the other lay flat behind him.

Bile rose in her throat.

"Dane?" Avi cried out.

"I'm here," Dane said, taking the man's hand in his own and briefly squeezing. "We're going to help you, Avi, all right? Can you tell me what happened?"

Avi let out a sob. "She came out of nowhere!"

Isobel stiffened.

"Who did?" Dane pressed as Dad knelt beside the pair of them. *Don't you dare say her name.*

"I don't know." Avi dug his fingernails into the already-damaged skin beneath his eye. When one of the flower stems popped free, he screamed in agony.

Dane pulled Avi's hands away from his face. "Was it Eva?" he harshed out, breathless.

"No," Isobel snapped, stunned at both the question and his coldness. *He doesn't get to say that.* He couldn't think that, after all they'd done to protect her from suspicion. Dane couldn't... He couldn't think...

Avi moaned. "She was made of trees, a-and roots..." he sobbed.

"Right," Dane muttered, flicking a look to Isobel. She'd spent years learning his tells, and yet she couldn't parse that expression. Her chest squeezed, the smell of mangled flesh and blood and flowers making her sick.

Dane shifted his focus to the wound on Avi's leg. Unhooking his belt, he wrapped a makeshift tourniquet around Avi's upper thigh. "There's a medical kit in the glove box," he said to Isobel.

She raced back to the patrol car and yanked the passenger door wide, crouching as she dug through the contents of the glove box, tearing out item after item. The car manual and registration. A notebook, pens, and... Isobel slowed, and lifted a small jam jar filled with a familiar shade of deep blue petals.

She knew this tea. It was the same blend Lenny had been sent to fetch from their house the day he and Arthur got into that fight.

"Isobel!"

Shaking herself, Isobel located a mini first aid kit from the depths of the glove box and raced back to the men just as Dane rolled Avi onto his back.

"Where is my brother?"

Avi let out a sob. "I-I don't know!"

"That's okay," Dad cut in, taking Avi's wrists and gently folding the man's arms across his chest. "Don't scratch now, son."

Isobel's heart pounded as she passed over the first aid kit.

"Lenny left me there to die," Avi moaned. "She-she came out of nowhere and" — his voice took on more volume and energy, his one good, bloodshot eye popping open — "he *left* me!"

Chapter 29

The Monster

There was once a lonely little boy who reached inside the deep and darker parts of his subconscious for a friend. What he dredged from the depths of his own mind was something else entirely, something that would have frightened other little lonely children like him.

But Arthur wasn't like other children. He never had been.

The monster worked itself into the cracks between their wills while Arthur slept, one arm slung around his bee girl. It put the monster at ease to see him finally rest. This mind had been made for both of them, no matter what Arthur had tried to convince himself of over the years, shoring up his mental defenses as though the monster was an enemy.

As though they had never been friends.

Filling the hollows Arthur left unchecked felt like sliding a hand into a glove. Despite what Arthur believed, the monster didn't relish making the boy feel helpless. It usually let Arthur guide the actions of their shared body.

But the monster always showed up when the boy needed it. Just as he did now.

Arthur twitched, unaware of the shift in control happening while he slumbered on. The monster slinked delicately into the notches of the boy's subconscious. It wasn't ready to wake him yet. The moment Arthur woke, he was sure to fight, and the monster wanted to use this time to plan their next step.

Most pressingly, they had to get off this mountain. Arthur's fever was worsening with every passing hour, and while the monster tried to soothe him and cool the heat burning him from the inside out, it didn't have the power to truly heal. It could numb, and for a short while it could shoulder a world of pain for the boy it loved so much.

But nothing would stop the march of death itself if they didn't get Arthur to a hospital soon. The boy likely had no idea of how much the monster was already carrying for him, or how much worse he could feel.

Cautiously, the monster blinked Arthur's eyes open. The room around them smeared, waterlogged and rheumy. One of Arthur's arms was still flung across Eva's waist. He'd wanted to keep her from falling off the cot. The other arm was currently serving as a pillow for her, Eva's cheek propped against the honeycomb tattoo. Some of her hair had found its way across Arthur's cheek and into his mouth, so tangled and folded together were their bodies.

The monster watched the rise and fall of Eva's chest. She sighed, as though she, too, were close to waking. Maybe that would be to their advantage. She needed to agree to the monster's plan, after all, but it was hard to wake her when she looked so peaceful.

Arthur's already aching body had been rendered more sensitive by infection. The monster stretched itself, feeling like a tentacled creature in its effort to cool and soothe all the places where Arthur's fever made it hard for his body to rest.

Eva's eyes fluttered.

The monster's awareness telescoped, and it took in the change of her heartbeat and breath with a new kind of fascination, flexing Arthur's hand and running a thumb over the soft, pale flesh of Eva's stomach.

"Hi." Eva's voice was dry and raspy. Her fingers knit into Arthur's as she let out a sigh, still sleepy. "The...storm?"

"It stopped." The words tasted strange on Arthur's tongue, causing a shiver of delight to run through the monster. It felt good to hear its voice through Arthur's vocal cords. It felt good to be *real*.

Eva stretched, her back arching as she yawned. "Finally."

The monster didn't usually get to be this near to her, to smell the damp of her hair or feel where her freckles lay flat against Arthur's skin. It loved her freckles.

Eva's touch had a tendency to push the monster back. At times, it had wondered if her absence had been the reason the monster had managed to slip past Arthur's defenses so completely after Charlotte died.

The monster held its breath as the acute sensation of summer grew heavy around the two of them, but the sunny feeling didn't hurt. It *hummed*.

Their eyes latched. Hers were summer-sky blue. The monster tenderly brushed a thumb across the dip in her waist again. Arthur's body was weak right now. He needed the monster. It would be...irresponsible to relinquish the helm before the boy was well and safe.

"Hungry?" Eva asked. "There might be something in that trunk."

The monster nodded, ignoring the physical protest of Arthur's sore muscles as it extricated itself limb by limb from Eva's embrace. She'd found one of Jack's old flannel shirts in the trunk. With the storm gone, a streak of sunlight turned the total blackness of the shed into a hazy gray. The monster could just make out where the buttons of Eva's shirt had been improperly aligned, exposing a bit of her stomach.

She lowered herself carefully to the floor again and fished through the trunk. There were more overlarge and musty clothes inside, including a weathered pair of hiking boots with a hole in the toe that must have belonged to Jack. They wouldn't fit Arthur quite right, but they would protect his feet better than nothing. Hiking without shoes had left Arthur's soles aching.

The monster fished a few things out for itself as well. The sun was leaking through the cracks in the shed walls, rapidly heating the space inside. It had to be...what, late morning maybe? They hadn't slept long.

The sounds of the soft fabric sliding over skin filled the tiny, quiet room.

"How did you sleep?" Eva asked.

The monster scratched a salt crystal out from the corner of its eye. *"Good,"* it said. A partial lie. It never slept, but Arthur did, and while the boy rested, the monster had run over again and again what Arthur had said.

You hurt me every time.

The words clanged inside its head. It was accustomed to being the thing Arthur rained his anger on, but those words — delivered so raw, so broken — had burrowed deep.

The monster touched the swirl of tattoos on Arthur's arm. The honeycomb hexagons. The dark, feathered songbirds. The starling on his tendon covered his first and deepest scar. The monster had spent a long time thinking about the night Arthur finally took a blade to his skin and tried to carve the monster out.

You hurt me every time.

He hadn't meant that. He was just upset. Arthur sharpened himself on the blade of guilt so often that living itself had become an open wound. The monster didn't want that for him. It was time for a change, time to write his boy a new story.

To do that, however, the monster needed to get Arthur medical aid and sustenance to help him heal. There was life to be devoured in that meadow, flowers and field mice and all kinds of creatures that Arthur hadn't let himself kill, too scared of what it would do to his soul to sacrifice another living thing to survive. The monster had no such problem. It had always done what it had to do to protect Arthur. From the moment the boy ripped the monster into existence, it had wanted nothing except to ease Arthur's troubles and pains.

To become the home Charlotte had denied him.

Eva scratched the back of Bug's head as she laid out more items from the trunk on the floor. She'd started on the task during the storm, before Arthur had coaxed her back to the cot, eager to sleep and arguing that they could hardly see the contents anyway.

Now in the light, the two of them cataloged their new inventory. There was a lighter, a first aid kit, a flashlight with dead batteries, and —

"Peppermints?" Eva laughed softly, crinkling something between her fingers. "Dad loves these!" She popped one out of its plastic pouch and held it out. Where her fingertips grazed Arthur's palm, an electric zing of awareness sparked, bright and tingling.

The monster worked the stale mint into Arthur's cheek and murmured its thanks, unable to stop the tug of its lips up into a smile. Bug seemed to have recovered from the state the storm had put her in, and she purred and pressed against Eva's leg.

"*Why did your dad create this place?*" the monster asked.

Eva bit her cheek. "I'm...not sure, honestly," she admitted. "I never went with him to harvest these flowers. Come to think of it, I think I tried to, once, and he didn't let me." She stilled, and a furrow knit between her brows. "I had no idea what he'd built up here," she said, turning her head up to the slanted roof of the little shed. "Must have taken him ages."

"*Must have.*"

Carefully, the monster rose to stretch, mindful of Arthur's weakened state. As expected, a dizzy spell made the room around them spin. The monster caught its balance on the wall.

Deep within, Arthur stirred, confused. The boy must be realizing that something felt wrong. The monster tried to soothe him, cooling the fever running through Arthur, but the moment it tried, something inside Arthur snapped to attention, and alarm collected inside their shared body. Arthur tried to push the monster out, but it was too deeply sunk in, firmly fitted inside its glove. Arthur's resistance was no more than a fly to skin.

Hush, now, little death-touch.

Though Arthur couldn't hear the monster, it hoped the boy would feel the care behind its calming words.

Arthur couldn't scream, couldn't voice even a single word, but his shiver of terror moved through the body the two of them shared. The monster knew this feeling. The fear of tight spaces, of feeling trapped, was an unfortunate side effect that had risen over the years as, from time to time, circumstances had forced the monster to take control in order to keep Arthur safe — from the world, and from himself.

It touched the scar on his forearm again, a grounding reminder to its purpose.

You're going to survive this too, it silently vowed.

When the boy tried to lash out again, the monster pushed back, hardening the barrier that enclosed him until it calcified.

The first aid kit allowed the monster to treat the lesser of Arthur's wounds. It used the pack of cleansing wipes to clean the dirt off the cuts in his skin, then applied a soothing balm that clearly hailed from the Moreau household. It came in the same shallow tins Eva used when she boiled down her beeswax, but the smell was different from her usual concoctions, too heavy on the lavender. The monster warmed the balm between its finger and thumb, and rubbed more over Arthur's bug bites, as Eva had done the summer they spent together.

"Let's go down to the river," Eva said as she wrapped Band-Aids over the still-healing blisters on her heels. "We can use those tablets and the canteen to purify some water."

The monster chose not to remind her how much of the river's *unpurified* water they had certainly swallowed when they fell in. It was as good an idea as any. But when it reached for the purifying tablets, something hard and compact slipped out from the pile of stacked, used clothing. The monster plucked it off the floor.

And froze.

Even with Arthur held perfectly still and quiet inside him, the monster felt the boy's shock when they registered what they were looking at.

A satellite phone.

The monster sucked a breath deep into Arthur's lungs, stunned, then pushed the ON button. Nothing. The battery inside the phone must be long dead. The monster all but launched itself toward the trunk and began digging out the few remaining contents, searching for a backup battery, a generator to recharge it, *something*.

"Whoa, what are you doing?"

The monster held up the satellite phone. *"If we can get this to work, we can call for help."*

Eva gasped. "Of course!"

Together, the two of them discarded a tube of rock-hard toothpaste, a bar of soap, a paper-wrapped roll of toilet paper, and at least two dozen more individually wrapped peppermints.

Frustrated, the monster tossed a pair of folded socks across the room. The loud *thunk* made the monster jump, and it looked back at the small cotton lump. That had been far too loud, and too heavy as well. It retrieved the socks and folded the cuffs down.

There, protected inside, was an unopened package containing a phone battery.

Eva gasped.

Delicately, the monster removed the old battery from the phone. There didn't seem to be any leakage or physical degradation inside the battery chamber — a miracle in and of itself. When was the last time Jack had been up here? Would the new battery even work?

The monster chewed on the inside of Arthur's cheek as it made the swap. Arthur had used phones like these before and knew how to operate them.

It held its breath as it pushed the ON button again.

A red light flashed, indicating a poor signal.

The monster shoved to its feet and stumbled outside, a furious hope coiling inside it as it blinked the bright sunlight out of its eyes. The storm had cleared the air, leaving a pristine scent of earth and minerals rising off the soil. The monster held the phone up. A step behind, Eva grabbed her makeshift walking stick.

The phone connected.

The monster let out a whoop of joy and tapped 9-1-1.

"It worked?" Eva exclaimed.

"It worked!" The monster couldn't believe their luck. It would have to deal with the sheriff and the mess of all they'd left behind, but that didn't matter, so long as it could get Arthur safe and well again. The rest they would figure out together, one step at a time.

"911, what's your emergency?" a voice buzzed, the connection crackling.

"Hello, can you hear me?" the monster said loudly. *"We need help out here!"*

"Can you identify your location for me?"

"I-I don't know. We're off-trail." The monster stumbled over its words, doubting itself in a way that felt unfamiliar.

"My dad will know how to find us," Eva said.

She was right. The monster gripped the phone, desperately blurting out, *"There's a man in the town of Audrey, Pennsylvania, named Jack Moreau. He'll know exactly where we are!"*

The operator's voice cut out before they could reply. Alarmed, the monster smacked the side of the phone. To its relief, the voice came back in. "Are there any injured in your party?"

The monster swallowed hard. *"My friend and I are both hurt. I don't know if we can make it back down."*

"All right, sir, I'm going to get you help. Just stay with me. Can you describe your location? Any landmarks nearb —?"

The phone cut out again. The monster shook it, then smacked the side, holding its breath. Instead of coming back, the operator's voice clicked out, and the red light started blinking again.

No signal.

Chapter 30

*Arthur,
Before*

"Truth or dare?" Eva lay face down on the sun-warmed dock in a bikini top and shorts, her hair spread loose over the slats of wood. She turned her head and considered. "Dare."

I grinned. "You sure?"

"What, do you finally have a good one?"

I guffawed. "Awful lot of talk from a girl who never picks *dare*."

She rolled onto her side to face me. "You never pick anything exciting."

My eyes cheated past her to the blue-green ripples of water slapping the side of the dock. I nodded to the pond. "I dare you to jump in."

Eva groaned. "Wait, no. I changed my mind."

I tsked. "No take-backs, bee girl."

"I am a lizard! I deserve to sun myself on a rock!"

"You mean dock."

She stuck out her tongue. "Tomato, potato."

I leaned over where my camera sat between us, close enough to let my breath heat the shell of her ear. "Eva Moreau," I murmured, "I dare you to skinny-dip with me."

Her lips rounded. "You don't skinny-dip."

"I don't?"

"You're too shy!" she said, gesturing with a hand.

I snorted. "Just what part of me are you pointing to?" Pushing to my feet, I peeled off my shirt and shorts, leaving me in nothing but my boxers. "I'm going to beat you into that water."

I needed a distraction anyway. It had been nearly six weeks since that farmers' market afternoon, and I hadn't relaxed for a second, worried I'd done the wrong thing by promising to keep what Lenny had tried to do in the Honey Shoppe a secret.

But the bee girl was in a good mood today, and I didn't want to ruin that.

Eva's cheeks pinked as her eyes slowly dragged up my body. Instead of shrinking, I arched a brow.

"I like this new you," the monster hummed. *"She's been very good for your confidence, hasn't she?"*

Maybe she had. I'd never given much thought to my appearance, too consumed with the monster beneath it, though I supposed I liked my eyes and the shade of my hair. I wasn't overly tall or brawny like the lords and dukes in her books — yes, I was a snoop, and I had no shame in peeking at her novels — but the way Eva looked at me now made me shiver pleasantly.

With her arms crossed under her chest like that, she gave me a rather stirring view herself.

"Fine." Eva popped to her feet and wriggled out of her shorts. Her swimsuit was the same deep cobalt as the sky above. I couldn't help the spread of my grin. "Why are you smiling?"

"You are very pale."

She swatted my arm. "I *freckle*."

"I know."

The monster snorted.

It wasn't lost on me what a gift it was that Eva trusted me enough to let her guard down like this.

"Well?" she asked. "What are you waiting for?"

I tore off my ball cap and tossed it aside with as much dramatic flair as I could muster.

Eva gave her belly laugh to the sky. It was pretty and honest and sexy as hell. I didn't stop to think then—I scooped her up and bolted down the dock. She screamed as we flew off the edge and plunged together into cold water. Together, we sank until our toes stirred mud. She scrambled for purchase, kicking hard and climbing me like a monkey until we broke free again.

"How *dare* you!" she coughed.

I cut her off with a splash to the face. Eva shrieked and splashed me back. Soon she was giggling, holding on to the edge of the dock for balance as she tried and failed to splash more than she laughed. She was so lovely I couldn't stand it; my cheeks hurt from smiling.

When her laugh dropped into the low spread of a hum in her chest, Eva reached behind herself and fiddled with the drawstrings of her swimsuit until the bikini popped free. Then she sank lower.

My mouth went dry. She'd turned the tables on whatever game I'd thought I was winning before. Her hands dipped below the water again, surfacing with a pair of bright blue swim bottoms. She flung the swimsuit onto the dock. "Dare," she chirped, a task complete, then twirled a finger in my direction. "Now, then. Boxers. Off."

I hitched a laugh.

Eva pushed off the dock toward me, both of us kicking our legs to tread water as she gently set her hands on my shoulders.

I'd promised myself I wouldn't touch her, but I hadn't prepared myself for what I would do if *she* touched *me*. At the graze of her fingertips, my stomach pebbled with goose bumps.

Eva moved closer. The blissful glide of her skin against mine was a sweet, delicious shock. We hadn't done this yet, not even close. Despite the cold water, my body hardened as she tugged the waistband down, tossed the boxers onto the dock and wound her legs around my waist.

"Hi," she whispered.

"Hey, bee girl."

She was so soft, the feeling of her breasts flattened against my chest the most erotic sensation I had ever experienced. Swallowing hard, I reminded myself to go slow.

I wanted her thighs in my hands. I wanted to kiss down her throat and taste the freckles on her skin. But even more, I wanted her to feel safe.

"This okay?" I whispered, keenly aware of the new territory we were approaching.

Eva nodded. "More than okay." She smoothed a drop of water off my cheek. "I like this." And then her lips moved sweetly against mine again, the slip of her tongue like a promise. I made a little sound and drew her hungrily against me. Eva's fingers combed back my hair as I deepened the kiss, a new desperation unfurling inside me.

I like this, too.

The words I wanted to say to her stuck like molasses in my throat—heady and dark, but oh, so sweet.

I like you.

When Eva flexed her thighs around my middle, we bobbed a little lower in the water, too distracted to tread properly.

The bank exploded with bright green reeds. Something slippery brushed my calf before it shrank back from my skin, dying beneath the water's surface. Nearby, green pads popped to the surface, pale pink and white lilies opening into full bloom.

When Eva saw them, she broke away. "Sorry."

"Don't be sorry," I rasped. "I like what you can do."

"Really?"

I nodded. Her tickling reeds wove through my toes before shriveling back at my touch. The slippery cold made me shiver, but so would any brush of a fish.

"You're not scared?" Eva asked in a too-small voice.

"No." Her gift was raw and wild. Sometimes it made me doubt that she was even real. But it didn't scare me.

I drew her arms back around my neck and gently pinched her stomach between my fingers. Eva's round lips puckered, and she squeezed her legs around my waist. "Touch me."

My thumb skimmed up her ribs, daring to brush the underside of her breast. "Where?"

I tracked the barest contraction of a swallow in her throat. "There," she whispered.

I was obscenely hard between her thighs. It should have been embarrassing how obviously I wanted her, but I couldn't find it in me to care. When we kissed again, I tasted the pond: silt, sunscreen, and *her*. My hand slipped higher, my thumb drawing a line up her sternum as I hesitantly cupped her breast in my hand.

The pitiful sound Eva made resonated in every crook of my body.

"Yeah?"

She felt so good, and I was high on the rush of her reactions.

Eva nodded, her nails digging into my skin. "Let's go to the bank."

I kicked to the dock and used the edge to haul us in until the water grew shallow, a slurry of mud squishing between our toes. We fell into a patch of grass, dripping and naked. A flood of green moss withered under my palm, but I didn't care. I only saw her.

"What now?" Eva said with a laugh.

My heart pounded. "What do you want now?"

A pretty blush stained Eva's cheeks as she bit her lip. "I don't know. I've never..."

"Me neither."

I drank in the sight of her sprawled beneath me, sun-rosed, freckled, and full of trust.

The grass had no idea what to do. At my touch, the plants withered and died, but Eva renewed them without a thought. The way the world transformed for her was art. She was art. My eyes followed the sparkling trail of a water droplet down her chest. She was a fucking masterpiece.

"Maybe we could...keep going where we left off?" Eva tentatively asked, drawing my hand back to her breast.

I squeezed on reflex. Nodded hard. "All right."

Sometimes I had a difficult time seeing myself as a good person. Good people, after all, didn't have death swirling inside them. But when my touch drew a gasp out of Eva, I didn't feel wicked. I felt alive. My death-touch ripped the life from the microgreens Eva's gift had coaxed to the surface, and for once I couldn't bring myself to care.

For once, I loved it.

The sun had touched her everywhere, constellating her skin in honey-colored freckles. I wanted to map her stars with my mouth the way a cartographer charts the heavens.

Eva's head fell back into the grass as she let out a sigh.

It was a breathless game, discovering what she liked. "Show me where else you want to be kissed, bee girl."

After a moment's pause, Eva's eyes fluttered shut, and she drew a little circle in the hollow of her throat.

I was a good student. Brushing a lock of hair off her neck, I lowered my weight onto her and gently kissed the spot. Eva's chest erupted in goose bumps. When she drew a line down the valley between her breasts, I followed, planting little kisses like seeds in soil. Maybe a garden would bloom from her skin, an Eden I couldn't destroy.

When I ran my tongue over her nipple, Eva let out a shocked, breathy laugh.

Pride swelled in my chest. *I'd done that.*

I crawled down her body, eager to touch and taste more of her. I kissed the soft, pale flesh of her stomach. Kissed the little mole beside her belly button. But when I found her hips, Eva stiffened. "Wait."

I pulled back immediately. "Sorry."

"Don't be sorry." Eva's eyes were glazed, her pupils wide and dark as she wove her fingers into my hair, keeping me still. Keeping me there.

"We can stop, Ev."

"No." Her voice cracked a little. "I don't want to stop."

We stared at each other, Eva's chest falling as she let out a shaky breath.

I swallowed. "Do you want me to kiss you there?"

A helpless sound slipped out of her. "I...I don't know. I want you."

"You can have me. Any way you want." The truth of that scared me a little. I'd never felt beholden to any kind of divinity, but kneeling between her thighs felt like worship. I'd do anything she commanded.

"You have me, Ev," I said again, more softly.

A flicker of vulnerability clouded her expression. "I'm not supposed to want that."

"Bullshit."

She laughed wetly.

Seriously, who had told her that? I hated seeing her embarrassed when she had no reason to be. Maybe neither of us had done this before, but I knew with every beat of my heart that it wasn't wrong. That loving her, learning her, couldn't be wrong.

I threaded my fingers with hers and bent to press our foreheads together. "It's just you and me, Ev. Nothing else matters."

When her lips parted, I watched something change behind her eyes. So I asked again. "What do you want?"

Without breaking my gaze, Eva slowly drew our intertwined hands to the hinge of her thigh. "Kiss me here."

Heat flamed inside me at the gentle order. I pressed a butterfly-soft kiss to her hip bone, then paused, awaiting further instruction.

"Here." Eva trailed a fingertip down her leg. She was meant to be savored, and I tried, I *tried*. But the line of stretch marks on her inner thigh pulled me in like a drug. *These thighs.* I eagerly kissed a path down to her knee, then higher and higher up the other side.

Eva's breaths turned ragged. "Where do you want to kiss me?"

"Everywhere, Ev."

Snarling her fingers in my hair, Eva dragged my face up to meet hers. "Truly?"

"Every inch of you."

Slowly, her trepidation eased into a smile. Eva bit her lip, then reached between her legs. "Here," she said softly.

When I closed my mouth on her, the wildflowers lining the bank burst into bloom. I wrapped an arm around her upper thigh and lost myself in skin, in sighs, in summer.

The pond lapped at my toes. Something green brushed my arm, but I couldn't focus on anything except her. Eva canted her hips, and I muffled a groan against her skin.

No. Not wicked at all. A rush of validation swept through me. This was worship of the softest kind, a prayer made of touches, an altar of flesh. Her sounds were benediction. When she pulled my hair, I kissed my way back up her body — the dip in her waist, the crook of her neck — finally sealing my mouth to hers once more. I loved that she kissed with her teeth. That I, too, was something to devour.

When I broke away, Eva laughed, breathless. "Wow."

"Wow." I grinned down at her.

Like this, our bodies were almost perfectly aligned. Eva's bright expression changed, growing more heated as she set her palms on my hips and urged me closer.

"You sure?" I whispered.

Before she could answer, the sound of voices in the trees startled us both. Eva and I jolted apart. They were coming down the path to the pond. I identified the low rumble as Jack Moreau's voice.

"Shit."

Eva pulled me back into the water. "Under the dock!"

We didn't have time to dress. Bubbles licked my ears as we submerged, surfacing beneath the dock's gooey underside. A green film dripped water onto my nose. "You didn't mention the slime," I muttered.

"Shh." Eva peered through the slats as the voices drew nearer. Although we couldn't make out the figures themselves very well, I did catch a glimpse of my camera, and realized too late that we'd left it and our clothes on the dock.

"Please, Jack." The voice was familiar, and after a moment I placed it as belonging to the older Walker brother, Dane. "Lenny's a good kid. He just needs another chance."

"Another *chance?*" Jack's voice was low, and terrifying.

"I thought you would understand that."

"Chances go to those who deserve them," Jack roughed out. "Not to those who brag about their exploits."

"Len wouldn't hurt her — "

"He sure ran his mouth off like he did!" Jack's voice, usually so warm, went hard and cold with anger. "You think Izzy would lie to me?"

Eva gasped.

"No," Dane said softly. "No, she wouldn't."

The color drained from Eva's cheeks. *I don't want to be another thing my neighbors talk about,* she'd said.

And now she was anyway.

I found her hand under the water, a knot forming in my throat. Gone was the giggling girl I'd run off the dock with. Gone was the pleasure she'd worn like the sun in the grass. This was the girl I'd seen in the Honey Shoppe, scared to be seen. The coating of slime on the dock's underbelly washed her in a sickly green, droplets streaking down her cheeks. My heart tugged as I thought of Lenny Walker pushing her against the counter. How many times had something like that happened and no one noticed? How many second chances had he already wasted?

"Dane," Jack said wearily. "This isn't who you want to be."

The words might as well have been an arrow straight to my own conscience. I'd made the wrong choice. I should have been the one to tell Jack what had happened in the Honey Shoppe.

There was a painful beat of silence. "I know," Dane finally said, sounding defeated. "But Jack... What am I supposed to do?"

"What you do for any other assault, Deputy," Jack said flatly. "Report it."

Dane's voice was raw, young. "He's my only family left."

The words hooked something deep inside me. Sometimes I couldn't chase away the panicky feeling that I was all alone in the world, that the heart of my family, my *only* family, had walked away from me without so much as a glance back.

The monster pulsed inside my chest. *"You have me."*

When a shadow fell over me, I squinted through the slats, trying to get a better look at the men on the dock. The rustle of fabric and clasping skin made it sound as though Jack had drawn Dane into an embrace. "You have us."

Dane let out a shaky, humorless laugh. "You shouldn't have to deal with this shit anymore," he said, his voice rough with emotion. "You've done so much for us already."

Under the water, a fish brushed my calf as it swam by. The slimy touch sent an unpleasant current of feeling up my leg before my deadly touch sucked the life from the creature.

"I don't know what to do with him, Jack."

"Yes, you do."

Eva's grip on my hand was starting to hurt. She had her eyes fixed on one of the dock floats, and I watched a tear slip down her cheek.

Jack's voice was firm. "Show him how to be a better man."

After Jack and Dane retreated, Eva and I hurried out from under the dock and quickly dressed, eyes on the trail they had taken. I lifted my Minolta from the dock and slung the strap over my shoulder. Had Jack, on seeing the camera and our discarded clothing, put two and two together? My stomach twisted at the thought. I wasn't sure I would've survived his discovery of his daughter and me under the dock in nothing but our skin.

"Are you okay?" I asked Eva.

"No."

I took a breath. "Did you tell Izzy?"

Eva stiffened, then slowly shook her head.

I could have left it there. But something was gnawing at me. I swallowed. "Maybe we should have."

Eva whipped around to face me. "What?"

"You have to be safe, Ev. That matters more."

"I can take care of myself."

"Can you?" I whispered.

Her eyes flashed, and she turned from me and stomped away.

Every step up to the house was a weight. When I caught sight of Eva's silhouette in the greenhouse, I angled toward it.

"No," the monster said. *"Give her a moment."*

"I just —"

"A moment, little death-touch."

Dejected, I stuck my hands in my pockets and passed the greenhouse over, leaving Eva to fume. When Hyssop saw me from where she was playing in the yard, she made a dash for the bushes.

I slipped inside and toed off my shoes in the mudroom.

"Arthur?" Jack's heavy steps made the floorboards creak as he peered down the hall.

I stiffened and tried to smooth my features. "Yes, sir?"

"We need to talk." Jack's low-drawn brows did nothing to reassure me as he nodded for me to follow him.

Shit.

I hesitated in the doorframe to the kitchen. The fixings for tea were out, splayed across the countertop. The kettle, the jars full of multicolored petals. Honey, gleaming in the light. I didn't know what it was about their honey I found so alluring, but my mouth watered at the sight.

Jack sat on the edge of a chair, frowning. "Take a seat."

I sat stiffly, my camera banging against my thigh. Jack's eyes dropped to it.

He'd seen our things at the pond, hadn't he? He'd seen our things, and now he was deciding how slowly I should die.

He passed me a cup of tea. "You've been spending a lot of time with Eva this summer."

I choked on the scalding liquid. "Y-yes, sir."

"Hmm."

So, this was how it ended. Over tea.

"Maybe he won't mind that you were... you know."

My neck burned. Maybe Jack did care for me, a little, but that didn't mean he'd let me stay if he knew I was sneaking around with his daughter. Why had I risked *everything*?

There was more on the line than a crush or a kiss. This place was a home. As long as the Moreaus let me borrow it, I could pretend to belong here, just as starlings did whenever they found a suitable nest. The Moreaus had burrowed through my defenses and shown me what a family could look like. I didn't ever want to give that up. I wanted to be here, on the farm. I wanted to feel, even for a summer, like I belonged somewhere good.

"I'm glad she has you," Jack said, and I blinked, surprised. "It's hard for a girl like her to grow up in a town this small."

I nodded cautiously, still waiting for my lecture.

Jack reached for a shoebox in the middle of the table and handed it to me. "I was saving these for you," he said. "For Dane and June's wedding."

I blinked in confusion, then gingerly lifted the lid. Inside, I found a pair of men's dress shoes exactly my size. They glistened, unscuffed. Perfect and new.

"There's something else." Jack fished a slip of paper from his front pocket. He looked strangely nervous.

What was going on? Why wasn't he yelling at me?

Jack set the paper on the tabletop. "I wasn't sure when to give you this."

My stomach did a little flip when I recognized my mother's handwriting, and I snatched it off the table.

"You can stay, if you want. You're always welcome here." Jack shifted in his chair. "I just want you to know that you have a choice."

I stared at the phone number scrawled on the wrinkled page, the careless loops of a name written in the bottom corner.

Lottie.

My throat got very tight, and I was taken back to the day she left. She'd written something down for Jack. Had he known how to reach her this whole time?

With one hand, I closed a fist around the paper and held it to my chest. With the other, my fingers beat a rapid rhythm against my thigh.

"Excuse me," I rasped, shoving to my feet.

"Arthur, wait."

I couldn't look at him right now. I didn't turn around, and in my frantic state I nearly barreled into Izzy as she turned a corner.

"Whoa!" she cried out in surprise.

The monster yanked me sideways, our shoulder slamming into one of the golden picture frames. Adrenaline beat heavy in my chest, flooding my body with panic.

But Izzy only laughed. "Sorry, Fairy."

When I realized what she was holding, my horror dissipated, replaced by hot embarrassment. Izzy extended a box of condoms with the cool arch of a brow, her quicksilver grin laced with danger. "Don't hurt my sister," she chirped politely, "or I'll peel your skin off from nail to armpit."

I blanched. "I...We're not—"

"Very subtle," Izzy finished firmly.

Heat crawled up my neck, but I accepted the box and ducked past her into the old sewing room. Then, slowly, I unclenched my fingers from around the crumpled paper. My chest hurt from too much swallowed feeling.

"Well?" the monster prodded me. *"Are you going to call?"*

"I don't know." Saying even that aloud felt like a betrayal. It should be easy, obvious. *Yes,* of course I was going to call. That's what I'd wanted all summer long. My home was a person. My home was her.

The monster turned our neck to look out the window, where a sea of coneflowers rippled across the hill leading down to the hive boxes. *"Or maybe,"* it hedged, *"home is here."*

Chapter 31

Eva

Arthur stared at the satellite phone in his hand, visibly distraught. "Hey. It's all right. We'll find a better spot for a signal," Eva said, touching the inside of his elbow and coaxing his attention back to her.

But the tension in Arthur didn't release. "You don't understand. He's not well, and I... I have to protect him."

She frowned. "What are you talking about?"

For a moment, Arthur didn't say anything, squeezing the phone in his grip as he took in a slow, steadying breath. "Nothing." He turned to her and nodded to the canteen and tablets in her hand. "Let's go down to the water."

The rain had given the vivid blue Lotties surrounding them quite a battering, knocking some of the petals loose. At the meadow's edge, Eva stopped and carefully bent over, plucking a clean, bright stem that had snapped at the base. She popped the whole thing into her mouth.

Arthur's eyebrows shot up.

"What?" she said. "It's the same flower as our tea, isn't it? I'm curious if it will help."

His expression shifted to intrigue. "How does it taste?"

Eva considered, tonguing a silken petal against the roof of her mouth. "Vegetal."

Arthur snorted a laugh.

Her ankle throbbed the whole way down the hill, the two of them retracing their steps back to the water. No doubt Izzy would caw after Eva to elevate her foot, and Eva would, after she let the cold river numb it up.

As they walked, she considered their options. There weren't many. The most pressing priority, of course, was to reconnect the satellite phone, but Eva was starving, and so thirsty her throat felt scraped raw. So, water first.

Arthur noticed her struggling to keep pace, and offered to let her lean on him again. They hobbled through the woods, he in her father's old boots and Eva in her still-damp tennis shoes.

When they reached the river, Eva sank onto the lip at the water's edge with a relieved sigh. Slowly, after removing her shoe, she eased her bare foot into the flow and winced. The pressure of the quickly rushing water hurt the sprain, but if she angled it just right, the cool temperature also provided relief. Soon her skin went slightly numb. It would hurt like hell when she had to stand and the blood rushed back down, but for now she would take the temporary relief.

"Toss me the canteen?"

Arthur did her one better, kneeling by the water's edge and filling the canteen nearly to the top. Eva dropped a water-purifying tablet in, her eyes sliding down his forearm. Heat flamed across her chest as she thought of how those same hands had sculpted so reverently over her curves. She looked up. Arthur's hazel eyes were even more brilliant in the sunlight, and the unspoken *something* between them glowed a little brighter as he screwed the lid to the canteen back on, meeting her gaze with a smile.

Goose bumps rose on her arms. Eva blamed the river's chill, and she turned from his steady gaze, leaning down to scoop a bit of water onto the back of her neck. "We have to wait thirty minutes for it to take full effect, I think," she said.

"I could drink twelve canteens in thirty minutes."

While they waited, Eva watched Bug pounce on little creatures in the grass, her tension slowly fading away. The river had been a good idea. Occasionally the ice-cold waves splashed droplets against Eva's face, refreshing her. The rainstorm had made the whole forest glow, the world dyed its deepest and most vibrant shades, like jewels in a box.

She dipped a finger into the rushing water, her mind drawn back to the man stretched out on the grass behind her. The color of his infected skin was an alarming shade of strawberry. He spun the satellite phone between his fingers, watching the red light *flick, flick, flick.*

Eva plucked a stray blue Lottie from the ground and tossed it his way. "Try this."

She expected his refusal. Arthur didn't like using the flowers that way. But to her surprise, he not only accepted the bloom but, like her, popped it straight into his mouth. His nose wrinkled.

"Your dad's tea is better." That startled a laugh out of her, and after a moment, Arthur's expression turned rueful. "What?"

"Nothing. You just...seem different."

She felt different too.

Something fundamental had changed between them, and not just because of what they'd done in the shed. After so many years of buried feelings, perhaps such a release was needed. Inevitable, even.

When a honeybee landed on Eva's knuckles, she smiled.

Wait.

Eva's eyes widened at the sight of more bees flying overhead. It wasn't unusual. She always had a few nearby, no matter where she went. They had likely sought out shelter during the storm and were now making their way back to their hives.

She drew in a breath.

"Eva," Arthur said slowly, staring at her hand. "Is that...?"

Like a bolt of lightning, the realization sent a shock straight through her. Eva launched upright, causing the bee to take flight with a startled buzz. "Wild hives!" she exclaimed. "They must be nearby!"

She couldn't believe she hadn't thought of it before.

Long before her ancestors had dipped their toes into beekeeping, these meadows — the whole mountain, the whole world — had flourished under the hand of nature herself. It was the natural state of things to survive, regardless of human interference. Sometimes in spite of it.

Another honeybee landed on the tip of her nose, making Eva laugh. She should have thought of this the moment she and Arthur found the hive boxes empty, but her grief had overwhelmed her judgment. She'd forgotten what her father had taught her, that where there is life, there are always bees.

When the bee on her nose took flight, Eva grabbed her walking stick in one arm, tucking Bug under the other as she hobbled after it.

Arthur followed close behind as the bees led them deeper into the belly of the woods, the meadow and river shrinking behind them. Eva knew they were close when the droning hive grew louder, and she held her breath as she approached a large, fallen chestnut and caught sight of tunnels of golden honeycomb constructed in its hollow.

There was a scar bisecting the trunk, the bark long split and overgrown with moss. The death of the great giant had given way to new life in all its forms. The never-ending cycle of death and rebirth had always been one of Eva's favorite things about the forest. She'd tried to show that to Arthur. He thought what he could do was wrong, wicked even. But a fallen tree wasn't wicked. Neither was mulch, or the rotting fertilizer under the leaves that turned dead things into new possibilities.

Arthur was just like that.

"We did it." Arthur sounded stunned as he stepped toward the wild hive.

"Wait." Eva held out a hand, eyeing the bees carefully. Some honeybees could learn the faces of their keepers. That had served Eva and her family well. But these bees didn't know them. They might draw near in curiosity, but they wouldn't trust Eva, especially once she and Arthur took what they'd come for.

The forest floor beneath her was saturating into a more vibrant shade of green, her rush of excitement pulling the plants into germination. There was a large branch from the same snag lying in the grass nearby. Eva knelt before it, sending insects squiggling away as she pried off a bit of the outer bark to use as a makeshift scoop.

The buzzing intensified.

"I can do it," Arthur said.

She wanted to kiss him. "Don't be stupid," she said, putting a hand to his chest and pushing him slightly back. He already looked ready to topple.

Arthur caught her wrist. "But you — "

"Haven't been stung in years," Eva said brightly, though she had a feeling that was about to change. But she was also the quicker healer between them, and something about this moment felt like it belonged to her. She'd been the one to suggest they find the honey in the first place.

A vision of Dad flashed before her eyes as she neared the hive and crouched beside the beautiful, intricate design of comb work. "I won't take much," she promised. Then she carved the bark into the honeycomb. The bees frenzied immediately, and just as Eva had expected, one of them stung her on the arm, then a second, then a third. She cried out, shoving to her feet and stepping back, back, back, into the safety of the trees. Sticky honey slid into the gaps between her fingers, but a large chunk of honeycomb sat glued to the section of bark she'd used.

Arthur's hands came around her upper arms. "Let's go," he said roughly.

Eva could already feel her stung skin beginning to swell, the bee venom triggering a rush of heat and pain. Tears came to her eyes.

But it was worth it.

Arthur guided her away from the hive, looping one arm around her shoulders to help Eva keep her weight off her foot. When she thought of Dad, her heart swelled. They'd done it. She couldn't believe it!

What are you doing?

Eva gasped and dropped the honeycomb. Lotties burst through the soil at her feet, startled into life with the force of Eva's surprise.

"Who's there?" Arthur demanded. He snatched the honeycomb off the ground.

The voice sighed, a hollow sadness spilling through the breeze around them. As Eva watched, the trees before them twisted their branches with a sharp, unnatural crack. It wasn't a gentle transformation but a brutal uprooting of parts. The aspens groaned as the branches reshaped into a nearly human form, fluttering leaves flattening themselves against the pale bark in an eldritch mockery of skin.

The figure cocked her head to one side. *You don't recognize me.*

Eva couldn't tell if there was a question in those words or not. "Who are you?" she asked, unable to keep the shake out of her voice.

We've met before, beekeeper. A slash opened where a mouth might have been had she been flesh instead of forest. The strange, almost Cheshire smile sent a bone-chilling shiver down Eva's back. *Or do you not remember?*

Eva's pulse raced. When she'd seen this creature at the edge of the river, she'd brushed it aside as a trick of the mind. Now she faltered.

I suppose it has been years.

Arthur stepped forward, taking Eva's hand in his as he put his body between her and the possibility of danger.

The figure seethed. *Creature of want. You think I don't see you behind his eyes?*

Arthur tightened his grip. "You," he said, disbelieving. His voice cracked. "How are you here?"

I belong to this wood. Now get out.

"I don't understand," Eva said.

I said GET OUT! A root snaked up from the soil and slithered toward her. Eva yelped and jumped back, landing too hard on her sprain. She let out a cry as a shock of pain shot up her leg.

Arthur ripped the root from the ground. It shriveled at his touch, slumping into a deadweight on the soil. Eva's gaze snapped back to the figure, expecting her to be affected.

But the figure didn't so much as flinch. I am the spirit of this wood, devil. Your tricks can't unmake me.

"I'm no devil," Arthur growled, sounding suddenly like a different person entirely. When Eva tugged on his arm, Arthur shucked her off.

This isn't what he wants.

"You don't know what Arthur wants," he snapped. "You know only the surface of a sea, but he is my entire ocean."

My son is —

"Not yours," Arthur spat. "Not anymore."

My son? Eva's heart beat faster as the words rolled through her mind. "Arthur?" she asked as she looked between him and the rustling creature. "Who is she?"

The instant the question dropped off her tongue, Eva knew. There was only one person who made Arthur feel the way he looked now. Small. Broken.

Eva sucked in a tight breath.

Lottie.

He broke his promise to me. He promised to scatter my ashes and tell the bees I was gone. The sound of the spirit's sorrow hurt, reaching into Eva's very skull.

Eva had met Charlotte Connoway only once, when she'd dropped Arthur off on their doorstep. That day was still so clear in her mind. Eva could still see Arthur exactly as he'd been when he'd thrown open the door to her greenhouse and shoved a box of tools into her hands, when he'd told her he was *no one*.

She'd made that moment a flashbulb memory, all the other details fading into the background. Over time, Charlotte had become less and less a real person to her, and more the memory of an obstacle. She was a thorn. She was an irritant.

She was a ghost.

"We were going to scatter your ashes," Eva said quickly, fear budding inside her as she pulled on Arthur's hand, tugging him back. But where could they go? "We were just... interrupted."

Lottie Connoway's spirit turned her strange, arborous face to the sky with a crackle of branches. She let out a wail.

The suffering didn't seem to move Arthur, his expression cold. "Why do you care?" he snarled. "Just let the boy go. Be done with this world." He was vicious with her, more than Eva had ever seen. At that moment, he hardly felt like her Arthur at all.

The leaves around the spirit's mouth curled back into a grimace. I need the bees. The echo of her voice swirled around Eva on the breeze, knitting into her hair and reaching deep into her chest.

There was pain in that reply, but an ugly part of Eva didn't want to hear it. She didn't want to see a softer side to the woman who'd so deeply neglected her best friend. Even when Eva and Arthur weren't speaking, resentment had fueled Eva's bitterness toward Lottie.

But bitterness, like fuel, burned out.

"Enough." Arthur turned, pressing the honeycomb to his chest so the viscous golden liquid seeped into his shirt. "Come on, Eva."

A feather of doubt touched the back of her mind.

He never called her *Eva*.

The figure called after them, as though she could see Eva's thoughts laid bare. Don't be fooled into seeing a man, beekeeper! Her voice sounded more inhuman in her agitation. He is something worse.

"Don't listen to her," Arthur snapped. Eva leaned against him for support as he led her away. She looked back, expecting the spirit to follow them, but the trees were already twisting back into place.

Her heart beat hard in her chest. Something was wrong with this forest.

"Damn woman can't just leave him alone," Arthur muttered.

Eva dug her nails into his side and looked up. From this angle, she could make out only the hard cut of Arthur's jaw.

Something was wrong with him too.

Chapter 32

Arthur, Before

Audrey was a petri dish for gossip.

The week before the Walker wedding, the whispers reached the shelves of the Honey Shoppe. I was in the back when a trio of girls I'd never met tucked themselves into a corner to sample our new ginger-infused honey. When they mentioned the Walkers, my ears perked up.

"Did you hear that Dane kicked Lenny out of their house?" the first asked, dipping her sample stick into the jar and swirling generously.

One of her companions gasped. "Really?"

"Long overdue, if you ask me," the third snorted.

"But why?"

The first girl shrugged. "Something about the girl he was seeing, I guess."

When the second girl dipped her actual finger into the honey jar, I decided I hated her a little.

The third member of their group flicked her friend's wrist. "Seriously, Mai, were you born in a barn? Use a toothpick." Then her voice dropped lower, forcing me to strain to hear. "I heard Lenny's not allowed at the wedding."

I'd been running a rag over the inside of a newly washed honey jar for at least a minute. At her words, I quietly set it back on the shelf.

I should have been relieved. Instead, Lenny's absence had made me nervous.

Where was he?

That had been nearly a week ago. Since then, Jack had somehow scrounged up a pair of slacks my size, to match his gift of shoes. As I waited for the girls to finish getting ready, I examined my reflection in the hallway mirror. It felt strange to be so dressed up, like a reptile molting its skin.

"I think you look good," the monster said.

I wasn't sure. The shirt hung a bit long, maybe? I ran my hands over the starched cotton.

"It suits you."

I whirled and found Eva leaning against the wall. At the sight of her, my heart damn near stopped. She wore a sage-green dress that came in at the waist and swished around her ankles. Embroidered flowers decorated the edges and sleeves, making her appear like spring itself.

"What?" Eva touched the low dip of her neckline. "Too much?"

"No!" I stepped toward her. "You look incredible, Ev."

Pink tinged her cheeks. "Thank you," she said softly, then she turned. "Will you zip me up?"

Goose bumps pebbled her skin as I slid the zipper, lingering at the top to brush a knuckle over the curve of her spine. After, Eva led me to the bathroom and wet a comb, attempting to smooth my hair into place. "You need a tie?" she asked. "Dad's got a whole drawer."

When I shook my head, Eva opened the top button and brushed the skin of my throat with her fingertips. It was gentle, and intimate, and I warmed at the sudden feeling of belonging.

But when she left to fetch a water bottle, my thoughts moved to the folded paper in my pocket. I hadn't called the number yet, but I couldn't stifle the budding fear that my time here was draining away like sand down an hourglass, whether I liked it or not.

The church itself was cold and drafty, the pews sardine-pressed with congregants in their finest hats and brightest shoes. I knew the instant I stepped inside that I'd made a mistake. With Eva's help, I'd made progress controlling the death-touch, yes, but I didn't want to test its limits. Especially not here.

Anxiety climbed my ribs as we slid into the back pew, the monster's awareness tuning my senses to the delicate heartbeats filling the crowded room. It would take so little to hurt them. Just one slip. One accident.

One touch.

They kept the ceremony short and sweet. Despite his best man's absence — or maybe because of it — Dane Walker looked more relaxed than I'd ever seen him. After "I do," his new bride squealed and jumped into his arms. The room stirred. Smiles, rouged cheeks, and rose petals painted the whitewashed chapel every shade of blush. I retreated to a shadowy corner with no one nearby, save a spider weaving its silk. I fiddled with a loose button on my cuff, giving curious passersby a polite, strained smile.

Jack found me and casually angled himself so anyone sliding down the side rows grazed him instead. Embarrassment and gratitude heated my face in equal measure. He had a way of noticing when I felt anxious.

Izzy was the last to go, dragging her sister behind her. Eva tossed me an exasperated smile. I matched it, but when the door slammed behind them, I accidentally popped the button off its cuff.

"*Breathe,*" the monster soothed. "*It's going to be fine.*"

Jack had cut himself shaving. I could see the line of red-green blood smeared over his jaw. "You all right?" he asked.

When I nodded, we made for the exit door and Jack shouldered it open.

"Wait..."

He paused. "Yes?"

We'd hardly spoken all week. I wasn't sure if he, or I, was avoiding this topic, but I had to know. "Have you really had a way to reach her, all this time?"

Jack took a deep breath. "Arthur—"

"Sorry," I said automatically. But I wasn't. I was confused, and hurt, though I didn't want to be. "I know you didn't ask for this." For me, here all summer. Heat rolled up my face, and my throat constricted. I just wanted to know why. Why he'd kept me here when he could have called her to come back for me.

"Listen." Jack's voice grew heavy. "My history with your mother is complicated. Maybe I should have told you sooner. You deserve that. But..." Here he faltered. "I'm also not sorry I waited."

"You're not?"

"Of course not." Jack stepped toward me and bucketed my shoulder with a giant hand, careful to touch only the fabric of my shirt. "We want you here, Arthur."

My throat ached with sudden feeling.

"You don't have to prove yourself." Jack smiled. "You can take up space."

Then he slipped out into the roar of festivities, and I was left with nothing but starlings in the rafters and a button clenched in my fist.

The reception went deep into the night, strings of fairy lights illuminating the clearing. Izzy seemed to gain more stamina with every new song, dragging her girlfriend, Priya Dawson, onto the dance floor and looping her arms around the shorter woman's neck.

Priya and June were cousins, I'd learned. They had the same dark eyes, the same warm brown skin with a shock of sleek dark hair. I would have thought them sisters.

Eva and I sat apart on a hay bale, sipping apple cider the Walkers had ordered all the way from some specialty cider mill in Michigan.

I'd caught more than one side-eye thrown in Eva's direction today, whispers passed about her possible connection to Lenny's disappearance. She'd kept her head high, but after one too many pointed fingers, I decided I couldn't take it anymore, so I popped to my feet and extended a hand.

"Dance with me?"

Eva's eyes dashed to the swollen crowd, surprised. "We can't."

"Sure we can."

I led her to where the shadows grew thick against the chapel's eastern wall, then caught her by the waist and swung her in a circle. Eva squealed, clinging tightly to me. When we slowed, her nails drew over my scalp, sending shivers down my spine.

She'd braided her hair half up and secured it with a dark green bow at the back of her head. I delicately tugged on the ribbon's end, careful not to pull too hard, as the band crooned a warm acoustic cover of the classic song "My Girl." Eva played with the empty place on my cuff where the button had broken free, her clean, earthy scent invading my senses.

"Come on." When the song ended, she dragged me to the front steps of the chapel. The door creaked when she pushed it in and poked her head inside.

"What are you doing?" I asked, bemused.

Eva pulled me in after her. "Kissing you, of course." She smoothed her palms up my chest and walked me back against a wall.

"*She likes this shirt,*" the monster noted. "*We're wearing it every day.*"

When Eva tugged my lip between her teeth, I let out a ragged breath. I couldn't get enough of her. I felt hungry all the time, but nothing satiated me like she did. Friction charged the space between us with desire. She could banish my darkness forever — I knew it. Her touch sanctified ordinary places. The greenhouse. The attic. The pantry. The pond. All christened with our stolen moments.

The landmarks on my skin had changed too. My scars no longer felt like accusations.

"Stay in Audrey," Eva murmured.

"What?" I asked.

"I know what you have in your pocket, Arthur." She bit her lip.

"Don't call her." Bewildered, I pulled back, but Eva took my face in her hands. "Stay here. With me."

"I..." I tried to say that I couldn't. I tried to explain this feeling in my chest that maybe I shouldn't. Maybe I needed to leave so I could come back, like a migrating bird sure of its place. "I don't want to leave you, bee girl."

That was an easier truth.

A mischievous grin spread across her cheeks. "Good." Then she was pulling me toward the pews. "Now come on."

I scanned the sanctuary. "Isn't this a bit irreverent?"

Eva shrugged. "I figure God's seen it all by now."

I wouldn't know. I'd never understood the concept of churches in the first place. It seemed a little strange to seek the divine indoors when the wilderness was practically bursting with it. I'd found God among the trees, where the sun touched my skin and the warblers sang.

A sudden flutter of wings drew our attention to the rafters, where a nest of oil-slick starlings flitted. "I'm surprised the pastor was able to focus with all that," Eva said.

"Don't talk birds to me, bee girl, or we'll never leave this room."

She laughed and pulled me down. I slipped a hand beneath the soft layers of her skirt and cupped a hand around the back of her thigh.

I loved her thighs.

When I took her mouth in a kiss, Eva made a satisfied sound. She tilted her head back to expose more of her skin to me, tugging her neckline down. Her neck tasted like salt, like *need*. I melted as I kissed my way down her jaw and collarbone. No one had ever needed me before.

Eva hooked her finger in my belt loop, her eyes a question in blue. I nodded, and she slid the buckle open. The graze of her fingers made me groan. "Way better than dancing," I husked.

Just then, the door behind us gave a whine. At first we froze, before jumping apart a moment later, scrambling to put our clothing to rights. "I thought you locked the door!" I whispered.

"I thought I did!"

A shadowed figure staggered inside, a flask dangling from his fingers. "Thought I saw you come in here," Lenny Walker slurred. Even in the shadows of the small chapel, it took him only a second to locate us. Startled. Wrecked. Lips puffy and clothes askew. Lenny sucked in a breath and stumbled forward a few steps. "You," he growled. "You let this piece of shit *touch* you?"

I stiffened.

"What gives him the right—" Lenny stumbled and had to catch his balance on the backrest of a nearby pew. I moved to stand between him and Eva. Lenny cut me a hard glare.

"Fuck off," I growled.

"I've been waiting"—Lenny smashed the flask on the wooden floorboards, and the sound made me flinch—"long enough."

Then he lunged forward.

"To your left."

I shifted obediently, pushing Eva to the side. *He won't get near her.* Lenny tripped over his own shoes and fell, feet upended, over a pew.

Eva tugged at my sleeve. "Let's just go."

No.

Adrenaline pumped inside me, and I clenched and opened my hands. Where were my gloves when I needed them?

"Arthur," Eva pleaded.

Lenny popped to his feet. "She's mine," he snarled.

The monster rushed forward, filling my hollows. I didn't remember choosing to lunge forward; I registered Eva's shout only when my shoulder slammed into Lenny. We hit the ground hard, knocking over a stack of hymnals.

Eva's shout found me in a sea of red feelings. Despite the monster's grip on me, her presence and fear pulled me back to the surface, where I gasped. *My gloves. I need my gloves!* The monster and I had shared space in moments of crisis before, but never like this, where I was nothing but a husk to its flame.

Pink spittle dribbled from Lenny's mouth. He spat out a tooth, and my thoughts slipped like sand through my fingers.

"That all you got, Connoway?"

This time, Lenny found skin, digging his nails into my cheek. Pain sliced through me where he scraped back flesh, followed by quick relief as a whisper of life stole out of him and into me. It took only an instant for my death-touch to start draining the life out of a person.

But an instant wasn't enough to kill.

The monster snapped our arm forward and shackled a hand around Lenny's throat, curving our lips into a smile.

The chapel door slammed open. I didn't care. I didn't look. Lenny clawed at my hands. My fingers bled, but the monster squeezed our grip tighter.

"Arthur, stop!" Eva pleaded.

I didn't. I tried, but my control over the death-touch weighed nothing against the monster's hate. A heavy cold bloomed inside my chest, spreading quickly down my limbs as the monster surged into every part of me. It wanted to take and take and take.

Someone shouted behind me, someone I knew. Lenny's stare blackened. He whipped something out of his pocket and slashed...

Silver flashed.

I let go, pain rearing through my arm and yanking me out of

the monster's icy grip. Eva screamed. Green vines rushed through my periphery, and a figure shoved between Lenny and me.

A slick and horrible squelch filled my ears as something dark and wet sprayed the chapel's plaster walls. It speckled my skin too. I smelled summer. I smelled iron. The world thinned to a ringing in my ears, and I blinked fast, trying and failing to process the scene before me. None of it made sense. A blanket of moss and wildflowers, spread over the pews. Lenny Walker, dry-heaving the contents of his stomach. Eva, my Eva, sobbing.

The real horror, however, was Dane Walker. He lay face up on the hardwood, eyes fixed on the rafter starlings, a bloodied vine impaling his chest.

Chapter 33

Isobel

The hospital waiting area was a quiet place, with nowhere near enough distractions. Every breath stung Isobel's nose with the sharp scent of hand sanitizer. She hung on to the steady sound of someone's heart monitor beeping down the hall as she bounced her knee, glancing up from her shoes to where the Dawson family was gathered, waiting for Avi to finish giving Dane his official statement.

Isobel couldn't stop seeing Avi's face. Whenever she closed her eyes, she saw the blood smeared down his cheek and pictured the flowers growing out of his empty eye socket as though he were already gone and ready for rotting, a corpse not yet decomposed.

But he wasn't a corpse. Whatever had happened up that trail, Avi had survived to tell it. Any minute, Dane would walk out of Avi's hospital room with answers that would finally calm her beating heart.

Isobel unscrewed the cap of the bottle between her knees and sucked down the last quarter cup until the plastic crackled. Her hangover migraine had thankfully downshifted into a dull throbbing behind her eyes. She was angry at herself for slipping at all.

Shame never did her any good — she knew that — but it was hard to resist giving in to its pull.

She would focus on what she could control. Tomorrow, she would attend the hospital's biweekly AA meeting. That was a step she could manage.

Her eyes lifted to the Dawson family again. Even June had come to support Priya, though June tellingly hadn't said a word to Isobel all night.

As though drawn by a magnet, her former best friend lifted her gaze from where Esther scribbled in a unicorn coloring book on the floor. June's expression stilled when it met Isobel's, instantly becoming more guarded.

For a moment, the pair of them simply stared at each other. Years ago, they would have been pressed tight, as close to sisters as friends could get. Neither would have let the other wait in a hospital room alone.

The hollow in Isobel's chest grew a little wider.

Across the hall, Avi's door clicked open, and Dane stepped out. The family leapt into motion, crossing the hall to replace him at Avi's side, a cluster of Mylar balloons trailing behind them.

Esther abandoned her crayons on the floor, leaving June to sweep them back into their canvas pouch while her daughter rushed to her dad. Dane picked Esther up and squeezed her tight, landing a kiss on her stickered cheek. "You good to keep her a little longer?" he asked June, who nodded, glancing back to where Isobel sat frozen.

"Yeah, I got her."

When the door closed behind the last of the Dawson clan, Dane sank hard into a chair next to Isobel, rubbing his face in his hands. He wore exhaustion like a coat.

"What did Avi say?" Isobel hadn't meant to jump on the question so fast, but she was practically vibrating with anxiety, the nerves running a current of stress down every one of her limbs. "Did he know where Lenny was going?"

He shook his head, not even bothering to look up. "They were following her trail," he muttered.

The trail of wildflowers.

"What happened?" Isobel pressed, laying a hand to the center of Dane's back as she forced her words to slow, to meet him where he was. Dane was grieving too, his brother's involvement its own kind of loss.

"They were attacked by something inhuman," he said slowly.

A chill skated down Isobel's spine. "What do you mean?"

"I don't know." Dane's lungs expanded beneath her touch as he turned his face. "Avi said it looked like a woman, but...wrong."

"I don't understand."

"Don't you?"

Something in his lowered tone made the hairs on Isobel's arms stand up.

"Do you remember the fight Lenny and I got into before the wedding?" A new weariness fell over Dane as the words rolled out. "After I learned what he did, or tried to do, to your sister, I reported him to the sheriff. Lenny got so angry with me. We fought, and I...I told him not to come to the wedding."

Isobel had forgotten about the tension between the two brothers in the days leading up to Dane's wedding.

"When I saw Lenny go into the chapel that night, I followed him. I wanted to believe he wouldn't hurt her."

"I know," Isobel said softly.

Dane squeezed his eyes shut and pressed his thumbs to his

eyelids in clear frustration. "I can still see her. So wild. Radiant and terrible... almost inhuman, the way she wielded the vines."

Isobel's heart tripped a beat, and she silently willed him to stop. *Don't say it.*

"What am I supposed to think, Isobel? Avi goes looking for Eva, and comes back with an unbelievable story and wounds no one in this damn hospital can explain!"

Isobel felt like a live wire, her panic sparking. "It wasn't her."

Dane searched her face with hungry eyes. "Tell me I'm crazy, then," he roughed out. "Tell me there isn't a glaring common thread in these stories." He glanced to the nurses' station and lowered his voice. "Tell me the missing puzzle piece isn't your sister."

Alarm beat a drum in her chest. He couldn't know this. She'd spent too many years covering Eva's tracks, afraid of what might happen if Dane Walker knew the truth about what had happened to him that night.

"You can't even say it," he breathed out.

"You're wrong."

"Am I?" Dane countered, growing more agitated. "Isobel, I woke up in this very hospital with a scar on my chest. No wound! I know you were there, and I know it was traumatic for you too. That's why I've let you dodge my questions. I thought it was too painful. I didn't want to make you relive it, because I love —" He broke off, but Isobel heard what he'd left unspoken.

I love you.

She swallowed hard. "You don't understand."

"Then help me understand!"

He looked worn and weathered by the weight of it all, and Isobel wanted to tell him, she did, but she was so afraid. If she told him the truth, it would be the end of them. He wouldn't forgive what she'd kept hidden all these years. She did love Dane Walker, but that love had been swallowed up time and time again by her choice to love Eva more, and to keep her secret.

"Don't I deserve to know the truth?" he asked her.

Before she could answer, a nurse wearing mint-green scrubs strode into the waiting area, lifting her gaze from her clipboard through a pair of tortoiseshell glasses. "Izzy Moreau?" she called out.

"Isobel," Dane quietly corrected.

"That's me." Isobel popped to her feet, her thoughts spinning. To her surprise, Dane stayed right at her side, jaw set in a stubborn scowl, his eyes pure steel.

"I'm coming with you."

After a moment, she gave him a sharp nod, and the two of them stepped into her father's room. Dr. Rosen swiveled to face them. The small, graying woman had a way of smiling with her eyes. She was the only doctor Isobel trusted with her father's care. Though many specialists had taken an interest in her father's sapling over the years, only Dr. Rosen seemed to care about his life outside the hospital. "Take a seat," she chirped. "I have good news."

The words took a minute to sink in as Isobel plopped into the chair nearest her father's hospital bed. Confusion stirred inside her. "Good news?" That certainly wasn't what she'd expected.

The doctor nodded and looked at Dad.

"I get to go home," he said, visibly stunned.

Isobel shook herself. "Wait, what?"

"Dr. Rosen says I am the picture of health."

The doctor clucked her tongue and shook her finger at him.

"Don't twist my words, Jack." She turned to Isobel. "I was just in the middle of telling your father that he's low enough on iron that I'd like to get him an infusion before he leaves and keep an eye on his blood work over the coming months."

Isobel blinked. "Is that... all?"

Her father reached to take her hand in his much larger one, squeezing slightly. The dry texture of his calluses was a familiar comfort to her, each rough place hardened into his skin by meaningful labor.

"What about the aspen?" Isobel's gaze landed on the stump still protruding from his sternum. Most of the branches were gone, but the base was still lodged inside him. They couldn't remove that without disrupting the complex network of roots and viscera in his chest cavity.

"It's remarkable," Dr. Rosen said. "I wouldn't have dared to follow such an aggressive course of treatment, snapping the branches off like that. The way the roots are webbed so near your heart and lungs, I would have thought such a shock too great a risk."

Dane had chosen a place by the door and stood with his arms crossed. "But?" he asked when Dr. Rosen paused.

"Given the circumstances, I'm very pleased with how well his body is adjusting to a new normal," Dr. Rosen said. "We knew that without intervention, the roots would reach his heart eventually, and that's still a possibility, so I want you in here every week, Jack." She turned a stern gaze on him. "No skipping appointments, you hear?"

Her father nodded. "All right."

"I'd also like to set up a meeting with our new occupational therapist to help you adjust to any changes."

"But he's going to be okay?" Isobel cut in, a wash of disbelief surging through her.

Dr. Rosen's crow's feet crinkled in a kindly smile. "He's going to be different from before. But different can be good. You're very lucky. Whatever halted the sapling's growth may have just saved your life."

Saved his life?

Isobel's body warmed in a flash of understanding, and she was suddenly glad to be sitting as a wave of dizziness passed over her.

Arthur had done this.

"Dr. Rosen, may we have a moment?" Dane asked. Despite the calm words, Isobel sensed the urgent current running beneath them. And just like that, all the unease she'd felt before they stepped into the room rushed back in.

"Of course."

The moment the doctor exited the room, Dane moved toward the hospital bed. "Jack," he said, and Isobel, sensing what was coming, did the only thing she could think of.

"Dane, wait." Her voice broke as she looked between the two men who meant the most to her, both of them preserved by a miracle. Both of them forever changed.

Dane was right.

Isobel met her father's gaze. They'd spent so long not talking about this, keeping their promise to conceal the truth so far that it had gone unacknowledged even between the two of them, for years. "He deserves to know," she said softly.

For a long moment, Dad didn't say anything, the beeping on his monitor the only sound in the room. Then he turned to where the sheriff was watching the two of them with the wariness of a cornered animal. "The tea I gave you to ease your chest pain," he murmured. "I never told you where it came from."

Isobel flashed to the jar of blue petals she'd found in the glove box of Dane's patrol car.

The blue tea had become a permanent fixture in her surroundings over the years, a jar always set in a place of honor in their pantry. How many times had she curled up beside her father and sister and a cup of that very tea while Dad regaled them with some new and tragic folktale about a honeyman whose venture into a magical world always seemed to end in tragedy?

"We call them Little Lotties. They only grow in the meadow I spoke of earlier."

Dane let out a breath and put a hand flat on the rolling tray beside the bed. "What does that have to do with me?"

Everything.

"When dried, they are not so different from any other herbal remedy, if a bit more impactful. But concentrated into honey, they give a person power over life itself."

Isobel cleared her throat. "There was an accident that night in the chapel," she said. "When you went in after your brother, you tried to break up a fight between him and Arthur. And you were..." She trailed off, unable to even say it.

"Hurt?" Dane finished.

"Killed," her father corrected.

Dane's attention snapped back to him, all the blood draining from his face. "What?"

"I'd only ever used the life-giving power for home remedies. To grow medicinal plants. To cultivate my garden. To expand the fields behind our house. There was always a cost, but I didn't mind the changes, at first." Dad set a hand to the base of the trunk in his chest. "Nature makes no distinction between flesh and earth. The ground is simply another skin we carve into, our bodies a garden to sow and harvest from."

The words sent a chill down Isobel's spine.

"I didn't know if it would work," Dad said more softly. "But I... I had to try. If I didn't" — his voice cracked, thick with emotion — "then my daughter would've been a killer."

Dane's knuckles were white. "So, what? You gave me some of that...honey?"

Her father shook his head. "I didn't have any on me," he admitted. "All I had was the spoonful of honey from my tea that morning still running in my veins. And it was enough."

"Enough...?" Dane whispered, his throat bobbing.

"To bring you back," Isobel said.

She'd never forget that night for as long as she lived. It wasn't just the horror of it all. She'd been holding her dead friend, anguishing, when her father knelt and placed his hands on the wound.

When Dane had gasped awake, his cheeks flushing with new life, something in her had changed too. His rebirth had re-curved the path of her life forever.

"And..." Dane struggled through the question. "Your tree?"

"The aspen started growing that very night. A tithe, I'd guess, to balance what I'd done. I was lucky it didn't kill me," he said with a laugh. But Isobel didn't feel like laughing.

A knock sounded on the door, and a nurse poked her head in. "Sheriff?"

"What is it?" Dane clipped. Then he caught himself and stood. "Forgive me. I'm...very tired."

"No problem," the nurse deadpanned in a tone that suggested she was used to people's bad attitudes.

Dane cleared his throat. "What's going on?" he asked, moving on instinct to straighten a tie that wasn't there.

The nurse's gaze flicked from him to Isobel and her father.

"Emergency Services just contacted us about a satellite phone call from some injured hikers in the mountains," she said. "They need to talk to Jack Moreau."

Chapter 34

Arthur

If I had the capacity to scream myself out of the monster's prison, I would have already torn my throat to shreds. Instead, I watched as the beast in control of my body stomped away from the wild hive, the spirit's accusation spinning through me.

Could that really be my mother? Was that how she saw me?

Not as a man. *He is something worse.*

She'd clearly upset the monster, if the pounding rhythm of our heart was any indication. Though I couldn't hear the monster's thoughts anymore, our body spoke a language we both understood. Our lungs were working overtime, and tension made our already sore muscles even stiffer.

Even in my frozen state, this body was still mine. I knew how it panicked.

The monster had tucked Eva under its arm as it guided her away from the spirit of the wood. Now it hurried her through the trees, so impatient to get back to the meadow that it didn't seem to notice Eva's limp or labored breathing until she pulled away at the base of the hill.

"What was all that?" Eva demanded.

The monster didn't stop walking. *"The hell if I know."*

Anger stretched a hollow in my empty chest. It couldn't talk to her like that.

When the monster didn't offer more, Eva lumbered behind. "What did she mean," she puffed, "when she called you a devil?"

An emotion I didn't recognize from the monster swirled in my belly. *"I am no devil,"* it snapped at her.

"Well, obviously," Eva muttered. Near the top of the hill, she caught up and snagged us by the sleeve. "Hey," she said. I took in her eyes, bright and bloodshot. One of the bees had stung her neck, leaving it swollen and red. "Will you please just talk to me?"

"Don't feel like talking."

"Well, I don't care," Eva snapped back. "Because *that* wasn't normal, Arthur!"

The monster snorted. *"Since when are we normal?"*

Honeybees swirled in the air overhead, calmer now that we were back in the meadow. Maybe they hadn't belonged to the hive we'd stolen from, or maybe they'd realized the harvester wasn't someone to be feared.

"When we were in the pit, you said something. We were sinking and you...you said there was *something* inside you."

The monster's alarm spiked inside our shared body.

"I don't know what you mean."

Her irises were a study in vivid blues, searching my face. "You're lying to me."

Everything inside me stretched to the verge of pain as I tried and failed to move something, anything, to scream, to whisper, to *be* in my body again. But it was useless.

"You were scared," Eva said softly, stepping closer. "And it wasn't just because of the pit, was it?"

She was so clever, so close to the truth, and I trembled inside my prison of ice, regretting every opportunity I'd ever had to tell her about the monster where I'd stopped myself because of shame. If she'd only known, maybe she could have helped me. Why was that so easy to see *now*, when I could do nothing about it?

The monster's nervous laughter sounded more like a stranger's than it did like mine. *"Eva, I don't think—"*

"You never call me *Eva*," she cut in. "You call me *Ev*. You and no one else." Her voice cracked, the confession suddenly, painfully intimate. She stepped forward with a wince, leaning her weight on her walking stick. "Who are you?"

The monster balked. *"What?"*

"You're not my Arthur." Her brows knit together. "He was right. I do know him. And you... you are someone else."

My heart beat a solid *thump, thump, thump.*

Eva took my hand and flipped it palm up. "You keep tapping on the side of your leg," she said, her blue eyes studying my face. "He's still in there, isn't he?"

A shiver of warmth rolled through me, reaching past the monster's ice.

She saw.

It didn't matter that I was hidden away; the bee girl *saw* me, just as she always had.

The monster's disbelief filled every hollow where our wills entwined. It yanked my hand out of hers, an instant loss of summer heat. *"He's not your puzzle to solve, Eva."*

When the monster stepped back, Eva followed as well as she

could, leaning on her walking stick. Bug hopped along behind her, meowing. "He's not yours either," she snapped.

Am I not?

I didn't know where or to whom I belonged. For a long time, I'd been a tetherless creature, as unbound as the air that carried a flock of migrating birds overhead, craving the very roots that my mother had seemed to fear so desperately.

"*No.*" The monster's voice took on an edge. "*But I am his.*"

Eva's eyes blew wide.

"*And I am taking him home.*" The monster turned and stomped in the direction of the shed. Its resolve settled inside my chest, but whatever it was thinking, whatever it was planning, was lost to me. I couldn't see the details of its thoughts anymore. I could only feel the way its intent manifested in the body we shared.

Eva followed close behind. "You're running again?"

Those words cut to the bone. I wanted to tell her, *No, I am here! I want to stay!* But the monster ignored her, stomping up over the crest of the hill and back into the meadow. The flowers seemed almost too brilliant now, a sickening sway of sugary cereal held in the meadow's bowl.

There was something else different too. I couldn't put my finger on it as the monster stomped up to the door of the shed, Eva puffing in close pursuit. I hated that it could be so petty as to leave her behind when it knew she was hurt.

I was so consumed with my thoughts that I almost missed the moment the monster brought our body to a rough halt. We stared, shocked, at the shadowed form sitting on the cot in the shed.

He cut a figure like a knife, his presence instantly ringing alarm bells inside me. The man sat on the edge of the cot, legs spread, his forearms resting on his thighs. One hand hung loosely over his knees, holding a gun.

The monster's disbelief bled into my own.

"Lenny?"

Chapter 35

Arthur, Before

Eva knelt in a pool of Dane Walker's blood, sobbing as she begged him to keep breathing. But her touch made the vines in his body twist deeper.

"Ev, stop."

"I can help him!" Her eyes were shot with a terror I'd never seen.

Jack must have followed Dane in, because he was suddenly there, peeling his daughter's grip off the dying man. "Get her out of here," he commanded. The chapel's front door creaked and Izzy stepped in. "Lock the door!"

"What's going on?" Izzy looked alarmed.

Little sprouts pushed from Jack's scalp. He cornered me with a hard look, eyes green with wildness. "Go out the back," he said. "Take the truck. Get Eva far away from this."

"No!" Eva wept openly. "No, we can fix this." She turned to me, desperate. "You can fix it!"

My eyes popped wide. "What?"

"Y-y-you've been practicing," she blubbered. "You're getting better. You can help him!"

My stomach flipped. I'd been practicing how to slow down the effects of my death-touch on plants, not...this. I shook my head. "Ev, I..."

"You can fix it!" she snapped. "Kill the vine!"

My body snapped to obedience at her command, my heart pounding with adrenaline as I snatched up Dane Walker's hand. Instantly, my death-touch woke at my fingertips. As power surged inside me, dark and familiar, I closed my eyes and did as we'd practiced, forcing my breaths to slow, forcing myself to hold back the hungry thing inside me that wanted to *take*.

"Arthur," Jack roughed out, his voice unsteady. Beyond him, Lenny knelt in a pool of his own vomit, panting and clawing his throat where the monster's poison had seeped into his skin until it blistered and bubbled.

A whisper of doubt moved through me. But...no. This was different. *I* was different. The monster had wanted to hurt Lenny, but I was in charge now, and I could help Dane if I chose. There was more to me than death.

"Arthur," Jack spoke a little louder. He pushed to his feet. "Step back."

But I couldn't. Not yet.

Blood dribbled from Dane Walker's mouth as he stared at the starlings in the rafters.

"Little one," the monster cautioned, but I flung its voice aside and clasped the vine, begging it to stop. I could do this. I had to do this. The vine withered under my command, verdant green giving way to a hard, knotted brown.

That was it. Relief unfurled in my ribs. I could do this. I just had to isolate the power, to kill the vine and not the man.

"Arthur!" Jack bellowed, wrapping both arms around my stomach and hauling me away. "I told you to stop!"

I startled, a wave of unchecked power rolling down my arm and into the vine still clutched in my hand. Dane gasped, and his eyes rolled back into his head.

The whole room stilled, and I stared, uncomprehending, until Jack dropped me and my body crumpled onto the bloodstained floor.

No.

I snatched up Dane Walker's wrist, seeking the slug of a pulse. Instead, the glow of life inside him — warmer and brighter than any plant, bird, or mouse I'd ever stolen from before — slipped from his grasp and crashed into me. Iron coated my tongue at the sudden rush of life blooming in my bones.

It tasted divine.

"Fuck." Jack stripped off his shirt and pressed it to the wound in the younger man's chest. He checked Dane's pulse, as I had done, but it was too late.

No, no, no.

There was no denying the horrible truth in front of us. The empty glaze in his eyes. The preternatural stillness of a man made into an empty shell. Dane Walker was dead.

Because of me.

Outside, the sounds of merriment died down and someone shook the chapel door. "What's going on in there?" they called.

Jack yanked a set of keys from his pocket and hurled them at me. "Go. Now." He sounded scared, and that more than anything finally pulled me out of my haze. Jack was staring at Eva, and Eva was staring at the body on the floor. "Go to the house and wash up. Burn your clothes. They can't connect her back to this. Do you understand?" When I didn't answer, he barked my name. "Arthur!"

I jolted. "Yes." Took her hand. "Ev. Come on."

"I killed him." Her voice was the smallest and weakest I'd ever heard it.

I shook my head violently. "No." I had done that. Jack had told me to stop and I wouldn't — couldn't — stop. My throat went hard with grief. He'd been so angry, and now he wouldn't even meet my gaze.

Why hadn't I stopped?

Izzy stayed with her father. Their voices dropped to a hush as I half walked, half dragged Eva to the back of the church. A layer of moss coated the pews, and wildflowers bloomed in every crack and crevice. A storm of honeybees filled the room. They were all I could hear, the hitch in Eva's breath all I could feel. Every step she took, more flowers bloomed.

Rough-cut pieces of a life-size nativity set filled the storage room in the back of the chapel. I shivered with cold as I led Eva through the labyrinth of painted plywood figurines.

She looked down at herself. "I'm... bleeding?"

"No," I said. "You're okay."

Put like that, it felt like a lie.

Eva licked a fleck of red off the bow of her lip. More blood smeared her cheeks and nose. Alarm rose in me. I couldn't let her or anyone else see her like this.

The voices at the chapel doors grew louder, knocking more insistently. When I snuck a look back, I saw moss sneaking under the storage room door. We slipped out the back into the shadows. The remaining partygoers had congregated at the front of the chapel, clearing a path. I took her hand, and we ran across the now-abandoned dance floor, my heart racing. I tasted copper on my tongue.

What would happen when the crowd finally made their way inside and found Jack and Izzy covered in a dead man's blood? Would Jack lie for me and call it an accident?

And what story would Lenny tell?

When we got to the truck, I yanked open the passenger door. Eva scrambled to click in her seat belt, hands shaking. When a sob escaped her, she covered her mouth with bloodstained knuckles, smearing red over her lips.

I took her face in my shaking hands. Even now, every touch between us felt like a battle won. Scars replacing wounds. It didn't feel right to find relief in her, not now, but the relief came anyway. "We have to go." I planted a rough kiss on her temple, then slammed the door and ran to the driver's side.

We made it halfway to the cottage before Eva rolled down the window. "I think I'm going to be sick."

I shot her a look. "You want me to pull over?"

"No."

The instant the house came into view, however, Eva tapped my leg urgently. I pumped the brakes, and we screeched to a stop, leaving a cloud of dust in our wake. Eva burst from the truck and vomited on the side of the road.

I was out the door and at her side in a moment. Helplessness flooded through me when I settled a hand between Eva's shoulder blades and she burst into sobs.

"I'm sorry," she wailed.

As I crushed her against my chest, Jack's instructions filled my mind. We had to wash off the blood. Get rid of the dress. My shirt. My pants. "Let's go inside, okay?"

"Okay." A soft, childlike response.

I cupped the back of her head and forced a bit of calm into my voice. "All right, honey. Arms around my neck."

Eva pressed her nose into my shoulder as she cried. Once inside, I carried her to the bathroom with the claw-foot tub and set her gently on the rim of it. Eva looked a little dazed.

"She's going into shock."

The faucet shrieked when I turned it, water plonking on the porcelain.

"I killed him," Eva whispered again.

My heart twisted as I slid the zipper down her back, a reversal of my role earlier that day.

"I'm a monster," she said in anguish.

"Don't say that."

I could still feel the rush of the withering vines in my palms. I could still hear them crackle as summer turned to autumn in Dane's rib cage, the monster parching him of life. I could still feel the final beat of his heart.

Maybe she'd landed a blow, but *I* had been the killer here.

"You did him a mercy," the monster said. *"He wouldn't have survived that anyway."*

Its callous words stunned me to the core. I'd never hated the creature, and myself, as much as I did right then.

Even though I knew it was right.

I raced down the hallway and fetched some towels from the closet. When I returned, Eva had peeled off her ruined dress. She perched on the edge of the tub in nothing but her underwear, eyes blank, knuckles white. Sweat plastered a blond strand to her cheek.

I shuddered. There was blood in her hair.

"Breathe through it. You need to stay calm for her."

Resentment rushed through me. How could I do that? The dreamy afternoon had twisted the world into a nightmare, and all because it

we

lost control!

"I'll help you," the monster reassured me, pouring itself into the cracks of my resolve as it had when it took me over at the chapel. I shuddered.

No. I didn't want that.

Closing my eyes, I pictured the sky and begged the clouds to clear away. I wasn't the storm. I was the whole damn sky, and I would not be made to shrink.

With a mighty shove, I threw off the creature's hold, setting the towels on the toilet and wetting a clean rag in the sink. Bile swirled in my stomach as I blotted the streaks of blood off Eva's skin. Her eyes looked dull, and she swayed a little. I took her face in my hands and softly brushed her cheeks with my thumbs until she met my gaze.

I couldn't smile, but I could be here, and maybe that was enough.

Her swollen eyes tugged at my guilt. I shouldn't have gone after Lenny. I should have just left the chapel like she'd wanted and gone straight home. But even in my darkest moments, I'd never thought to fear *this*. Never this.

Never her.

Eva licked her lips. "Can I brush my teeth?"

I snatched her toothbrush off the counter. Eva used twice the amount of toothpaste needed as I ran a wet rag over the cut in my arm. Lenny's knife had grazed me, but adrenaline masked the pain, for now.

After she stood to spit her toothpaste into the sink, I handed Eva a cup of water. "Here. Drink this."

She drained it in one go.

"Let's clean you up." I turned off the tap and helped her step in, then dragged over a footstool. I sat beside the tub just behind her and, using the cup on the ledge, scooped water onto her skin until the blood sloughed away, turning the water pink.

This would've been so much easier if the cottage had a shower.

I pumped the shampoo bottle and worked it through her tangles as best as I could. The scent of coconut dispelled the taint of iron, but only just. Eva brought her knees to her chest, quiet sobs racking her body.

I wrapped my arms around her and let her cry until the tears ran out and Eva sagged against me.

"Let's rinse your hair, honey."

She nodded and sank below the surface, bubbles churning as she scrubbed the lather out. Water slapped against the porcelain as she climbed out of the tub, and I wrapped a towel around her, using a second one to scrunch her hair dry, as I'd seen her do.

After putting on pajamas, Eva crawled into bed, clearly exhausted. When she tried to pull me down onto the mattress with her, I resisted. "I'll be right back, bee girl."

I had to burn the clothes.

Careful not to get any blood on her sheets, I wadded up the towel and retreated to the parlor. There, I set the paper with my mother's number on the mantel and knelt by the fireplace. There was blood on my shirt. I could smell it, and I wanted it off.

Jack was right: We couldn't let anyone tie her back to what I had done. My hands shook as I arranged the kindling and struck a match. The monster steadied my movements.

Its presence in the body we shared revolted me. I didn't want to be this way. I didn't want its help! But I could no longer fight its invasion either.

I wasn't sure I even knew how.

Chapter 36

The Monster

The monster let out a huff of surprise when Eva collided with its back. Instinctively, it reached to block her from entering the shed. Under Lenny's glare, the monster's shock turned quickly to venom.

"What...?" Eva started.

"*Stay back.*" Even to the monster's ears, the harsh words sounded foreign. Arthur never let himself surrender to his fury like this, and it felt wrong to dredge up the darker, angrier parts of him, but the monster wanted to feel its rage.

What had the spirit of the wood called it? A *creature of want*? She'd been right. It wanted so much. To kill. To consume.

Lenny stood slowly, a predator's rise that also revealed some stiffness in his muscles. The shadows of the little shed cut a harsh line across his face, obscuring his eyes and the intent within. The hard-set line of his mouth pulled back into a sneer.

"Outside," he commanded, the words full of quiet malice.

Eva tensed at the monster's back. It nudged her to go. When her warmth disappeared, the monster took a careful step back, then another, its gaze fixed on Lenny's gun as he followed them out into the light.

The sight of him in broad daylight sent a ripple of shock through the monster. Lenny's arm hung limp and heavy from a shoulder clearly dislocated out of its socket. His sleeve had been ripped wide-open, exposing a deep gash down his arm, the wound weeping dark vermilion blood. The cuts weren't clean and precise, like those made by a knife. Instead, the flesh looked as though it had been twisted into and ripped free.

The monster wrinkled its nose at the rank iron scent.

"One of you is going to tell me what the fuck is going on." Lenny's other hand shook as he swung the gun from Arthur's chest to Eva's. "Or I shoot."

Arthur's heartbeat sped to a gallop inside their shared body, his panic cracking through.

The monster lifted its hands, palms out. Despite the instinct to reach for the bastard's throat, the monster knew that if provoked, Lenny might very well make good on his promise to pull that trigger.

The monster had to wait for the right moment.

"How did you find us?" Eva asked, her voice thin.

Lenny sneered. "You leave an easy trail."

The wildflowers. Of course. The monster cursed inwardly.

"I have to admit, I never thought I'd see you again, Connoway," Lenny said, waving the gun in a loose figure eight as his head tilted to the side. "And then you just...reappeared."

Without taking its eyes off the man, the monster steadied its feet in the soil beneath it. If Lenny provided an opening, it had to be ready to strike.

"You always do that, you know. You show up where you aren't wanted," Lenny spat. "It doesn't matter what damage you do, does it? People keep giving you chances to fix it."

"*What are you talking about?*"

Lenny harshed out a laugh. "What, you gonna pretend you don't love that? Starting over, only to screw with the people around you again? I know who you are, Connoway. I know what you can do." Lenny spat in the dirt. "And I know you tried to kill me."

A delicious sensation stole across the monster's tongue as the memory unspooled in its mind. That night may have haunted Arthur, but the monster savored how closely it had dragged Lenny Walker to the edge of death.

"You don't get to start over. You don't get to pretend that never happened!" In his agitation, Lenny's aim swung from Arthur to Eva. The monster stiffened, and its voice dropped low in warning.

"*Put the gun down.*"

But a craze seemed to have taken Lenny over. "Do you have any idea how you fucked with my life that night?" he said to Eva, staring at her now with eyes starting to shine. "I saw everything, you know, but no one believes me. Your family made sure they wouldn't. They said I was drunk—"

"*You* were *drunk*," the monster shot back, losing an inch of control.

Lenny flinched but didn't tear his gaze off Eva. "Funny that your daddy's tea is the only thing that eases my brother's chest pains."

Eva blinked. "What?"

"Oh, you didn't know that?" Lenny taunted. "They like keeping their secrets from you, don't they? Poor Eva, fragile as a bomb. Of course they didn't want to risk you blowing up again."

"*That's enough,*" the monster growled.

"He bleeds green now!" Lenny shouted. Red bloomed down his neck in a flush.

The monster flicked a look to Eva, whose eyes were now shining with horror.

"My brother, he's... not the same," Lenny said, pained.

"I'm sorry." A little sob slipped out of Eva.

"No," the monster graveled. "*Don't apologize to him.*"

Lenny swung the gun back toward Arthur, his bad arm dangling heavy and loose from the shoulder joint. *Like a broken doll.*

"Stop!" Eva cried out.

And maybe it was foolish, with the barrel of a gun aimed straight at its heart, but the monster couldn't help the tug of its smile as it stared at the vile man, knowing Lenny's life was quickly coming to a close.

Lenny scowled. "There's something wrong with you."

"*I know.*"

Lenny huffed. "You're just going to stand there while I kill you?"

The monster cocked its head. "*You don't want to shoot.*" It could tell by the shake of the gun, the crack in Lenny's voice, the delays, one after another. The coward wanted to scare them, but he didn't actually want to kill.

Not like the monster did.

A muscle twitched in Lenny's jaw. The monster glanced at the faded scars marring Lenny's throat, remembering how it had felt to hurt him all those years ago.

Its mouth watered.

Eva made a pitiful sound of protest as the monster took a step closer to the barrel of Lenny's gun. The monster was made of hunger, all the want consuming the body it shared with Arthur forming a tight knot in their belly.

Confusion flickered over Lenny's face.

How would it do it? The monster had tried to cut Lenny's life short once before, and had nearly succeeded. Now death by its touch felt like a mercy after all the monster had imagined doing to Lenny over the years.

Arthur's dread fluttered in the monster's chest, so much like the wings of an injured bird.

Of course the boy's moral compass would put up a fight. Though unable to hear his thoughts, the monster knew Arthur well enough to guess exactly how he felt about this, the tension in their shared body making it clear that Arthur was still *here*.

The monster growled under its breath and tried to ignore the feeling as it prepared to lunge forward. It would grab Lenny's arm and thrust it skyward before he could get a shot off. Humans were complex. Like any animal, they took more time to poison than any weed or flower. The monster would have to hold on for several seconds, maybe more, for its deadly touch to take hold.

You hurt me every time.

The monster ground its teeth together, hating how the words pressed and pounded within its skull. Even frozen inside, locked away where the monster couldn't hear his protests, Arthur was everywhere, his soft heart pounding in the monster's chest and his goodness leaking into its veins.

The monster loosed a harsh exhale.

"What are you doing?" Lenny asked uneasily. Blood from the cuts on his arms wept down his sleeve.

You hurt me every time.

The monster could kill him so easily. If only it could tuck Arthur away where he wouldn't see. It took a step forward.

"Stay back!" Suspicion and fear bled into Lenny's voice. He was close now, and the monster lurched forward, digging an elbow into Lenny's ribs and forcing him to the ground with a howl.

The tussle had brought their skin into contact, and the brief touch woke the monster's hunger. It wanted more. It wanted to consume, to kill this pathetic creature that had brought so much ruin to their lives.

You hurt me every time.

With a growl of frustration, the monster shoved Lenny away, flinging his gun into the grass. Denial was an agony, and the monster's chest crowded with a sudden mix of love and resentment.

There was one thing it wanted more than vengeance.

Damn you, little death-touch. A stinging sensation heated the bridge of Arthur's nose, a sure sign of swallowed emotion. But this was not the boy. No. This was something else. Something raw and unfamiliar.

"Go back to your brother," the monster snapped.

It could spare one life, not for Lenny's sake but for the boy the monster loved so much.

Lenny seethed up at both of them, his bad arm twisted wrong in the grass. For a moment the monster saw itself as though through Lenny's eyes, a wicked slash of lips curving Arthur's mouth into a grin. What had the spirit of the wood called the monster?

Something worse than a man.

Maybe she was right.

When Lenny stood, the grass beneath him lengthened, stretching up past his knees, where it swirled, ropelike, around his legs. Alarmed, Lenny kicked the grass off with a shout.

"Leave," Eva echoed, her voice small but steady.

The monster watched, moved by her grit.

"I don't care where you go," Eva said, "but I don't want to see you ever again."

How remarkable she was. Full of admiration, the monster shot her a brief look of approval.

A mistake.

In that split second of distraction, Lenny flung his body to one side. The monster's attention snapped back to him just in time to catch a flying stone to the side of the face. Pain erupted in the monster's skull. The stitches split open, the already tender, swollen skin stinging as it wept hot, new blood. The monster's ears rang with tinnitus, and its knees hit the dirt.

Lenny rolled to his feet again, breathless. The gun was back in his good hand, and he pointed it at Arthur's face.

"No!" Eva lunged toward the monster just as Lenny fired.

Chapter 37

The Monster

The gunshot split the air like glass, the force of the bullet throwing Eva's body into the monster, where she crumpled like a rag doll, heavy and warm. The whine in the monster's ears stole every sound but the pounding of its own heartbeat.

Birds exploded from the canopy overhead.

So many feathers.

So much life.

For several seconds, the shock of it stole the monster's breath, and it lay there, stunned. When it set its hands on Eva's waist, something warm and wet slicked between its fingers. The tang of iron filled its nose.

"Eva?" it whispered as it blinked very slowly, finding it hard to arrange its thoughts.

Then everything rushed in all at once. With a gasp, the monster gripping the fabric of Eva's shirt and rolled her over, confusion melting into fear as it realized what she'd done by jumping between Arthur and the bullet.

"I-I didn't mean..."

The monster's gaze snapped to where Lenny stood frozen, staring at them. He stammered, his voice breaking.

The sound that came from the monster wasn't human at all but the furious cry of an animal. *"Go,"* it seethed.

Lenny stepped back, startled. He looked suddenly younger. "I didn't mean to hurt her."

The monster roared. *"GO!"*

And Lenny did, stumbling into the woods. The monster held Eva close, searching with trembling fingers for where the bullet had lodged itself in her flesh, like a seed planted in soil. Red bloomed from the wound in her side, flowing too fast and covering both of them in blood.

Her blood.

"Eva?" the monster whispered, feathering a panicked touch to her cheek. Her color was fading, a deathly pallor swallowing the rosy hue of sun-touched skin. *"Wake up,"* it pleaded weakly, cradling the back of her neck to prevent her head from lolling.

Salt burned the corners of its eyes. Strange, how tears could hurt sometimes.

With a little sob, the monster repositioned Eva on the grass and pressed both palms to the wound in her side. The gentle pressure made Eva convulse, her eyes slitting open.

She moaned.

"I'm sorry." The monster couldn't tell where its panic ended and Arthur's began. The level of terror coursing through their shared being was so violent it made the monster nauseous. *"I'm so sorry. But you've got to stay awake for me."* It scrubbed under its eyes, clearing the blurriness away, tasting salt. *"You have to stay."*

Eva's lips parted, but no sound came out. The monster stripped off Arthur's shirt and balled it up, then pressed it to her wound. "*Come on, Freckles,*" it choked out.

The monster had never prayed before. What was a creature like it supposed to do with God, anyway? But it firmly believed that if anyone should curry divine favor, it was Arthur's bee girl. A plea kept beating in the monster's head, finding release the way Arthur did with his tapping. *Not her, not her.* It was an ancient rhythm full of pain. *Not her, not her, PLEASE.*

It reached into the dark of its mind as a sob tightened in its throat. But Arthur wasn't there.

"*Please,*" the monster whispered as it bowed over her bleeding body. This wasn't supposed to happen. All it had wanted was to protect Arthur, but this would break him.

Not her, not her. The monster's plea fell in sync with its pulse. It had never wanted their bee girl to become another one of Arthur's scars.

The forest seemed to mirror the sounds of Eva's body: the river's rush like her blood, the beat of life underground like the thump of her heart, and the rustling wind like the gasp on her lips.

Tears striped down Arthur's cheeks. Even trapped inside his own mind, Arthur was nothing but heart, and the monster could do nothing to stop the pain when the same slide of grief was pulling it down too, a tar pit of panic drawing it lower with every passing second. When Eva's breaths became a wheeze, the monster broke.

This couldn't be happening. They couldn't lose her!

But they already were.

The hard reality made a bout of nauseating fear roll over the monster. This was why it kept Arthur numb, because feeling *this* was agony. A love like theirs shouldn't end in loss like this!

But that's what all love stories did.

A sob ratcheted the tightness in the monster's chest. Had it made things worse? It wanted to be a balm, but maybe it had simply become another burden for Arthur to carry.

He would never forgive the monster if it let Eva die.

The monster wouldn't forgive itself either.

Eva twitched a little gasp beneath the pressure of the monster's touch. She looked so delicate, so unlike herself. She was usually a force of nature. Now she was a greenhouse. A whole world trapped in glass bones far too fragile to keep her safe. Not even her uncanny ability to heal could pull her back from a wound this deep.

Her skin was graying fast, her hairline drenched in sweat.

I can help you.

The voice startled the monster, drawing its gaze to where the spirit of the wood stood nearby. How long had she been there?

You can save her, devil, the spirit said. *If you heed my instructions.*

The monster's jaws snapped. "How?" They were running out of time, and it could do nothing to help her! It was a creature of death, born to take. Not to heal.

We bring my son back. The spirit's leaves rippled, her tone cool and firm. *For good, this time.*

The words dropped a pit into the monster's stomach. "Arthur needs me," it rasped.

But a whisper of doubt moved through the body they shared, and suddenly... the monster wasn't sure that was true. It helped Arthur survive, but even it knew there was a difference between survival and truly living. Arthur wanted to live. He wanted to feel.

The monster was useless to Eva. It could feel her life draining out. Eva needed a champion, someone soft and brave enough to face grief even when it hurt.

She needed Arthur.

"*Okay,*" it whispered. "*What do I do?*"

First, promise to tell the bees that I am gone.

"*Fine,*" the monster snapped. "*I'll tell them anything you want. Just help me save her!*"

The spirit nodded, as though she had expected this reaction. She extended a hand covered in delicate aspen leaves. In the place where a palm might be, she held out the chunks of honeycomb Eva had broken off from the wild hive.

Eat.

The monster frowned. "*I can't just give it to her?*"

She's spent a lifetime drinking tea from these flowers. It won't be enough.

"*Fine.*" The monster wiped the sweat off Arthur's upper lip. *Push me out, little death-touch,* it silently pleaded as it took the honeycomb from the spirit.

There will be a cost, the spirit of the wood said in warning as the monster brought the bit of comb to Arthur's lips.

"*There always is,*" it whispered, squeezing its eyes shut in surrender.

And suddenly the monster understood that it had been wrong, all along. It was never meant to prevent Arthur from feeling all the pain in his world. It was meant to stand by him. To witness. To weep. It was meant to be for him what Jack and Izzy and Eva had been.

It couldn't put its own fear of pain in front of Arthur's heart anymore. The monster knew Arthur's every desire. It knew what the bee girl meant to him, and so it knew that the price didn't matter. Arthur would pay it every time, to save her.

The monster plopped the honeycomb onto its tongue, and bit down.

Chapter 38

Arthur

There was nothing quite like honeycomb. Still warm from the sun, the hexagonal cells split under my teeth. The rich, sweet flavor slicked back over my tongue and into my cheek in a sugared burst, viscous and heady.

It was summer.

And summer melted ice.

The wall holding me captive in my own mind dissolved in a trickle, the return to myself painful in the way of a numb limb reexperiencing the rush of blood flow. I gasped, biting my tongue in surprise as the monster's hold sloughed off, leaving me heavy instead of weightless, my head pounding.

And I was reminded at once that sometimes it hurts to exist.

"Help her," the monster begged aloud, and I didn't know if it was speaking to me or to the spirit of the wood, *my mother*, who still watched silently, but the instant I took a breath, relief and agony twining with the swell of my lungs, something changed.

It started as a glow deep within my ribs. Over the years, I had gotten used to the monster's awareness tuning my senses to the beating life surrounding us, but this awakening was different. Not a hunger to take but the pressure to grow. To create.

When I gasped, the ground at my feet burst into life with a crackle, daffodils jutting their thin green necks past the press of my knees, their sepals opening bright yellow faces to the sun. My heart pounded, a newborn power pulsing beneath my skin. It sang in my ears, sunlight spilling like a cracked yolk over the hills at dawn.

Shock rippled through me. This wasn't Eva's magic.

It was mine.

Human beings are not meant to hold the forest inside them, the spirit of the wood said, her voice gentler now than it had been before. *That's why it hurts, at first.*

I looked at her and tried, for a moment, to see the mother I wanted to remember. She'd been the whole world to me, once. Now she was a stranger, pulling more questions to the surface than answers.

"What do I do?" I begged.

The aspens forming the shape of her groaned as she raised a bark-covered finger and pointed to the wound in Eva's side. *You heal.*

I blanched. "I don't know how!"

The spirit of the wood shrugged.

Eva's words came back to me in a flash, stolen from years ago. *I mend things,* she'd said.

Her eyelids had closed and I felt her pulse growing ever fainter. There was no room for error, no time for mistakes. She had seconds, minutes at most.

Tenderly, I lifted a lock of hair out of her eyes. "You have to live,

Ev." A scant, delicate whisper as tears slid down my cheeks and dripped into her hair. "Please. Stay with me."

I gathered her against me, my desperation lancing down into the rootscapes below, wilting the grass, then restoring it over and over. I was undone, unleashed, more broken than I had ever been. I was life and death, unbound by the sharp cut of my grief.

"Stay with me now," I hoarsed out. "Stay with me forever, bee girl. I need to make things right between us. Don't leave me before I get the chance."

A nearby oak gave a loud moan as it crashed to the forest floor, the split of its trunk like snapping celery. Honeybees buzzed furiously overhead. One of them landed on Eva's shoulder. Then another, in her hair. I held my breath and watched them gather, landing on her one by one. It was a strange and beautiful sight, and I watched, immobilized by the sudden, overwhelming feeling of sacredness settling around us.

Something changed.

The glow in my chest ballooned down to my fingertips. I couldn't feel the monster, nor could I hear its voice, as sunshine and power poured into my limbs, filling my heart to bursting. I gathered all the love I could muster for Eva, all the years spent missing her, all the ways she'd changed me and made me new. The flowers around us seemed to sigh, the heartbeat of the earth so close I could taste it. I could *take* it.

But I didn't want to take things anymore. I wanted to mend.

A heady sensation filled the gaps in my mind where the darkness lay. But this was not my monster. It was sweet, and it poured through me, through Eva too, bright and sweet as sticky, sugary gold. Every breath was honeyed. Every breath was life.

With a guttural pop, Eva's ribs snapped back into place, expelling the lodged bullet into my palm. I gasped and dropped it in the grass.

Eva's cheeks flushed pink. Her eyelids fluttered as she arched off the grass. I watched in awe as the skin around her wound knit itself closed, leaving behind a pale pink scar. Tears pooled in my eyes. Scars were okay. Scars were beautiful. Scars meant you still got to live.

"Ev?" I whispered, my voice shaking as I dragged her close. The world seemed to hold its breath as her eyelids fluttered, then opened.

"Arthur?"

With a sob, I gathered her to my chest. Eva clung to me, crying too.

My life had been a series of unsure things, the ground beneath me always shifting. I'd traversed the dark more nights than I could count and knew too well the clawing pain of doubt and self-loathing. But she was soil, a place where I could put down roots. I'd known eight years ago as surely as I knew it now, because even then, when I saw only the parts of me that were hungry and lacking and frail, she saw *me*.

"You're okay," I promised. "We're okay, bee girl."

It took a minute for the panic to leave her eyes as she looked from me to the empty clearing. "But...Lenny?"

"Ran off," I murmured, thumbing the soft apple of her cheek.

Eva's gaze flicked to my face, and she touched the trail of blood running down my temple. "Your stitches..."

"I don't even feel them," I said reassuringly.

Eva shook her head and touched my brow. "No, I mean they're gone."

"What?"

"The infection," she said in growing confusion, her brows knitting as she sat up. "It's healed."

I lifted my hand to touch where she pointed, and felt my lips pucker in surprise. She was right. Where the skin had been swollen and hot to the touch, now I felt only the smooth slice of a healed scar cutting through my eyebrow.

The honey had worked.

A meow drew my attention to where Bug was bolting toward us through the grass. The sight took me so by surprise that I didn't even have time to retract my hand before she bumped her forehead against my knuckles.

Too late, I snatched my hand away.

But the snuggly fur ball didn't seem fazed. She didn't seize up in sudden rictus, and her heart beat fast as she leapt onto my lap.

The monster swirled around my spine, as stunned as I was.

"How...?" The words had hardly left my tongue before Bug dug her claws into my leg. "Ouch! No claws, please!"

Eva laughed in disbelief. "You can touch her!"

I blinked. *I can touch her.*

An idea formed, and I palmed the grass below me.

At first, the tendrils woke and swirled up over my fingers. I passed Bug to Eva and closed my eyes, reaching for the monster in my depths. I'd never tried to use the death-touch of my own accord, but I had to know something. Slowly, it rose to the surface. As one, the blades of grass shriveled back into crisp yellow weeds.

I took a breath. When I let it go, the monster pulled back, working with me. The glow in my ribs pulsed like a tiny sun, and the grass grew back.

The spirit of the wood shifted, her leaves rippling over her torso in an illusion of hair as she held out the honeycomb again. Her breath filled the whole glade with the sound of rushing wind. For Jack, she said, the words sounding unsteady for the first time.

I accepted the proffered gift, a strange ache in my chest. It took me a moment to register it as gratitude. It wasn't an emotion I was used to feeling when it came to the woman who'd raised me. I'd loved her forever and hated her nearly as long for not loving me back.

Or not loving me *right*.

But as I stared at the spirit of the wood, the curl of her shoulders surprisingly human, something in me softened.

I didn't want to bear the weight of our bad days anymore. I didn't know if I could forgive her yet, but for the first time in a long time, I knew I wanted to someday. There was a good person wrapped in all her mistakes. Just like me.

The monster swirled in my depths, calm and content for the first time in months as I resolved to try to let it all go, start anew, and plant a fresh beginning.

Remember your promise, said the spirit of the wood as she began to unravel, the cracking of branches and rustle of leaves an almost violent unmaking. Tell the bees.

"I will." I stared, squeezing Eva's hand, until the spirit was gone and the groan of the woods gave way to a new sound. I frowned, trying to place the distant thrum.

"What is that?" Eva asked, following my gaze.

My heart leapt in my chest.

There, beyond where the treetops met a saffron sky, a helicopter was pointed our way.

Chapter 39

Arthur

Eva flapped her arms like a bird.

"We're over here!" she called out, her voice still hoarse as she scooped Bug up from the grass and stumbled to the center of the meadow. Her limp was gone, the cuts in her skin and her blisters wiped away by magic, but still I saw the drain. Blood loss, I guessed. We weren't out of the woods yet.

"Over here!" I echoed.

The moment I lifted my arms over my head, I knew something was wrong.

At first, the pain was just a pinch, like the kind of cramp I got when running. I winced. Little Lotties burst to life, doubling the meadow's vivid blue hues as the helicopter drew nearer, its blades abuzz in a deafening roar.

In seconds, the discomfort worsened and I was breathless.

When I came to a halt, Eva turned. "What's wrong?" she shouted over the din, but I couldn't answer. I couldn't speak, let alone breathe through the agony slicing me up from the inside, wriggling and twisting through muscle and sinew. I slapped a hand to the place beneath my ribs where the pain grew hot and bright, flashing to when I'd witnessed Jack Moreau doubled over in torment just like this.

"*There's something inside us,*" the monster said, with none of the awe it had felt that night as it had watched the seed of Jack's aspen crack open, pushing a thin sprout skinward.

Above us, the helicopter lowered, its blades cutting the sky. They'd seen us.

My vision blurred with pain as the *something* inside me snaked outward, determined to see the light. I cried out, sinking to my knees as my peripheral vision filled with sudden dark spots.

"Arthur?" Eva sounded panicked now. "What's happening?"

"Side," I groaned. The nucleus of heat pulsed low in my ribs. It writhed upward, reaching for a surface where it could crack me open, splitting layers of skin like soil.

A whoosh of air threw back the petals and grass filling the meadow as the helicopter descended, the force sufficient to lift one of the frames of the broken hive boxes into the air, blowing it several feet away before it tumbled down again.

Eva knelt and tore my hand from where I clutched the same place on my side where the bullet had struck her. The skin was bruise-dark and swollen.

"What —?" Eva sounded stunned. When she grazed my ribs, the sprout's wriggling intensified, seeking her like it would the sun. I cried out in pain and slumped against her, dizzy.

There will be a cost.

That's what my mother's spirit had said. Now I understood: Every time I would use the honey magic to heal someone or make something grow, the sprout in me would grow too, just as the tree had done inside Jack.

A few people dismounted from the helicopter and ran toward

us. Surprise filled me when I recognized Dane Walker among the faces. The EMT who reached us crouched and began peppering Eva with questions.

I didn't hear her responses. My eyes were fixed on where Dane Walker had paused in his tracks, staring at something in the grass. He bent and picked it up. I blinked through the haze and realized it was Lenny's gun, discarded in the weeds.

Someone peeled my hand off my side to look at the wound. It took me a moment to realize the bellow of pain had come from me. I felt out of control, my throat choked with fear as the newborn gift inside me pulled flower after flower into bloom until—

"I don't think so." The monster yanked the sprout in my ribs back down. *"I said I wouldn't control you again, and I won't,"* it promised as it twined itself around the sprout and sucked the life from it. *"But I won't let you die either, little death-touch."*

I trembled as they loaded me into the helicopter. All the way down the mountain, Eva held my hand. Her eyes were drooping. The paramedics spoke in low voices, confused to find us covered in blood without a scratch on our bodies.

"Was there anyone else with you?" one asked.

"Yes," Dane said.

"And where are they now?"

Dane looked at me. The monster didn't want to answer, sensing a trap, but it didn't prevent me from speaking either. "He ran off," I mumbled. "Gone."

The medics shared a quiet look, but I didn't have a spare thought left for Lenny Walker. The hike, the fight, and the drain of new magic were taking their toll on me. I wanted to rest, but it felt as though the moment I closed my eyes we were touching down on the helipad of a hospital. Eva and I were rushed down different hallways. I drifted in a fog as doctors worked around me, prodding my side and slipping an IV needle into my arm. A nurse brought me a large mug of ice water, and I sipped until my eyes were drooping. Then, unable to fight it any longer, I curled onto my side and finally slept.

I woke to a deep timbre. The voice was familiar, the rolling cadence reaching into my fog and pulling me up, up, up. Drowsy, I groaned and scrubbed my eyes.

Jack Moreau stood in the doorway to my room, speaking to someone just outside.

I snapped to attention, upending the tray at my bedside in my haste. My heart monitor sped its beeping. Jack glanced at me, then held up a hand, pausing whatever conversation he'd been having as he stepped into the room. My gaze dropped to his chest, anxious to see if the honey we'd brought with us had worked.

But what I saw confused me.

It wasn't the tree anymore, not exactly. The branches were pruned back to the base. Only a nub remained, pushing out of his sternum like the stubs of a fruit tree in winter.

"Don't look so worried." Jack sank into a chair at my bedside and pulled a thermos from his jacket. He passed it over. "And drink this. You need it."

Hesitantly, I unscrewed the cap. It was still warm, but not so hot it would burn my tongue. Steam lifted, wetting my cheeks.

Tea.

Not just any tea. I knew the faint notes of this flower, both from the summer I'd spent spooning honey and tea into mugs and the hours spent in that meadow, surrounded by thousands of the living blue-violet clusters. *Little Lotties.* I took a sip.

"The wild honey you found has a twofold ability," Jack said. "As long as it runs in your veins, you'll wield the same green magic I did for years. Your body will also heal itself." His eyes dropped to the place in my side still throbbing, caught between wanting to grow and wanting to yield to the death that lived in my every cell. "It will be harder to fight that off soon. Unfortunately, nature does not discriminate between soil and human flesh. It will grow through you, as my tithe has done."

"Your tithe," I whispered, putting a name to this new thing we shared.

Jack nodded. "There is a price for breaking the rules of nature. We can only borrow creative power, not wield it against death. If we try... well" — he touched the base of his tree — "it grows in us instead."

"So he says. But he doesn't have me," the monster said, preening. *"I won't let this so-called tithe get anywhere near your heart."*

Jack's expression softened. "I'm sorry. You've only just woken. If this is too much, I can let you rest."

"No!" I tried to sit up, and a rush of exhaustion poured vertigo into my vision. I closed my hand around the side rail of the hospital bed and breathed until the ringing in my ears cleared, then I met Jack's even gaze. "Eva?" I said raggedly.

"She's okay."

Relief was a crashing train. I fell back against the pillow, squeezing my eyes shut for a moment.

"There was a lot of blood on your clothes," Jack said. "The medics who picked you up thought it might belong to the missing member of your party."

"It wasn't Lenny's."

Jack accepted that with a nod, then paused. "I know what you did for my daughter."

A swallow lodged in my throat. "She was dying. I-I had to — "

"I know." And then he did something I didn't expect. The giant honeyman moved closer and pulled me into a crushing hug. "Trust me, I know."

It shouldn't have been possible for us to embrace this way without my death-touch drawing Jack's life out second by second. But just as it had when I'd tested it in the meadow, the monster remained calm and contained, keeping its promise.

After a stunned moment, I gripped Jack by the shoulders and hugged him back, a hot tear rolling down to my chin. I didn't have words for this. The casual, easy press of affection reached deep to the core of me, spreading a balm over my heart.

"Thank you, son," he whispered.

A lump balled in my throat. When Jack pulled away, the pressure uncorked and tears spilled down my cheeks, hot and healing. Behind his glasses, Jack's eyes were shining too.

The door behind him opened, and Izzy popped her head inside. "If things are getting sappy, I want in." She stepped into the room, carrying a bundle under her arm. "Got a change of clothes for you, Fairy," she said, setting the bundle on the tray before she plopped herself at the end of my bed, landing right on my foot.

"Ow," I said indignantly.

Izzy ignored my sound of protest and pointed at my chest. "You broke your promise," she said. "You weren't supposed to leave before we talked."

I swallowed hard. "You're right. I'm sorry."

To my relief, she accepted my apology with a nod. "I guess that means dinner is on you tonight."

I blinked. "Dinner?"

Before she could reply, Jack cut in. "Eva still in with the sheriff?" Izzy nodded. "Why don't you two go on ahead and pick up the food, then? I'll drive her home when they're done."

"Perfect." Izzy opened her purse and passed over a pink bundle to Jack. "I brought her a clean dress."

"Wait a second," I blurted out, trying to catch up. I looked between her and Jack, my mind clogging with questions I wanted to ask, apologies I wanted to give, and too many other important things I'd left unsaid.

Izzy's expression softened. "What'll it be then, Fairy? Cheeseburgers?"

"I... What?"

"Chicken? Pizza?" She raised her eyebrows. "What are you hungry for?"

I felt as though I'd been transported out of my body and was hovering above, watching the scene play out beneath me. The easy back-and-forth was strangely comforting, and between Jack's grounding presence and Izzy's lighthearted banter I felt real in a way I hadn't for a long time.

So I told the truth.

"Cheeseburgers. And fries. Thick, salty fries."

Izzy smiled. "You got it. Dad?"

"I was thinking ice cream."

Chapter 10

Arthur

The smell of burgers filled the cab of the truck as we drove up the mountain, the outside world passing in a peripheral blur of deep pine green. Izzy cranked up the radio and wound down the windows as we drove, content to let conversation slough away. She swayed with the music and belted out the lyrics she knew, and some others she clearly didn't.

I couldn't help but smile.

When we passed through Audrey's single, blinking stoplight, my eyes snagged on the old white chapel. I leaned forward. "Iz?" I asked softly.

"Yeah?"

"Can we stop here?"

She eyed me curiously as she pulled off to the side of the road just in front of the battered church. I pressed my eyes shut and gathered a breath. Only days ago, I would have sworn that I never wanted to see this building again. I'd thought there was nothing I wanted to remember tucked behind its walls.

Before I could second-guess the tug pulling me forward, I unbuckled my seat belt and slipped out. The chapel had felt bigger to me when I was seventeen. Now it just felt quiet, not at all the beast it had become in memory, but wounded in the way of old abandoned places.

I quickened my step. If I could just see the pews, the rafters, the place where everything had changed... if I could just see it, maybe the shadow of this place would stop looming over me.

I pushed inside, surprised to find the door unlocked. Izzy followed a few steps behind. Her presence was lightweight, a comfort I didn't realize I'd needed. She didn't ask questions or watch me too closely, instead turning her eyes up in curiosity.

"There's a nest up there," she said, squinting.

"Sure is." I didn't have to check to know the species. Even if the last time I looked up into these rafters hadn't been burned into my memory, their familiar call would have sent a chill along my skin. "Starlings."

The stark emptiness within struck me as odd, though really, what had I expected to find? A wilderness of moss-covered wallpaper, with lichen riming the pulpit and flowers spilling across the pews? Time and someone's obvious attention had worked here as it had on me, clearing out a mass of detritus and leaving it once again fresh and clean. The walls of the chapel had been scrubbed, the floors swept and weeds pulled out of the cracks. It was strangely cold, pale as bone, and eerily sterile.

A dead place.

"It took a while to clean out the garden she made," Izzy mused, drawing a fingertip over a layer of dust on the back of a bench.

I looked at her. "You cleaned it up?"

She gave me a strange look. "Who else?"

I didn't think the question was intended as a barb, but it did hold weight.

"Can I ask you something?" Izzy said. I nodded. "Why *did* you come back to us? I know, I know, you wanted to bring your mom's ashes here," she said, waving the reason away before I could give it, as though it wasn't enough. As though she knew there was something more.

I'd thought I'd come to appease the monster and regain some control of my mind. But now? "I...don't know."

Izzy cocked her head. "I think you do."

I thought of the monster's gnawing hunger that had pushed me into the woods time and time again, looking for something neither one of us had ever been able to find. I thought of the way it had pushed me out of my own head, taking lives to keep me going, deer and bird and badger. So many flowers. So many trees. I wasn't a hunter, but I felt like one all the same, with the taste of hides and hearts locked under my tongue.

I hadn't wanted to lose myself. That's why I'd come back, or at least it was part of it. Death was an endless slope, and I was so tired of climbing that hill. I just wanted peace again. I wanted —

"To live," I said. The confession felt like a weight, handed over. I was almost dizzy from it. "I wanted to live again."

Izzy nodded, a smile crimping the sides of her mouth. "Do you know how scion cuts work, Fairy?"

I blinked. "Scion cuts? Like, in tree grafting?"

Izzy nodded. "They don't just help the scion survive. Both the rootstock and the plant cutting join together and become something new." She shifted to face me more fully as she put a hand on her hip. "Love is like that too. You don't pay it back. It transforms everyone it touches, so that rootstock and graft can grow into something better than before."

I let out a breath, words spoken long ago whispering softly in my ear. *Home is a thing that grows.* "You know, Eva said something like that to me once."

"'Bout time you listen, then, isn't it?" Izzy cocked her head toward the door. "Let's go. I have a bag of crinkle-cut fries with my name on it."

It was a short walk back to the truck. To my surprise, instead of turning onto the road that would lead up to the Moreau farm, Izzy pulled up to the neighboring Walker farmhouse. When she put on the brakes, I turned to her with a frown. "What are we doing here?"

"Dane's got enough spare rooms for us all," she said. "And don't worry. We'll figure out what happens next, you know, with the whole *breaking out of jail* thing. He wants to help."

I didn't relish that conversation, but her response hadn't exactly answered my question.

"But... why aren't we staying at the cottage?"

"Oh!" Izzy cut in. "You don't know!"

"Know what?"

She bit her lip as she extricated herself from the vehicle, a brown paper sack full of our food tucked under her arm. "So much has happened," she murmured, her heels clicking over the pavement. She tried to use her hip to nudge the front door open. "The cottage isn't... Well, this is a little hard to explain."

I followed, grabbing the door and widening it for her. The two of us slipped inside. I blinked, struck by the sudden rush of AC. "The cottage isn't what?"

"Well." She set down the bags. "It's not exactly there anymore."

"What do you mean?" I asked, frowning.

"Do you think Dad and Eva would be upset if we ate without them?" Izzy tossed a fry into her mouth. "I can't imagine they're far behind us, but it feels like a sin to let these get cold."

"Isobel," I begged.

I'd never said her full name before. I hadn't thought it would feel natural, but in my frustration it had rolled off my tongue, and to my surprise, it fit.

She sighed. "Come on. I'll show you."

Chapter 41

Isobel

Isobel watched Arthur take in the cottage's ruined state with an ache in her chest. The house, at least, had finally stopped sinking, the front door half buried in moss and soil. They could walk onto the roof if they wanted, though doing so seemed ill-advised.

The smokeless chimney was a lonely beacon.

Isobel could tell by the stiff way Arthur walked that his side was still aching, though he didn't say so. He never was one to complain.

"You okay?" she asked.

"It's all gone," he whispered, a ragged, broken sound that cracked something right in the center of Isobel's chest.

"Not gone completely," she said, thinking back to what Dr. Rosen had said about her father. "Just…different. But different can be good." All of their possessions were buried beneath a thick layer of overturned soil, yes, but that didn't mean they couldn't rebuild. Hell, maybe Dane could urge the judge to slap Arthur and Eva with nothing more than a bit of community service, and they could all dig out the past together.

Isobel knew that in the coming days the grief of losing this place would catch up with her, but right now all she felt was a weight being lifted off her chest. She and Dane would need to sit down and talk, once everything calmed down. She wasn't sure how that conversation would go. Maybe he would sever things between them. She had, after all, spent the last eight years lying about what she remembered from that night, afraid of exposing Eva's involvement. Maybe her full confession had come too late.

But for the first time, Isobel felt peace. It had been the right thing, telling him. Maybe it had been the right thing a long time ago, but that didn't dilute her relief at finally having done it.

"How..." Arthur said, a vulnerable sound pushing past his lips. It made him sound younger. "How did this happen?"

"I'm not really sure," Isobel admitted, sidling up next to him. "The earth just opened up and...swallowed it." She let out a rueful laugh, hearing the words spoken aloud. "That probably sounds ridiculous."

"No." Arthur met her gaze, his expression shifting to one of understanding. "It doesn't."

Isobel's brows came together, and she cocked her head, curious at the sudden tightness in his jaw.

"Was anyone hurt?" Arthur asked.

Isobel could still hear her father's bellow of pain when he'd snapped his branches clean off, just to get out the window in time. "We're okay now."

Arthur's face was the picture of grief. Of course. This had been his home too, for a time. There was always more to a house than brick and mortar and stone. Hope lived there too.

"We'll dig out what we can," she said. "Or start anew..." Isobel trailed off when she noted Arthur running his palm down the steep gable. He didn't wear gloves, and a thick layer of moss had grown over the roof tiles. It didn't shrivel back at his touch.

She cocked her head. "What are you doing?"

"Where are my mother's ashes?"

Isobel didn't like where this was going. "They're in Eva's room," she hedged. "But it's not safe to go in. The roof could collapse."

"I need those ashes, Iz."

The weight in his voice took Isobel back to when she'd lost her own mother. "She's at rest, under there," she said softly.

"Actually," he murmured, "she's not."

Isobel's nose wrinkled. "What do you mean?"

But Arthur was already circling the cottage, quiet as the kitten he and Eva had insisted on bringing back with them in the helicopter. Isobel glanced back toward the Walker farmhouse. They'd left the rescue sleeping on a soft rug in a ray of sunlight in the den.

"Here?" Arthur asked, pointing to Eva's partially buried bedroom window.

"That's the one," she admitted.

This was a bad idea.

Butterflies and honeybees stirred the air overhead as Arthur ran a hand along the lichen-covered sill, his eyebrows drawing together in contemplation. Though the window was still open from their earlier escape, it was now so deeply buried that the chances of his fitting through the slot seemed slim.

As Arthur bent to study the opening, his knees pressed into the earth and tiny green blades of grass pushed through the soil. Isobel drew in a sharp breath. Was it *him* doing that?

He drew back. "Help me dig?"

Isobel laughed. When she saw he was serious, the sound went flat. Make that two for two on bad ideas. "Oh. I, um, don't think that's the best idea, Fairy."

"Please." He stared at her, eyes pleading. Isobel was struck suddenly by how well the expression matched that of a very sad puppy.

She sighed. "Who can say no to that face? Go. There are shovels in the greenhouse." Her sister's sanctuary had somehow survived the earth's shaking, its glass walls miraculously intact.

Arthur popped to his feet and dashed off in the direction she indicated, and soon the sounds of rifling metal and wood met Isobel's ear. He returned holding a garden hoe in one hand, a shovel in the other. He passed the latter to her.

They dug as one, widening the opening until it was sufficiently large for Arthur to squeeze his body through.

"Don't hurt yourself," Isobel said uneasily as he disappeared out of her line of view into the bedroom within. When she heard the sound of books being lifted and discarded as he searched, Isobel got down on her hands and knees, craning for a better view of the dimly lit room. She could just see Arthur's silhouette, but the angle strained her neck.

"Watch the floor," she called out. "It might not hold." As soon as the words were out of her mouth, Isobel's chest tightened. Why had she agreed to this? They could have waited until they had more help, more equipment, more —

"Found it!" Arthur's silhouette lifted an arm in triumph.

Isobel sighed and sat up, cricking her back from side to side to make it pop. A door slammed in the near distance, and she looked up in time to see her sister stomping toward them through the rows of pear trees in the pink sundress Isobel had brought to the hospital for her to change into.

"You might want to hurry," Isobel said as the storm of Eva's emotions flooded the grass at her feet in furious thistles. "Someone is here to see you."

"What? Who?"

But Eva was already there. "Where is he, Iz?" she called out. "Where's that son of a—"

"I'm here, Ev," Arthur called out, waving a hand through the window's opening.

Eva came to a sudden halt, and her eyes bulged, her apple cheeks wearing the sun in pink confession. "What the hell is this?"

"I'll be up in a minute."

Isobel had never seen her sister look so murderous. "Is that all you have to say?" her sister shouted. "'I'll be up in a minute'? 'I'm here, Ev'? Why the hell are you *here*, Arthur? You're supposed to be in a hospital bed!"

Arthur handed the box of ashes up to Isobel, then tried once to lift himself out, grunting as his ascent proved significantly more difficult than his descent had been.

His touch should have made the grass under his palms wither and die. Instead, tiny yellow chamomile flowers bloomed around his hands.

He'd hugged her father at the hospital, too.

Isobel sucked in a breath as the pieces clicked into place. She didn't know what had happened up that mountain or how this was possible, but just now, she didn't care. Setting down the ashes, she grasped Arthur by the arm and hauled him up. His skin was smooth and slightly chilled, his body smudged in dirt.

She laughed, delighted. She'd never been able to touch him before, and she wanted a moment to take in this new revelation.

Or better yet.

Isobel threw her arms around him, squeezing tight. After a few prolonged seconds, Arthur hugged her back. She didn't miss the shake in his breath. "Fries are getting cold," she reminded him. "Don't take too long." Then she retrieved the box of ashes off the ground. "I'll take these back to the house."

Chapter 42

Arthur

She was radiant. Furious and bright, just how the sun should be. I brushed the dirt off my palms as she stepped closer and shoved her hand against my chest. I caught her by the elbows. "The last I saw you, you were writhing in agony."

My heart fluttered. "I'm okay now."

For the first time in my life, I knew I would tell her about the monster. What it had done for me. What it had become for me.

Eva's hands settled on my biceps, holding me as I held her. "You left," she said again, her voice cracking.

My chest ached as I flashed back to another night. I hadn't even said a real goodbye when I'd left eight years ago, leaving her only a roll of film negatives, our memories trapped on acetate. It was a pittance, just like the Polaroids Mom had left me whenever she'd gone away. The coward's goodbye.

But I wasn't running this time.

Eva looked past me to the ruin of her home, dejection flashing across her face. "It's so much worse than Dad described."

What could Jack have even said? I wasn't sure it was possible to convey this level of devastation without seeing it yourself. To lose a home was to lose a sanctuary. I would know.

"We can rebuild it," I said.

Eva sniffed. "What are you even doing here?"

The promise I'd made sat at the very front of my mind. Maybe I'd initially come to Audrey for selfish reasons, but now? I truly wanted to let Mom go. I was ready.

"I had to get her ashes." A swallow bobbed in my throat. "I'm going to fix things."

Maybe it was wishful thinking, but I could have sworn Eva's gaze dipped to my mouth. A heaviness weighed in the center of my chest as I flashed back to the meadow, to the wilted crook of her body in the grass. I'd thought I'd lost her, and for a moment, the world had collapsed. I wasn't going to let her go so easily now. If she made me beg, I'd get down on my knees.

I drew her closer. "I meant what I said before, bee girl. I want to earn your trust again." I softly squeezed her upper arms. "Can I try?"

Eva grabbed my shirt and pressed onto her toes. Our lips met once, then again with more hunger. My hands clutched the bend in her waist. But too soon, Eva pulled back. "You want to stay?" she choked out.

"Of course I want to stay."

She cupped the back of my head, fitting her thumb just under my ear as she dragged me down to her. This close, I could feel the trip of her heart, and tenderness welled inside me.

"You don't owe me anything," I husked out. "What happened at the meadow ... If you don't want this, we don't have to — "

"Arthur." Her voice dropped a register, and she shook her head slowly, the tip of her nose teasing mine. Behind her, the colorful pots of garden herbs swelled and stretched. "I do. I want this."

I stared, letting the words crack open inside me, like seeds in fallow soil. Pleasure warmed the center of my chest, and I pushed away my instinct to flee.

I let myself be wanted.

"You do?"

Eva nodded. "I want so much from you it hurts."

She looked so vulnerable in her confession. She looked so brave.

"Come on." Knitting our fingers, she walked backward, leading me toward the greenhouse. I nearly tripped over my feet to keep up with her determined pace, a laugh huffing out of me.

"What are we doing?" I asked.

"Fixing things."

"What —"

Eva cut off my question. "Do you remember the day we met?" she asked, pushing the door open and dragging me in with her. I flashed to the meadow, to the way she'd pushed me against the door, cool against my feverish skin, rain scudding down her arms and the damp of that old sweatshirt.

Eva pulled me forward a few steps, then stopped. "It was right here," she said softly.

"I remember. Your rake broke my nose."

"And you refused to let me apologize," she said with a grin. "You didn't want to know me then."

My heart beat hard in my chest. "I want to know you now, bee girl." I moved one of my hands back into her loose waves, grasping her nape. The bow of her lips was ripe and pink, like something to pluck and devour. When I kissed along the ridge of her jaw, Eva sighed.

The smell of the sun on her skin assaulted my senses. I tugged her hair at the roots, tilting her head back as I planted warm, open-mouthed kisses down her neck. "I tried to stop wanting you."

"Me too," Eva whispered.

Maybe it was the wild honey lingering in my system, or the throb of her pulse and the spark of desire heating between us, but something in the room *changed*. I felt it before I looked up and saw the sway of potted herbs stretching new growth out in thin blades of bright green. My nose filled with the smell of summer. It was mortars and pestles, freshly ground basil, the bleed of petals down scissor blades as Eva prepped her worktable for some new infusion she wanted to try.

"And did you?" I asked softly. "Stop wanting me?"

Her swallow transfixed me, the way it moved down her throat in delicious confession. I wanted to eat it, to suck the skin until she was strawberry red, bruised and wanted and mine. Maybe I was depraved. Maybe all the time we'd lost was catching up to me at once, waking my baser desires. She made me want to worship things. The sun. The soil. Her.

"I thought I had," Eva said. "Until you came back."

My eyes shuttered. "I'm sorry I left."

"I know."

This time would be different. I was already different, because of her. Long after I'd left, the memory of her had become my anchor whenever I'd felt myself slipping back into the dark. It wasn't just how I'd loved her. She'd woken up my hunger for life and made me believe, deep down, that I was worth my own fight.

She'd made me want to live again.

Eva slipped her hand beneath my shirt, so near to where the sprout had bruised my ribs. Her eyes shone with questions. "It's okay," I murmured, not wanting to discuss my tithe. Instead, I took her by the hips and swung her so her back faced the counter.

Ours had been a soft love, and I'd often let Eva lead. Something in the bite of her nails told me she didn't want that right now. Maybe I didn't either. For the first time, I trusted myself to fully let go and need her irreverently. I wanted to be hers again, to show her how well she undid me with a single command.

Suffer me, then.

I'd never forgotten that instruction, and the spell of it wrapped around me now.

Bending, I wrapped one hand around the back of her thigh. Eva gasped, then palmed the counter behind her and lifted herself onto it, knocking planting cups, seed bags, and photographs onto the concrete below. My heart tripped when I recognized the images as those we'd taken together that summer.

Eva spread her knees and tugged me closer. She met my kiss with a vow of teeth, as though I, too, were something to devour.

"Get this off," Eva husked, already lifting the hem of my shirt. "I want to touch you."

I forgot my anxiety about the sprout and shucked the shirt off, already reaching for the neckline of her sundress and tugging it down. Eva's sigh when I cupped her breast made me lightheaded. Fuck, I'd missed this. Missed *us*.

"You scared me, back at the meadow." Eva skimmed a thumb down my side, her eyes glistening. "I don't want you to hurt for me."

Tenderly, I took her face in my hands. For so long, I'd lived beneath a cloud of the monster's protection, turning numb whenever the world became too much. I didn't want that anymore. I wanted to feel everything, even if it hurt.

"I'll be all right, Ev."

A tear slipped down her cheek. "You'll scar."

"It wouldn't be the first time." I echoed what I'd said to her only days before. Somehow, it didn't hurt so much anymore.

Scars were for survivors. And while mine used to make me feel weak and ashamed, now I saw only the courage it had taken to keep on fighting.

"Besides," I murmured. "Now we match."

She'd always been my opposite, the sun that gave shape to my shadow. So what if now we had twin marks to show for it?

Eva laughed wetly. I tucked a blond strand behind her ear and leaned in. Her lips parted under mine. Strange, how quickly sadness could pour its way into desire. In seconds, the drag of her tongue woke a pleasant shiver over my skin. I took her lower lip in mine, and her answering moan sent a stroke of heat down my body.

Eva's fingers skated down my stomach, over the center thatch of hair at my navel to the skin at the top of my jeans. Her sundress was bunched down to her waist now. The lovely scrunch of color beckoned me, and I dragged her to the edge of the counter, loving my mouth over every exposed inch of her I could reach.

It wasn't enough.

I hit my knees, desperately pushing the soft cotton skirt up her thighs. "Please. Let me," I begged.

Eva nodded, lifting her hips as I adjusted the dress to allow her to better spread her knees. She swayed above me, the sun backlighting her curves and catching in the gold of her hair.

She was everything holy. Everything I wanted. I disappeared beneath her dress, kissing her inner thigh. Heat washed over me. The humid greenhouse. The burn of so much desire. Her body, warm and wet and wonderful.

When I closed my mouth between her legs, Eva gasped, arching against me.

I'd missed this, too.

She knit her fingers into my hair. I lost track of the minutes as the greenhouse frenzied around us, plants overgrowing their pots and tipping off their purchases. The shatter of terra-cotta made Eva jump. I flicked my tongue. She cried out. "Arthur," she pleaded, rucking up the skirt of her sundress farther. "I...I need—"

"I know what you need, bee girl." I threw her legs over my shoulders, keeping her steady with one hand braced on the top of her thigh, my other arm curling around her. With my face buried deep, I sucked and kissed her until I couldn't breathe.

Eva's thighs pinned tighter against my ears. "Please," she whimpered. "Don't stop."

My jaw ached, but I stayed my course, my fingers digging into her soft, warm skin. She was so obviously close to the edge, and my whole body thrilled to her groans. I'd never been able to make her finish with just this before, and I wanted to, badly.

"Arthur." The sound of my name on her lips, soft as prayer, nearly undid me. I dragged my tongue up her center.

Eva bucked. She came hard and fast, hips lifting, head tilted back in absolute bliss.

I'd seen a lot of beautiful things. Earth, sky, sea. But no wonder of the world compared to this.

When her body slackened, I snatched the old picnic blanket from its place on the bottom shelf and spread it on the concrete, keeping one hand behind the small of her back as I gently guided her down. Eva's exhale was almost a laugh, full of relief and shaking emotion. Her hands found my chest, and she buried her face in the crook of my neck as we stretched out together, our chests moving in breathless tandem.

"My legs feel like Jell-O," she whispered into my skin.

"Good." I pulled her closer, tenderness swelling inside me. For a long moment, we simply held each other, tangled and sweating, my fingers woven through her hair.

I thumbed her cheek, searching her eyes for regret.

"What is it?" she asked, her expression soft and open.

"It's just…" I swallowed hard, a decade of loving her crowding its way into my throat. "You're the whole sky, Ev."

Slowly, her cheeks spread in a smile, her eyes silver with unshed tears. A strange feeling washed over me. Not déjà vu, not quite. We'd never been *here*, though we'd fooled around enough in the greenhouse to walk the line.

Eva touched the scruff on my jaw. "I do like this," she whispered. "It suits you."

"I'm glad you think so."

She nodded, trailing her fingers down my jaw, then lower. She stalled with her palm to my chest, then she pushed me flat onto the blanket and swung a leg over my knees. Her pupils were dilated, her throat still flushed with climax and desire as she unbuckled my belt.

"Pants off."

I was already hard, but her gentle order heavied the ache. When I fell back against the blanket, Eva took me in her warm, firm grip. I gasped, instinctively thrusting into her touch. "Fuck."

"I'd like to," she muttered.

"I don't have a condom."

And yes, she might have been sacred, but that was a wicked grin. "I do." Eva let me go, tugging her scrunched-up sundress over her head. She held up a foil square.

I gaped at her. "How did you...?"

"Izzy left it in one of the pockets."

I barked a laugh. It felt so good to laugh, after everything.

Eva tore the packet open and crawled back over me. I helped her roll it into place. I felt electric, my skin buzzing, my body tight and full with need. Eva sank her teeth into her bottom lip as she fit herself against me. One nudge and our bodies would join.

"Keep touching me," she instructed.

I ran my palms up her sides, slowing to pinch her stomach softly between my forefinger and thumb. "I love how soft you are," I murmured.

She laughed, a little self-conscious. "I've, um, gotten a little softer."

"And I love it." I cupped the bend of her hip. "You're so beautiful, Ev."

She leaned down to steal a kiss. Time slowed, even as our bodies quickened, the inches between us ripe with desire. Green tendrils brushed my arms. The greenhouse had overgrown itself.

Eva flicked a glance at the flora, then grinned. She plucked a leaf off a nearby lemon verbena and held it just over my lips. I took it between my teeth and bit down. Its flavor spread over my tongue as she sank onto me, sheathing me inside her. Pleasure was a shock. I gripped her hips.

"*Oh.*" Eva's voice piqued with surprise. "You feel good."

"You feel amazing." I groaned when she pressed her lips to mine, tasting lemon verbena and her, her, her.

Eva braced a hand on the floor as we moved together, moss growing under her fingertips. I wrapped my hands around the small of her back, touching her everywhere I could reach. It was strange to return to each other this way, to remember each other so easily when all we'd ever had was a single summer. So little time to memorize and learn the shape of each other. Back then, I'd thought I knew what love was. I'd thought it was this. Needing. Giving. Seeing.

And maybe it was that simple. Maybe love was simply putting yourself on the altar of being known.

Eva gave me a watery smile as I thumbed a rogue tear sliding down her nose. There were no words for this tender ache. It hurt to love so deeply. It used to scare me how loving left me vulnerable. I never realized until I saw it splayed across her features that it also made me brave.

Eva braced her palms on my shoulders, eyes shining. The windows of the greenhouse had long since fogged over, leaving us sweating. This little room was the birthplace to so many important firsts. First glances. First touches.

I'd never known how sacred a *second* could be, or that coming home could feel so much like rebirth.

"Stay with me," she whispered.

"Yes." I twisted, wincing from the sudden, breathless pain in my side as I pulled her beneath me, both of us sweat-glossed and smeared in dust. "Yes, always." With one hand to the base of her spine, I rolled against her faster. Eva hitched a moan and bit my ear. The smell of green things filled the room, intoxicating me. She was warm and wonderful, summer incarnate.

Her body grew frantic, her movements less precise. "Arthur," she whimpered.

"I'm here," I promised.

This time, her peak rose like a tide, a flush spreading across her chest like watercolor on a page. Eva held her breath, tear-streaked, smiling. Tiny gasps marked the path of her release. I kissed a constellation of freckles, my own body reduced to snatches of sensation. A tug on my hair. A breath in my ear. Her legs wrapped around mine.

But it was her laugh that sent me over the edge. I groaned at the honest, golden sound, taking in the sight of her bright and free and happy.

Happy with *me*.

When I gasped her name, Eva grabbed my face and kissed me through the end.

Chapter 43

Isobel

Isobel found Dane sitting on the steps of the front porch, staring blankly at the long, empty street. Dad was in the bathroom, taking a shower, having already wolfed down the first of the two cheeseburgers she'd gotten him.

Isobel stepped out onto the porch. "Hey, Charming," she said softly.

He didn't look back, but the curve of his spine straightened a little as Isobel gingerly sat on the porch step beside him.

She'd made a mental log over the years of the emotions he kept under lock and key, but this expression was a stranger to her, new and raw and more than a little bit lost.

"I really wanted to believe he'd changed," Dane finally said, the words coming out flat. "I thought he could, Isobel. Even after… everything." He drew in a long, heavy breath. When he let it out, Isobel set a hand on his knee.

"You've given him every chance," she said just as softly.

Dane hung his head, deflated. Gone was the authoritative lawman who'd kept order and clarity moving as they coordinated the search for Eva and Arthur, and in his place was a very tired, and very worried, older brother.

"Do you think Lenny's alive?"

Isobel chewed her bottom lip. She knew why he was asking, after what had happened to Avi. There was a mystery hidden in those woods. Maybe her father had been right about ancient places creating unusual things.

"I hope he is," she said honestly.

Dane nodded at his shoes a moment, then covered her hand on his knee with one of his own. There was a small cut on his arm. Isobel's focus contracted on the smudge of red-green, long dried now.

"Jack gave me that tea a month after what happened," Dane said. "I told him I was having chest pains. You know how he is with herbs. I thought he could suggest something. But I never thought...All this, it's unbelievable, Isobel." He turned to look at her.

"I know." Turning her hand over, she clasped his hand with her own, heart in her throat. "I'm sorry I didn't tell you sooner."

"Why didn't you?"

The simple, earnest question could have been a cut thread between them. Instead, the way he'd said it felt like a lifeline.

Dane Walker was one of her oldest friends, and time and time again, he'd shown Isobel that he could adapt to remarkable truths about her family. He and June had been there for every major milestone since Isobel was young. It was always the three of them.

"I didn't want to lose you too," she said, looking away. "And that is selfish."

The silence stretched between them as Dane sat without answering, simply considering. Finally, he spoke. "I should have done more for your sister."

Isobel's eyebrows arched in surprise.

"I was so desperate to see the best in my brother, I refused to see anything wrong. I didn't want to accept the truth."

Isobel knew the texture of remorse. Her own regrets were like an itch she could never fully scratch, especially when it concerned Eva.

"No more secrets." The words were out before Isobel could fully plan what she wanted to say. But this felt right. "No more lies."

She didn't miss the flash of relief in Dane's eyes. He turned to face her. "No more lies."

Isobel arched an eyebrow. "And?"

"Well, I do have one more secret, actually." Dane reached into his pocket and drew something out, pressing it firmly into her palm. The ring was a simple band of gold, warmed by his touch.

"What are you doing?" Isobel croaked out.

"I've been carrying this around for months," Dane said, his eyes soft and hopeful. The words struck her like a bell, leaving her ringing. He sandwiched her hand in both of his. "I love how much you care, Isobel, and how hard you fight for the people you love. You are the most extraordinary person I know." A smile pulled up the corners of his mouth. "You are already my family, but I want — I hope — that you will let me be even more. That you will let me be yours."

It was getting more difficult to keep the moisture out of her eyes. "Are you...?" She could hardly get the words out, but Dane must have heard the nervous catch in her voice, because he tilted her chin up and kissed her softly, just once.

"Proposing?" he asked, his voice deepening in a way that sent a pleasant shiver over Isobel's skin. When she nodded, he shook his head. "Not yet."

It wasn't fair that she could feel both disappointment and relief at once.

"I want to, love." Dane laid another, longer kiss on one side of her mouth. "I want it all. To go to bed with you"—he kissed the other side—"and to wake up together. I want to bear your burdens, to love those you love and protect them as my own."

A tear slipped from the corner of Isobel's eye. It was so rare for her to cry.

"I want my daughter to know how wildly obsessed with her you are," Dane said, his tone changing to something more playful. "Did you know Esther thinks the tooth fairy stocks our cookie jar with honey sticks?"

Isobel let out a weak laugh. "I love her." The words came surprisingly easily. They'd been living inside her for ages, unsaid.

"She's a good kid," Dane said softly, as though he knew the ache in Isobel's chest.

"The best."

Dane ran his thumb over the line of her jaw, slowly taking in every inch of her face. "I'm not asking yet, Isobel, because I want you to be ready. To be sure. But this"—he smiled as he slid his hand back into her hair, anchoring her—"is where I hope we land."

The sudden roll of tires over gravel drew both of their attention to the black car sliding into the drive. Isobel shoved to her feet, Dane's words ringing in her ears, her heart soft and pliant.

All thoughts of proposals and futures dissipated, however, at the sight of the driver. A pair of thick dark sunglasses helped conceal June's expression from where she sat behind the wheel.

Heat stung Isobel's cheeks.

Esther threw her door open and came barreling toward them. "Hi, Dad! Bye, Dad!" she called out as she rushed up the steps.

"What's she after?" Dane grunted.

"Popsicle," June said coolly.

Dane shot Isobel a quick look and rose to his feet. "Better monitor that," he said, following his daughter inside and leaving Isobel and June alone.

Awkwardness thickened between them, made worse when Isobel realized she still had Dane's ring trapped in her fist.

"Didn't know you'd be here," June said.

Isobel nodded, not sure what else to do. But when June turned back to the car, that steady ache opened up in her chest again. Maybe Arthur had awakened something in her with his return, because suddenly the years of estrangement between Isobel and her former friend seemed like such a waste, and that gave her courage.

"June, wait," she called, feeling uncharacteristically nervous. There weren't many people who could make her shrink. June certainly didn't try. She was calm, if cold. "Please," Isobel said.

"What is it?"

June's hesitation made all the old, comforting memories they shared rise to the surface. Isobel wanted to confide in June, to spill her every thought and worry. She wanted to tell June she was sorry, that she was confused, that she was very afraid June hated her now.

Instead, what came out was "Are you free tomorrow?"

June blinked. "What?"

"I was just thinking, maybe I could buy you a coffee?" The

second the words were out, a wave of insecurity washed over Isobel. "We can catch up," she offered weakly.

"Catch up?"

"Only if you aren't busy," Isobel blurted. "It's just that it's been a long time, and I..." Oh, this was mortifying. Was this how Eva felt in social situations? "I miss you, Junie."

As June's eyes strayed to the farmhouse, Isobel held her breath, feeling oddly similar to how she'd felt the first time she'd asked a girl on a date. Only this was June, who'd always been a fixture in her life. Isobel wanted to believe that a bond like that, though wounded, could be healed with time.

When Esther's giggle filtered through the walls, June's expression softened into something more bittersweet. "Nine o'clock," she said. "And you're buying me breakfast too."

"Done," Isobel breathed.

An odd feeling collected in her chest as she watched June get into the car, adjust her sunglasses, and drive away.

Inside, Esther had removed her backpack — a spotted pink-and-white bag with unicorn pins pushed into the vinyl — and was seated beside her father, licking an ice pop. Strawberry juice stained the corners of her mouth. Dane held a matching ice pop, his sleeves uncuffed and pushed to his elbows.

At first, neither father nor daughter saw her. Isobel tucked the ring into her pocket and knocked softly, trying not to feel like an intruder. Dane waved her in with a smile.

"Daddy says you can choose any flavor you want."

Isobel bent to ruffle the little girl's hair. "Do you have any green ones?"

"No. Only strawberry left," Esther chirped. "We have ice cream too, but we can't eat it yet."

Dane and Isobel shared a look of amusement. "A strawberry pop sounds perfect." Isobel opened the freezer and dug one out. "What have the two of you got planned next?" she asked, her eyes on Esther, though she felt Dane's curious study of her face. A warmth spread where his gaze touched her skin.

Esther wiggled in her chair. "Pear time!"

"Oh?" Isobel asked, bemused.

"The storm knocked some of the harvest off the branches," Dane explained. "They'll be too bruised to sell fresh, but we can freeze some and make jam with the rest."

Isobel could still remember stirring a mixture of pears and sugar on jam-making days with her mother. It was those little memories she'd clung to most as time went by and other details of her childhood faded away. It put an ache in Isobel's chest now, and she almost drew away, tempted to let Dane and Esther work alone. Though small, their family was as full of love as the one she'd grown up with. Isobel didn't want to insert herself where she didn't belong, or to complicate things for Esther.

Dane's words resurfaced in her mind, a balm for worry. *You are already my family.*

Gathering her courage, Isobel offered the two of them a hesitant smile. "Mind if I join you?"

Chapter 44

Eva

Esther Walker's giggle grew louder as Eva and Arthur approached the farmhouse. The little girl was outside, curled up in the grass with a small gray kitten on her chest. Bug was licking what looked like Popsicle juice off Esther's face. Beside her sat a basket slowly filling with golden pears. Dane and Izzy were busy nearby, walking the rows and collecting pears off the ground and into their own wicker baskets.

Arthur took Eva's hand in his, and together they crossed over the fence joining the two properties. "I really do like this dress," he murmured.

She hummed. "It's the pockets."

And just as she'd hoped, Arthur laughed.

"Food is inside," Izzy called out when they drew closer. Eva felt a little flushed, certain she looked as disheveled as she felt, but her sister didn't comment.

"Where's Dad?" Eva asked.

"Picking a movie for Esther." Izzy tucked a loose strand of raven-dark hair behind her ear. "We'll be in soon too. Light's fading."

She was right. Dusk was stealing away the last golden dregs of daylight.

Eva hadn't been to the farmhouse in a long, long time. The kitchen was the picture of clean lines and minimalist decor, granite countertops accented by stained, reclaimed wooden cupboards. It was comforting in an empty, unburdened way. It was manicured, clean, and, to Eva's relief, didn't feel like Lenny at all.

"You want to shower?" Arthur asked.

She did, desperately, but her growling stomach took priority. "Let's eat first."

Eva wasn't a fan of hot, limp lettuce, which she pulled off her burger before sticking the rest in the microwave, watching the turntable rotate. The sheriff's massive leather couch proved a formidable temptation. Maybe she'd forgo the shower altogether and curl up on one of those vast leather cushions. The doctor she'd spoken with before she was discharged had told her that it would take a while for her energy to be restored, after all the blood she'd lost.

Arthur filled a few glasses with water from the tap, looking as out of place as she felt. "This is weird."

Eva nodded. "Really weird."

The microwave dinged.

The tomato in her burger hadn't been picked off the vine at peak ripeness. Eva could tell the moment she sank her teeth into her food, but for once she didn't care, stuffing the whole meal into her mouth in just a few bites. Arthur ate just as ravenously.

"Ice cream is in the freezer."

Eva whipped around. The floorboards in the Walker house didn't creak the way they did at the cottage, and despite his size, she'd somehow missed her father's approach entirely.

"Dad." Eva slipped from her place at the table and went to him, wrapping her arms around his middle as much as the trunk of his aspen allowed. She held on to him, breathing in his forest scent and sagging with relief at the slow, steady beat of his heart under her ear.

"What is it, honeybee?"

Eva took a breath. "I'm sorry."

She'd tried to say it on their drive home from the hospital, but the apology had felt like such a weight on her chest, unable to take shape while the car was still moving, her world upended and unsure. Now she felt rooted again. She cut a look to Arthur as he stood and gathered their plates off the table. Now she felt safe.

"I shouldn't have left the way I did. I know I made you worry, and I just…" Eva had to stop herself and take a breath, a lump forming in her throat. "I'm so sorry."

"My tenacious girl." The bellows of his lungs were a comfort as he sighed and gently cupped the back of her head.

"We lost the honey," she said raggedly.

They'd dropped it in the rush to the helicopter, returning empty-handed in the end.

Her father drew back. "I wouldn't have eaten it."

Arthur dropped the dishes into the sink with a loud clatter. "What?"

"Why not?" Eva's jaw hung. But the resolute acceptance of his fate that she had begun to fear was nowhere in her father's soft expression.

"The wilderness took root in me long before my tree began to sprout. At times, I saw it as a gift. Other times, a curse." His eyes moved from her face to Arthur's. "But it took you killing the tree for me to understand what it really was."

He led Eva around the counter, where she took Arthur's hand in her own. "What it really was?" Arthur echoed.

Arthur had eaten the honey, after all. He'd chosen this same fate.

"An ending," Dad said. When Arthur's shoulders slumped, he offered an encouraging smile. "A beginning, too. Just as winter melts for spring. After so many years with the forest pressing on my lungs, I almost forgot how it felt to breathe without it. But now?" Dad's smile sparkled with the promise of tears. "I can breathe again, Arthur. Because of you."

Later that night, when their bellies were stretched full, Arthur leaned down and whispered in Eva's ear. "Will you take a walk with me?"

He held the wooden box of ashes in one hand. Eva followed him down the rows of Walker pear trees, deeper and deeper into the cradle of cricket song, past the fence, the greenhouse, then down the trail to the pond.

Her eyes dropped to the ground at his feet. Even in the dark, she could see the earth respond to him. Long-forgotten bulbs pushed through the dark, wet soil. His wilderness stunned her. It — *he* — was breathtaking. Leaves clung to Arthur's skin without dying. Smudged in soil, raw as rain, he looked to her like a god of the woods.

And she wanted every part of him.

When they reached the dock, Arthur stopped and knelt. "Here."

She dropped to her knees beside him, her eyes tracing the path of the bird carved into the lid of the box. It was beautiful. She hadn't noticed that before. The last time they'd tried to do this, she'd been so angry that all she saw was him, him, him.

Now she realized exactly what she was looking at, and she reached to touch the intricately carved design. "Is this...a starling?"

Arthur nodded once, a tug to his lips. "Her favorite bird."

Then he undid the latch and lifted the top of the box, exposing what remained of the pale gray ashes. Eva pictured the spirit of the wood, and the strange, arborous form she'd taken to communicate with her son again.

There was nothing so strange about these remains, save one thing. When Eva looked down, she saw a honeybee, out far too late, sitting on the dock. She lifted it onto her fingertip just as the wind picked up and stole the ashes from the box, chasing them across the rippled surface of the pond.

"So, now you know." After a moment, Eva realized Arthur was addressing the little insect she held. "She's gone."

Eva bit her lip and lifted the honeybee into the air. As far as eulogies went, it wasn't much, but then, Arthur Connoway did a lot of speaking without words.

He leaned against her. "Hey, Ev?"

"Yeah?"

Arthur kept his eyes on the water, softly rubbing her skirt between his forefinger and thumb as he spoke. "I didn't like to talk about her much before."

"I know."

After a long silence, Arthur turned his face to hers. The last sun streak lit the jeweled hazel tones in his eyes. He was earth and fire, passion and depth. "I think I'd like to tell you about her now," he said. "If that's okay."

Pressure built behind her eyes. Eva lifted the now-empty box and set it on the dock, crawling into Arthur's lap and folding her arms around his neck. His hands came around her, and together, they breathed, slow and steady. They had the time, after all.

"Yes," she whispered. "Tell me everything."

Epilogue

One Year Later

I groaned, clutching the dark gold mess of Eva's hair. "We have to go, bee girl."

Eva used one arm to swipe her tangle over one shoulder. "You want me to stop?"

"No."

She grinned, crawling back up and fitting her body to mine in a warm, sloppy kiss. I hadn't slept well in the tent, and drowsiness made the pleasure of her touch harder to resist, especially when she rolled her hips against mine like that.

The alarm sounded.

"Ignore it," Eva said into my neck, squeezing her thighs against me. I fumbled for the SNOOZE button again.

"Five minutes," I mumbled, rolling her over and kicking off the sleeping bag.

We didn't really have five minutes. Blue hour would come and go in a flash, and if we weren't ready, we wouldn't make it to the proposal spot by sunrise.

But then Eva wriggled out of her shorts.

With a growl, I sat up and took her by the hips. She rode me with her hands on my shoulders, my face buried in her breasts and my hands at her waist to control the rhythm.

It drove me wild. And she knew it.

"You are resplendent," I murmured against her skin.

Eva laughed. "You're easy to please."

"Hardly." I moved a hand between us. Despite the chilly mountain morning, my body was overwarm. Eva's stomach was slicked with sweat. "I have very discerning taste, and you"—I pressed a thumb to the place where our body joined, drawing her gasp—"are exquisite."

When I circled the same spot, Eva thrust an arm out for balance, knocking into the tent pole with a laugh.

I smirked. "Careful."

"You've gotten cocky," she panted.

"*Cocky*, Ev? Really, right now?"

"I don't see a better time."

I pressed a smile to her lips. All this time, and still it felt like coming home. We'd learned to love each other this way before we really knew what we were doing, learning each other by touch and trial and trust. Now my body woke to her like the world to the dawn, aching for warmth. I was soothed by every familiar curve and groove, by the hush of her voice and the hitch in her breath.

The alarm went off again. Eva smacked it.

I pulled her down to me and we fell into a now-familiar rhythm, the push and pull of our bodies a song I'd never forget so long as I lived. The hum of it lived in my bones.

When she collapsed against my chest, panting and satisfied, my cheeks pulled into a grin.

I loved blue hour.

Eva looked at me. "When do we need to leave?"

"Four alarms ago."

With a little sound and a nose nuzzle into my chest, Eva rolled away. She unzipped the door to the tent and stuck her head out.

"Got your jacket?" I asked.

"Yeah, but I want food."

With a smile, I fished out a granola bar from our overnight pack and tossed it her way. We'd pack up the tent on the way back.

To my chagrin, Jack and Esther had beat us to the lookout. Eva felt no shame in her tardiness, waving to Esther with vigor as the little girl bounced on the balls of her feet, waving back.

Sweet kid.

When we reached them, Jack passed me a thermos. It was too much to hope he'd opted for coffee. The man had a strong palate for worry, and even after all our talks, I knew he didn't fully believe the monster would hold back the sprout forever. He was always pushing tea in my face. Just in case, he said.

I took a sip and smiled my gratitude.

"Okay, they'll be here any minute. Everyone needs to find their hiding place, and stay there," Eva said.

Jack lifted an eyebrow. "We know, honeybee. We've been here for half an hour waiting on you. What held you up?"

"Would you believe the alarm never went off?" she said, feigning annoyance.

I choked on my tea. Beautiful liar.

At the sound of nearing voices, however, Eva put a finger to her lips and motioned for us to get into position. I caught her by the hand, warming a kiss to the center of her palm. When she pinked, I stepped back into the bush. "Hide," I mouthed.

Flustered, Eva hurried into the trees, but I didn't miss the lift of her smile.

The lookout spot was a local secret, situated in a broad strip of trees that overlooked the northernmost tip of the Blue Ridge Mountains. The view stole my breath every time.

For a moment, I felt an itch to reach for gloves I no longer had any need for, but I forced the feeling down and ran my fingers over a soft fern, releasing the dew caught in its leaves. Would I ever get used to this? Touching the world, and letting it touch me?

At the call of a nuthatch, I shivered with pleasure. I hoped not.

I wedged myself back against a wide cedar, where I had a clean view of the overlook, and quietly adjusted the settings on my DSLR one more time. I liked controlling my Kelvin temperature in camera, rather than in post, and with the rising sun, that meant little adjustments every few minutes to accommodate the change from cool tones to warm.

The others tucked themselves somewhere between the trees as I eyed the path. The pale violet sky was a stunning backdrop, but if they didn't make it here soon, they'd miss the sunrise altogether. Not that Isobel would care, but I did. She'd put me in charge of this. I had to make it perfect for her.

As though summoned, her bright laughter filtered through the trees. I straightened, and when she and Dane came into view, I raised the lens and blew out an even breath. They were both casually dressed, though Isobel, I noted, wore a full face of makeup. Maybe she didn't want the full party, but she was still her, always prepared, and it didn't surprise me at all that she wanted to look her best, even if that best was slightly glazed in sweat from a steep morning hike.

"Let's stop here. Take in the view," Dane said, slinging an arm over her shoulders. Sweet but annoying. He was blocking her face. I'd spent far too many hours waiting for a bird to surface from its nest only for the stubborn thing to come out facing away from me. No one was impressed by a catalog of nothing but tail feathers.

"Move," I muttered.

They took a drink from their water bottles. "You're right," Dane said. "This was a good idea. It's beautiful."

"It is." Isobel flashed a look to the trees. "Charming, I—"

A twig snapped under my foot. *Damn it.*

"What was that?" Dane turned.

"Nothing!" Isobel grabbed his face and pulled him back toward her just as Esther's giggle sounded from the bush.

"I heard someone." That wasn't Dane; that was the *sheriff* speaking now.

"I have something to say to you!" Isobel dug something small out of the pocket of her yoga pants and stuck it on her finger, then held it up for him to see.

I raised my camera again. *There. Finally, the shot.*

Dane stared at her, perplexed. "Your...ring?"

"Yes!"

"Why are—"

"I'm going to marry you!" Isobel shouted in his face.

Eva's laugh slipped through the trees as I fired off a volley of accidental shots. Dane must not have heard it, however, because he was still looking at Isobel, stunned. "What did you say?"

"I want to marry you," Isobel said more softly, taking his hands in her own. "I'm sorry it's taken me so long and I'm sorry I've been scared, but I..." Her voice shook. "I want you forever, Dane."

He laughed in obvious relief. "Thank God." Then he drew her close, searing a kiss to her lips. "This has been the longest year of my life, Isobel."

"I'm sorry."

"Don't be sorry, wife."

Isobel tipped her head back in a laugh. I snapped photograph after photograph.

But perfectionism was a funny thing. I knew going into this that portrait photography wasn't my specialty, but still, it drove me mad that I could have gotten a better angle if only I'd planted myself a few feet to the left. In this spot, a tree slightly blocked my view.

I could do this. I just had to move slowly. Holding my breath, I leaned to the left —

SNAP

— and fell gracelessly into the bush.

Dane pushed Isobel behind him. "Who's there?" he called out.

"Stop!" Isobel pulled his arm down. "It's fine! I invited them!"

"You invited...?" Dane's tone lost its edge, sounding more confused than angry now.

"Could you wave, Fairy?"

I obliged, throwing my hand out of the tangle of branches and leaves I'd gotten myself stuck in. "Pictures look great, Iz."

She clapped her hands as Eva dropped down beside me, grasping me by the forearm and hauling me out of the bush. "You are so consistent," she murmured.

It sounded to my ear like *Take me back into the trees.*

Esther bounded out from behind a pine tree. "Hi, Dad!" she sang as she barreled into her father's middle, drawing a startled *"Oomph"* from him.

"What, Esther...?" Dane twisted in bewilderment. "How many of you are there?"

"Just four," Jack said, bringing up the rear.

Dane's mouth dropped open, and then he turned to Isobel. "You... planned this?"

She cleared her throat. "The thing is... I want to be your wife, but I'm not really sure about a giant wedding. I..." She stumbled over her words. "I didn't like how your last one ended."

Dane took her in his arms more fully. "Is that what the delay has been, love? It wouldn't be like that."

"No. It won't. I've made sure of it." Isobel nodded to our motley crew. "I want to marry you here. Now. Well, in ten minutes. I do have a dress I want to change into, after all."

Dane's mouth fell open again, and a slow smile spread over his face. "You sure? Here?"

"It's perfect," Isobel rushed on. "Just you, me, and the people we love most." She held out a hand and knit her fingers with Esther's. "What do you say?"

It was a rare sight to see Isobel Moreau look nervous. Did she think he'd say no?

"Isobel," Dane softly said, cupping her cheek in one hand, then cutting us a quick glance before deciding he didn't care about an audience. With the other hand, he held his daughter, as he dragged Isobel in for a kiss.

Eva bumped me with her hip. "Money shot," she whispered as I snapped the photo.

Esther pushed them apart. "So, will you marry her or not, Dad?"

I'd never seen the man smile so wide. "I thought she'd never ask."

Isobel gave us ten minutes, during which Eva did indeed haul me back into the privacy of the trees, but only to change. From our overnight pack, she dug out a slightly wrinkled sundress.

I warmed. This was the pink one. With the pockets.

"Am I clear?" she asked, already peeling off her T-shirt.

"You're good."

She tugged the dress over her biking shorts. This was one of my favorites. It was loose and pretty, perfect for summer. Best of all, it fell slightly off her shoulders. I loved that.

Eva tossed me a look. "Are you staring?"

"Oh, absolutely."

She laughed, a little self-conscious.

I watched her freckles disappear beneath a layer of cotton. "When you blush," I said as she tossed me a shirt of my own, "you match your dress."

Her reaction only proved my point.

At Isobel's request, there was no apparel in our party finer than a dusty pair of tennis shoes and a pair of suspenders Jack wore over his flannel shirt. As officiant, he stood at the edge of the overlook, his back to the sky. Affection swelled within me as I watched him pull a notecard from his pocket and mouth a few words.

It had been nine years since Dane Walker's first wedding. That day had transformed all our lives. For a long time, I'd thought the only thing I would remember was the pain of how it had ended. Looking at the honeyman before me, however, what came to mind were the words Jack had spoken just before we'd left the chapel that day.

You can take up space.

And I was, now.

I'd taken a job as a freelance photographer for a local wildlife magazine. It paid very little, but I loved every part of it. Sometimes I traveled for an assignment, but mostly I stayed in Audrey and did what the court had instructed: helping Jack and his family clear out the debris on their property and rebuild, stone by stone.

I'd spoiled my kitten rotten.

I'd even found myself a therapist, by which I meant that Isobel had done a deep dive into therapists in Cumberland Valley and found me someone she swore I would like. I'd shown up, for her, and to my surprise, she was right.

We'd faced the hard things too. Jack had let me read through my mother's old letters. Dane had grieved a brother whose body they never found. We'd all touched the darkness.

But there was still light. The best things in life, after all, often find their beginning in the smallest seeds. I still held hope that one day my grief would find a shape that I could better hold. Maybe it would even grow to be as beautiful as the gardens Eva grew under our feet now, moss and chamomile forming a circle around the bride and groom's hiking shoes.

Jack cleared his throat. He had gotten ordained for this and was clearly excited, if a little nervous, rubbing the spot on his chest where the stump of his tree still extended.

Eva held Esther's hand as songbirds filled the air with music.

"My Isobel," Jack started, then promptly stopped, his voice already shaking. "Shoot, I promised you I wouldn't cry."

"It's okay, Dad," she said.

Jack took a breath and started again. "You're better at this kind of thing than I am anyway, so I'll keep this brief." He kept his eyes on her, his expression soft and serious. "When I met your mother, I had no idea that I'd met two of the greatest loves of my life. Her, of course," he said with a smile. "And you."

Isobel let out a weak laugh.

"My girl," Jack said. "You snuck into my heart. There's no one who knows better how to choose the ones we love, but the truth is, I never needed to choose you. From the moment you first asked if you could call me Dad, I *knew*—" He choked on the words. "I knew you were mine."

Looking around, I saw not a dry eye in our circle.

"Now." Jack cleared his throat and smoothed out the paper he held. "You never know how vast a heart can be until you crack it open," he read.

"If you compare me to a seed, Dad, I swear…" Isobel cut in.

"It's a perfect metaphor!" Jack countered.

All of us laughed then. My cheeks ached from smiling so much. When we settled, Jack took Dane's and Isobel's hands in each of his. "You never know what will grow when you let the light in."

Their vows were brief, unscripted, and perfect. When Esther rushed her father for a hug, I wrapped an arm around Eva's shoulders and rested my chin on her head. She leaned back against my chest with a sigh.

For a moment, the future stretched out as vast and endless as the overlook before us, begging me to fly, to leap toward the light and let love fill every crack in my heart.

Eva craned her neck up and grinned. "Hey," she whispered, just for me.

Light. Hope. Home. Autumn was coming, but with her by my side, the promise of summer spread its wings in me. I would hold on to that and fight for this life I wanted until I had no more breath inside me.

I pressed a kiss to Eva's nose and grinned.

"Hey, bee girl."

Author's Note

In her lifetime, the average honeybee will produce only one-twelfth of a teaspoon of honey. When I think about how often I drizzle honey over toast or into tea, the life and impact of such a small creature seems inconsequential. But I hope you find the opposite is true: that every life is precious, impactful, and worthy of care.

I inherited many things from my botanist father, not least of which is a deep well of respect and love for the earth. Perhaps that is because, to me, we are not so different from it. We are of the earth. We are mineral and magic, carbon and creation.

And like the little honeybee, we matter.

A large part of my inspiration for *Honey in Her Veins* stems from my obsession with the Celtic belief that honeybees serve as a bridge between the natural world and the afterlife. It is tradition for a beekeeper to tell their hives when a member of their household dies, so that the bees can guide their soul. This, combined with studies suggesting that honeybees can not only differentiate between human faces but also recognize their beekeepers, stirred my storyteller brain, planting the seed of an idea that grew into *the bee girl*.

Too often, I think, we are overwhelmed by all we cannot do when it comes to making an impact on a personal, social, and environmental level. But just like the tiny honeybee whose entire life produces only one-twelfth of a teaspoon, we can make a difference by loving fiercely and trying hard to make the world a better place. We, like the bee girl in this story, can choose to live vibrantly, creating life and color with every footstep.

We can choose rebirth, again and again. For at its heart, this is a tale about metamorphosis, about all the ways we put down roots, and about the people and places that make us want to live again.

Acknowledgments

Love is an ecosystem.

We are all interconnected, in need of one another to thrive, sharing an environment that can be at times both beautiful and terrifying. Writing this book opened my eyes to all the ways the people in my ecosystem made life possible for me through years of unknowns, hard work, and all the tears I cried as, word by word, I wrapped this story around myself like a cocoon, unsure how it would change me.

But change me it did. And metamorphosis demands thanks.

To begin, my heart and thanks go to Jacob, my love, for always being my safe place, and for showing me a kind of love that feels like roots.

Thank you to my agent, Amanda Jain, for pulling this story out of the slush pile and seeing its heart. You have been a grounding presence from the start of our partnership.

Thank you to my dream editor, Julia DeVarti, for your passion and the care you bring to my stories. I could not ask for a more intelligent and thoughtful advocate of my work.

Thank you to my incredible team at Little, Brown, whose open-armed welcome has been such an immense support in my publishing experience.

My ecosystem would collapse without the many readers and writers who have left a mark on me and on this story. So, I want to thank my friends, who have shown up for me time and time again.

To Taylor, whose ability to draw the fire and passion out of me and my stories changed the direction of my life.

To Erynne, who steadies my chaos and always meets me where I am. Your depth and sensitivity as a human and as a storyteller enrich my work at every turn.

To Kayley, who always fills my well, and is the first I turn to when I need to cry, to breathe, or to brainstorm. Your love is all over this book.

To Carly, whose resilience and courage astound me, and whose deep understanding of craft makes me a better writer all the time.

To Kayla, for being a light in every way to my stories and my soul.

To Ghabiba, for being my snack buddy, for reading and loving every version, and for lighting up every space you fill.

To Nadine, who single-handedly refused to let me give up on this story and saw magic in it long before I did.

To Jamie, whose love for storytelling lives in her bones.

To Gina, who moves like a storm through the world and whose stories enchant me.

To Jessie and Briana, the world's most enthusiastic hype readers.

To Don and Pamela Laidley, whose expertise as beekeepers was an immense support to my research when writing this book.

To Adrienne Young, who has given so much back to the writing world by creating spaces for community and growth in our craft.

To my Writing With The Soul friends, who were there for me

at a pivotal crossroads in my life and career. You will forever be a large reason I took the road I did.

To the many readers who have read and loved Eva and Arthur's story, I thank you. I hope you find a friend in the dark parts of your mind. I hope you feel the support of your own ecosystem moving around you. I hope you set down roots in people and places that feel like home.

And to bees: I've been crushing on you for years.

Content Warnings

This is a story about hope, and choosing life even when it feels too heavy to go on. While I have tried to create a bridge where mental health and magic meet, I know some of the elements of this story may be triggering for some, so I have included a list of content warnings to help my readers navigate with peace of mind.

Content warnings include:

- Parental neglect
- Death of a parent (off page)
- References to self-harm (off page)
- Blood and mild violence
- Botanical body horror
- Alcoholism
- Depression
- Anxiety attacks
- Attempted sexual assault

About the Author

Ruth McKell writes haunting, romantic fiction designed to break and mend her readers' hearts. When she's not channeling her passion for mental health awareness into magic-touched worlds on the page, you can find her sipping on tea from her at-home apothecary, haunting her local indie bookstores, and exploring the mountains with her husband and son.

RAISING READERS
Books Build Bright Futures

Thank you for reading this book and for being a reader of books in general. We are so grateful to share being part of a community of readers with you, and we hope you will join us in passing our love of books on to the next generation of readers.

Did you know that reading for enjoyment is the single biggest predictor of a child's future happiness and success?

More than family circumstances, parents' educational background, or income, reading impacts a child's future academic performance, emotional well-being, communication skills, economic security, ambition, and happiness.

Studies show that kids reading for enjoyment in the US is in rapid decline:

- In 2012, 53% of 9-year-olds read almost every day. Just 10 years later, in 2022, the number had fallen to 39%.
- In 2012, 27% of 13-year-olds read for fun daily. By 2023, that number was just 14%.

Together, we can commit to **Raising Readers** and change this trend. How?

- Read to children in your life daily.
- Model reading as a fun activity.
- Reduce screen time.
- Start a family, school, or community book club.
- Visit bookstores and libraries regularly.
- Listen to audiobooks.
- Read the book before you see the movie.
- Encourage your child to read aloud to a pet or stuffed animal.
- Give books as gifts.
- Donate books to families and communities in need.

Books build bright futures, and **Raising Readers** is our shared responsibility.

For more information, visit **JoinRaisingReaders.com**

Sources: National Endowment for the Arts, National Assessment of Educational Progress, WorldBookDay.com, Nielsen BookData's 2023 "Understanding the Children's Book Consumer"

Praise for Ruth McKell's
Honey in Her Veins

"*Honey in Her Veins* is an atmospheric fantasy steeped in the kind of magic that grows wild in the cracks of broken things. With lyrical prose, aching romance, and a world humming with bees and ghosts, this story will burrow into your heart and bloom."
— Adrienne Young, *New York Times* bestselling author

"Deliciously atmospheric, *Honey in Her Veins* is a stunning tale of a death-touched boy and a honey-kissed girl defying every darkness. This debut is absolutely mesmerizing."
— Sydney J. Shields, author of *The Honey Witch*

"As sweet as honey and as sharp as bone, *Honey in Her Veins* will leave you breathless. My heart blossomed with every page, even as I clutched my copy with whitened knuckles. Magical, lyrical, and deeply resonant — I savored every moment inside this story."
— Taylor Grothe, author of *Lethal Kiss*

"Infused with magic, *Honey in Her Veins* is a stunning genre-blend of a debut. With delicate prose, a tender love story, and monstrous undertones, this story will hook its claws into you...and you'll be glad." — Amanda Linsmeier, author of *A Dance with Death*

"A masterwork. Ruth McKell's breathtaking debut delivers achingly beautiful prose, deliciously complex characters, and a deeply moving second-chance romance with all the heated longing readers thirst for. No one pines quite like Arthur Connoway. *Honey in Her Veins* is the kind of book you keep on your bedside table long after you've closed it so that you can relive the tale over and over again. I was spellbound from the first honey-soaked page. Prepare yourself for a lifelong love affair." —Taylor J. LaRue, author of *Steelborn*